WITHDRAWN

LEAVING
the LAND

a novel

by DOUGLAS UNGER

University of Nebraska Press
Lincoln and London

♻ The paper in this book meets the minimum requirements of
American National Standard for Information Sciences—Permanence
of Paper for Printed Library Materials, ANSI Z39.48-1984.

First Bison Books printing: 1995

Library of Congress Cataloging-in-Publication Data
Unger, Douglas.
Leaving the land: a novel / by Douglas Unger.
p.   cm.
ISBN 0-8032-9560-X (pbk.: alk. paper)
I. Title.
PS3571.N45L4   1995
813′.54—dc20
95-10945   CIP

Reprinted from the original 1984 edition by Harper & Row,
Publishers, New York.

For Amy and her sisters

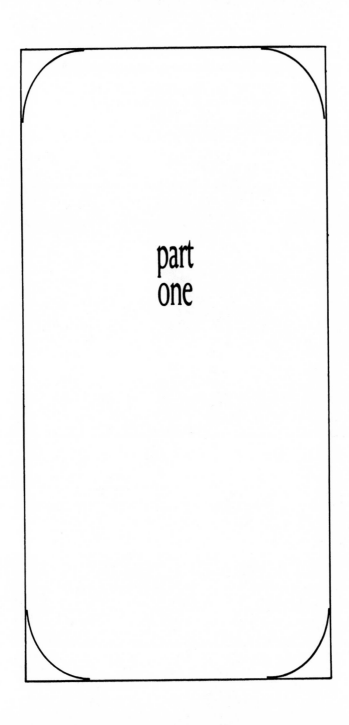

part
one

1

The years immediately following the war were fertile for weeds. There was a kind of plague of them. The white fluff seeds of the Canadian thistle and of the milkweed and dogbane filled the air like an invasion of tiny white parachutes. Hot winds swirled them through the streets so thickly that Marge gave up trying to pick them off her dress. She walked down the main street of Nowell, collecting seeds.

She hated this town. She hated the way the sun blinded her, glaring off the white adobe storefronts. She passed the high square wooden false front of the Baker Hotel and gazed up at five dark windows, one with an old white head leaning on the sill next to a box of withering geraniums. Clumps of cheat grass made a shambles of the sidewalk as they broke through the concrete and spilled in wild tufts toward the curb. Weeds scratched at her ankles as she walked. Sharp seeds prickled under the collar of her dress. She would have to comb them out of her hair like wedding rice.

White, she thought, *white . . .*

Marge had trouble with her high heels as she stepped off the curbs, crossing unpaved sidestreets more like ruts with manes of weeds. Houses along those streets were mostly white, save the few that were left an unpainted gray, with rusted tin where they ought to have shingles. If she watched for them, she might see a yellow house with black shutters, a small brown house with white shutters. She hated the thought of houses. She passed the double doors of the municipal bar with its black-on-white sign that read *Nowell* hung over the wide frames of screen. She glanced in at the men shooting pool. Somebody hooted. She had no way to tell if that

3

sound was meant for her, but whenever there was hooting she liked to believe it was meant for her. She moved her body in a certain way when she heard it, not even sure there was someone watching her in the street.

Marge didn't believe in love. She hadn't believed in love since Thursday. That was the day she decided to accept Burt Cooney's proposal for marriage. Now it was Monday. She was on her way to his mother's house to fit her wedding dress. She walked, alone in thought that love was over before it had ever been. She used to think love was a feeling of romance. Both romance and what she had been taught to believe of love—that all love was somehow the same as a spirit in her hands as she worked, as she curried the sides of a show heifer and shaved the face just right, even when she was sure she couldn't do anything right; or in her hands as they toughened with other chores, getting the bum lambs through the last suckling weeks, working in the dust and swelter of the fields, cooking her family's breakfast when her mother was ailing. Years ago, she believed all love was the same as the love in the rhythm of her mother's sewing machine long into the nights, as in the early morning sound of her father's bootsteps amid the high, sirenlike whining of the cream separator. Years later, alone in darkness, she discovered other meanings.

Burt Cooney was just a boy. All she had ever known were boys. He was like the boy she had gone to the movies with and didn't go with anymore because once he brought a jar of pig's knuckles along and offered one to her as if it was popcorn. He was like a boy at a party once who sat on the log next to her. He slugged down whiskey out of a pint bottle. He stared down for a long time as if at the stitching of his cowboy boots. Then mumbling into the firelight, he tried taking her hand, afraid to look her in the eye. And when she so much as squeezed his hand back, he asked her to marry him. He was like the boy she used to cruise with from the blacktop junction and back to the Dairy Freeze at least once a day, parking somewhere so he could cup her breasts, suck her neck, ply her clumsily with his fingers. She might have gone all the way with him if he hadn't told the whole damn town it had already happened. He talked the way boys did of how many beers he'd had

4

that day or he offered to drive on out to the butte for a sloe gin screw under the northern lights. Or he told her for the umpteenth time how he'd shot the front tire of his truck out from under him huntin' jacks or how next month's winner-take-all jackpot rodeo was gonna be another story, and on and on he went until she thought she was fit to die of boredom. There was nothing better to do than give in to him, but only up to a certain point. She draped her arms over his shoulders and kissed him. Her nostrils filled with the acrid odors of sweat and shaving lotion. Her lips recoiled at the bitter tastes of beer, smoking, cheap whiskey. She carefully raised an elbow to protect her breasts. She rested her head against his neck, wiping her lips on his shirt in the process. She felt a film of hair oil on her face and hands.

"Shit," Burt Cooney complained. "We been at this three months now, three damn months now, honey! What in hell's wrong with you?"

She gave in and kissed him again. They fought each other on the musty carseats. As much as she wished it were different, her mind was always somewhere else.

She usually had him drive her home as early as possible. Then she lay awake in her bedroom, trying to imagine her lover as almost anyone else. She imagined him with her in that small, orderly bedroom. Then he led her out to some weedless pasture all high brome and crested wheat grass, and like in the movies, he spread his coat in that deep rug of grass. She heard the high-pitched drone of the insects in waves of sound. There was a sudden, high chattering as a covey of mourning doves exploded up out of the pasture. They lay down on his coat. He played a kind of game in which he knelt over her and spread the long grass around her face, weaving it over her cheeks and over her eyes. She tasted it. She ate a little grass. He gripped her hands with a strength almost painful. He kissed her and it was different, as if the sun shone with a summer's wholeness in sunflower gold. She raised one bare knee, imagined he set his chin there on it and eyed her deeply. Then the image dissolved, a palmful of chaff scattered in the winds.

Sometimes he was comforting. Nights when the yapping chorus

of the coyotes kept on because there was no answering call. She had heard that sound all her life. But she found herself turning on the lamp to search her room, turning it off again to settle into her bedsheets, then a howl might burst out closer, just beyond the yard fence, the family dogs in a sudden uproar, and she'd reach for the lamp again. Sitting up, she'd try to imagine her lover there so she could hide her face in the muscles of his chest. She wanted anyone's voice in that room, in that old clapboard house where her father and mother slept, scratching themselves, tossing in their sleep. Sometimes, it was enough to close her eyes and think he was with her, warm and holding her close into sleep, his voice a comfort to her until he had gone. Other times, nothing helped. She lost all vision of what it was she really wanted. She lay awake and dreamless, filled with the unhappy sense that she would always be alone.

Mornings after a night out were always the same. She faced her parents.

"You been out some," said her father. He was at the breakfast table, scooping eggs into his mouth with a spoon. "You got home awful early." He glowered up at her. "You won't get nobody, you come home so early."

"There's nobody to get," she said. She picked the biscuit plate up off the table.

"You go on and say that now. You just go on and keep telling me that!"

"There's no more than that to tell," she said.

"I don't like you 'round here like you are."

"Then I'll move on into town."

"Now that ain't what I mean," he said.

"You won't have nobody to cook your breakfast!" she snapped. She watched her father nod his head back toward his plate, using a knife to chase a fried potato through the grease. She shrugged. She went into the living room to fetch her mother's plate. Her mother held the plate stiffly in her hands. Her head was laid on the chairback, eyes wide to the ceiling as if it might fall with the pressure of the next rain.

6

"You can't get a thing done here without me," Marge told him. "Who's going to help you herd them turkeys out of the rain?"

"I expect that won't make no difference soon," he said.

"Well, it sure as hell better," she said. "When I'm done sticking you in the grave, I want to have something."

"Shiiiiiit . . ." Ben Hogan said, and laughed.

"I mean it," she said.

"But that's what I been telling you all along for, damnit!" he shouted.

"Well, then why don't *you* try riding around with him?" she shouted back. "Go on now! You just try an evening with Burt Cooney! Go on! That boy doesn't know scours from hoofrot! He'll tell you about the way he rides, sure he will. He couldn't stay on a corral fence! He doesn't know a solenoid from a voltage regulator! There just isn't nobody . . ."

Ben Hogan coughed and laughed at the same time. "That's what your own ma kept telling her folks about me," he said. "And all the while, we was spending nights in her daddy's harness shop. He's all right, that Burt Cooney. He just needs feeding up some. He'll show right. Now you might have to teach him how, but he'll take to it. Besides, I think I'm getting me a bit of the emphysema. . . ."

"You hush up," she said. "We'll do just fine on our own."

"Marge." Her mother's cracked voice came from the living room. "Marge, you got the Gel-u-siiil? . . ."

Ben Hogan sighed and rose from the table. He hooked the straps of his overalls up and over his shoulders, then stretched and yawned. He caught his daughter by the arm on her way with the medicine.

"You be out in a minute and help with them turkeys," he said in his gentlest voice, playfully slapping her behind.

2

The Hogan family farm was a good farm. It had a tight board house that had once been a railroad station. Ben Hogan moved that house on rollers eighteen miles from the town of Nowell. He built a high, shake-shingled barn behind it, cutting the logs himself in the Black Hills, milling the logs into rough boards still covered with bark at the edges and honing them into beams. He kept that barn painted bright red with white windowframes. One broad side of it was half covered by his white-painted stock brand, ᗡꓤ. Sometimes, when he looked up at it doing chores, or when it passed him as a hairy scar on the hips of his stock, he muttered it to himself, *"lazy you are, lazy you are,"* as if that made him work all the more. Out drinking, he was known to complain, "What I really wanted when I first homesteaded these parts was a brand a fellah could feel outright proud of. Now, that *lazy you are* ain't too bad, it does have some kick to it. But that wasn't the one I wanted. Old Sy Lockhard beat me to it for the *P over U* brand. That's the piss on you ranch, goddamnit," he said. "Then one time up in Aberdeen, I met a man like to sell me the *2 lazy 2 P* brand, but it was registered by the time I got smart enough to rustle me up some stock."

The ᗡꓤ brand was burned into the corral boards, into the sides of his cows, the hips of his horses, painted on the wool of his sheep, clipped to the ears of his hogs. Wherever he walked on his place, it stared back at him. For a time, it even stared back at him from Marge. She helped him brand one of the workhorses used to pull the haysled in winter. They both fought the two-thousand-pound animal into the loading chute. They scotch-hobbled it with ropes so that if it reared too much or tried to break through the chute, it

8

would fall right on its nose. Marge held the rope tightly, leaning out over the chute. When the horse smelled the hot brand coming in for its hip, it did rear up and fall on its nose. Then instead of letting the rope go, Marge got her hand caught in it. She was pulled down with the horse and in the confusion of smoke, dust, Marge screams, horse screams, Ben Hogan reached in with the brand.

Marge's two brothers chased her for a week to get a look at the welts. They finally caught her in the barn. They wrestled her through the straw and stripped her clothes. She did a *boom cha cha, boom cha cha* dance for them in the barn loft and the way her brothers treated her after that, she began to hope those red welts might stay for the rest of her life, but they finally faded.

"That's my daughter there," Ben Hogan confided to his neighbors every chance he got. He pointed to the seat of his daughter's jeans. "I don't have no bill of sale to prove it," he said, "but I won't have no trouble with the state inspector once I get her in the ring."

Ben Hogan ran a successful business. He kept his fences horse high, bull strong and hog tight. When he first homesteaded, those fences only closed in a hundred sixty acres. But over the years, he avoided borrowing too much money because of his talent for constructing new machinery from pieces of old machinery and because of his foresight in raising beans when everyone else was raising corn, raising corn when everyone else was raising beans, raising milk cows when everyone else was raising sheep, raising sheep when everyone else was milking cows. So by the time the war came along, he had bought up three of his less successful neighbors who had gone under during the Great Depression. To buy those spreads, he had to borrow a lot of money from David Whitcomb at the First Bank of Belle Fourche. But to a man with four hundred eighty acres of the finest gumbo in the county, the future looked prosperous. He figured he had to gamble on his credit every once in a while.

Ben Hogan worked. He worked and never slowed. He bulled his way through the house before sunrise each morning, growling to his sons to get out of bed and do the chores. Almost every morning of her youth, Marge woke up to see his stubbled face press in to kiss her forehead as he grumbled, ''Where's the goddamned breakfast?'' Then he stomped around in his hip-high rubber boots, snuffling at the pots and pans, shouting, ''Where the hell y'all hide my diggers? What in God's name your good shoes doing where the mice can get 'em? For pity's sake, can't you make no damned coffee that don't take the hair right off'n my tongue!''

He milked in the barn. He leaned his head against the cow's flank and bellowed with some old song in his mind, or with pieces of many old songs that he strung together. His hands squeezed and pulled in rhythm to that horrendous hour or so of out-of-tune yodeling. When Marge's pet hen exploded into a cloud of blood and feathers in the old threshing machine, he made up a song about it. When she helped him milk, he sang that song for her in a teasing tone of voice: *"Cockle Doodle Dandy, my old hen, laid her eggs in the thrashing bin, ohhhhh first she laid eight, and then she laid ten . . . ohhhhh poor old Cockle Doodle Dandy, my old hennnnnn . . ."* followed by a blast of that same out-of-tune yodeling.

She helped him separate the milk into skim and cream each morning before school with a machine he had partly built himself. Then he fired up one of his tractors and headed into his fields. Ben Hogan had modified his tractor engines to run faster than the normal RPMs recommended by the owner's manuals, so he could plow or disc or cultivate more acres per day than anyone else in the county. When Marge watched him build a fenceline, it was like watching a dance. He dug holes with a double-bladed shovel. He lifted the blades up and pumped them down into the ground, spilling the earth in a pile beside the hole in the upswing, never breaking his rhythm, never stopping despite the sun that made him glisten with sweat. The wiry muscles on his bare chest sprang and trembled, the tight knots of muscles in his arms mottled with pulsing veins as the shovel blades came down again, as he pumped them up and down for an entire day, stopping to rest only once, as was his custom, to eat dinner, then stretch out to sleep through exactly the hottest hours.

His sons shared his working constitution. He and his sons could stack up to ten tons of hay in one day, scooping it up with tractors, pitching it up onto the stack under a steady rain of dust and prickling leaves. He and his sons could keep two hundred acres irrigated throughout the summer. They walked the earth to judge the contours. They studied the slow curves of the muddy creek that bordered their land. Each morning, they dragged shovels out into the fields and built earth dams across main ditches as wide as their outstretched arms, digging networks of small connecting ditches as wide as their hands, each with a mouth trickling water down the rows of corn. Like sharp tongues, those cornleaves stood out luxuriously with health. Ben Hogan and his boys moved their system of ditches all summer long along the creek, over the wide, rolling sweep of their best fields. They worked in water that steamed off the sun-hardened clay soil like off the floor of an adobe oven. They tasted their cornleaves in passing. They sucked on the spade-shaped leaves of the great northerns, spit and chewed the sweet purple alfalfa flowers like fragrant tobacco. They cut alfalfa tops for the evening greens. Then came the week spent tinkering with the rakes, sweeps and mowers up to that morning when Ben Hogan stormed through the house, brandishing a ripe sprig of alfalfa like a club. He announced the time: ''Get the hell out of bed! There's hay out there! We got *hay* out there! It'll likely rain before you get your shoes on!''

Their machines moved out over the fields, the mower clattering, breaking down at least twice a day. The old man stomped and swore. He nicked his hands replacing sharp steel teeth. The hay-rakes followed his mower, his sons turning the dried hay into neat, continuous piles that looked like whorls of a huge thumbprint in the fields. Ben Hogan and his sons moved like parts of the same machine to stack that hay in high, tangled mounds in the stackyards. They ran from mower to rake to plunger to haywagon to pitchfork for four weeks straight, moving ton after ton of dried grass and clover. There were times when they leapt on each other in the anger of frustration over somebody screwing a wrong bolt in somewhere or some backward adjustment; and once, Mike Hogan accidentally hooked a chain on the wrong sprocket so the gears of the haymower were sheared off with a high-speed shriek of disintegrating steel. Marge watched the three men shouting. They wrestled each other on the stacks. They strained, vise-gripped heads and privates, tangled in wrestling, then they rolled over the edge and tumbled down the long slope of the stack. By then they were laughing, stretched out with chests heaving skyward, exhausted in the shadows until Ben Hogan put his boys back to work again by telling them, "You're the laziest damned rednecks I ever laid eyes on. You're the weakest goddamned mollycoddles I ever seen!"

"A mollycoddle," Ben Hogan explained, out drinking with his friends, "hell, that's any man who *sits down* to take a piss!"

3

Marge grew up mostly with her brothers. Summers, they smoked rolled cornsilk behind the barn. Winters, they trudged over the snowcrust dragging wooden sleds to the manure hill by the corral. They tried bronco-busting calves, sheep and each other. George was huge, with broad shoulders and a dark head of curls. Mike was thinner, more like his father, and whenever he talked to anyone, his eyes were somewhere else. Marge hunted with her brothers. One side of the barn was covered with the stretched white skins of rabbits they sold for about thirty cents apiece at the wool exchange in town. Marge followed behind them, bundled up and doing the stiff snowshoe slide over the snow-covered prairie.

Once, on purpose, the boys shot one of their father's buck sheep with the twenty-two. They couldn't find any rabbits that day. She followed them as usual, punching at their shoulders from time to time to get a chance to shoot. They spent the entire afternoon target-shooting at bits of brush that poked up out of the snow. It began to get darker. She listened to the crunching sound of their snowshoes breaking through. Her hands were numb. She curled them tighter into her pockets. "I'm cold," she moaned, trying to keep up with them. George was out in front with the rifle. Mike shuffled just in front of her, peering around under his sheepskin hood to make sure she was keeping up. "I'm cold," she moaned again.

"Hush up," spat George. "We ain't going back until we get us something."

"I'll take her back," said Mike. George stopped and glowered at them.

"Aw, the hell with you both," said George.

They began the long shuffle back to the house, Mike leading this time with the rifle. They crossed two barbed-wire fences. Dark, jagged post tops were all that showed above the snow, without sign of the wires connecting them. Marge kept telling herself it was only one more fence to cross, just one more fence to cross and they were almost home. Her feet were numb. She bent against the wind and let her mind fill with the rhythmic, crunching sound of her feet.

"Well, if that don't beat it," said George. Marge raised her head. George pointed to one of her father's buck sheep, loose from the corral and in the neighbor's pasture. "That sonofabitch has broke out again," he said. He looked back at Mike, who stood silently, meekly holding out the rifle.

"Best idea you've had in a week," said George. He reached for the gun. "Now, Petie," he said. He always called her Petie or Margie-Pete when he wanted something. "Now, Petie," he cooed, moving close enough to take her by the shoulders. "You don't tell nobody about this, you hear? We're going to do ourselves some target-shooting. I don't aim to chase that buck back one more time. No, honey, I don't. You tell, and we'll fix your ass but good."

"That's Papa's," she said.

"He won't know the difference," said Mike. "He'll think the coyotes got it. Won't he, George?"

She watched the young buck move slowly toward the pink line of the sunset. It broke through the snow to its shoulders, then it jumped out of the hole and broke through the crust again. His wool was just a shade darker than the snow. The shadows of the evening blue almost swallowed him whole. He was trying to run. He plunged up and down powerfully, spraying snow out around him. He threw his front hooves up high, bounding through the waves of snow. He stopped. He heaved a vapor trail and licked his nostrils. He turned his head toward them, the ears raised. George knelt and dropped his gloves. He brought the rifle stock to his shoulder. The sound of the gunshot was distant, muffled by the wind. The white body tumbled over itself and kicked dead in the snow.

When they reached the house, the first thing Marge did was tell on them. George and Mike got the whipping of their lives. Ben Hogan chased his sons out of the house, smashing a chair thrown against the door. The boys didn't turn up again until the middle of the night, lips blue, their knuckles bleeding from trying to skin and butcher the already frozen carcass of the sheep. They stood on the porch half frost-bitten and George in tears.

They caught up with Marge after breakfast. They took her out to the manure pile and buried her. For a month after that, they refused to take her along with them to the movies in town. George and Mike were her only way to get to town but for the schoolbus and the times she went with her mother, shopping. Getting to town was most important to her then. Town was the place to buy things, or at least to try on outfits she couldn't afford. It was a meeting hall for the 4-H dances and the Grange. It was the place where the town kids lived. She often envied the life of the town kids and did her best to make friends with them. But even when she was with them, in school, they were always the same eighteen miles distant.

Her brothers had owned a car from the time George was sixteen. She had watched them build it from pieces of old cars and had learned to hold the wrenches. It seemed that ever since they could talk, her brothers were holding tools. They were always pounding at machinery. Mike even managed to kill her pet hen because of his interest in machinery. One Christmas, the family gave her that hen as a present. She waited in her bedroom, imagining clothes and records or something so large that she couldn't possibly need it. For days, George and Mike had been clucking their tongues at her as if that was some hint at what it was, then on Christmas morning, they made her stay behind her closed door until it was ready. George opened the door and pushed his head in.

"It's all yours, Pete!"

A hen circled the Christmas tree, bobbing its head, pecking at a can of corn set there for it. A long red ribbon trailed from one yellow foot to a limb of the blue spruce. That bird was a gray leghorn, a breed with unusually long legs and striped gray feathers, which had been sent all the way from England. Marge fell in love with it immediately. It was the most beautiful bird she had ever seen. She cradled it for a week, stroking the feathers, letting it peck at the disordered blond hairs falling down over her nose. But that hen wouldn't roost with the other hens. It preferred to build its own nest out in the cold, in an old threshing machine behind the barn. Each morning, Marge climbed up over the bin and reached down through the wooden spokes to collect the eggs. The hen complained at her, but if she talked at it like speaking at a doll, it didn't peck her hand. The eggs were usually brown. But sometimes, she found an egg that was green-speckled or bright orange. She brought them to the house and showed them to her mother. "You just might win a prize at the 4-H with eggs like that," Vera Hogan said. "They sure are curiosities." She held them up to the light to check for spots. "Go on and see what they hatch into," she said, putting them back in her daughter's palm.

Marge began to imagine they had other meanings. She imagined that if the eggs were green enough times, it was a sign she wouldn't pass the sixth grade that year and if enough of them were orange, Ron Ballock would discover that he had always loved her secretly. Come next summer's Farmers' Union picnic, he would want to lead her into the willows. Then one afternoon, Mike bought an old gas engine at a farm auction. He was excited to try it out, hooking up a belt and pulley to the threshing machine, then pulling the cord. The bin heaved once, the wooden spokes clattering, spinning noisily around on their track. A tiny cloud of gray and white feathers drifted out of the chute. Mike had forgotten Marge's hen liked to roost inside.

He didn't tell her right away. He waited almost until supper, when Marge was sent out for an extra egg for the potato salad. "Now, Margie," he said, catching her on the back porch. He held out a small paper sack, heavy at the bottom, a dark stain starting to show through the paper. "Aw, I'm sorry, Petie," he said, handing her the sack. "But it served that dumb bird right if you ask me."

Walking out through the pasture behind the barn with the sack and a shovel, the shadows of the cottonwoods long over the short green grass of the meadow in spring, the sunlight fading to an eerie yellow in the immense rolling distance to the horizon, she was resigned to the loss. The family dog followed behind her, snuffling at the bag until she swung the shovel at him. She had seen death since she was born—the dogs and cats that had died, her father shooting his steers or the same bum lambs she had bottle fed through the winter, then hanging them up and bleeding them out; and other deaths: the cow that had coughed hoarsely until it lay down and refused to eat, and once, only partly remembered when she was a little girl peeking out through the screen door, the Reary boy had been loaded into her father's pickup after he caught his shoelace in a horse-drawn combine by the south fence.

The birds were singing from the cottonwood undisturbed and took flight only when she started to dig, brown explosions out of the half-bare branches. She cut a square in the sod, chopping through it, peeling it aside in one heavy piece and then scooping into the dark soil, cussing at the tree roots in the way, dirt spilling over her heavy shoes. She dug until she hit the hardpan, until she couldn't dig anymore. She dropped the sack into the hole in a lump, like a sack of peelings. On second thought, she reached down into the hole and opened the sack a little, not wanting to look, feeling around inside until she pulled out a long gray striped feather. She filled the hole. She found a small stone and weighed the feather down over the grave. Her family's voices came in bits and pieces across the field, carried on the breeze, her brothers hungry and too impatient to wait for her even with the stern voice of her mother. She wondered what it would be like to grow up somewhere else, wishing she'd been born in town.

George and Mike were always building something. It took them only two months that spring to build the car that changed all their lives. Their car made it possible for Marge to go to town sometimes without her mother and not only have that snot Carol Hinkle who lived just down the road as her only friend, someone she couldn't talk to except of kitchens. It was the car that made it possible for Marge to get close to her town friend, Rae Ott, who could describe the desired subject even if she was a minister's granddaughter. Rae swore it was possible to hold her fingers out like witching rods and make boys fall over themselves in the school halls. Rae and Marge spent afternoons talking about boys, trying out makeup and cigarettes. They positioned themselves at The Cove Café in tight sweaters and jitterbug skirts. They pretended to ignore all boys. Then they made plans to flunk the seventh grade so they could stay back with the boys they knew they loved forever. They spent weekend nights at each other's houses, sighing at the phonograph and at pictures of movie stars. Rae wasn't allowed to go to most movies due to a Calvinist streak in her family's religion, so Marge described them to her scene by scene. One Sunday, Rae switched a *Star & Screen* article Marge had brought to her for her grandfather's sermon on the rostrum. The article contained a full-page, smoky photo of Robert Taylor with his arms languidly draped around the bare shoulders of Greta Garbo, Garbo's expression a mixture of ecstasy and dying. The Reverend Charles G. Ott normally delivered his sermons in a dry clear monotone as if reading directly from his notes. That morning, as he took the rostrum and held out his arms over the assembled families of the Church of Christ Reformed, the look on his face, the high cackling in his voice, made the girls sink down in the back pew, choking, biting their lips. In short, Marge and Rae became best friends. And it was all because of her brothers' car.

She watched George and Mike building it piece by piece. George drew up a design with a crayon on a piece of cardboard. He hung it over a window of the machinery shop, raving on and on about how they would paint that car a gleaming silver so it would look like a fighter plane without wings. While George talked, laughing and spreading his arms, jumping around over the scattered parts,

Mike was busy quietly inspecting each part, holding it close to his eyes and up to the light of the single bulb that hung from the rafters. He made a list of all they would need. Ben Hogan paid out more than thirty dollars for parts because the boys had worked so hard in the fields. It wasn't easy for Marge to imagine all those pieces of scrap iron would ever look like George's picture. She came to watch them work on it every afternoon and fetched things for them. Sometimes, when the boys were up against a tough adjustment and shouting at each other, the both of them sprawled under the chassis at cross-purposes, they stopped work for a while. They crawled out from under their gutted machine, covered with grease, and partly to keep from slugging each other, partly for lack of anything better to do, they played catch with Marge. She grew to love their playing catch with her, as long as they didn't throw her high enough to hit the shop beams.

Marge went to town sometimes with her mother, Saturdays after morning chores. Most of her chores were in the kitchen with her mother. Vera Hogan had spent most of her life in the kitchen except for twice a week, when she became like a whirlwind that moved through the house to battle the dust and manure tracked in by her family. She was a stern woman who hardly ever spoke. Sometimes, when Ben Hogan came back from a night at the Nowell municipal bar, she made him sleep in the barn, the kind of woman who could do this without uttering a word. She owned two hats for town. The summer hat was black straw with a wide, flopping brim. She wore it with a cluster of fresh flowers pinned to one side of the crown. The winter hat was made of stiff felt, with a short brim like a bowler hat and with a square silver buckle in front as if to match the right angles of her face. She was a heavyset woman who had never been pretty, or had never seemed pretty to Marge, especially in town among the women who dressed with style, who didn't show a trace of dried mud on their fashionable shoes. Marge tried to get her mother to take off her hats, but Vera claimed she didn't feel comfortable without one. In town, Marge felt embarrassed by her mother's hats, that made her look somehow more plain than she was, older than she was, and that made them both stick out unmistakably as hicks from the gumbo. As she grew older, she began to feel sorry that her mother was the kind of woman who thought she had to hide under them.

Vera Hogan almost never complained, though she was ailing even as she cooked, cleaned, hauled, did heavy lifting when her kids were in school and there was no one else to help her husband. She had had surgery several times. Most people said the experience had touched her some. Marge eventually had to take on most of the house chores, though her mother never asked her directly to do them. When her mother was ailing and wanted Marge to help around the house, she took down her jar of gallstones. She claimed those gallstones were "the smallest and most painful Doc Monahan had ever committed surgery upon." They were the size of coarse grains of sand and there were enough of those tiny mud-brown pebbles to fill a small canning jar almost halfway. Vera Hogan used to spill them carefully out on the kitchen table and count them. Her hand, which was like a pack of loose bones in an old leather purse, moved each gallstone slowly from one pile into another. By the time the count was finished, Marge had already swept the carpet or cleaned the stove or was hanging wet clothes on the line to dry. Her mother's count almost never came out the same from one day to the next.

"Will you look at that," she said. "There's a hundred twenty-two of 'em. Yesterday, there was a hundred thirty-six of 'em. I just can't figure it. I keep thinking maybe one of you kids has been messing with my jar...."

Marge continued on about her work without answering. She watched her mother shake her head, then begin to count the brown pebbles back into her canning jar. And as the years passed, Vera Hogan spent more and more time ailing. Marge began to wake up early, leaving her mother sleep, to fix breakfasts of oatmeal, eggs, bacon, sausage, pancakes, home fries, a whole tableful of food for the men. She washed up the dishes. Then if it was summer, she made the bag lunches and sugared tea she brought out to her men in the fields. She spent afternoons standing over a deep boiling kettle, dropping in jars filled from the garden and lifting them out according to the clock. She tapped the shiny lids to make sure they were sealed. This sometimes went on long into the nights. But there was a satisfaction at the end of the season in seeing so many jars packed onto the back porch shelves like the ranks and files of a colorful army of fat glass soldiers on parade.

She didn't mind cooking, cleaning and canning, would never have thought to mind it, but she felt imprisoned by the kitchen as her men worked. She would much rather have been out there with them, working like a man, if she couldn't live in town. Ben Hogan thought it was unladylike for his daughter to work in the fields. He only let her work out there if she was truly needed, during the four weeks of haying season. Marge drove the tractor that pulled the haywagon. She learned to use a pitchfork that toughened her hands. She grew to love it out there, working with her brothers. Her brothers played catch with her, just resting. She chewed their tobacco. She felt playfully at their jeans. She pestered them constantly for rides when they went to town. Then one day, she was with her brothers when they shot that buck sheep on purpose and they refused to take her to town anymore. She spent the next full month pretending she didn't care. Then for her birthday, George and Mike built her a bicycle from pieces of old bicycles so when the snow cleared she could get there on her own.

4

Pearl Harbor was bombed and war was declared. In remote South Dakota, a place where the chance passage of an airplane still brought people out of their homes to marvel at the sky, the news of war was received with an outward sense of calm. Many had been expecting war and out here, on what had once been a vast plain of buffalo grass thousands of miles from the gravity of events, few doubted what the outcome would be. Lives changed overnight, with crops, livestock and machinery left in the care of wives and daughters as men presented themselves to defend Old Glory from the "yellow peril" and the "Nazi blitzkrieg." Or so they viewed it, as simply as that, like a mass boxing match with everyone cheering for the hometown boys. George and Mike joined the service the week after Christmas and were soon shipped out to training camp. Ben Hogan, unlike his neighbors, told them not to go, to stay and work the farm, they were surely eligible for agricultural deferments. But nothing could keep them home. They saw a great adventure overtaking them.

Almost since the day the boys left the homeplace, things went wrong. The priorities of wartime farming gave Ben Hogan the choice of raising either sugar beets or turkeys. He could raise enough corn to feed his turkeys and maybe have enough left over for local sale, or he could plow his cornfields under and plant row upon row of difficult sugar beets. He could have tried selling his corn at the local elevator so it might join the great rivers of western grain pouring east and west through feedlots and mills. But the Department of Agriculture, which claimed, "Victory is a question of stamina" in many wartime pamphlets, was struggling to provide enough meats and sugars for the crisis overseas. The USDA recommended in its many wartime directives that the coarse gray soil known colloquially as "gumbo" was best utilized when sapped by the gnarled, gray-brown roots of the sugar beet. During the first year of the war, a huge government loan helped to expand and improve the Great Westward sugar refinery in the town of Belle Fourche, forty miles away. The Nowell-Safebuy turkey processing plant, eighteen miles away, had been steadily increasing production for years before the war began.

Ben Hogan couldn't figure it. There was supposed to be a corn shortage for the alcohol industry, alcohol necessary for the manufacture of explosives. But the USDA kept telling farmers here that it was simply good sense for a man to raise either beets or turkeys, since both could be processed right away, packed and made ready locally for immediate use. A man was free to raise just corn or wheat or beans, or other livestock animals than turkeys, free to raise many different crops at once in diversified farming, he really was, there wasn't any law against it. He just wouldn't get much government subsidy money through the Farmers and Ranchers Stabilization Board for those crops, and there were also certain priorities at the Belle Fourche & Western Railroad shipping office. The rails were under strict government supervision. Sugar and canned turkey were already piled up on the loading docks, and they were soon declared top-priority commodities. It was considered a waste of good boxcars to ship corn that could be raised more efficiently elsewhere hundreds of miles to feedlots, mills and distilleries before it could be turned into a finished product. So if a man in Wovoka County wanted to keep raising corn, wheat, beans, beef—diversified crops—just as he always had, he would have to wait several months or more before he could ship his harvest. He might have to sell what grain he could to local turkey growers who didn't have enough feed, then leave the rest to the chance that it might take on too much moisture in storage, steadily growing worse in nutritional values and lower in price per bushel until it was sold and, well, *there was a war on.* As Buster Hill, local manager of the Nowell-Safebuy plant, said, ''The boys overseas need beets and turkeys to win this war.''

There were problems with beets. They grew up so thickly after planting that the rows had to be thinned, and it was hard to cultivate them properly with tractors. A good beet crop required hundreds of hours of hand labor. So if a man raised beets, he needed labor to thin the rows and hoe the weeds and to cut tops during the harvest. That first year of the war, there was very little labor available. There were a few Brûlé Sioux up from the Rosebud reservation and about a hundred or so Mexicans who came up all the way from Texas. But that ramshackle force produced much less than the government expected. Something had to be done. The first shipment of German prisoners of war came in during 1943, sent as top priority in fine Pullman railroad cars. The seemingly endless rows of small, bushlike, green leafy plants could be finally thinned and cleaned of weeds by line after line of bluejeaned men sweating under the hot sun. At night, those men were kept in a huge wire cage called the Orman Camp. They could be herded around like turkeys by the army guards, mostly men not fit for combat, older men with years of service and a connection to get stationed stateside, or younger men who were just lucky.

By the time the first shipment of prisoners of war was expected, Ben Hogan had decided to raise turkeys, partly because he knew a lot of farmers who had gone with sugar beets and he had always been one to move in the other direction. But the main reason he had decided to raise turkeys was that he didn't want to have anything to do with Germans. His son George was off fighting them. He didn't want to have to look out in his fields and see the enemy working there, eating his food, watching his daughter. It was tempting, though. From a purely business point of view, the price of prisoner of war labor just couldn't be beat. He would only have to pay about eighteen cents an hour for every man, an extremely low price for farm labor, and with that kind of a deal, he might really make out raising sugar beets. All he had to do was plant the beets, irrigate, then he could sit back and watch the prisoners working his crop for a free lunch and a small check at the end of every week made payable to the army's provost marshal at the Orman Camp. And if any one of the prisoners didn't want to work to Ben Hogan's satisfaction, he wouldn't have to feed him or pay for him.

Prisoners were something to consider, but Ben Hogan didn't consider them for long. He decided he would rather farm turkeys by himself, his daughter helping, if that's what had to be done to win the war. He and his daughter launched into the turkey business with a sense of purpose which people mistook for enthusiasm. As far as Marge was concerned, she prayed for a quick victory overseas. Victory seemed like the only thing that could save them.

5

When she finished working turkeys on summer days, after the sun drew in its orange scarves and sank into the evening violet, her father sometimes let Marge out of chores so she could take the pickup into town. She spent a good hour or more at The Cove Café relaxing, sitting in a booth listening to the jukebox or the radio among crowds of women. She sipped at a tall iced tea and waved away the flies that used to plague that place during the years when the Nilsen family owned it. Summers, this town was filled with flies. It was also filled with bats, tiny bats about the size of a dimestore mouse. Bats swirled above the streets like whirling clouds of leaves. There was a constant chattering through the nights. Rapid shadows flickered against the storefronts as bats dove down suddenly under the six bare bulbs that were the only streetlights in the municipal lighting system.

Marge sat surrounded by women. It seemed that Nowell had become a town of women overnight. Most of them had driven in from the farms the same as she had, after a long day's work. They kept each other company, dressed in their diesel-stained clothes smelling of sweat and turkey manure, some of them with unaccustomed hands still bandaged from working in the fields. There were a few old Nowell farmers among them, a few old range boys, but The Cove Café and the municipal bar were mostly filled with women. They drank and shot pool just like their husbands. They talked ration tickets and government subsidies in the same careful tones as they talked about changes in the weather. That talk was a comfort to them, as if they might stay close to the men who had left them by living that way themselves.

This town was gripped by a pervasive fear. Everyone expected a telegram. Everyone listened intently to the radio at The Cove. There were four bodies shipped home during 1943. Marge went to the funerals, always with the sense that it could have been her brothers. Mose Johnson, foreman at the Nowell-Safebuy turkey plant, usually helped to organize the transportation. He commandeered an army bus to drive the hundred miles to the national cemetery at Sturgis and sometimes he rode along. He dressed in his black pants and shirt, his brown dress Stetson, consoling everyone, doing his best to support the grieving family along with the Right Reverend Charles G. Ott. He was one of the few men who stood in silence with the women, watching the coffin lowered into that green tailored hill that was covered with white crosses as far as the eye could see.

It didn't make sense to Marge the way some women turned their fears into lust. That was the word for it. She could feel it happening at those funerals, was embarrassed some by it. And yet she often found herself wishing it for them—that all their fear and grief, for most of them a grieving in anticipation, might turn to some momentary passion for Mose Johnson or any other man. She remembered what her father had said about Mose: "He couldn't pour piss out of a boot if there was directions printed on the heel." But he was one of the only unmarried men, and she had seen it more than once at graveside, among that crowd of women dressed in mourning. The color rose in their cheeks as Mose responded, his arm supporting them with a gentle and stupid kind of innocence. She watched those women flushing at his touch and presence even as they muttered, wept, drew close around the grave. And as she stood on with them, she felt angry at Mose Johnson for being the kind of man who would never know their needs.

Carol McCann, who was notorious for sacking with a half-breed drunkard like Charlie Gooch, with a dull-witted packing plant butcher like Dale Rynning, with a hopeless case like Sheriff Meeker or with any old fogy she could find, the raunchier the better, a list of one-night stands as long as her arm, sat in The Cove talking on at Marge in a wistful, sentimental tone of voice as if Marge's youth somehow reminded her of her own. She talked always of the first man she had ever loved, her husband Jody, away in the navy, and always in the past tense as if he had already died.

Mary Wasiolek was a small, humble woman, gray at a young age and a woman who had long remained faithful to her husband. She was so faithful that she even insisted on washing his GI socks. Every month or so, she received a package of dirty socks in the mail and claimed that was one way she reminded herself she was married. She washed those socks, wrote passionate letters and sent them back. Then Ben Wasiolek was killed in action. For several months after that, Mary kept getting his packages of dirty socks in the mail. Marge shared her grief. She sat across a table from her at The Cove Café. She held her hands and agreed with her compassionately that there was nothing else a woman could do but keep washing her husband's socks, sending them back overseas. When the last package was finally mailed, Mary Wasiolek gave up farming two thousand turkeys all on her own. She sold the Wasiolek family farm to the Nowell-Safebuy. She left town with a traveling salesman for the Mason Shoe Company and was never heard from again.

Anita Foos, who in those days was pursued by every old boy in town, though it was well known she was happily married to a man who settled scores, often spent her hours at The Cove passing around the one photograph of her husband. Marge had always admired Larry Foos from a distance. He was that boy who had won the state wrestling championships, that boy sure to make his mark as the best mechanic this town had ever seen. During their senior year, Anita and Larry were voted the couple most likely to succeed. Marge stared into the photograph. Larry was in a large group of marines, a suntanned face third row to the left against a gray, numbered background. The only hint of where he might be was a single withered palm leaf intruding into the top left edge of the frame. Anita kept telling everyone in a voice filled with celebration that Larry was coming home soon. He had written two months ago that he might because he had malaria. Nobody said anything. They let her go on believing that she hadn't heard from him since because he must be bound on some shipment home.

Marge sat among the women. She studied them, their work

clothes somehow reminding her all the more of what they looked like underneath. She was saddened by them. At the same time, she began to resent her own treatment. They treated her like some favorite niece at The Cove. The way those women talked to her, they made her feel too much like what she knew she was—a girl who didn't know any more about love than some boy pinching at her and fondling her hair. Or some old boy like Mose Johnson joking with her how much he hated ponytails because they made him think of what was under a pony's tail. It might have been enough if she could just flirt with a man, take his arm as the jukebox went on raving its love songs. Mose Johnson, Charlie Gooch, Dale Rynning, anyone, but the times she had tried, it was always the same reaction. She took Mose's eyes on directly. He smiled. He turned away shyly, giving her a look she knew was different than the one he might have given someone else. Then he always turned the conversation back to working. ''How you been making out with them turkeys?'' he'd ask. ''You ought to have near three thousand pullets out there. Some of the damndest ugliest birds I ever seen. But one thing I got to say for them. I ain't never seen turkeys grow as fast during the pullet stage. Ain't that right? Has old Ben remarked how fast they grow?''

She gave up trying to flirt with him. She drank her iced tea, pumping nickels hopelessly into the jukebox. It was getting impossible to hear the songs. There was too much conversation and the radio was usually on full blast, the jukebox unplugged at the first sign of any news announcement. She couldn't help but begin to hate that crowd of women. It was even getting hard to go to the movies anymore. Thursday nights, when the film of the week passed through on the Jack Rabbit bus lines, the Arcade Bingo & Theater was filled with the shouts, hoots, and wolf whistles of women. As Marge sat at The Cove sucking sugar off the icecubes from her glass, she wondered just what it was those women knew of love that she did not. The way they talked, she began to doubt any of them had ever really loved.

She strolled out into the street. The nights were cool and there was a constant chattering overhead. She savored the night air. But just savoring the night air was never enough. She picked up a dirt clod and threw it high into a circling cloud of bats. She watched the small dark shapes swarm in around the clod and follow it down in swift, chattering dives as if not quite sure of what it was until it hit the ground. She watched the bare bulbs of the streetlights swimming with insects. She continued on to her father's battered pickup and drove the eighteen miles home.

6

The third Christmas of the war, George and Mike each sent the family a photograph. Mike sent one of himself in his tailor-made blues, leaning with one elbow against an engine and hefting a wrench as long as his arm. George sent a photo showing a hill of burned treestumps and himself in a foxhole, arm over a buddy, both of them wearing sunglasses, both of them presenting rifles with youthful smirks. Mike's photo ran half a page in the Nowell *Enterprise* after the U.S.S. *South Dakota* was bombed. Later that summer, George was missing in action. His body was never found.

"Goddamn turkeys," said Ben Hogan. His old leather boots kicked out at clods of soil. He held the President's yellow telegram, the news of George crumpled in his fist. "They got us chasing birds." She watched him say it with a tired voice. He stared out over his acre of white fluttering turkeys. "I don't think they ever would've done it," he said. "Too much goddamned work in it for 'em. That's right. They never would've stood these turkeys. They always was that way. They'd've rigged up some kind of *power* herder. You betcha. . . . It ain't possible, no kind of power herder. . . ."

The old car her brothers had built from pieces of other cars sat glaring under the sun, parked on a corner of the meadow where they had left it. It didn't run anymore. A pair of spurs dangled, rusting, from the rearview mirror. Crumpled beer cans and an old stained horse blanket swirled in the back seat, gathering dust, and became the home of mice and insects. The tires the boys had painted white cracked and flattened gradually under the sun. Their gleaming silver car turned a uniform color of rust and sagged into the earth. On summer mornings, before her father could drag himself out alone into his fields, he made a habit of tying his horse to the bumper, sitting on one fender snapping the long lead rope into the swaying grass, talking to himself as if his boys were listening.

Marge's mother drew circles in the flour dust on the table. Her mother scratched at the disordered hair over her eyes and leaned into her palm. The yellow light from the ceiling lamps made her features look waxen, sharpened as if they were carved out by a pocket knife. Chokecherry pies reminded her too much of her sons. She still hadn't cleaned the room where they had last left socks crumpled under the beds, their straw work hats scattered with a pile of empty clothes.

"You get yourself married," she said, with an expression hardened by realities. "Your papa can't work this place on his own."

Marge sipped at her coffee without answering.

"I ain't worth much no more," her mother said. "I can't do it for him no more."

"I'll fix me up some dresses," Marge answered, finally, smelling the sweet, heavy odor of the pies.

7

Marge helped her father herd turkeys. They moved the flock out of the pens Ben had built in the barn, using short poles to push the birds into the near pasture after grasshoppers. They walked through the cool grass swinging poles, signaling to each other if small groups of turkeys wanted to split off and slip through or over the barbed-wire fence. Then Marge was left to tend them while her father put up enough corn to feed them. They were strange-looking turkeys, in Ben Hogan's opinion—a pure White Holland variety that came in crateloads of tiny squeaking poults from the Nowell-Safebuy every spring. Ben knew something about turkeys. For many years, he had raised a few out back for family consumption, mostly mixed range varieties—the dark gray Slate, the black English, the Narragansett with its bright coppery plumage, the Bourbon Red and the Bronze. Marge grew up watching the tall scrawny toms chasing the hens around the backyard, pinning them to the earth in explosions of feathers. But this new White Holland variety was different. The poults grew to unbelievable sizes during the first few weeks, or at least the percentage of them that survived to the pullet stage. The toms stood about waist high to Marge, gleaming white birds that thrust their breasts out and strutted proudly in their pens. She watched one in courtship. It danced. It spread its white wings and jumped up wildly, clawing at the dust. It stretched its red neck high and called out to the hens. It slowly began circling, wings stretched out, and first one wingtip then the other wingtip touched the earth with fast steady rhythm, lifting its body just a few inches off the ground before it circled again, Marge thinking she could hear a farcical music in its dance. The tom turkey settled, huffed out its breast and fanned a pure white tail into the sun. It stood, head erect, proud.

Each day through the summer, Marge moved the turkeys out of their pens and into the pasture. She watched the awkward way the pullets pranced around, bald red heads in constant motion as in some strange Egyptian dance, the thousands of quick dark eyes like a small nation in search of food. In the fall, she helped her father load the birds onto trucks and ship them off to town. That turkey check was "decent," in Ben's words—the mortgage payment was made, the fuel bill, parts bill, seed bill, everything was paid up by Christmas with enough left over for the winter. Then when the creek began flowing in spring, Marge had to be up before dawn again working poults, repairing pens. She vaccinated thousands upon thousands of feeble balls of gray down she could hold in the palm of one hand. She put young chickens in the pens with them. Turkey poults could only learn to peck by watching chickens. Without chickens, they stood in piles of grain and died of starvation.

They died in swarms anyway. She collected them in a disinfected box. She spent hours on her hands and knees, scrubbing the pens with iodine and a wire brush. She burned the dead and quarantined the living. By summer, she worked sunup to sundown tending the survivors. She let the pullets out of the barn to follow swarms of grasshoppers through the fields. She had to keep that huge gobbling herd of pure white turkeys moving through the fields by day and had to chase them back to shelter again before night brought out the foxes, skunks, wild dogs and coyotes that had begun to develop a special appetite for turkeys. While herding them, it was almost impossible to keep the flock together. Many of the stronger birds wanted to lead groups through and over the fences as if to some strange attraction on the horizon. The flock might break up into dozens of smaller flocks, all headed in different directions. And herding turkeys was difficult because many of the more aggressive toms attacked whoever was making them move. They tossed their bright red crops around. They pranced ridiculously and slashed out with their beaks, gobbling war cries as they launched right into Marge. In the ensuing violence of her swinging pole and some clawing tom, hundreds of birds scattered in panic, flapping in all directions through the fields, and it took up to several hours to round them all up again. There was also a problem with cannibalism, the occasional turkey that ruthlessly attacked any bird that came too close. Turkeys nearest the action rushed in to devour the victims and that soon caused a chain reaction until the flock was mad with the smell of its own blood. Marge had to butcher or isolate any cannibalistic birds right away.

Not only that: there were diseases, serious diseases. She had to check to make sure the manure of the flock had the proper consistency. She wandered through more than an acre of pure White Holland turkeys. From time to time she stopped, when she saw the gray-brown manure dribbling out from under a tail. She bent down and poked the end of her pole into it, then raised it for inspection. She had to catch any signs of the turkey blackhead disease right away. That disease not only might kill most of the flock; it could also infest the meat of the survivors. Then the USDA might come in and ruin them financially by ordering them to slaughter and burn every turkey they owned. There was another disease called salmonella, which was even worse. That disease made turkeys suddenly drop their necks to the ground, their bodies listing drunkenly as they struggled to walk while dragging their beaks along beside them or between their legs. The entire flock soon grew too weak to hold up their heads and in a matter of hours they died of green runny scouring and high fevers. Salmonella could also make a man's family miserable with the same symptoms, though few people ever died. Then whenever it threatened to rain, Marge and her father had to rush out into the fields to herd their turkeys back into the barn or under shelter quickly, because sometimes a whole flock might stop chasing grasshoppers to stand in a kind of religious silence and watch the rain ball up in the dust. Looking hypnotized, turkeys peered down at the bouncing raindrops despite someone beating at them to move. At first, they pecked cautiously at the droplets as if they were insects. Then after the slow realization that it was water, not food, moving on the ground, all of them, gobbling festively and testing their short wings, prancing a bit as if to brace themselves, that entire flock in an incredibly orchestrated movement raised their scraggly necks from the ground, tilted their bald red heads to face the sky, and opened their beaks wide to the falling rain until they drowned.

Marge would watch her father moving after his flock. He had begun to walk with stiffness in his legs. Sometimes, he just sat down in the middle of a field for more than an hour, scratching the end of his pole through the dirt, staring into the distance. Marge had never seen him sit that way before. It seemed as if each time he did, it took him longer to stand up again and help her chase the scattered birds. Marge hated chasing turkeys. She hated the sound they made, the whole flock screaming all at once when a hawk dove low or a dog barked too close to them. At times she felt a listlessness in their mood affect her own.

Nights, she worked for hours sewing clothes. She bought what new materials she could but there wasn't much available. She made one dress out of five and dime material. She dyed simple cotton sacking cloth and hemmed it into skirts. Her mother watched over her shoulder, giving advice, helping to press stubborn edges home with her knotty fingers.

"That's good," she told Marge as they sewed. "That'll draw the eyes. I had me somethin' like that once. It drew me the eyes. . . ."

Marge wondered who he would be. She talked it over with Rae Ott, who was already engaged to an army corporal and was soon moving to California. She and Rae spent time searching the pages of the Ward's, Sears and Spiegel catalogues for bedroom sets, matching couches and loveseats for the living room, drapes, modern appliances, things Marge was sure inside that she would never own. As they turned the pages of the catalogues, Rae agreed with her that if Ron Ballock came home, he was the best choice. He had the welding trade and he could farm. He had always made her laugh with his jokes, like how the old sheepherder wakes up ever' mornin' with a cup of coffee and a piece of ewe and as he said this he would laugh at his own joke and try to see how far he could get with her. But no matter how hard she tried, and even though she used to dream of him years ago, Marge couldn't get excited about Ron Ballock now. She told herself she would just have to learn to make him happy. He was still the best choice. And if Ron Ballock didn't ask her, there was always Burt Cooney. Burt Cooney, all weasel-like and clamping his bony arms around her waist, jiggling her on his knee and telling her, "Now, Margie, this here knee may be a joint, but it sure as hell ain't no place of entertainment!"

Well, there'd be somebody. She was sure of that. There had to be *some*body. . . .

She began to have trouble sleeping. She'd usually been able to stagger in from supper, flop down in bed and the next thing she knew, the cocks were crowing mercilessly into the predawn grayness. But as the war drew closer to its end, it was harder to sleep. Her mornings seemed to pass much faster than she had ever remembered, her afternoons much more slowly, her mind and body steadily grinding down into those nights when she lay back not wanting to move. She could never tell how long it took until she fell asleep. She felt her back heating the sheets and mattress. She shifted around uncomfortably, looking for a cooler strip. She closed her eyes but it was no use. She sat up and turned on her lamp. She smoked a long time, filling her ashtray with brown, unfurling butts. She turned off her lamp. She closed her eyes and tried to imagine her lover there with her, but it was getting harder each time. She turned on her lamp again and tried to drink herself to sleep. Carol McCann had bought her a bottle that she used for that purpose, but she soon found that intoxication only seemed to keep her awake all the more. She turned off her lamp again. She lay back remembering the sound at The Cove of the random, distant radio station. . . . *in valiant street-to-street fighting, the Allied forces captured the city of Caen today.* . . .

She stared off through the darkness.

. . . inflicting heavy casualties and firmly establishing the flow of men and equipment into Europe. . . .

She wished she had a radio of her own and could fade into the news or dreamlike violin music or even the usual persistent static of the summer lightning.

. . . "Monty" announces that he'll reach Berlin by Christmas. . . .

She remembered how in the booth at The Cove, she had assured Anita Foos again that her husband was surely coming home. All the while, Carol McCann had her arm around Mose Johnson. She had watched the front of Carol's overalls, barely hiding what Marge thought were humongously large breasts, slowly heaving in and out as if powered by hydraulic overdrive. She lay awake wondering what that woman was doing now. She wished again that she had a radio of her own and resolved to get one as soon as the war came to an end. She slapped uselessly at the mosquitoes. She closed her eyes and tried to conjure her lover there again and found she could no longer imagine him. She was terrified. She grew convinced, for the first time, that she was doomed to live as a solitary woman for the rest of her life.

. . . . meanwhile in the wake of victory all was quiet in the Pacific. . . . Admiral "Bull" Halsey reports the only activity on his screens this week was Hedy Lamarr. . . .

8

When the boys started coming home, Marge tried her best to get married. She put on her new clothes. She drove her father's pickup to the municipal bar. She perched on a stool, her legs held in perfect S-curves sheathed in seductive nylon, her elbow gracefully leaning next to her drink. She did her hair like the movie star Veronica Lake so that it covered one eye, swept over the point of her cheek and spilled smoothly over her bared shoulders. Silver and turquoise dangled from her ears. She drew her lips in deep red and powdered her face. She flared her nostrils. She exuded clouds of L'Origan and Lilac Mist and dragon trails of smoke. She left the top of her dress unhooked to suggest encounter. She fluttered her eyes. One night, she even pretended there was hayseed in one of her eyes so Ron Ballock could lean in close, probing with a corner of his oil-stained handkerchief and listing drunkenly on his heels.

"There now," he said. "That's got it, I betcha." He patted her on the head like a dog. Then he hobbled back to his game of pool, feeling his war wounds.

Marge tried learning to shoot pool, rolling the soft melons of her behind with each ridiculous shot, peering down the length of her cue at the impossible angles.

"You go on and leave the table to the boys," Ron Ballock grumbled. "Either that, or put up your five bucks just like everybody else."

Marge lost twenty dollars that way.

Burt Cooney started coming in nights, covered with diesel, the grasshoppers crawling in his pockets. He sat up at the barstool next to Marge. He bought her beers and sloe gin cocktails. He swaggered around the pool table, spitting tobacco and teaching her how. Marge won back her twenty dollars. Burt Cooney invited her to the dance in Whitewood.

She went with him. It was a forty-mile drive, south into the tree-covered hills. They passed a pint bottle. He belched at the wheel. He pounded his hand on the dash in rhythm to the crackling of the radio. He threw his chest out proudly under the pink flowers of his western shirt. Before they left the car to join the folks packed into the main street of that town, wildly kicking their heels to the music of fiddles and Hawaiian guitars, Burt Cooney arranged each grease-coated strand of hair in the rearview mirror, pushing his thick glasses higher on his nose.

They danced. He waved his hat like they were riding in the rodeo. He did tiny quick steps to either side, gripped her hands, then he swung her dizzily on the axis of his cowboy heels. He pressed in closely for the slower numbers, oblivious of the elbow raised to protect her breasts. That street was too crowded with hooting range boys tossing women in bright clothes and the music was usually too fast to keep up with unless Marge let Burt Cooney drag her in circles or lift her perilously in his tottering arms. He grinned each time he lifted her, as if surprised at himself, then he bore in to try again until he tossed her up just a bit too far and with a high-pitched scream of amazement he fell on top of her, as stiff and heavy as a pine log.

"Marry me," he said, parked under the fireworks of the northern lights on the way home. Marge still held an icepack to her head. "I love you, gal . . ." he moaned.

"I'm not any goddamned *gal*," she muttered, then lit a cigarette.

She tried another man. He was a huge bear of a man named Clemmie Bosserd. He worked for the Homestake Gold Mine in the town of Deadwood, fifty miles south, but he had grown up on Marge Hogan's mail route out of Nowell. He stopped for Marge one day to help her change a tire. He invited her up to the historic mining town in the picturesque holy hills of the Sioux for drinks and dinner, for an evening spent reaching a compromise while holding hands and exchanging personal histories. His eyes were the color of blue steel. They looked her over through the dim amber candlelight of the restaurant as if she were a piece of fruit.

He told her his war story. She laughed at how he had been standing in the noncom club when it was bombed. He dove under a table. The sergeant cowering with him had a Scotch in his hand and there was a full bottle of it on the table above their heads. He was ordered to rescue the bottle. He reached up to grab for it just as a bomb sent a shower of fragments through the canvas walls. He wondered how he would ever explain to his kids that he had received the Purple Heart while reaching for a Scotch.

She pressed him at the mention of children. He said he wanted at least ten, though he couldn't afford them. She sympathized with his hard life in the mines, his days spent using a steel bar to pry loose rock down from the shaft ceilings. She told him about her father's farm, his predicament, the deaths of her brothers. Clemmie listened quietly for a long time.

"There just doesn't seem to be a man worth the bother," she said.

"You come home with me now," Clemmie said, "and I'll show you who to bother with."

She rose immediately to go to the "gal's" room. She was in there long enough to smoke four cigarettes and by the time she was back at the table, her fingers working nervously at the clasp of her purse, she had made her decision.

"Let's go now," she whispered hoarsely.

There was a long walk half up a mountain through that old western town with its brightly painted buildings, each with an old hitching post anchored to the sidewalk in front of a brass plaque to explain which gunfighter had bit the dust in that very location. Clemmie Bosserd pulled her along as she tried to stop and read each memorial. He drew a finger like a gun and playfully pushed the barrel against her back.

His small cabin smelled of the sour union suits hanging on the door. It was lit by a glass lantern filled with green oil, swinging slowly from a beam near the old blackened coal stove where bacon rinds and potato skins sat molding in a skillet. Marge stumbled over the rough, unpainted floorboards, looking for a place to hang her hat and purse. Clemmie began to shed his clothes quickly, with his back to her, tossing them in a pile on the floor, then he turned, raising his eyebrows like some comedian in the movies, as if surprised she hadn't undressed the same way. Her fingers went cold on her neck as they worked at the hook of her dress.

"That's it now," he said. "You ain't scared. You're the gamest woman in these hills, that's a fact. And one of the prettiest I ever seen. Don't think old Clemmie here don't know. You're the kind of woman that jumps on a man like a dog jumps on a bone." He laughed. He sat down on his narrow cot like some four-limbed fish, dangling his hands between his knees. She turned her back to him. She spent an interminable minute picking at the elastic of her garters with hesitant thumbs.

"Come on over here now," he said. He stretched his arms out. She froze. Then she thought what the hell. She looked over her shoulder at him perversely. She peeled off her underwear and faced him. She moved shyly toward him a few steps, then she spread her smooth legs up over his knees and folded herself into his arms. He wrestled her to her back, throwing her giddily over his mountainous body. She was breathless under his weight. She felt him try for her immediately, probing and missing at least twice before he grumbled, "What in the hell can't you gimme some *help* now, baby. . . ."

She felt a warm trickling in the creases of her thighs.

"I never been with a man," she said, and felt him stiffen. With sudden revulsion, she tried to push him away. "What in hell do you think I am?"

"Shiiiiiiit," he groaned, a sound she felt as much as heard by a violent movement in his guts. He vise-gripped her arms. "Shiiiiiiit," he said again. He turned her body like a shock of straw. He pressed his weight so hard against her she couldn't move.

"Let me go!" she screamed. She squirmed, used her nails, kicked her feet at him wildly. One of her feet landed home. He responded with a blow into her side. She saw the next blow coming at her head and her body went suddenly limp in a dense, ringing whiteness. . . .

Arms about her breasts, Marge weaved like a spinster's shadow through her room. She began to give up hope for any love but the love in dreams. Her parents rocking in the living room wouldn't say it, as though they thought it was a kindness not to, as though their silence wouldn't do the same. She slept each night curving her spine a little more, curling her body into its own warmth. Sometimes, she wept. Other times, she beat her pillow, crying *Damn, damn,* and still she didn't say it even to herself, that, loveless, nothing could make her beautiful again.

"Marry me!" shouted Burt Cooney in front of the municipal bar. He followed her down the sidewalk on his knees. Sick from drinking, she was searching for some bushes, anyplace, to relieve herself discreetly.

"Noooooo," she croaked, staggering down the walk.

She decided to give herself at least a year before she married him. Exactly one year from that hopeless night. She circled the date on her calendar. It was a Thursday in the hot month of August.

9

"Omaha!" shouted Ben Hogan. "That's where we'll make out! There ain't no sense getting twenty cents a pound for 'em! No, sir! Not when you and me can get us twenty-four or -five in old Omaha!"

His neighbors and fellow members of the Nowell Farmers' Organization—an activist splinter group of the old Farmers' Union—Jake Ballock, Will Hartley, Don Hinkle, Pearly Cyrus Green and son William Green, all stood around Ben Hogan at the municipal bar. They scraped their boots on the brass footrail. They rolled fat cigarettes and smoked, staring pensively into the scarred oakwood of the bar. Jake Ballock had just finished selling his October turkeys to Buster Hill at the Nowell-Safebuy for twenty cents a pound.

"It'll cost you near that much to ship," said Jake, slugging confidently at his beer. "There ain't no sense to bother. You can git a fair price out o' the Safebuy."

"Fair price! Fair price!" shouted Hogan. "Fair price *my ass!*"

"They don't credit you for 'em down in Omaha," said Jake. "They don't unload 'em right down in Omaha."

"They screw your weights down there, sure's right they do," said Don Hinkle. "I don't trust nobody down in Omaha."

"But it's the same sonofabitchin' outfit," said Pearly Green.

"That's right," said Ben Hogan. "They give you twenty cents here and twenty-five cents there. You go on now and figure it. Somebody's getting screwed without getting *kissed* is what I say."

"Them's pretty serious words, Hogan," said Jake Ballock. "Them's enough words to ruin this whole damned town now that we got it steady. Them's enough words to take the check right out o' my pocket!"

"He's right, Hogan," said Don Hinkle. "We start shippin' to Omaha, there's no tellin' where it might lead."

"We got the process here," added Jake. "We always got us a place to sell turkeys. At twenty cents or any other price. We always got us a place."

"To hell with the process! It don't cost that much to ship turkeys!"

"I can drive one o' them tractor trailers," said William Green.

"I don't like this idea at all," said Jake Ballock. "Not at all."

"I'll get me the figures," said Ben Hogan. "That's right. I'll get me some figures!"

Ben Hogan spent two entire days scribbling with a pencil stub and making long-distance calls to Rapid City, to Omaha, and to independent truck owners clear to Cheyenne before he finally came up with the figures he needed. At the cost of diesel truck rental, assuming all liabilities in case of accident, plus some extra hourly pay for Will Green over what his share of his father's turkey crop might be, plus what Ben Hogan guessed to be the number of dead birds in shipping, which he doubled to be on the safe side, and at the calculated price at the end of the week told to him over the phone by a turkey processor in Omaha, from which he subtracted a full cent per pound just to be sure, he would wind up with twenty-one and three-quarters cents per pound after his costs had been paid. But they might all come out much better than that on the return trip if Will Green used some cash from the turkey sale to buy as much cheap wire as they might need in the coming year, though he might violate interstate transport regulations because a livestock trailer didn't have the proper license to haul wire in commercial quantities, or something like that as he understood the law. They might also make out well if Will Green loaded up some high-nutritional poult feeds down in Omaha, enough even to sell to their neighbors, even though the truck and trailer wouldn't carry the proper inspection sticker for the interstate transportation of feed grains. Will Green would have to take the chance of getting fined and drive the trip mostly at night. But even if he was fined, they would still make out because Omaha prices were so much better than the Nowell-Safebuy's.

Even with his figures, Ben Hogan couldn't convince his neighbors. Only Pearly Green would commit his turkeys to the enterprise. Most farmers here were clearly scared of crossing Buster Hill. Will Hartley and some of the others who had never been scared of anyone, including Buster Hill, preferred simply to sit on their hands, holding back the sale of their turkey crop on principle, just to wait and see what might happen.

Marge helped the Greens and her father load the truck. The long steel trailer jutted out from the Hogan corral, half filled with the Green family's crop. Turkeys were driven out of their pens into the corral and coaxed up the loading chute, one continuous line of gobbling birds that fought at each other and flapped their wings in hopeless attempts to fly. Ben culled out his best birds for shipment—mainly plump hen turkeys for fresh market sale—wanting to send his finest with the first truckload, as Pearly had. The turkeys were stacked in makeshift tiers five layers high inside the trailer, which was broken into tiny compartments by means of movable wood panels to pack the birds in as closely as possible. The old men figured all day, arranging and rearranging the load amid turkeys suddenly breaking over the wooden partitions, mixing themselves up as the men moved the panels around like the pieces of a huge jigsaw puzzle. That truck steamed under the autumnal sun. The noise inside was deafening, a huge steel drum of shrieking sound. At one point, Ben and Pearly realized how mixed up their turkeys were, all of them looking so much alike. They shouted at each other, one loud moment of obscene name-calling before they agreed on how many turkeys there actually were and just who owned which ones. They each had a little under half their crop in the first truckload, their finest grade A birds. The two men stooped around through the trailer, haranguing over this or that identically large White Holland turkey, before they agreed the numbers were close enough they might just as well split all profits down the middle. Then Will Green climbed into the truck cab and had trouble figuring all the gears out exactly. He swore at them, pumped the clutch several times, the gears grinding as the truck finally lurched out onto the gravel lane.

"That's the better half of one whole year riding there," said

Ben Hogan, slapping Pearly around the shoulders in brotherly fashion. "You'll see we done it right. Ignorant sonsabitches around here anyway. . . . They'll see we done it right!"

Before William Green left for Omaha, Marge took a walk around the farm with him. Will, a small man with red-orange hair, was much older than she was and unusually quiet. She hardly knew him from school and had never seen him at the municipal bar. When he spoke, he showed the space where he had lost his front teeth. But he claimed to know everything there was to know about the grass. The postwar weed plague was just setting in. He pointed to the patches of bromegrass in the weed-choked fields waiting for next year's herbicides, fields still teeming with grasshoppers. He pulled a brome plant out of the earth to show Marge how each leaf had the initial *M* etched onto the base just above where it joined the stalk.

"That's your grass there," he said. "It's got your monogram right there on it." He nodded matter-of-factly and handed it to her like a flower. He stepped back from Marge and considered her head to foot. He grinned like in the old miners' song, the way the freckles played tag with the mole on his chin. She thought he was almost stupid, somebody who grins the way he shuffles his feet, somebody who grins because he doesn't quite understand a question. The sun was setting, the pink clouds fading into the evening blue, the huge orange disc of a hunter's moon just starting up over the horizon. The temperature began to drop as the few evening stars instantly sharpened.

"I been shearin' sheep 'fore this weed season," he began, as if this would somehow introduce himself. "Ten an hour. That's good. Twenty-five cent apiece. That ain't bad."

"That where you been keeping yourself?" she asked. "With the sheep?"

"Oh well, now I wouldn't quite say keepin' myself." He hemmed and hawed, watched his toes scraping the dirt. "Oh, you know, to get the down payment for the old man's place. Sheep's my line, though. That's what I'd like to raise out here, once a fellah can get at the weeds."

"They always seemed so stupid," she said.

"Oh yeah, well, I kind of figure . . . You know the way they . . . Well, I don't rightly know. I just figure they're easy."

"All that dirt and that greasy wool?"

"Don't bother me none. No, that don't bother me none."

"I can tell you just *love* it out there with your sheep."

"I guess I do, yeah, I guess I do. They carry the mortgage on their backs."

"So practical," she said. He grinned then and moved close enough to reach for her hand. She let him have it without a reciprocal squeeze.

"Got me two thousand dollars from 'em in the bank," he went on, "for the down payment. Won't get no loan till I get three. So the old man can retire, you know." His voice was almost singing it to her as they crossed the creek bridge into the dry, ripened cornfield.

"Just look at that pheasant!" he hissed, and pointed. She watched the rich green of a ring-necked pheasant diving into the withered cornleaves.

"You go dancing?" she asked. "Or I suppose you're just too busy with all them sheep."

"Oh, I ain't too much for it," he said.

"They got dances in Whitewood now, for that school they're building. A dollar for the music and you bring your own beer."

"I ain't too much for dancing," he said.

"You look like a dancer."

He let her hand loose and spun around, laughing.

"Now what makes you think that? What makes you say a thing like that?"

She pretended to stare off into the dark ripples of the creek for a long time.

"C'mon now!" he said. "How come you think I look like one? I don't think I ever danced two steps in my life!"

"You jump around those turkeys like a dance," she said, then she turned and fluttered her eyes at him until he broke out laughing again. He jumped back from her and stretched out his arms between the cornstalks. He began to kick up dirt clods with his heavy shoes. "Like this!" he shouted, battering his soles together with a loud, heavy thumping sound. Then he began to spin his small body around, wildly hawing with laughter.

"Like this!" he shouted again, and jumped up to touch his heels to his outstretched hands once, then he spun around again wildly and took a running leap right at her eyes. She ducked her head. She squealed with fright as he hurtled past her. When she looked up again, he was rolling over himself in the plowed earth, crying with laughter. She made like she was going to pounce on him, curling her fingers into claws, but he grabbed out fast enough to pull her feet out from under her. They rolled together through the dirt. Then he pinned her down with his knees and strained a handful of dirt through the hole of his fist, over her face and down the open neck of her blouse. She sputtered and spat dirt back at him. She snarled and bared her teeth as if she might take a piece out of his throat. He rolled back over himself and set her free. Then he continued rolling through the field, his arms tight to his sides, his face redder than his ruffled hair as he toppled a row of cornstalks.

"Take me dancing!" she shouted after him. "Take me dancing or I'll see you don't get your supper!"

She stood up and brushed herself off, shivering a little in the evening cold. She turned her head from him as if indignant, then she swayed her body over the creek bridge, headed back for the house. She expected him to run up behind her any second screaming yes, half expected him to knock her off the creek bridge into the freezing water, but when she turned to look back at him, he was still sprawled in a nest of crumpled cornstalks, his arms outstretched, laughing at the sky.

The truck never made it to Omaha. In the darkest hours of the morning, the truck was stopped just short of the Nebraska border along the south fork of the White River, a country of receding sand dunes and sparse sagebrush clumps just north of the Rosebud reservation. It was on a seldom traveled road. Desolate, uninhabited country, nothing for miles around. Will came up on a pickup half across the road, its hood up, a man standing beside it and waving him down. He pulled over to help. Then a gang of three men Will had never seen made him get out of the truck and open the lock on the trailer gate. He was tied up, blindfolded, gagged, then dumped into a roadside ditch. He heard the sound of wooden partitions thrown out onto the road. Gasoline was spilled through the trailer, a loud panicky squawking as white feathers soaked it in, then over the hood of the truck, over the tires, in the cab, everywhere. Then somebody tossed in a match.

It took Will Green until dawn to get loose. He might have freed himself earlier, the fire still burning, when two carloads of reservation Indians pulled over and stopped, or at least their voices sounded like Indians to Will. He tried to make sounds and roll himself out of the ditch. Bottles smashed on the pavement. Will quit making sounds. He heard drunken laughter and what sounded to him like men going over the truck to see if they could take anything with them. He lay quietly a long time, until the cars drove off. By the time he had freed himself, hitched a ride into the town of Wood and phoned the sheriff, it was too late. Nothing was left of his father's venture but a smoldering heap. He had to pay a hundred and thirty dollars cash for a tow truck to haul the wreckage into Wood. Will turned up at his father's house the next day, his wrists burned, his mouth swollen, all the money he had ever saved in an envelope he set on the kitchen table.

As Pearly told it, it was a fight that had been building for years—Will working for his dad and having his own ideas about the farm, never quite able to act them out, never given the chance to be his own boss. Then the hijacking and losing everything. When Pearly responded to the news with what kind of a dumb shit would pull a truckload of turkeys over for a stranded pickup, Will slammed him against a wall. He made a fist with the strength of six years of sheep shearing and started in. He might have killed Pearly. Will's brother Tom pulled him off. Then Will tossed some clothes into an old sack. He left every dollar he had ever saved on the kitchen table and took off down the road.

"So that's the finish," said Pearly, his left eye purple and swollen shut. He passed the bottle to Ben at the Hogan table. "I just hope that boy of mine's got the good sense to come back and finish what he started."

"Hell, you got other boys," said Ben Hogan. "It's me that owes ten thousand bucks."

"I'm sorry about that, Ben," said Pearly. "But we ain't the only ones. Ben Reary's entire crop went out and drowned in the rain."

"I expect Buster Hill had his hand in this, him and them sons-abitches with the company," said Ben. "Maybe even Jake Ballock. Don't Jake have relations down by the White River?" Pearly just shook his head. "Hell, there ain't no way to tell now. The worst thing is we'll have to swallow bile and deliver what we got left to the Safebuy. I couldn't rent another truck right now if life depended on it. And Buster's got the price dropped down to eighteen cents this week," he said, turning to look at the women behind him in the kitchen. Marge wiped the same plate dry twice, three times, anything to keep from facing that table. "*Ten thousand bucks* . . . That's near the kind of money a fellah could get for this place. That's more money than I'm likely to see in two years of work. Well, you got that two thousand belonged to your boy. You can hang on. I expect I can another year. I got half a bunker of corn I can sell. I got six beef out back, I'll sell them too ; won't be the first winter we ate antelope. And I got a few cows I can milk for pin money. I just got to get the bank to take part payments. Then I'll get me a crop. That's what I got to do. No more goddamned turkeys. I'll build me one of them boom sprayers. It'll clean out an acre a turn. I'll raise me a crop even if I don't get no government loan. I'll get the cash to put a crop in somehow. Maybe wheat. The price of wheat just might hold steady," he said, turning to his women again. "You betcha. Y'all don't worry about nothing. Next year's gonna be the year. You betcha. Next year's gonna be the year. . . ."

10

Marge didn't believe in love. She hadn't believed in love since Thursday. She continued down the main street of Nowell, collecting seeds. It was useless to pick them off her dress, her blue flowered dress sewn from five and dime material. Hot winds swirled the tiny white parachutes by the thousands through the streets. She would have to comb them out like wedding rice.

She walked past The Cove Café with its door fan blowing hotly at her legs. She walked past Foos's garage, past the voices of men with wrenches and the clanging of machinery. Buster Hill stood huge in the parking lot. He tipped his straw hat. She tried walking past him like he wasn't there. She tried walking through the whole town as if it wasn't there. Burt Cooney's mother waited in her white house at the end of town. As she drew closer to the house, she knew more and more inside that she could never marry him. And there was nobody else.

She slowed her pace. She stopped and spent a long time adjusting the straps of her shoes. Breathing was hard. Thick air pushed her diaphragm slowly and forcefully inward. She felt faint as she stared off into the hot white grain of the shimmering sidewalk. Grasshoppers hummed. She was stopped there, sweating, unable to move.

Suddenly, she heard the distant throbbing sound of machinery. Her hand moved to straighten her dress, then fluttered nervously at her hair. She started toward the Cooney house again. The Cooney house was just down from the Dairy Freeze. She saw the drive-in had a half dozen cars parked around it. She felt she was being watched from them.

The Cooney house was just across the street in the shadows of its elm. Marge stepped off the curb and felt one of her heels slip in the gravel. She bent over to fix her shoe again, then stopped. She looked around in the middle of the street. There was a loud noise coming from somewhere. Horns were honking from over the rise of the highway that skirted town just past the Cooney house, big diesel truck horns. Everyone at the Dairy Freeze heard it. The high school kids were leaving their cars to stand out closer to the highway, sipping their milkshakes and jabbing at each other, asking, *What's that? What is that sound?* Her eyes found the roll of prairie over which the blacktop disappeared and from which the sound of horns and clattering steel rose to a deafening pitch.

The lead bulldozer, pulled along on its trailer, a gleaming yellow in the afternoon sun, rolled up over the hill. Then one by one, a convoy slowly appeared—three bulldozers, several trucks larger than she had ever seen and loaded with bulk under gray canvas, a long road grader, three tank trucks marked with flammable-liquid warnings, two trailer houses as wide as both lanes of the road, then several smaller trucks loaded with tools and materials of construction followed by a tractor trailer pulling the two halves of a high steel tower decked with red flags. And in the middle of it all, looking as if he couldn't possibly belong there, thick brown scarves of dust rising up around and nearly covering him, a man in a black convertible wove in and out of that line of machinery in search of some way to pass on down the hill, but the trucks weren't leaving him any room.

Marge watched that man from a distance. His image wavered in the heat. She could see him shout something to one of the truck-drivers ahead of him. He leaned on his horn. He wove out again wildly, trying to pass, and the truck moved over to block his way. He gave up and pulled back into line. Dust shrouded him. A pair of sunglasses covered his eyes with glaring reflections. She could just make out a sports jacket thrown over the seatback next to him, and the way he used its sleeve to wipe the sweat and dust from his face. He turned his head stiffly. He stretched his neck as if it pained. He drew close enough so that she could see his hands beating a tattoo on the wheel in impatience, his mouth set grimly, one hand raking through his gray hair, his features badly sunburned and looking worn by an early middle age.

The lead bulldozer was pulled off the highway onto the main

street of town, followed by the convoy. She was surprised to see that small black convertible make the turn with it onto Main. The car slowly approached the Dairy Freeze. She watched the man in it turn his head and consider the small crowd gathered there. She was close enough to notice the gray shadow of his beard, the rings on his hands, his crumpled necktie draped over the rearview mirror. She felt his eyes pass first over her and for an instant, through his sunglasses, she caught his eyes with her own. She looked back at him weakly as he grinned, then he faced the crowd of high schoolers in the parking lot behind her, raising one hand to wave at them energetically and with a politician's smile.

The horns trumpeted and the engines boomed. Huge tires dug furrows in the gravel streets. It looked like a circus parade of caged machines. As the convoy moved down Main, the drivers shouted, waving their arms out the truck windows. The sidewalks filled with people. Knots of children ran out of the houses and down the street. A group of farmers shuffled out of The Cove, even Mrs. Nilsen out there with them, wiping her hands on a flowered apron. Then closer up the street, Larry Foos and his mechanics stood, apelike, and watched, tools in their hands. Sheriff Meeker, farther down, staggered through the double doors of the municipal bar. Jim Fuller stood wiping shaving cream off onto his jeans. An old man with a pool cue climbed up on a bench and shaded his eyes.

Marge stood on her toes to catch sight of that man again. His car pulled up in front of the Baker Hotel. He climbed out of it and stretched his legs a minute, walking stiffly in a small, casual circle, then he moved around to the trunk for his luggage. The convoy passed on its way to the turkey yards at the end of Main, everyone out there gaping at all the new Nowell-Safebuy plant machinery. Nobody was there to greet him. Nobody waved or shouted at him. It seemed as if no one knew this man.

She looked around her then, amazed. She found that she had followed the trucks down Main Street almost one full block. She stood there, sweating. Her head ached. The damp straps of her brassiere dug into her skin. She started for the Cooney house. She stopped. It was early yet. There was bound to be some uncommon action at the municipal bar. She told herself that she had the time at least for one drink, just one drink before Mrs. Cooney's fitting. Around her eyes, internal tremors suddenly inflamed her eyelids. She felt the tears about to burst over her cheeks.

Somebody hooted. She turned on down the street and saw an arm waving at her from a truck window. She swore at it under her breath. She caught her heel in the gravel again and stumbled. She threw off her shoes. In bare feet, she elbowed through the mechanics in front of Foos's garage. She pushed her way through them and came up against the crowd in front of the municipal saloon.

Mose Johnson, just retired from the Nowell-Safebuy, stood at the center of the crowd. He tottered drunkenly. He opened and closed his fists like he was ready for a bar fight. He waved a fist at that caravan of machines, pointing them out for the turkey farmers gathered around him, grumbling something that she couldn't hear. Across the street, the man in the car was setting his bags in front of the Baker Hotel for Hiram Baker to carry up the stairs. Hiram said something, and the man looked toward the crowd in front of the saloon.

The commotion gathered force. Marge pressed in to listen. Whatever Mose Johnson was telling them, something about a speed-up at the plant and the loss of jobs, the others reacted with laughter, cussing, an uproar of disbelief. Then Will Hartley, as if convinced enough to humor him, reached an arm out to steady Mose and guide him back through the door. "Why I'll be damned, Mose," he said. "Why I'll be damned."

11

The man sat on the edge of his bed. He clutched a sheet to his body like a freezing man's blanket and with what she thought was a womanly modesty. She didn't know what else to think, remembering her brothers comparing certain measurements behind the barn and all the other men she knew who flexed and posed like tom turkeys showing off their plumes. This man couldn't start off for the bathroom without covering himself. He found his boxer shorts on the floor by the bed and sneaked them on under the sheet. He rose and quickly pulled on a soft red bathrobe. He wrapped a clean towel around his neck and strutted off with a dignity all too fierce.

She thought of her own clothes. She couldn't see them anywhere in a half sleep and the dim light showing through the nicks and tatters of the hotel curtains. But she felt somehow free at the thought that she was naked. There was a satisfaction in simply waking up that way, without knowledge of her clothes, fuzzy memories of the night before slowly coming to her like so many stray dogs turning up at home. She remembered shooting game after game of stripes and solids, or maybe it was only one long game, the old boys lining up seven 'n' sevens for her in a sickly sweet darkness of sweating men. She was all liquid with the cue, she couldn't miss. She even won the beaded pouch Charlie Gooch kept all his money in and as a kind of compensation sat on his lap in a corner booth and kissed him on the mouth. The municipal bar was packed for a Monday, every stool taken at the bar. She watched a man in a fresh white shirt and heavy tweed jacket lean into the bar, looking around uncomfortably. She remembered sauntering over to him and touching his jacket. She fell into him a little to keep her balance. She threw an arm around his waist, pulling them both up closer to the bar, a hand with Charlie Gooch's money in it waving for Dolores Moss. He began to say something about himself but the room was suddenly rolling. She reached for his glass. At the first taste of his martini, she rushed for the front door, not wanting to make a sight of herself in the washroom.

He caught up with her around the corner. She was leaning her head against a wall and staring downward into whirling bushes. She remembered falling to her hands and knees in the prickly junipers and wishing she could die. She might have tried to tell him this; it was important he know how she got into this condition. She couldn't remember. She cried. He held her head. Later, past the point of caring, she tore at his clothes.

They slept well past dawn. He awoke first and acted as embarrassed as if they were strangers. She listened to his shower, closing her eyes and hoping she could fall asleep for just five more minutes.

"I want to have a talk," he said, scrubbing his hair with a towel. He pulled back the curtains with a rude inrush of light. She could see he wanted her to get up. As solemn as a witness, she stood, shakily, out of bed. She made it as far as a chair across the room. On second thought, she went back for the sheet he'd left rumpled on the floor and covered herself.

"Good," he said. "We can talk now." She smiled. He looked at her carefully for the first time. "What I told you last night is true," he said. "I don't want any strings. I was tied down once and vowed never again." She noticed the monograms on the heels of his dark leather slippers, a pair of little silver V's he dragged across the braided rug. "And then there's my age," he said. "I could show you the plates I have instead of teeth. Here. For God's sake, can you imagine waking up each morning to this?"

"I'm not sure I'm awake right now," she said. Her head felt packed with hot steaming rags. The sight of his bridgework didn't help. She turned her eyes away quickly, thinking her tongue could barely feel her own teeth. "You got any aspirin?" she asked. "Jesus. At least a cup of coffee or something."

"Right," he said. He went to the bureau and shook out some

aspirin. Then he found two glasses and poured some whiskey into them.

"Oh, no," she said. "Not for me."

"Drink it. Straight down. It'll make you feel better," he said. He pressed the glass and the aspirin into her hands. "Go on."

She did. She felt an almost immediate warm and drowsy feeling.

"I . . . I don't know what I told you last night," he said. "I've been known to say some pretty wild things under the right conditions."

"It's O.K.," she said. "You're not the first."

"Now don't misunderstand me," he said. Something, a sudden shyness at his intent, made her laugh at him. Then the serious look on his face made her stop laughing.

"You're a young girl," he said. "A night like last night, well, it happens. And I can't say I'm sorry it did. But a man my age wouldn't live long enough to make you happy."

"I've known lots of men," she said. "Seems like the trouble with a good share of them's that they live too long."

"Then I haven't compromised you in any way," he said.

"Nobody takes advantage of me," she said. She sensed a power in the way she let her sheet slip just a little. "Nobody," she said.

That morning, though it was supposed to be his first day, Jim Vogel didn't get dressed and go to work. He pulled on pants and a T-shirt and left the room to use the telephone and ask for sick leave. The Nowell-Safebuy gave it to him. He returned with coffee and rolls from The Cove. But they didn't drink the coffee and the butter on the rolls melted away completely. They made love again. It felt good to her to make love, no other thought in her mind but the new sensations in her body, a feeling of being transported into a focused instant of time with no one in the world to tell her when to come home. She didn't give a damn about the consequences. It felt best of all to her not to give a damn anymore. Afterwards, they dozed through most of the morning. But men came knocking at the door to his room. Sam Carlson, manager of the turkey slaughtering division, came by on the pretense of asking about Jim's health. She hid in the bathroom. Jim let Sam in, pretending to be stuffed up and miserable with a fever. He answered a question on an immediate insurance matter for Sam and got rid of him. They fell back into bed. Then Hiram Baker came upstairs from the front desk to slip messages under the door. One concerned a case later in the month, information about a chemical company that had accidentally mixed certain poisons in place of fertilizers for the Nowell-Safebuy's contract cornfields. Another was from Harold Rosengrin, a lawyer who had just moved into Belle Fourche, trying to set up a social call. Buster Hill came in the afternoon. Marge swore she could hear Buster sneak around out there in the hall, breathing heavily, listening. He knocked. She hid in the bathroom again. The two men held a short conference after which Jim had to rush downstairs to make long-distance phone calls. He returned with supper in boxes from The Cove. The most he told her by way of explanation was that a buy order for a pound of turkey now was worth two sell orders come next July. But they didn't talk much about his business. They ate supper in bed and finished his bottle. He wanted to make love again. She didn't, wanting to talk awhile or, better, to go out somewhere together, but she said nothing. He turned out the light and shed his robe. Hazily, dreamily, she closed her eyes and gave in, some small part of her wondering just how it was she had ended up in this position.

Wednesday morning, he awoke in a rage. He kicked his scattered books and clothes. With one violent sweep of his arm, he knocked ashtrays, bottles, glasses, shaving kit from his table. Then there was a frantic searching on his hands and knees for his shoes, in every pocket for his car keys. He pulled on a set of mismatching clothes and left her alone without a word.

She made his bed. She picked up after him, his clothes, books and shaving kit. She used the edge of a magazine to sweep his room, using a box lid as a dustpan. Then, alone in that room, she sat until she swore she could hear the paint peeling from the walls and hear the electric wires humming in the antique fixtures. She wondered how in the world she had ever wound up in this mess, in this fleabag hotel with her reputation absolutely ruined. Absolutely ruined. She tried to be honest with herself. He probably wanted to dump her off at the next crossing. So if he planned to dump her off, then let him. She was bound to make sure he left her with enough money to get to Rapid City or Cheyenne. She deserved that much at least. Maybe she could even convince him to leave town in the middle of the night and take them both to Cheyenne. *Jesus,* she thought, *at least out to dinner or something.* She decided she would have to be stronger with him. No matter what happened, she would make herself strong. Anything he dealt out, she resolved to deal straight back at him in spades.

She put on her own clothes. She crept down the hotel stairs, moving cautiously through the lobby filled with old folks who had something new to talk about. Hiram Baker gave her a strangely dirty look and a stingy, woodchuck smile that made her want to spit. Marge slammed out of the Baker Hotel and up the street to the Nowell Grocery thinking she didn't give a damn. The few town women out shopping seemed to forget what they were buying, watching Marge rattling her own basket up and down the aisles. She fumed, muttered, cussed. Nobody said anything. She brought back meat, bread, juice, mustard, grapes and peaches, plates and cups, knives and forks, and a broom. She spent a long time figuring a way to warm canned beans and soup in the peat block heating stove—a kind of coat hanger harness she lowered into the flames.

He came back from work sooner than she expected. The evening shift whistle hadn't even sounded from the Nowell-Safebuy. Supper was hardly warm. He didn't seem to notice the fact there was any supper at all. He carried bottles clinking together in his arms. He kicked the door closed behind him and slammed the bottles on his small, rickety table.

"So how was work?" she asked.

He turned to her and said almost bitterly, almost a formal greeting, "Come on. You're going to burn yourself over there. I've brought us something to drink."

He drank either Scotch or martinis. Marge decided she couldn't stand the taste of either and started drinking straight white vermouth. Something bothered him. He paced up and back, his shirt tail out, his feet in mismatched socks fitted into his slippers. Everything about him looked a chaos compared to two days ago. "You've got no business with a man like me," he said. His voice had tremors in it that made her afraid he was going to throw something. "And even if that weren't the case, even if this could have happened twenty years ago for me, it still wouldn't be right. It wouldn't be right for you. You're the kind of woman who deserves someone who's willing to tear down the walls. I've never been much of one for tearing walls down. Besides, for my part, I think the old saying is true—'The maid is May when she's a maiden and becomes December when she's wed.'"

He seemed pleased enough with this. He changed his course back toward the gin in celebration. She lounged on the bed. She remembered the pose of a pinup at Foos's garage and she languidly assumed this posture. "Honey," she said, slowly unbuttoning her blouse, "it might as well be December now."

Jim Vogel turned a thousand-yard stare off toward the wall.

"I could love you, surely," he confessed, later that night. "And God knows I'm attracted to you. But, Marge . . . I just can't believe you have enough experience in this world. Surely not enough to take this seriously. Listen. An aunt of mine told me something once. Something her father told her when she was a young girl. Let's just call it a wisdom from another world, a wisdom from her people. 'When you want a bowl of soup, you shouldn't go out and buy yourself an ox.' There. It's said. I think you know what that means." He lay there quietly depressed for a long time before he added in a softer voice, "What's troubling is that you'll never know how different it is for me."

She was almost asleep. The room was dark and his voice blended with the night sounds, the sounds of rusted hotel plumbing, someone coughing in the next room, a radio playing down the hall. Marge didn't know what to say to him. She moved her body closer, drew the blankets high and held him close. He must have been the saddest man she had ever known. Somehow, that made her want him all the more. Or maybe he was right. Maybe it could have been anyone. She felt a satisfaction at this thought, as if the world suddenly held possibilities she hadn't dreamed. She considered his body. It was the body of a man who might have gone hungry more than once, a body that had known loneliness, the rain, the roads. His skin was pale white. His ribs showed and his shoulderblades stuck out as rudely as a cow's hips. There were scars on his back. When she mentioned them, he told her they were due to a form of severe sun poisoning. Later, he told her that on a beach in Italy he had lain face down for six hours under the sun. He wasn't wounded seriously. He had lost most of his shirt in an artillery shell explosion that left a piece of shrapnel in his arm and his back peppered with sand an inch deep. Gray hair covered his body. He told her that during his third year as a captain in the army, all his hair had grayed.

Time passed. He phoned in sick again on Thursday. There was a fog between the day and the alcohol of days. By then nothing could get her to leave his room. She imagined the worst, imagined she was already pregnant and would surely be stuck with it. She'd heard of a home in Cheyenne where they sent such girls. And if by sheer blind luck she wasn't, there was nowhere else she could think of to go. Just staying put was a kind of solution. And she wasn't about to leave as long as he wanted her to stay.

Early Saturday morning, five days after she first kissed him, they lay asleep. The room looked stormbeaten with empty bottles, scattered books and clothes. The curtains were drawn. A welcome cool wind had sprung up suddenly the night before, drowning out the hooting range boys, the horn-honking on Main, the roaring engines of Friday night. The wind died and left the morning still. Marge heard it only faintly, a distant stumbling. She settled deeper into the covers. The Baker Hotel was full of sounds. The lock on the door rolled once and loudly clicked. The lights went on. They both sat bolt upright, crying out in a nightmare.

"Jesus, Burt!" she shouted. "Burt!"

Burt Cooney hugged a shotgun uncertainly. He staggered, leaning over the foot of the bed.

"Why, shit," he said. He reached for a handful of bedclothes to keep his balance. "They told me you was with somebody. But this here's just a damned old rag. He's just a damned old rag!"

Jim stiffened. She felt his body arching against the mattress, ready to spring at Burt Cooney.

"Marge, how could you lie with a rag like that?" he asked. Then something changed in him. He searched them both closely in that way drunk men have, as if on the verge of some deep revelation that never comes. He turned his gaze fully on Jim, slowly raising the barrels of his shotgun.

Marge threw herself to his side of the bed. She screamed.

"Get out of the way!" shouted Burt Cooney. "Get out of the way!"

"Do as he says," Jim said, trying to break her hold. He was trying to roll off the bed onto the floor, but she hooked a foot over the brass bedrail and pressed her body hard against him. She knew Hiram Baker must have started up the stairs. Outside, she heard a siren wailing in the street.

"Goddamnit!" shouted Burt Cooney.

Burt slapped at her anchored foot. She kicked the free one at him and screamed. She was losing hold. Jim gouged her hard in the ribs and was rolling free. . . .

The gun went off. She felt the wind of it. Plaster rained down on them. She screamed and kept screaming. Somewhere in that white dust cloud Jim Vogel kicked free onto the floor. She found him on his knees, reaching for the shotgun. Burt Cooney was doubled over, emitting a high, shrill sound, a sound like the weak bleating of a calf lost in the brush, the wind knocked out of him.

Jim was outraged when Sheriff Meeker didn't throw Burt Cooney in jail on charges of attempted murder. The sheriff only held Burt at the office until he sobered up a little, then he telephoned Mrs. Cooney to come get her son. The most he was going to do was lock up the shotgun. Marge was grateful the sheriff at least pulled Burt off into a back room and shut the door. She couldn't face him. It was enough to have to listen to the sound of his crying from there.

Jim began to shout at the sheriff about every last dime he had and the county elections if no charges were filed. Sheriff Meeker leaned back, resting his boots up on the big desk as he scrutinized them both a minute with an amused expression. "Sir," he said, "this town don't have a law yet against the friendly discharge of firearms. But I'd like to tell you right now, *right damn now,* that it does have express written statutes against fornication outside the holy sanctuary of marriage. Now I think you know what getting throwed in jail could do to your kind of employment. So I don't want no more trouble. There ain't nobody getting arrested here. Not if you'll just get the hell out of my office and leave the public sleep."

Marge managed to get Jim out just in time to avoid a disastrous confrontation with Mrs. Cooney. In front of the Baker Hotel, they stood together in the street.

"I'm finished," he said. He faced her, his jaw trembling. Both hands gripped her hard by the shoulders. "I can't go on like this," he said.

She clung to his arms, resolving not to let go of him. Her knees were shaking. The memory of the gunshot rang out over and over again in her mind. She felt lost in time. It was shortly before dawn on Saturday. The only people out were two old men dressed in coats, pajamas and slippers, still sitting in front of the hotel, waiting to see what else would happen. The street was a dust-covered plain of blue dawn and shadows. She was getting nervous. They must have stood in the street five minutes, not moving once.

"Honey . . ." she started.

"I can't be destroyed like this," he said. "I can't. . . ."

He started to lead her across the street. She was suddenly aware that she had no shoes on. Each new footstep in the gravel was a kind of shock. He swore under his breath. He stopped them both abruptly in the middle of the street.

"Not for any woman!" he shouted. "Do you understand!"

He shook her roughly by the shoulders. Her head jerked violently up and down. She felt her body going limp, unable to respond. He made her feel the full strength of his grip as he dragged her the rest of the way across, straight for his car in front of the Baker Hotel. She stood on in silence, nervous, unsure.

"Get in," he said. He opened the car door for her from the inside. Marge slid into the seat. She watched him staring morbidly into the instruments, squinting at them due to his nearsightedness. Over the wheel, he rubbed his hands together as if they were numb and cold.

"Maybe we should go up and get your glasses," said Marge, thinking of her shoes.

"Glasses!" he shouted. "Glasses? We don't have the *time* for glasses!"

The car engine groaned a few seconds before it caught. He shivered. He plunged the car into gear. The tires whined in the gravel, the car lurching, skidding half sideways down the street. Marge pulled away from him, clutching at the door handle in preparation for jumping.

"Where are we going?" she asked, softly.

Jim Vogel laughed. It was a sound that made her skin crawl, a cynical laughter, a laughter at the preposterous world. Then the sound of his laughter began to change. "I'm doing the right thing," he said, suddenly calm, even blissful, as he reached his arm across the carseat to draw her close. "Before it's too late. We're getting married."

"Who the hell ever asked you?" she said after a moment, after the shock. "Did you ever think of that? Just who in the hell did?"

"I . . . I thought that's what you want," he said.

"What *I* want? Stop the car now," she said. "I'm getting out."

After a moment, when he didn't stop the car, she balled up her fists and started hitting him about the head and arms. "Let me out!" she screamed. She grabbed for the wheel. "Damn you, stop this car!"

The car rolled to a slow stop in the middle of the road. Marge pushed the door handle and jumped out. She landed in a crow hop, skinning her knees. She stood up and lost control. She kicked his fender once, twice, screaming. By the third kick, her bare heel cracking as it sank into his door, he ground the gears angrily and drove off in the direction of Belle Fourche.

She sat down in the weeds by the side of the road. She rested her head and arms on her knees and closed her eyes. That's all she wanted, just to close her eyes and rest. Nothing else mattered, not any of the wishes she had spent in dreams, not that she was like a leaf fallen in the creek and turning, turning aimlessly into the rocks. There was nowhere else to go. Her feet were cold, one of them throbbing from kicking his car. Her knees burned under her arms but she was too tired, too tired to lift her arms. She sat that way a long time. She heard the sound of an engine pulling up, the crackling of tires slowing in the gravel. She raised her head and looked in the sudden wild hope that it was her father. The passenger door swung open on the pickup. Will Hartley was behind the wheel, just able to make out her features in the dim light. "Marge Hogan, is that you?" he asked. "What are you doing out at this hour? You should be home."

The engine popped and hummed. The seat looked friendly in the smoke of Will's pipe.

"Please, Mr. Hartley," she said. She hugged her knees. "Go on and take me home."

12

The autumn earth was hardest. Summer had baked it hard. The seasonal drought was at its peak and gray chips of earth peeled back like old shingles. The ripe wheat had stood its last days, then was planed over by harvesters with wooden arms beating the golden heads into their teeth. Trucks with tires spinning under five-ton mounds of grain moved across the fields onto the gravel roads, groaned over the blacktop highway day and night and mile after mile to the scales. Weight was somehow converted into money according to the day, according to the whims and forces of a market no one had quite foreseen. Brush was cleared from the ditches around the fields, torches set to the stubble on windless days, and straight walls of flame made their own winds across the fields. Smoke rolled and tumbled up like black tornadoes whirling into the deep autumnal blues. Men ran along beside the fields with cans of fuel to keep the fires going, calling out to each other, waving their arms, watching out for maverick flames ripping off like orange flags into the surrounding pastures.

They chased after those wild fires with blankets, fire extinguishers strapped to their backs like aqualungs. Such range fires were mostly beaten out, but one or two each year grew too wild to contain, swirled off through the dry autumn grass burning out the fencelines, leaping off to where they crackled through the brush, continuing onward to some prairie desolation where they slowed and died.

Marge struggled over a ditch and across the black strip of burned grass at the edge of a freshly harrowed field, feeling the earth hard as stones under the soles of her tennis shoes. She stopped to catch her breath and set down a heavy can of tractor fuel. She spat into the palms of her hands, using a finger to rub saliva over the red welts on her palms. She changed hands on the bare wire handle of the fuel can and started walking again. She looked out at her father shuffling slowly toward her from his empty tractor. From the house, she had seen his tractor run empty. She figured her father would start back to the house for fuel and she would have the time to fill the can and meet him halfway. But it seemed that once he had seen her coming, Ben Hogan took his own sweet time. She was almost all the way to the tractor before she met up with him. She set the fuel can at his feet.

"Not a bad day for a walk," he said as he took up the can.

Marge followed him to the tractor and helped him lift the can up on the hood. She listened to the bass drum sound of the tank drinking in the fuel, and shielded her eyes from the sun as she stared up into her father's face, all shadows under the odd angles of his hat. The old man threw the can out away from him on the ground. She started after the can, still rattling over the furrows. As she bent down for it, she caught sight of a moving column of sun-gilded dust from just over the rise of the field, a car of some sort driving up the homeplace lane. She heard her father snort once contemptuously.

"What the hell is it now?" he said.

"You go on ahead and find out," she said. She stood a minute wondering if she might go a few turns. But ever since she'd come home from five days gone he had been distant, not liking to have her around. He didn't even wake her up to cook his breakfast. He hadn't said a word about where she'd been, not one word. It was as if he knew he had no right to say anything, he'd encouraged her all along.

"I'll go a few," she said.

She watched her father think about it as he checked the seed in the bins of his grain drill. It was an old grain drill, raised up on steel-rimmed wheels once used on a horse-drawn machine. It looked like some kind of wide, midget's buggy with four wood boxes instead of seats and a bright-red hydraulic cylinder mounted in front that had two cracked rubber hoses plugged up into the tractor. Under the four square wooden bins for the seed, it dangled long rusted drills for spitting the seeds into the earth. A row of dual steel disc arms, gleaming white in the sun, was set behind those drills to rake over the seeds. Ben Hogan was proud of that machine. Marge knew he wasn't sure he could trust her with it. He had spent several weeks constructing it himself on an old John Deere frame, complete with hydraulic lift that raised the discs and drills up out of the soil. She knew he was thinking that if she held the hydraulic lever the wrong way too long, the pressure might make the old rubber hoses explode. Or if she didn't watch right she might hit a rock. She could tell by the look he was giving her that he imagined a pile of scrap clanking along and digging a shallow trench across his field.

The seed bins looked full enough from where she stood. Ben Hogan slammed the bin lids closed. His boots shuffled slowly toward her through the gray dirt clods. He had an expression on his face that showed all the work he had left to do. Marge pulled up on the hot steel tractor, heaved a white denim thigh across to straddle the seat and pumped the throttle lever several times.

"C'mon down," he grunted. "We'll fetch more seed."

"I can go a few turns," she said.

He gave her a look that made her climb down off the tractor. She followed him toward the house feeling like the same little girl who had left the gate open when the cows got loose. When she reached the top of the rise, she saw a small black convertible almost run straight through the yard fence. The old white Judas goat tied to a clothesline in the overgrown weeds went wild kicking around, thwanging its bell and pulling hard against the rope. She recognized both the man and his car. She wanted to hide right there in the soil, planting herself like some small white knuckle of seed potato. He hadn't so much as telephoned in three weeks. She wasn't about to telephone him, not even if her only good shoes were still in his room. She didn't know what to do now. She watched him get out of his car. She thought of what she must look like without a dress on. She walked faster across the field, sweating, her hair flying in a mess.

"It's the new man in town," she said.

Ben Hogan spat. They passed George and Mike's rusting car half fallen into the earth. Her father was moving fast enough that Marge had trouble keeping up with him. He slammed the wire gate coming through the yard. He was half up the steps in a rage ahead of her when he stopped an instant, turning to her and telling her, "*Pete,* you go on now a minute. Just leave him to me. Give them brood hens their happy hour!"

He slammed the door of the house. Marge waited a minute in the yard wondering whether or not she should go inside or do what her father told her. She had no idea what he might say to the man. Her father had never been friendly to strangers and this man was something far worse. "Damn," she said to herself. She turned and ran off as fast as she could to the chicken coop. The chicken coop was a red-painted shack all the way behind the barn. She ran over the hard ruts of the machinery road thinking that her ragged blouse with the hundreds of faded pink flowers on it wasn't passable. She slowed down some, rolling her head around, impossibly trying to check her blouse for diesel stains. Then leaping over the mudholes made by the leaking stock trough, she wondered if maybe she could sneak by the man somehow and put something else on. She figured he would be sitting in the living room and would surely see her before she could. The only way to avoid that was to use the paint ladder and go in through her bedroom window.

She skidded around the corner of the barn gasping for breath, reaching back to pull at her red hair ribbon and shake out her hair. She took the short ramp of the coop in a single athletic bound and threw open the bolted door. She ducked into the hot, compressed atmosphere of chickens. She shouted and waved her arms around, chasing those ragged, molting hens into a frenzy of squawks and winged explosions out of the imposed darkness, out into an hour's free-for-all scratching in the manure.

On her way racing down the ramp, she caught one of her tennis shoe laces on an exposed nail and she stumbled, pitching forward, crying out as she belly-flopped straight into a sea of organic fertilizer in the chicken yard.

13

Ben Hogan stood in his doorway inspecting the man. He saw a tall man with sharply hewn features and a body as lean as any range beef. He also saw one of those *pleased to find you in* expressions that made him think of courtrooms.

"How do you do?" the man started, extending his hand. "My name is Vogel. . . ."

Ben Hogan pushed right past the hand, spinning his hat in a neat curve across the room onto the sofa. He stomped through the wide arch from the living room into the kitchen, where he reached his mouth up under the sink faucet and turned it on, letting the cool, glowing shaft of water stream out over his face, ducking his head in under it and ruffling the water through his hair.

Vera was busy dropping icecubes into a pitcher of tea she was cooling for her guest.

"Get on outa here," she snapped. "You're sweatin' all over my dishes!"

The man stood in the archway observing them.

"Good afternoon, Mr. Hogan," he tried again. "I wonder if I might have a few minutes of your time?"

"Set down there!" Ben Hogan snarled. He strode back into the living room, jabbing a finger rudely toward the wingchair. The man nodded his head formally and sat down. "Now what in the hell you got to say?" Ben Hogan asked, collapsing in the middle of the living room floor, then stretching out in his usual afternoon resting position, flat on his back, arms spread wide, eyes focused straight at the ceiling. "You want to declare your intentions, it's O.K. by me. Not that it's going to get you anywhere."

"I'm sorry, Mr. Hogan," Jim Vogel answered. "That's not the reason I'm here. I'm in the position, reluctant as I am, considering your feelings and ah . . . everything . . . ," he said. He looked at Ben Hogan for some reaction. Nothing. "I'm sorry to have to ask you several questions more of a business nature," he said.

"Just give me the straight shit. I've answered too many goddamned questions."

"I'm here representing the Nowell-Safebuy," Jim said.

"Ha!" Ben Hogan raised his head up some. "Don't think that's gonna get you someplace. I don't like *you* much and Buster Hill's *a hard-mouthed bushwhacking sonofabitch. . . .*"

Jim wiped his face with his handkerchief, pulling it out of his shirt pocket in a crumpled ball that he stared into morosely. Ben Hogan finished describing Buster Hill, then settled his head back the short distance to the floor, his eyes closing as if he meant to sleep.

"Shoot." The old man smiled cynically. "Go on and try me."

Jim searched nervously through his disorganized, overstuffed folder for a legal-sized page. He pulled the page only partway out, then seemed to have second thoughts. He set the folder on the carpet near his feet.

"Mr. Hogan," he started. He cleared his throat. He licked his dry lips. "Mr. Hogan, I'm terribly sorry to disturb you this afternoon. But I've come a long way out here. . . ." He stopped. He looked hard at Ben Hogan. He made a small effort to collect his folder and rise out of his chair, then gave it up, sitting back down again. "More people know the fool than the fool knows people," he said. "You know who I am. With your kind of unfriendliness, I'd pack up and leave right now if I could. Especially in light of your daughter. I don't like this business any more than you do. . . ."

The man was interrupted by a sudden tremendous crash, the

unmistakable sound of glass shattering. Ben Hogan jumped to his feet.

"Ohh . . ."

Ben Hogan leaped across to his daughter's bedroom. He threw the door wide. Jim peered out over Ben's shoulder at what appeared to be a woman, her face a tangle of dripping hair, the whole front of her one dull brown stain. She hung with one arm oddly twisted through the rungs of a paint ladder jutting through the broken window.

"Ohh . . ." she moaned again, and looked as if she were trying to swim through the shattered glass. She held up her arm and there was blood pumping everywhere.

"Vera! Vera!" shouted Ben Hogan. "Fetch one of them bridle leathers!"

"Ohh . . ."

"Chickenshit," Ben Hogan marveled. "Pete, what in the *hell* have you been up to?"

He started to use both hands to squeeze the wound closed. Jim stepped in quickly beside him.

"Not there," he said. Ben Hogan's fingers were slick with blood. Jim reached a hand up and clamped it tightly in the underarm. The bleeding slowed.

"Get her down . . . get her down . . ." he said, and Ben helped him disentangle her from the ladder, then carry her over to the bed.

". . . Ohh, noo . . ."

"Relax . . . relax . . ." Jim chanted close to her pallid, sweating face and her eyes fluttered open, locking themselves directly into his own, two star-fractured circles of agonized green suddenly wide with recognition. She let out a quiet sobbing. Her eyes rolled in a dead faint.

Vera Hogan rushed in with a leather strap. The man stretched the arm out delicately as Ben cinched the strap around the underarm.

"Alcohol," Jim said. "We'll need some alcohol. And a pair of tweezers."

Ben reached in under his overalls for his pint. The man rolled up his sleeves and doused his hands with the whiskey, scrubbing them together and holding them out to dry like a surgeon's hands. He bent down close to the wound, pulling a clean handkerchief out of his back pocket and daubing at the blood. He peered in through the intricate, swirling fibers, that knot of muscle bulging through the torn skin like a butchered rose. He probed two fingers in gently to spread the wound. He took his time. He lifted a small, ragged white belt of severed tendon as if he might know its name. He probed in more deeply until he struck a nerve. She stiffened. He paused, inspecting more closely for bits of glass, but couldn't find them. He moved aside frayed ends of skin and her body shivered with a cold sweat that must have radiated through his palms, feeling the rapid pulsing of that arm in his hands.

Vera Hogan leaned in and undid several buttons on Marge's blouse to free the arm up and a petite, unmoored breast fell into view. The man breathed with even concentration through his nose. He daubed in again with his handkerchief, soaking out the blood. He must have seen it then. He had a chance at it then. He eased in with the tweezers as gently as he could, probing, spreading the hot muscular tissues aside slowly, slowly until he found it, wet and gleaming against a streak of bone. He removed a large sliver of glass. He pressed back in to determine the severage, bending even closer to the wound, and when he touched the torn end of her artery, a weak spray of blood rained up into his face, drying quickly, tiny flecks of dried blood on his nose, chin and lips.

"It's a small artery." He pronounced it solemnly. "We should get her to a hospital."

Vera couldn't find anything better to bandage her up with but clean white cotton socks and black tire tape. Jim rigged up a rope suspension from the roof of Ben's old Ford pickup so the arm hung above her head. He loaded Marge into the cab and strung up the arm. She was dazed and humiliated. He pushed her head down so it rode between her knees.

Ben tried his pickup with his daughter moaning, semiconscious, on the seat beside him. He pumped the accelerator several times and the old engine began whining dryly. Ben cussed in rhythm to the ignition's siren as the engine turned over and over again with short desperate coughs and asthmatic lurchings. He turned the key off and waited. He tried again. The pickup heaved forward, popped once and clattered, then its engine suddenly died.

14

Jim Vogel was called upon to drive Marge and Ben Hogan the eighteen miles in his cramped black convertible, the top in place, to the town of Nowell and the office of Doc Monahan. He had Marge to Nowell in almost no time. Ben jumped out of the car and pounded on Doc's glass office door, without any answer. The blinds were drawn. The Doc might have been out making a house call. But maybe not, because on house calls he usually left a small dusty blackboard hanging in front of the blinds with a phone number written in his hurried scrawl. The other possibility was that as sometimes happened with him, in his fortieth-some-odd year of practice, he had closed shop on this town again for good.

About three times a year, Doc Monahan used a scalpel to hack his account books to bits that he maniacally scattered around his office. Then he stretched out on his own examination table with a bottle of medicinal alcohol, his wire-rimmed spectacles dangling from an ear like a busted swingset, his bald pink head shaking miserably as he calculated his life's fees into the usual two dollars a head plus so many vegetables or turkeys or hundred-pound sacks of potatoes and once even a pair of raw horsehide boots he hadn't known what else to do with but wear. At times like these, he refused to answer any calls. He telephoned Dolores Moss at the municipal bar and told her to spread the word that he had had it with this town.

Dolores Moss always listened to the Doc awhile, then she phoned up Beatrice Ott and told her to get someone in the women's auxiliary out to bake him some kind of pie. After that, she blew the crumbs out of an old cigar box and set it up on the bar. That was the collection box for the Doc's eventual retirement to Florida. Dolores started the collection off by putting in ten dollars from municipal funds. Then anybody who wanted a drink that day would have to face the woman's unflinching thumb jabbing down into the box. Those days-off tantrums were unpredictable. But even as he neared retirement, three or so days a year were the only days Doc Monahan didn't work. And the morning after every one of them, a knot of women from the Church of Christ Reformed invaded his office with bottles of homemade hangover cures, brooms and mops and buckets to clean the place up a bit, pies and assorted confections Doc Monahan had trouble resisting, and that box of his Florida retirement money he would likely use to pay last month's installment on the X-ray machine. Doc Monahan usually tried to throw those women out in a bachelor's rage until he finally had to give in, muttering to himself, taking up his bag and limping out to make just one more call. . . .

Jim was called upon to drive the forty miles all the way to the hospital in Deadwood. He pushed his car as fast as it could go, winding along the highway that climbed into the tree-covered hills. In the back seat, she opened her eyes and rolled her head around, overwhelmed by dizziness, then closed her eyes again with a moan. Pine trees passed her by like flashing spokes. The bare granite rocks that had tumbled from the twisting canyon walls lay rounded and polished like huge stone bearings in the Deadwood River, white water cascading over them with a rush that made her want to drop her head between her knees. She pressed her knees hard against her ears, her arm suspended miserably from the makeshift harness above her head. She felt the sensations of his driving, accelerating smoothly through the mountain turns, down-shifting in perfect rhythm to the road's erratic grades. He drove on in a thoughtful silence but for the few times that he turned to check on her condition. "Relax . . . Relax . . ." he chanted back at her from time to time. "And if you feel faint, breathe in deeply. That's it. Deeply. We'll be there soon. Just close your eyes and relax . . ."

She barely heard him. But something remotely bothered her in his tone of voice. He sounded almost cheerful as he was telling her what to do.

After running two red lights in the mining town of Deadwood, the two men unloaded Marge at the hospital emergency room. They sat waiting for her in the lounge. The lounge was one of those haphazardly donated collections of furniture, a mixture of old yellowed wicker and washable blues, a knee-high brass howitzer shell for a standing ashtray and assorted western pastoral pastels hanging on the sea-green walls—an Indian on a plunging white horse lancing a buffalo against a background of purple mountains; four ragged, fringed pioneers in a buffalo-hide dinghy, poling across the Missouri like the crossing of the Delaware; an old weathered range boy with chaps and lariat, staring out lonesomely over his branding fire; and a genuine framed replica of Wild Bill Hickok's last poker hand, fanned out on a red velvet field.

Ben sat smoking quietly in a wicker basket chair, staring up at the paintings on the walls or watching out meekly at Jim Vogel, who seemed to want to contain himself in the silence of his thoughts.

"I'm grateful to you," Ben said. "If you wouldn't have been there, I'd have had to drive her all the way on the tractor. Did that myself some years back. Near died from loss of blood before I got there."

"Don't mention it," Jim said. He stared out the window into the Deadwood Memorial Gardens.

"Well, I'm grateful to you."

Jim waved a hand in a gesture of indifference.

"Well, when a fellah . . ."

"There's no need for thanks, Mr. Hogan."

"Shit." The old man spat once. Then he jumped out of his chair and kicked around over the beef-hide carpet. "Now a while back, you was saying something about some damned business . . ."

"That's correct," said Jim Vogel. "And I could see you'd rather go under in court than do business with me."

Ben stopped in his tracks.

"A bad year don't mean a man's gone under," he said.

"Then it really doesn't matter, Mr. Hogan. We're not pushing you."

"The hell you ain't," said Ben. "Just how long have you been here? Thirty days? Thirty days! And you expect to come marching onto a man's place and he'll peel his drawers!"

The man made a sarcasm of his silence.

"Ha!" Ben spat into the ashtray. "The trouble with folks here is they don't have no guts. Every one of 'em's running scared to death or worse. Hell yes, worse than that! They're scared they won't get no *loans* for next harvest. No Nowell-Safebuy loans. No new government subsidy loans. A man can't make it without loans. Then Buster Hill sends you out there to take his land from him."

"We're not taking your land," Jim said. "We're doing our best to buy it from you. The Nowell-Safebuy has made an offer to purchase your mortgage from the bank. You must know the bank is going to force you to sell some part of your land, sooner or later. We're prepared to offer you the highest possible price. . . ."

"High price! High price!" Ben shouted. "High price my ass!"

"I'm sorry," Jim said. "I don't mean to bring up an unpleasant subject, at least not under these circumstances. We're not pushing you, Mr. Hogan. We don't have to do business with you. There are other alternatives."

Ben stood watching the man for a long time and the spirit drained out of him some. He slowly sat back down and rested his head in his hands. "You don't know what happens," he said. "I'm in trouble for some time now. Another farmer and me thought to buck the Nowell-Safebuy and ship to Omaha for a better price. I lost my crop and I quit raising turkeys. I thought I'd try gambling on wheat this year and had me a good crop, but there ain't no market for it now. You could stuff every hungry belly in this world and not get rid of all the wheat. Buster Hill has that government loan board sewn up shut. I can't get no loans to support my crop and it ain't worth raising if I can't. So I put a hundred acres of good crop land up for sale and see what happens. Just who's going to come and buy it from me? You think some dirt farmer's going to scrape up ten thousand cash and hand it to me? You think

Sy Lockhard or Will Hartley down the road's going to buy it? You think Don Hinkle's going to come return my combine and even have the rent he owes me on it? There ain't a dirt farmer got a pot to piss in, what with prices are this year. . . . So the place sits up for sale until the bank won't wait much longer. Then the No-well-Safebuy comes out and makes an offer for it at about half the price I need. That's just how it happens. A man either keeps raising turkeys or he don't get no loans. That's the way it works. A man can't make it without loans. There's no telling how many farms gone under that way since the war. And the Nowell-Safebuy ends up with 'em all.''

"I don't know what you're talking about," said Jim Vogel. "You act as if you were forced into something. And besides that, if you don't sell to us, there are hundreds of buyers in the market!"

"The hell there are," said Ben Hogan. He sat pondering the man in front of him a minute. "How long you been here? Thirty days?" he asked. "There's a nursing station on down the hall. You go on there now and get us some coffee. Then I'll tell you just how it happens."

15

Marge felt ridiculous. The hospital had given her a white smock to replace her soiled blouse and it floated on her body like a feedsack. Her ankle was sore and she limped on it down the long sterile hallway, a white prescription slip waving in her good hand, her mind in a turmoil with just what she could tell her father had happened. She reached the small waiting room. She stood outside the door a minute getting her courage up. Her father was pacing back and forth in front of Jim and talking on at him. Ben turned on his heel and spotted her in the hall. She sensed the anger in him.

What could she tell him? That she was knocking the mud nests of the barn swallows from the eaves? That she'd kicked Mike's football up on the roof again? Or maybe looking for a good place to hang herself so she'd finally lack enough sense to make the perfect wife for that four-eyed, weasely Burt Cooney, can't tell a piston from a woman's breast? She felt ridiculous. She limped more than necessary into the waiting room. Jim Vogel stood off his couch with a military stiffness.

Ben started right in at her. "What was you doing with my paint ladder anyhow? Your ma and me are sick of this kind of foolishness! First that week you're gone and now this! Like we don't have enough to worry us as it is!"

Jim took a step between them and interrupted. "Maybe we should leave now, Mr. Hogan?"

He steadied her good arm and leaned his terrifying face in close to hers. "Would you like some coffee?" he asked. "Or we could go somewhere for a drink?"

Ben gave them both a look that said he couldn't waste the whole afternoon.

"I guess my stomach isn't quite up to it," she said. "I'm still a little woozy." She leaned a little more firmly against him. He led her to his car, walking close beside her as if he belonged there somehow, measuring his strides to fit her own. Then he took her arm again as he led her down the steps. She felt some importance in his hand. She had already given up on the idea that he could be anything but annoyed or worse, even laughing at her foolishness. She was sick with embarrassment. He opened the car door for her like a gentleman. She wanted to curl around herself, withering like a sun-fried moth as he helped her into the back seat. He started the engine. The drab gray miners' shacks of Deadwood began racing past her like a painful newsreel. The mouth of the canyon loomed ahead with its insane grades and corkscrewing course down into the plains. It was only then she began to notice it, his eyes filling the rearview mirror intensely, asking questions as if he didn't mean to ask them, taking her in as if despite himself and as much as he could without the car going off the road.

Ben Hogan was in a terrible mood.

"Goddamnit, Marge! Answer me now! How much is this

damned foolishness going to cost us now! What was you doing out there? Answer once, goddamnit. Just what in the hell . . ."

She couldn't care by then. She was too busy at some kind of game in which every time he looked back at her in his rearview mirror, she turned her head away coyly as if more interested in the canyon walls. Then she put on what she thought was a teasing expression, gazing through his stern profile until he tried again. She beat him to it. She turned away smiling, giddily, filled with a sense of confidence as fearless as the wind in the evergreens she watched through the moving car windows. She began to test her arm, still painless from the doctor's injection but getting stiff now, the sling chafing her neck. She thought of just how long she would have to carry it like an ugly chicken wing. Otherwise, she felt surprisingly relaxed, sleepy, pleased. She watched him, his jaw muscles flinching nervously at every turn, that overly serious twist of his mouth as if he had been born with a frown. His eyes shifted toward her again. It was more than just a mild interest. She quickly turned away to watch the battered guardrail passing by her in a blur against the massive cliffside, feeling his gaze burning straight through into her mind, the warmth riding down in tremulous sensations through her limbs.

Her arm hurt fiercely by the time they reached the house. She had just managed to close her eyes and sleep when she was startled awake by the ruts of the homeplace lane. She sat up straight. Her stomach turned with the sudden thought that she didn't know how to get him back again. She knew he wouldn't ask to see her on his own. What could she tell him? Could she knock at his door some evening and tell him then? What was there to say now? That she loved him, or felt as close to love as she had ever felt with anyone? She wasn't even sure of that herself. But if she let him just drive off, she knew she'd feel as if she had loved and lost that man in an afternoon. As he was helping her out at the house, the most she could think of doing was to ask him in to supper by way of thanking him.

"Won't you come in to supper now?" she asked.

"I don't know," he said. "I have my schedule."

He looked like a box turtle wanting to pull back into his skin.

Vera Hogan began insisting on it as she helped Jim collect his papers. She was all but stripping him with her bare hands to get him to let her launder his bloodstained clothes. Ben was shaking his head violently no, his wife ignoring him completely. Marge sat hopelessly on the couch, watching the man have a hard time ducking out from under her mother's arms.

"Please come to dinner Sunday then," she asked him. She kicked herself for her pleading tone of voice.

Jim was too busy using his folder like a shield at Vera Hogan to notice tones of voice, politely stumbling back across the living room, confused, helpless under the circumstances. He apologized. He told her absolutely not. He sidestepped, fandangoed, jigged around, but nothing worked. Then he turned to Marge as if he expected her to do something. She stared back at him with a look of mocking incomprehension in her eyes and a triumphant grin. He laughed. He let loose. He bared his teeth in outbursting, incredulous laughter and she knew he was coming.

"All right!" He said it over his shoulder at her. "Sunday!" There was exasperation in it. "Sunday!"

The old woman stood on the front porch calling out to him.

"Eight o'clock! Eight o'clock now! Bring somebody if you like! Eight o'clock now! Eight o'clock! Eight o'clock now. . . . "

Marge watched him drive away the way he'd come.

16

She lay back dreaming in her room. Morning dreams, when the sun turned the cardboard over her window into an amber screen and the shadows of the autumn tree branches shone on it, dark shapes falling slowly as the sun rose above the house until the noon. She imagined the smell of him, a pleasant odor of his sweat mixing with the faint bitterness of his lemon shaving soap, the smell up against his clothes like the sensuous odor of a tobacco pouch or some other fragrant bits of leaf she could close her eyes and breathe in deeply. She imagined his face as strong as the faces men were busy carving in the granite hills when she was young—a sandblasted, monumental face, a face that had seen the rain, the roads. As a detail in a photograph can focus that photograph, her image of his face was always focused by the eyes. She loved the intensity of his eyes, almost content to lie alone with its memory and let it draw her through visions of how they shared their love. Then she imagined their love more distantly. They were like two beautiful twins gazing at each other in a sea of grass, passing hours chasing through it like children in a hiding game. She sat up in bed with the pillows bunched against the wall, daydreaming until the pale smooth plain of her abdomen stretched tautly and began to move under the hothouse of her sheets. She closed her eyes, her fingers gliding slowly, sensually downward until they touched.

She could die then just to hold him. She dreamed of herself dying there, a lovers' tragedy. Something had ruptured inside and Doc Monahan was already closing his bag and demanding his fee. Her father and mother weeping out of control, her mother even drinking to strengthen herself. George and Mike returning from the dead like in the movie *The Fighting Sullivans,* in full uniform marching in on a bank of clouds and reaching out mischievously toward her the way they used to, as if to yank the covers tented on her knees. In her daydream, she was hopelessly lost in unimaginably painful death throes. She came out of them cradling her lover's face, kissing and mothering him, feverish but speaking calmly. She told him he had to continue on after she was in the ground. He gritted his teeth. It was all he could do to keep from crying out like a wounded animal. He said he could never make it on his own. He showed her a solid gold locket full of poison. He planned to join her soon. His wife as always. Such a love as theirs . . .

As her last wish, she made him promise not to take the poison. Then she told him that after a full year of mourning passed, it was fine for him to lie with other women, "but, honey, only if you really need to,'' she said, ''and as long as it's never the same one two nights in a row.''

Her daydreams broke when her mother slammed in at noon calling her to the dinner table. Marge pulled herself reluctantly out of her sickbed. It was the first time she could remember clearly that she had ever been allowed to lie around like that. Then she had to go in and eat the same old meat and potatoes. She found her father already there, hardly looking at her across the table. He gummed at his food. She felt as tarnished in his eyes as the silverware in his fists. She watched the blunt strokes of his silverware as he scraped his plate. He squinted up at her once or twice to say something.

''You don't get up and around soon,'' he said, ''I'll have to give you a shot of the damned cow serum. You ain't that sick you got to lie around the whole day.''

He pushed back to roll himself a smoke.

''Just leave her be,'' her mother said. ''I expect she's done enough already.''

''Used to be ten minutes after birthing, a woman was up and sweeping the floor!''

''Hush up now.''

''Ha! The week after you had George, you was out shocking grain.''

''It wouldn't have got done if I didn't.''

''Ha! I had me a hired man all set to do it. You was bored to tears lying around the house like that. You was bored to tears!''

Marge listened to their talk. She knew it was all just talk between them. Even the times they complained at her it seemed like talk between them. Lately, it had been her father's complaint: ''Don't you just set around the house now! Just because you drag one wing don't mean you can't do no work!''

Then when she tried to help him with his work, he told her there was nothing she could do. And there was nothing she could do. She could never be his little girl again. Yet he acted as if he was complaining because he was having so much trouble rebuilding his pickup. Out there all day squinting at the numbers on the salvaged engine parts and none of them ever fit right. He had to take it out on somebody. But there was something else going on in him. It was a wound she had inflicted as surely as if she'd taken an ax to him. Even with his encouragement that she should stay out late with boys, even with his own frank and jocular humor at the facts of nature ever since she could remember, he seemed to take the new change in her the same way he sometimes took the adverse truth of a sudden and disastrous change in a season, knowing full well it was coming but still brought low when it finally arrived. She felt looked upon like a cornseed he had planted that had grown tall, strong and green, that had tasseled out as expected but had finally borne no fruit. It was the kind of cornstalk that her father went through his fields looking for and tore up by the roots. In some ways, for a brief time at least, she must have been nearly as much a grief to him as the loss of his sons. And there was nothing she could do to change that now. She couldn't even sit at the same table without setting his teeth on edge. *That's no grief of mine,* she thought, *that's sure no grief of mine. . . .*

She ate dinner as fast as she could. She leaned down close to her food, wishing she had a free hand just once to wave away the flies. Every noontime was the same. The same food, the same complaints, then she cleared the table and did the dishes one-handed as Ben lay down for his afternoon rest on the living room floor because he claimed the bare boards were good for his back. He closed his eyes and napped for about half an hour, then he slowly stood up, hooked the straps of his overalls up over his shoulders and pushed his way out the screen door without a word. Marge slapped a broom around the house thinking she couldn't stand it, the way her mother sat in the wingchair in her tattered blue robe, giving advice as she sipped at her tea.

"Mrs. Cooney called."

Marge wiped the table with a rag. She set the bowl of plastic flowers on it, the yellow heads drooping over the edges of the bowl.

"Mrs. Cooney called to invite you in to supper."

The pipes groaned when she turned the faucet on. She scoured out the sinks. She carried the bucket of scraps and garbage to the back porch.

"They ain't give up on you yet. That family's got the good

Lord's patience! You owe it to that boy to talk things over!"

Marge beat the broom at the floor. She raised a layer of dust up to her knees. With great swirling one-handed strokes, she beat the field dirt into a pile. The house was filled with it. In every crack between the boards. In every weave of the balding carpet. She swished and beat the broom around in a violent pattern across the kitchen. She beat a rhythm through the living room toward the door. She threw that door wide and sent the dirt flying out over the porch.

The young dog asleep on the porch shook itself under a dust cloud and sulked away.

"Mrs. Cooney called to invite you in to supper."

"That don't mean I'm still going to marry him!"

"An invite to supper don't mean that either," her mother said. Vera settled back, pleased enough at her reasoning.

"I'm not going," said Marge.

"What if there ain't nobody have you now but him?" her mother asked. "Now you know plain as rain what I mean. You're just lucky that family's willing to give you a second chance."

"But I don't love him, Mama," said Marge. "What do you do, Mama, when you put your arms around a man, when you kiss him with everything you got, when you want to give everything to him, and still you don't feel a thing? What do you do? I always thought I'd feel butterflies in my stomach. There's got to be that much, Mama. There's got to be."

"Nobody goes through life with butterflies," her mother said. "Butterflies are the first things to go. The rest is just hard work and endless days."

"Oh, Mama, how could you say that? How could you say that about Papa?"

"There's a lot more to life than the kind of love you mean," Vera said. "There's having a home. There's having a life with both feet planted. A dignified life, even with all the worries about money and bills and things like that. There's children and dogs and a garden to water. There's having a house and all the things that go with it, and all the work to keep that house a place where people want to come to your door, that's what there is. Now, honey, this is a hard thing to say. I know what you're thinking and it breaks my heart. It cuts my heart in two. But you already give that other man what he wants. Don't you see? No matter what we do now, the general truth about men is, after that, they won't give you any kind of life.''

''Who in hell wants any kind of life?'' Marge shouted. ''I want to die! You hear that, Mama? I just want to die!''

Marge went slamming out of the house.

''You owe it to that boy to talk it over!'' Vera shouted after her. Then ten minutes later, she heard her mother on the phone to Mrs. Cooney. ''You know how it was when she was born. I fell off the corral fence and Ben near had to birth her in the trough. Sometimes, I tell myself it's 'cause I fell off that fence. You know they come out ornery when you fall like that. There's some that come out red-haired, too. . . .''

Marge couldn't stand it. She slammed off the front porch to see what she could do to help her father. He usually just kept right on driving his tractor, doing what he was doing, giving her a look that as much as said if she stood in his way long enough, for sure she was going to end up harrowed. That hurt her deeply, though she knew if he really needed her as a pair of hands to extend his own, as someone to drive into town for parts, he'd call for her all right.

In the afternoons, after she had checked on her father, Marge took long walks along the wild ditchbanks, along fencelines that served as green viny latticeworks for the weeds. When the mosquitoes weren't too bad, she sat in the shade of the willows along the creek bottom. Her tennis shoes sounded with a quiet hollow clumping over the boards of the rickety bridge. She danced up and down on the boards as if not satisfied until she heard one crack. She jumped off the bridge onto the bank. The bank was narrow. She had to hug in closely to the mud under the yellow whips of the willow scrub. She pushed her way through to a private place, a small clearing where she used to hide sometimes from her brothers. Tendrils of brambles crawled out from the willow thickets, browning in autumn, but in summer the purple flowers of foxglove and thistles, the white trumpets of the creeping jenny tried to overrun the dark green grass. But along the edge of the clearing there was a tiny border of wild roses—not the pale lavender she had seen elsewhere, but little yellow roses, profuse in July, scattered to the winds by now but for a single late blossom or two that seemed to have no inkling of the approach of winter. She remembered how she used to kneel close to this spread of thorns that left red scratches on her ankles and wrists as she watched the armies of tiny gray insects harvesting some mysterious yield at the very center of the buds, scrambling over one another the closer to the center they came, reaching the summit of a petal's curve and sliding, tumbling, the horde disappearing in a chaotic fall into the dark center of the rose's fruit. She was alone, flat against the earth, able to distinguish each strand of grass from the next in a tiny clump, able to pursue the sudden leap of a frog in flight toward the creek and to capture it, give it a name then set it free in the deepest pool of the creek, where she knew that, even in drought, its children would live. Her clearing was a private place. Though her brothers, her father, everyone must have known the times she was there, no one ever disturbed her. It was a place where the world became suddenly clear from three inches away. Or overwhelming from the same distance. She rolled to her back. She lay there in the cool dampness of the earth and smoked, letting the smoke burn her lungs and rasp out in unutterable words of relaxation. She unbuttoned her blouse. She let the sun burn her, her green, gloomy eyes slowly closing to the sound of skittering birds.

It was always the same thinking now. She told herself she had to leave. Especially if her mother was right, she couldn't stand it anymore. She could join the Waves or something and get sent out of this place. She could apply to beauty school in Rapid City as her friend Carol Hinkle had done, if there would ever be any money for that, if she could ever get up the nerve just to pack up and leave. To get herself a job . . .

Her mind filled with thoughts of leaving. She would find a place as new and citified and colorful as in her travel magazines. She would never have to think of this farm again. This farm her family now had no money to make the payments on. This farm that, once he lost it, piece by piece, would likely kill the only man she really knew. Her father, whose arms would never ever hold her the same way again. Her father, who used to swear and spit and rage at her, then give her a fiver for the dance. She remembered the last gift she had given him, a red-and-green-checkered sports cap like maybe only the tourists wore and in a hard moment when she had wanted to hide at the way he looked at it, he stuck out his tongue, screwed up his nose and pulled the bill down over his ear to make her laugh. She saw his face press in to kiss her like his lady. She saw him dancing with her at the Grange Hall dance when there had been nobody else, him reeling around her room when she was still half dressed for a night on the town, slapping her behind and telling her, "Look what a sight you are! Look what a sight you are! One of these days your mama's going to the devil and you're coming with me, goddamnit. . . ."

She lay back smoking, knowing she had to leave yet caught by the stillness of the afternoon. Or by simply lying out there, alone and still.

17

Marge waited five long days. She lay in her bed turning the pages of magazines and listening to the radio that never seemed to get any station in clearly. She'd bought it after the war ended, one of those obsolete wooden boxes with a tortoiseshell finish and f-hole design in front carved as fancy as a cathedral door. She only paid a dollar fifty for it at Simon Lisky's farm auction, following his funeral; "looting the funeral," her father called such auctions, when there were no working heirs and the land was due to be sold to strangers. Neighbors descended on the Lisky place like a flock of crows. They carried off whatever they could—machinery, livestock, even furnishings and glassware from the widow's house, bidding only pennies on the dollar for what things were worth. Widow Lisky had sold the farm anyway and was soon to leave for a rest home in Belle Fourche. What remained of the homestead was a farmer's quiet legacy to his neighbors.

There were only two stations the radio picked up regularly and they overlapped each other on the dial. One station broadcast through scratchy static the voices of farm news announcers giving commodity prices or some woman yapping about her favorite piecrust, followed by the usual faith messages from the Right Reverend Charles G. Ott of the Church of Christ Reformed—that best-friend voice talking fire and brimstone with dramatic pauses for the organ chords. Marge did her best to dial it out or listen through it to the other station. The other station played her music, the seductive four-part harmonies heavy enough on the bass so the wood in the old radio was buzzing like a split cane pole with the new electric Hawaiian style of groups like the Sons of the Pioneers, then touring the Plains, the Rock Country Boys, strictly two-bit Rapid City, tolerably relieved by the occasional Hank Williams or Bob Wills and the Texas Playboys on that chance station that bounced in all the way from Tulsa.

She wasn't in much of a mood for music anyway. She had the radio on low across the room as a kind of company, a faint rhythm to serenade away the hours. After a while, the high-throated faces in her magazines gradually began to look the same, or the model was throwing her arms around the same gray, dimensionless leading man with sketched-in outlines, kicking one leg up high to show the flare of a skirt that nobody could ever get away with wearing in Nowell. Marge lay through the afternoons in her piles of magazines feeling bored and hopeless. She picked at the bandage on her arm. The stitches itched under the gauze. She tried to scratch over the bandage but that hurt too much. She tried slipping a nailfile in to scratch and it was even worse. She either had to lie back in boredom and irritation, scratching until it bled, or she had to try and forget the slow passage of her days by sleeping most of the time, waking to those same myopic dreams that blurred into a jittering and impatience that drove her out of her senses with anticipation. At the same time, she had no faith at all in anticipation.

Jim arrived three hours early to supper. She was already sitting in front of her mirror, trying to put on a face. She had barely finished the eyes, hard to do with her left hand. She heard an engine puttering like a fly in a jug down the lane. She ran to the front-room window and saw it was him. She experienced an attack of nerves. How could he have dared to come so early? She knew the calico dress she had on made her look matronly, deformed in the shoulders, pregnant. She wished there was time enough to go through the torture of pulling it off and putting on something else. That was impossible, in her mind. She searched through the sparse hangings of her closet. She thought of how few clothes she had as if it were a moment of high personal tragedy. His bootsteps drummed ominously on the porch.

She rushed into the living room. He was already standing there with her mother. He didn't look anything like the man she remembered, the man she had imagined.

"You're so early now!" said Vera, flustered, wiping her hands on her apron.

"Isn't it five o'clock?" he asked.

"You told him five o'clock, Mama," said Marge, pinching her mother at the waist.

"Well, come on in," Vera said. "It won't be ready for hours yet. Don't blame me for that! You go on and get Ben now, Marge. . . ."

She wondered. Now that he stepped in from the shadows of the porch, it wasn't surprising that she could hardly recognize him. He was duded up, hat to boots. A gleaming silver bolo in the shape of a bull's head hung down over his starched, embroidered shirt. He had a cowboy hat in hand. It wasn't like any hat Marge had ever seen, almost a Cheyenne style but made of some off-white, furlike material, flat-brimmed, flat-crowned, more like a riverboat gambler's hat. He carried a bottle of fine Scotch under his arm. She was mortified for him. Some old high-rolling range boy might have been able to get away with wearing that outfit, but on him it looked as if he stood too close to a shooting gallery, folks just might mistake him for a painted target. And there was something else about him—she figured he'd likely been drinking since noon.

"How are you?" he exclaimed over Vera Hogan. "I have something for you!"

He took a few unsteady strides toward her, then reached under the flap of his jacket for a bunch of roses.

She didn't know what to do. She wondered how far he must have driven to get them; the nearest flower shop was forty miles away. She was touched at them, speechless, extending a girl's hand out hesitantly. She hid her face in them.

"Why, thank you," said Vera. "But you shouldn't have done it! Thank you so much. . . . But he shouldn't have, ain't that right, Marge? Say, thank you, Marge!"

"Thank you," she said. "Very much."

"You're very welcome," he said, smiling. He reached out quickly to take her hand. Her hand was hog-tied in the sling and bandages. He closed his fingers around it, squeezing once.

"I'm really terribly sorry about what happened the other day," he said, wavering, rocking back and forth in his new boots that looked as if they must be causing him blisters. "But, Mrs. Hogan . . ." he said. He took Vera's arm just above the elbow. "I can tell you that I've never seen anyone endure pain more beautifully."

"Why, that's very kind of you," Vera said. "Ain't that kind of him, Marge?"

She met his eyes once over her roses.

"But you know, she's been using this as an excuse to take a vacation," her mother said. "And God knows she's been needing one. She works so hard around this house!"

Jim was picking nervously at the elkhorn buttons of his jacket, yet he looked pleased. His rust-brown eyes were taking her in jubilantly, calling forth some bright emotion that made him happy enough this afternoon. She was suddenly irritated at him. She felt as if he was staring right through her clothes.

"Mama, will you put these in some water?" she said, brushing quickly past him, her cheeks burning as she leaped down off the porch.

It wasn't long before they were both sitting in the shade of the weathered back porch. Vera set a table out there. Jim and Ben Hogan started drinking shots of Scotch neat and exchanging man talk as Marge sat in the old gray porch swing, the hardware creaking, creaking, marking time. Her mother left them to put the supper on. Marge found her attention wandering out through the crooked latticeworks that looked held together by the gray vines growing through them. Time seemed peculiarly slowed. She suffered the intervals between each spade-shaped, waxen-yellow leaf as it dropped from the vines, spinning in wild acceleration into the yard. The sun hung suspended over the barn as if it wouldn't move. The weathervane was listing, windless. Ben finally excused himself, stiff and unfriendly, she thought, as he went off loudly into the house meaning to change his greasy clothes. The screen door shut by its spring with two quick slaps. She still watched out away from him across the yard when they were alone.

"Does it hurt very much?" he asked, bottle in hand, walking toward her across the porch.

"Naw, it don't hurt," she said.

He sat down next to her on the porch swing, the chains pulling taut with a crackling sound.

"I was wounded in the arm once," he said. "Shrapnel . . . Really kind of a grim feeling."

"That's too bad," she said. "You should thank your stars it's not somewhere else."

He laughed and she laughed with him once. Then he reached a hand down, squeezing her knee in a fatherly gesture. She watched it there like some small repulsive animal until he took it back again, curling it around his bottle.

"Pardon *me*," he said. "I don't mean to take any liberties."

"You're a man who's used to taking liberties," she said.

"Oh, not really," he said. "Not really. Nobody really understands what I do. I was just trying to be friendly," he said. He stared for a moment into the orange glare of the sunset with a sad look on his face. "Well, perhaps more than that," he said. "Maybe I just can't help myself with you."

She knew he was going to say something like that before he did.

She sat there frozen, wishing he would lean over and kiss her full on the mouth. That feeling passed. Crawlers moved in her stomach. She had no idea what to say to him. "You said you been married," she said. "But you never said a thing more about it. I mean the subject just didn't come up." She paused a moment, not quite able to believe she had actually slept with this man sitting next to her. Maybe it was something about him, a distance on the world, a look in his eyes that reminded her of the look of order buyers appraising the weight of a steer at auction. "But then again maybe I don't want to know about it," she said.

"Of course you do," he said. "But it's a sad story, truly sad. I've had thirteen wives. This is true. No less than thirteen of them." He held his fingers up and began to count off each one. "Twenty-three miserable kids scattered from hell to breakfast. . . ."

"Don't go doing that to me," she said.

"No!" He waved his hand, protesting. "No! This is true!" He laughed morosely, the alcohol working in his laugh. He poured himself another Scotch. "Don't worry about nothing," he said. "From my end, it seems like I've had thirteen wives. Hell, sometimes I can sit with a woman five minutes and feel like we've lived through twenty-five years of marriage."

"You must be a strong believer in divorce," she said.

"Look. The first and only time I was married, it didn't work out," he said. "That was a long time ago. I can't even remember what she looked like anymore."

"I don't believe you," she said.

"You don't believe what?"

"That you can't remember what she looked like anymore."

"Oh, really? Well, don't kid yourself. With the right kind of woman, it's easy."

"That's a terrible thing to say," she said.

"Well, I'm sorry," he said. "Just think of me as a man who's reached that stage in life when he's learned to forget certain things."

"That's a crock of you-know-what," she said.

"Look," he said. He smiled. "I'll demonstrate for you." He

leaned his head against the porch swing and tightly shut his eyes. "Right now, right at this moment, I'm trying to remember what she looked like. I can see our wedding. Me, the bride and her parents in the dining room of a first-class hotel. It's the kind of place with crystal chandeliers and a thirty-piece dance band. Waiters are running back and forth with champagne. Her father—I can remember him very clearly, a heavyset, balding man—he's shouting bloody murder about the fact that he ordered a seven-course menu and only six courses were served at the reception. Everyone is in a major stew over this problem. It's like the worst thing that could have happened as far as they're concerned, a bad omen for the rest of our lives. Her mother, a tall, elegant woman in every respect, her mother is sitting next to me so nervous that she's picked a linen napkin to bits with her fingernails. On the other side of me, the bride, my wife, mind you, *my wife* . . . When I think of her, all I see is a very small empty space. That's all. If I try to get any closer, I sense the kind of hysteria that wants to pull the world in with it. So there's nothing. When I think about the next few years, that same small empty space is in all my memories. No ghosts, no bad dreams, nothing. It's really better that way. You don't have to hate anyone for wasted years, for lost opportunities. But her folks did put me through school and I'm grateful to them. Maybe that's why I remember what they look like. After I got out of school, nothing went right with us. Mainly it was money. I was just starting out in practice and even taking stuff in trade, garden vegetables and things like that. She was born and raised on the champagne trail and I just couldn't keep up. That's one way to put it. And her parents kept buying us things, expensive china and furniture, only the best. They'd put money down and stick me with the monthly payments. But that's just what we argued about. We were just kids. We tried to do the right thing and got married after the third date. We lived through a brief violent divorce that ended in me breaking her eardrum with a telephone directory. She broke my nose with a wine bottle. Right here." He pointed to a jagged white scar on the bridge of his nose. "That's partly why I've got a nose like a chewed-up potato. It was broken again in the army. I saw the war coming and joined the army after our divorce, three months before Pearl Harbor. I spent eight years in the army, most of them as an officer in the supply corps but close enough to the action that I didn't stop covering my head long enough to remember much of anything. During the occupation, I was almost married again . . . *almost*. Hell, about all a guy had to do was grab a shovel and help some poor woman dig out and he was as good as married. She was a very beautiful German girl; I can remember exactly what she looked like in every detail. . . .''

He had opened his eyes by this time. His eyes searched her out as if his thoughts were stampeding behind them. She felt as if all the women he had ever known were passing through his mind like a deck of snapshots. She could see them. Not any of them right for him. She saw him counting back the months since his departure, since the last swollen, red-light evening among the ruins. Some night of gutter love in a room full of smuggled nylon stockings dangling over chairs and wooden clothes hangers, of treasured cigarettes, brandy, tins of food in hands grown used to the occupation.

''But for some reason,'' he said, ''it never worked. I ran out on her, in the end. I was a kind of bad risk prospect, as it turns out. And there are other, more complicated reasons. Maybe as I'm getting older the price of the whole catastrophe keeps going up. I don't know,'' he said. It seemed to her his mood quickly changed, the tone of his voice suddenly optimistic. ''That's why I'm glad you settled things the way you did. Nice and clean. Short, sweet and clean, that's the only way to handle a guy like me,'' he said. ''You jumping out of the car like that saved us both from a big mistake,'' he said.

She licked her dry lips. She tasted something bitter.

''You're damn right I did,'' she said. ''I thank my lucky stars I did.''

''Damn straight,'' he said after a minute, staring off into the shallow swirling puddle of Scotch in the bottom of his glass.

''Well, you got what you wanted anyway,'' she said.

''Ho, ho,'' he said. Then he looked at her coldly and said, ''Yes, I did.''

"Well, why in hell did you ever come out here then?" She started to shout but caught her voice before it rose too far. She took a deep breath. "I'm sorry I invited you here," she said. "It's just another big mistake. Now if you'll excuse me ..." She started to rise up out of the swing but he caught her by her good arm before she could.

"Wait a minute," he said. "I didn't drive out here the other day to see you. I came out strictly on business."

"Let go of my arm, damn you," she said, and he quickly let go.

"For Christ's sake," he said. "Do you mean nobody's told you?"

"Hell, no," she said. "They've hardly had a thing to say to me all week long. And for reasons you might well understand."

"I'm sorry," he said. "You poor darling."

"I ain't no goddamned darling!"

"Wait a minute, wait a minute," he said. "I don't mean to bring up an unpleasant subject, but the reason I came out here the other day had nothing to do with you. It was to talk about writing up a long-term sales contract between your dad and the company. Don't get me wrong. There are a lot of things in this business I don't like doing and that was one of them. Your father has to sell out, you know. He can do it a piece at a time and sort of stretch the whole process out. But he stands a chance of losing everything if he doesn't sell about a hundred acres soon, and on generous terms. I was hoping he'd told you. We really have to have his decision soon." She looked as if she'd had the wind kicked out of her. "I'm sorry," he said. "I don't mean to be the one to break the news. It was wrong of me to say anything. This is neither the time nor the place."

"It's all right," she said. "It's all right. He never said a damn thing to me."

"I'm terribly sorry," he said.

"That's no grief of mine," she said. "That's sure no grief of mine."

"That's true," said Jim Vogel after a minute, pouring himself another Scotch. He sat for a long time staring at the horizon as if he saw the sun as sinking stupidly into the plains. "I'm not a man without some influence, you know," he said. "I could probably make a phone call and on my say-so your dad could get an extension. But all that would accomplish is to buy him some time. His farm will end up the same either way. You just won't be able to make a profit on this kind of a place anymore."

She hated him. She tried to think of something to say to him, anything just to get rid of him, trying to find the words exactly in her mind but choking on them before she could. The afternoon seemed endless. She wished she could fly on out of there, wished she were anything but herself, wanting to flutter into the mud nests with the barn swallows under the eaves, wanting to range out and be rattling a suckle pail like the calf tied to the shed behind the yard or just to sail off through the blond hay meadow and join in a dark violet shape of cloud that was slowly passing over the horizon.

"Would you like to come to town with me," he asked, "later this evening? Maybe if we could talk things over somewhere alone," he said. "Who knows? Between the two of us, we might come up with some kind of arrangement."

She turned at him violently, then met his eyes, an unmoving seriousness in them, a hard expression in his eyes as if presenting his case to her right then and there. She was suddenly terrified.

"I came out today to see you, you know," he said.

"Get me a glass of that Scotch, will you?"

He just then noticed her hands were empty.

"Of course!" He spouted it joyously. She nearly jumped right out of her seat. "How could I have neglected you? Of course. Forgive me. Here I've been hogging it all. . . . And thinking myself a gentleman to boot!"

His mood changed. He leaped out of the porch swing and all but danced over to the table. His blue suit gleamed in the fading light as if covered with a frost. He was smiling now, a different person from one moment to the next. She thought he was the strangest man she had ever laid eyes on. She had no way to think of him in terms she knew, in terms of his sheep, his rounds, his pool shots, his muscular attitudes, some hell-raising quality she could ride out in time, or even in terms of her own attractions to him.

"Here it is!" he shouted. "A glass! How fortunate! There's even a glass set out here for you!"

He held the glass up like a showman, bowing, waiting for her applause.

"All I wanted was a drink!"

"So here it is!" he said, and laughed. "Look! I'm pouring it for you! Marvelous! Here it is. . . ."

"Jesus," she said. "Jesus Christ . . ."

He was startled by the sudden high squawking of chickens. Vera Hogan came through the backyard gate carrying three chickens by the feet. The old woman stopped then and ruffled her fingers through the white feathers of the breasts, inspecting them, holding them up so her guest could see. She grinned with celebration. She shook the birds a little and smiled toward the porch. She straightened her thick, rounded body up more than usual, as if for him, moving self-consciously along the fence.

"Marge!" she called up at her from the yard.

Marge excused herself to him. She joined her mother in the yard, taking two of the struggling chickens, holding them way out from her dress.

Vera took one chicken under her arm, constraining the feet and wings so only the head could move. She tapped a finger along the comb and beak, a kind of hypnotizing until the lids closed over the eyes. She bent over for a stick lying at her feet. She laid the chicken's head between her feet, pinning the stick against its neck, holding the ends of the the stick down with her feet. She pulled the bird back slowly until the head was left between her feet. She carried the chicken flapping headless to the side and hung it up-side down on the fence, bleeding it out.

"Bring that bucket now!" she called to Marge. Marge started into the house to fetch a bucket of boiling water from the stove, her mother bending over with the other birds.

18

Vera called everyone to the table as she hefted a large steel pot and set it down. She waved them to their places, the fat jiggling on her arms, her face set with counting to herself to see if what she needed was there—the stale piece of toast under one leg of her round plank table, to counter the warp in the floor; the chairs, of mixed sizes; the dishes, each with a different landscape or sprayed with different-colored flowers and marked at the edges with wear; the tall blue tumblers, compliments of Neil's Texaco; the mixed set of silverware, bought piece by piece through the mails. There was an embroidered linen tablecloth to make the atmosphere special for the brown crusted loaves of her fry bread, the breaded zucchini squash, a bowl of creamed onions, the spinach leaves steamed in milk, the small potatoes with the skins still on laced with chopped scallions under a melting fist of butter, the tiny, transparent green watermelon-rind spice pickles in her mason jars. An old pocket watch was set by her plate to remind her of the pies in her coal-smoke-blackened oven. That meal was celebrated by Vera's massive presence and by the twist of her mouth that almost never smiled despite herself, all of it arranged around the chicken steaming in a tomato and hot pepper sauce, dominating the room with its pungent sweet hot odor, and the curved end of the ladle waiting for her hand.

She served the food. She heaped the plates high with chicken and greens. Marge passed one next to her down the table to Jim. Jim pressed his face in close to his plate and marveled at it properly. In doing so, he nearly dragged his bolo tie through the sauce. He reached out reflexively at his swinging tie and dipped the buttons of his jacket sleeve in the onions. He and Ben had finished the Scotch by then and Ben was dipping glasses full from his crocks of potato wine that he kept bubbling in a yeasty corner behind the stove. Ben was leaning against his fist like he was trying to keep his head on straight. He had only one of his sleeves rolled, as if he was drunk enough now that he would have to eat one-handed.

"Now don't you wait on it! Just go ahead. . . ." Vera watched around at her men.

For a long time, there was nothing but the sound of men eating. Her father sucking on the bones. Her father jabbing way out across the table with his knife. Jim sitting next to her picking delicately with his utensils as if they were a scalpel and forceps. He leaned back from time to time as though hunger was something foreign to him, as if eating was a form of contract to be drawn out and reconsidered. He poked through his food with enough patience that by the time her father was working on his third portion, he was still rearranging his first.

"Hell there!" Ben shouted, waving his knife out over the table. "I always say, 'For chicken and women, a man's got to use his fingers.' Use yer shittin' fingers! Ain't that right, Vera?"

Vera gave him a hard look. Then Ben looked a little too quickly across the table at Marge and remembered himself.

Marge played with her food like it was poisoned. She listened to the men eating. It seemed to her that that was what men did best. A man's function was to eat. If he could only eat, he might damn the whole rest of this world. She hated the sound of it, the scraping silverware, the glasses slamming on the table. Then Jim leaned back from time to time and started talking on at her father, mostly about what he had learned of farming in his thirty-some-odd days with the Nowell-Safebuy, about the new miracle grains, new miracle fungicides, new miracle ten-ton tractors and planting techniques, his voice sounding totally self-assured, pleased enough at his own expertise.

"There's nothing that can't be done, Mr. Hogan," he said. "I'll give you an example. . . . *Hormones*." He paused to look teacherlike around the table. He must have realized none of them knew the meaning of the word. "Chemicals, like vaccines, injected into the birds.'' He made injecting gestures with his hands. ''Someday, with the new miracle hormones, farmers are going to raise turkeys that weigh *a hundred pounds or more*.''

''Yer shittin' me,'' said Ben Hogan.

''No, no! This is true, Mr. Hogan. Absolutely true. It was talked about at the Safebuy convention in Chicago.''

''Don't seem like there'd ever be enough roasting ovens'd *cook* that sized bird,'' said Ben.

''No, you don't understand,'' said Jim with no little frustration. ''It's very simple. They just bone the turkeys and make something called a *turkey roll,* a huge, boneless roast. They get the housewife convinced that a turkey is just as good without the bones, and the Nowell-Safebuy is going to raise *hundred-pound birds. . . .*''

Marge lost her appetite. She excused herself to sit in the relative silence of the bathroom. She sat down on the cold stool and lit a cigarette. She threw the window open, propping it with a stick. There was a terrible sound. Cows at night in the barn. Her father was drunk enough to have given up on milking them. That wasn't like him, she thought. The cows were still locked in the barn, lowing in a sad chorus that made her skin rise. There must have been a horse in there too, whinnying in the still air, a high-pitched and forlorn sound among the rest. If that old plug stayed in there too long, she thought, he would likely get smart enough to break into the feed crib and founder.

She felt alone. There was no comfort in the night air through the window as she sat shivering in it. It felt as if it would frost again that night. She could imagine the cows still standing there in the crystalline dawn, their bags swelled up taut and the milk draining out of them on its own. She listened to the sounds of dinner a long time. She avoided the bathroom mirror as best she could. She slapped the string of the bare bulb that lit the room. She stared into the sink basin, which had a permanent line of smudge from men's hands, stared downward into the gray linoleum, which was stained and peeling in the corners from years of men aiming wrong. She felt assailed by the sounds from the barn and from the table, coming at her from all directions at once.

She thought of her father leaning back now the way he did, belching, drumming his swollen belly before he rolled a smoke. She told herself she had to leave. There was no sense in her staying any longer. She felt she hated the only man she had ever loved. Or if she didn't hate him, she knew he would never live up to her visions of a life together, and that much she had resolved to keep. She decided to pack her bag that night after he was gone. There wasn't any way to explain it to her parents. She'd turn down his offer to go out, and if she had to, she'd load up her bicycle in the dead of night and pedal in to the bus depot on her own. She had about twenty dollars in her jar. That was enough to get her to Rapid City. God knew what she was going to do from there, but she resolved to leave, finally, pondering life in erratic and tearful breaths of smoke. She rose. She dried her eyes and fixed her makeup. Then before she left the bathroom, she remembered to flush the toilet, as if to make sure that man would think she was really up to business in there, not just sitting there wondering what to do.

She stood leaning on her chairback a minute at the table. Jim had already finished with his pie and was carrying plates to the sink, juggling them up high over Vera Hogan's reach as he insisted on helping her with the dishes. Her father scowled at him.

"A working man don't do no dishes!" he shouted. "We don't do no goddamned dishes around here!"

"I haven't done any real work in years, Mr. Hogan," said Jim Vogel, setting his dishes in the sink as if that proved something.

"Papa, you left the cows locked in the barn," she said. "I'll go on and let 'em out."

She turned her back on him and left the room. She stood on the porch a minute, shivering. It was getting cold, as it does in these parts whenever the sun goes down, as if the land doesn't want to hold the heat once its source is gone, so it spits it back in a powerful draft that mixes the winds in all directions. Stock in the fields don't know which way to turn to keep their hindquarters to the winds, so they begin a constant circling. Human skin rises to it, shocked by the radical difference day to night, sometimes more than thirty degrees in a few hours' time. The autumn season was the hardest, most unpredictable. Some days, the sweat burned into every crease of flesh and a man's mouth dropped wide just trying to breathe, then in the darkest hours of the morning, a thin layer of ice formed over the stock troughs and damp rags stiffened on the tractor seats. It was going to snow out there soon.

Marge sneaked back into the house for her jacket. She waited on the porch again, letting her eyes adjust to the darkness. She couldn't get her jacket closed because of her arm in its sling. Even with the jacket, she was cold. She felt her breath coming harshly, as if coating her lungs with frost. She started down the steps. The old goat in the yard suddenly raised its head, the eyes two glowing amber coals, its bell clapping strangely and muffled like a spoon beating quick dancing rhythms on a tin drum, so fast she was startled. She waited. The goat lowered its head back into the grass. She walked carefully down the yard path, her feet sinking unsteadily into the damp freezing earth. She stopped. She felt watched from out of the darkness. A small animal scurried down the lane. She sucked her breath through her teeth. When she reached the yard, she closed the gate behind her and it rang out loudly in the night. She stood, rooted, watching out fearfully in all directions, then leaned her head back and faced the sky. . . .

It was a clear autumn sky, a deep and highlit blue in which the moon shone white gold in a partial phase. There was a full spread of constellations, more stars than were ever shown in George's book. She remembered how she and George used to lie on the haystacks, staring up at the stars. She followed his finger across the sky, looking from it to the pages of the book opened on his chest. There was a constellation the scoutbook showed as a flying horse, but on the page George had redrawn it to the slick curves of a '36 Packard. There was the constellation he drew to the shape of a pair of fine embroidered boots complete with riding spurs like in the catalogue. There was the one with stars connected in pencil like dot drawings to look like a haywagon with Papa on it, bullwhip in hand, giving George hell again. Her brother had described them all to her once. She stopped. The Little Dipper still hung there as George had drawn it once, like a man's private parts at the center of the sky, the stark North Star marking where his notion of love began and ended.

She walked on down the lane. The rails of the corral were a

gleaming silvery gray in the moonlight. She saw how the rails had bowed, had been left to splinter from neglect, and how the manure pile loomed high behind the corral fence waiting to be spread on the fields, a shape like a huge black skull with shovels driven through its eyes. The cows called out again. Rapid hoofbeats sounded distantly from the barn. She took a few more steps and turned. Something moved. A small shout escaped her. Nothing answered. She waited. Still nothing. She walked faster, her speed increasing until she ran. When she reached the barn, she slid the door wide in panic, reaching in desperately for the light-switch. . . .

She shrieked, jumping to hug the barn wall.

"Are you all right?"

"Jesus," she said. "You scared me."

"I did?"

"You sure as hell did! Who taught you to sneak up on folks that way? I'd like to have shot you!"

"That badly?" he asked.

She collapsed against the barn wall.

"I decided to come out for a bit of fresh air and to see if I could help you," he said.

"Just run the cows out the other end," she said, breathless, pointing to the cows. Most of the cows had poked their heads dutifully into the stanchions at the sight of people. There were only a few of them, mixed dairy and range breeds milked mainly out of habit for a few dollars on sour cream, the skim used to fatten hogs and steers before butchering. Ben was letting them go dry before winter. They were ragged-looking cows with hides sucked in over their hipbones like sunken landscapes, mottled red-and-white or black-and-white cows with horns either half sawed off or growing around in curves to meet the eyes and awaiting pruning. The cows lowed. They stretched out their necks and raised their noses high, the pitch ascending to an ear-splitting call.

"Run them out!" shouted Marge.

"That door?" he asked.

"You see any other door big enough?"

He stood a minute, gazing at her curiously. Then he nodded his head once, as if he was at her service. He picked his way carefully through the manure. He paused before the door where the cows raised their tails in a last evacuation before they were milked. He danced from side to side over the cow flops. His two-toned alligator boots were splattered to the ankle. He stopped. He looked around at her again. He bent his knees. He wavered a little and tried to jump out over the flops. He missed by a good few inches at least. She heard him cussing under his breath. He slid the huge barn door open.

He made it back over the pool, hugging the barn wall toward the cows. All the cows but two were in the stanchions. The two that weren't stood side by side, watching this stranger with careful rumination. He stood before them a minute, the muscles in his cheeks pulsing nervously. He raised his hands at them.

"Out!" he shouted crisply. "Out! Out!"

The cows lowered their heads some and stared at him.

"Out!" he shouted again. "Out!"

The two heads turned in unison. One of them looped a long pink tongue around and started cleaning its flank.

"Jesus. Just slap 'em on the ass," said Marge.

Jim opened and closed his fists. He nodded his head at her again. He marched a couple of steps closer to the cows. He raised his boot. He wasn't close enough. He took one more step gingerly forward. He raised his boot and toed one of them in the haunch. It switched its tail.

"Go on," she said, trying not to laugh. "She's not going to kill you or anything."

Jim leaned his body forward some, gauging the distance. He gathered his forces. He let loose with a full precise kick, then jumped back against the barn wall. The cow that was kicked started whipping its tail around, the both of them lumbering slowly toward the door.

"Get the others out of the stanchions now," said Marge.

He stared at the line of apparently headless beasts, the tails swinging, the hooves shifting nervously.

"How . . . how do I do that?" he asked.

"What the hell's the matter with you?" she said, and laughed. "Haven't you ever seen a cow before?"

"Yes," he said. "But as a matter of fact, this is the closest I've ever been to one."

"Now ain't that something? Mister Agricultural Expert here . . . Use your sense once! Step around in front there and slap 'em on the nose!"

Jim started uncertainly down the line of cows. He leaned in over the first stanchion. He reached in delicately with his open hand.

"Slap her on the nose!" she shouted.

He flexed his hand once. He held his hand up for her to see so he could be sure. He raised his hand high and slapped it down hard enough on the cow's nose so that it made a hollow, thumping sound. The cow pulled out fast and trotted for the open door.

"Don't scare her half to death," said Marge.

He looked pleased. He went on to the next stanchion. He hit more gently this time, just a little pat. It worked again. He watched the cow let loose its flops and jump off into the night. He went on to the next cow, approaching it with confidence, popping it once on the nose as if he had it down to a system. He leaned out over the last cow, slapping once. Nothing happened. He slapped again and again, raising his hand a little higher each time until he finally looked around for her assistance. She watched him battering the cow's nose. Horns clattered dangerously against the stanchion boards. Marge watched the cow's back slowly arching, the hind legs buckling under it like it was ready for a spring. . . .

"Open the stanchion first!" she shouted. "Open the stanchion first!"

He looked around at her with an expression of surprise. He jumped out of the way just in time as the cow heaved its large body backward with a basso scream. The stanchion was torn off its nails. The cow leaped around in panic with a piece of stanchion caught over its neck and back like a yoke. Then it smashed head-long into the barn wall, letting forth an eerie bellowing like a railroad horn.

Marge jumped out in front of the cow, waving her arm. The cow bucked up high and a barn board came crashing down. Blood spurted from the cow's nose. Marge danced around in its path. She ran to beat it to the barn door so she could keep it in long enough to get the splinters of wood that hung like a collar from around its neck, sliding the door closed just as the cow rammed through it into the darkness, the yoke of stanchion exploding over its neck and back in a confusion of cow screams, hay and manure tossed up everywhere, the barn door cascading off its hinges.

"Out!" shouted Jim Vogel. "Out!" still waving his arms twenty feet behind.

Marge stomped back through the barn, fuming, slamming through into the grain room. She dragged Ben's gelding out by an ear. The horse shook its head wildly, its hooves pounding the floorboards, its eyes rolling white with fear and resistance. Marge dragged the horse, kicking and raging at it, clear out of the barn. She came back in. The man looked to her like he was watching it all with an amused expression, even laughing at her rage.

Marge leaned over and picked up a piece of broken stanchion as long as her good arm. Jim Vogel stopped laughing.

"Maybe we should go back to the house?" he asked.

She swung the two-by-four through the air.

"What are you doing?" He backed off now, seeing the other barn door was latched behind him. "Are you all right?" he asked. He ducked it just in time. The piece of wood slammed into the wall behind him. He crouched there with a face transformed into an expression of violence.

"I'm fine!" she screamed. "I'm goddamned fine! Look at me! Don't I look fine enough to you! Look at me! You sonofabitch! Don't I now. . . . Just don't I now. . . ."

She collapsed against a barn beam.

"You come all the way," she said, "all the way out here. All the way . . ." She closed her eyes. It wasn't him. It was as if the fields themselves had turned their backs. And she was about to do the same to them. "Why don't you just get out of here. Go on now. I don't know why you came out. Get out of here now. Go on. Get out of here."

She rocked back and forth against the beam. Then she buried her face in her arms and wept. The sound must have pierced through him. He looked unsure of what to do. He stood there as if his desire to comfort might drift out across the barn. But he must have realized she no longer wanted any comfort from him.

"I'm sorry," he said. "All I meant to do was help."

When there was no response, he turned. He started slowly out of the barn. The barn lights overhead were dim enough that he must hardly have been able to see. He had trouble with his balance in those unaccustomed boots, in that shifting landscape of hand-hewn planks, piled hay, an old barn floor. He stopped. It was over now. He lifted the doorlatch. He didn't hear her stand up behind him or her quiet footsteps. Her arm was suddenly moving around his waist, her fingers bunching at his clothes. She pressed her face hard between his shoulders. "Please," she said. "Not like this."

Without a word, he turned and held her. They braced themselves. The dim barn lights darkened entirely in her mind.

19

The photograph of their wedding, taken less than two months after she first kissed him, shows the groom as looking startled, caught in mid-turn from the altar. He's reaching out with both hands toward her dark blue waist as if about to pull her to the ground in the sudden panic of an air raid.

She's a step ahead—a long, bright step—her eyes looking dreamy and unconcerned, her hat and veil tipped a little to one side, her small bouquet and a couple of pink roses pinned to her hat the only color to relieve the matching dark blues of her businesslike wedding outfit, a practical jacket and mid-length skirt she would wear again many times. The aisle of the Rock Creek Church is decorated with flowers in simple metal holders, bright explosions of color at the ends of the pews. The heads and faces of the crowd are upraised, turning to follow the couple back up the aisle. There's a look of distance about the crowd, and of awe, as if watching some strange new crossbreed brought before them at auction—the kind of people naturally suspicious of any farm girl who marries so above her age, to a stranger to boot and a man rumored by some to be Jewish, or atheist, which amounted to the same thing in this town. In writing up the wedding announcement, Willa Mason at the Nowell *Enterprise* asked, "Is a birthdate soon to follow?" in the caption under the portrait photos on the social page.

Three o'clock in the afternoon. Married life felt suspended interminably at three o'clock. Especially in summer, when it was too early yet to water the garden, too early to put his supper on. She had done almost everything else. She had run through their new little crackerbox house on Yampa Street with her dustcloth and carpet sweeper. She had picked through the laundry, scrubbed and slapped it clean in the bathtub, then hung it up to dry, had ironed his shirts off the line from yesterday and folded them neatly, stacking them in his drawer. She had made a sandwich for her lunch and had eaten it on the back steps under a high summer sun in a heat that even drove the insects to silence. Then she had taken her one main outing for the day, pulling her hair out of curlers and putting on slacks, a light blouse, lipstick. She fell in behind the wheel of the old Ford her father had found for Jim to buy for her, complete with patched-up gas tank, loose steering, gauges ticking wildly in the dash, a radio that didn't work. But the musty odor of the old carseats was a kind of comfort, the feeling she had walking out down the gravel driveway was a kind of song, and even the sun-baked, steaming atmosphere inside that car that was all her own was a recreation. The new freedom of her car kept her from really minding that she had to grip the wheel firmly to keep it from rattling, that she had to reach down quickly at times and use her fingers to pry up a sticky accelerator, then pump the brake pedal at least twice before the system caught and slowed her through the intersection at the end of the street and through a broad turn across Main. She pulled into the same parking space that always seemed to be waiting for her at the Nowell Grocery.

She shopped. She dawdled under the fans, leaned more than

pushed her basket along the colorful aisles. She lingered in the cool damp company of the produce until she ran into them—Anita Foos, Bonna St. Louis, Constance Gamble and the others. It was a hot day in town. The men were out working double shifts at the turkey plant and in the fields. One of the girls collected change and made the trip to the pop machine. Just after noon, they gathered over their mostly empty baskets and talked.

"Well, girls, it's liver and onions tonight," said Bonna St. Louis. "If Erwin don't get what he wants, he's a bastard on wheels. But they're running seven thousand birds through today and he's got six hours overtime. So I guess he needs his something special."

"You know my Larry's just the same way," said Anita Foos, "what with breakdowns from haying keeping the garage so busy. We won't even likely make it to the movie tonight because he just can't take the time. I hear it's a good one, too, with Dana Andrews," she said. "I don't want to miss one with Dana Andrews. But now on top of it all, Larry's promised to help out haying fifty acres of his dad's this year, and you know how haying always brings back the effects of his malaria. . . ."

"Thank the stars my Bruce is no farmer and closes the store when he wants," said Constance Gamble. "At least we got in one night alone this week. I can't complain compared to the rest of you. We're even planning on paying a visit to the new smorgasbord up in Whitewood. They say that's some deal, all you can eat for only a dollar a head."

"The best I can hope for is that Larry might recover in time for the Grange dance. You know how I get about a Grange dance. You know, Marge, I got some new patterns? You should come over and see my new patterns. I need an opinion."

"Just give me a call," said Marge. "I'd be glad to any afternoon."

"Well, I'm too busy this week," Anita said. "How's about beginning of next?"

"That's fine," Marge said. "Love to."

"You go on and do that, honey," Anita said.

"Speaking of opinions," said Constance, "I heard Ruth Collins was drunk as a post the other night and let old Charlie Gooch take her home. Can you imagine? Chippying around like that on poor old Ron, and for some sixty-year-old half-breed? Bruce says Ron ain't ever going to live that one down."

"Well, she always was that way," Anita said. "Or I always heard she was that way."

"When poor old Ron gets released from the VA this time, he'll have a real fight on his hands," Constance said.

"Could be a sixty-year-old half-breed's better than a limp ex-marine any day."

"You always did have the foulest mouth in town, Bonna," Anita said.

"She's darned proud of it, too," said Constance. "Ain't that right, Bonna?"

"I guess she ought to know," Marge said. "If I remember correctly, Ron Collins was one of her high school sweethearts."

"Well, that ain't any cause to know," Bonna said. "Or not when it comes to Ron Collins anyway."

"I don't see why not," Anita said. "I could always tell. I could tell just by looking."

"Nobody can tell by looking," said Bonna. "You might think you can, but you can't."

"God help us if we could," said Marge. "We'd all likely still be looking!" She laughed. The others stopped a beat. Then Anita was the first to join in, Marge grateful that she did. "But I don't know," Marge said. "We can all find things to complain about."

"That's true," said Constance. "But I don't think we have all that much to complain about. The truth is, a man changes. My Bruce courted me at first. He jumped around me like a flea in a frying pan. Then I used to feel when my Bruce was home, he was home. The kids too. Now he's got his stamp collection to keep him company. He sits in a corner of the bedroom all night sometimes, just tying little bundles of stamps together or pasting them in his albums. He's so careful about it. Know what I mean? Everything's got to be done just so. And that's all he thinks about. Stamps from all over the world. Now it's summer and the kids are out doing God knows what at all hours. It's hard enough to get them in to eat. Lately, I begin to feel like I'm the only one home. But I been married a lot longer than you have and we got the kids. Maybe it's just getting a whole lot quieter the older they get. I guess it's really the kids that make the difference.''

''We plan to have kids,'' said Marge. ''Jim's just waiting until he feels secure at his job. At least until he can set up his own practice.''

''Don't wait for a paycheck to have kids,'' Anita piped in. ''That's the wrong reason for having 'em in the first place. Go on and have kids whenever you want 'em. The old grumpies can't hold back a sea.''

''You listen to them and you got trouble,'' said Bonna. ''You don't know how lucky you are! I can't even sit down and read a magazine once without Mama do this, Mama do that, Mama spoon me up more liver and onions. That reminds me. I got to get over to the lockers and get some fresh. The shift changes at three-thirty. That goddamned whistle blows and I know Erwin's only got a half hour to eat in. Three-thirty's a hell of a time for a decent supper. Then I got to feed the kids. These double shifts are murder, just plain murder. But Lord knows we can use the overtime. . . .''

They began to disperse just as suddenly as they had gathered, each pushing her basket off in a different direction through the store. As Marge was on her way to the checkout counter, Anita Foos cut her off. ''You just go on and leave your diaphragm tucked in the drawer,'' Anita said. ''That's the way to do it. He'll never know the difference until it's too late,'' she said.

Marge went through the checkout and carried her single bag of groceries to her car. Then she usually drove the short distance home. Or sometimes, she didn't go directly home. She drove a half mile to the Dairy Freeze for a Coke. She loved to sit in that narrow parking lot, one elbow slowly baking on the doorsill as she watched the high school kids free for the summer on noon breaktime from their jobs or just back from parking the way she had done once with Rae Ott, Ron Ballock and Burt Cooney on the dusty back roads of summer, cutting off their boyish attentions just in time with the excuse of an ice-cold Coke or double order of fries and onion rings at The Cove. She ordered. She watched a group of young girls posing under the window fans. She remembered the times she had bicycled into town to do just that, how her brothers used to drive her in on breaktime from the fields. She paid for her Coke and took the first cooling pull at it, swishing the ice around in her mouth and letting it trickle down her throat. She settled deeper into the carseat. She remembered how she used to wait for hours before the boys came. Whole carloads of them, bluejeans and T-shirts caked with dust and diesel, forearms bleeding from bale-bucking scratches, hatbrims pulled down low over their eyes in that way they had. Now she watched boys she hardly knew as they cruised back and forth in front of the drive-in, cat-calling, shouting at the girls, tires tossing up clouds of gravel as their cars skidded into the tropical orange haze under the drive-in awning.

Most of them were new boys, boys just moved into town with fathers working turkeys at an expanded Nowell-Safebuy. Marge watched on from a distance. She always parked under the sun despite the heat, way back near the street edge of the parking lot as if to remind herself that she no longer really belonged with them. But she generally found some old jalopy circling her car flirtatiously, engine smoking, tires laying patches in the gravel, tanned, sweating faces hanging out the windows and peering in at her with hellbent masculine curiosity before they knew by her hairstyle, her lipstick, her sack of groceries, her wedding ring. She always smiled at them when they knew, not daring to look them square on before that, but playing with them just a little, just a glance or two out the window of her car as they were giving up. She made sure the tiny glittering shackle on her left hand was visible as she dangled it out over the door. She finished her Coke, taking the time to chew each sliver of ice until the cup was empty. Then she drove the short distance home.

Three o'clock in the afternoon. By that time she had finished leafing through her magazines, her Sears and Ward's catalogues, until even the daydreaming in them had become repetitive, gone stale somehow once she had come to believe anything in them was possible. Not now, but possible. She sat at the kitchen table, smoking. She found herself staring at the walls. She found herself listening for any sound at all in their little house, the pipes knocking, the toilet running, the screen door clapping in the afternoon breeze that always turned the house downwind of the turkey yards. Despite the heat, Marge went through the house shutting all the doors and windows. She sat back down at the kitchen table, the ingredients for supper spread neatly before her and waiting for the pan. She crossed her legs. She drew a face with her thumbnail in the soft white meat of a peeled potato. She rolled it back and forth on the table. She used a paring knife so she could stand him on his head. She sat straight up again. She lit another cigarette and saw the clock had moved.

Jim came in as he usually did, energetically, striding down the hallway to check his mail and toss his briefcase into the armchair. He stood scratching his chin in front of the hallway mirror a minute before he moved into the kitchen to kiss her once, then wash and sit down to eat. He wasn't in the house five minutes before he was eating.

"We have cash flow problems," he said that night at dinner. "Everyone's in the same boat. All equity and no cash. That's like having all your money in the bank and the bank's always closed. I guess that's hard for you to understand," he said.

"I just don't see how it makes any difference," she said.

"Look. Just give me two years," he said. "Two years is all I ask."

"Two years won't make any difference to you," she said. She was suddenly irritated at a quick nervousness she saw in him. "You look like you want to jump right out of your skin," she said.

"Aw, honey, please," he said.

"People think there's something wrong with us, you know," she said.

"Ho, ho. Since when do you care about what people think?"

"Well, two years'll be too late for my dad to get any time with them," she said. "That's half the point."

"We've been over it and over it," he said. "I've got to get a practice going first. Do you want to depend on the Safebuy the rest of our lives? Listen. We sacrifice a little now, just a little, and later we won't have to sacrifice. We're going to build a house so we'll have the room. We're both going to get some new clothes while we can, and take a trip or two before we're tied down. We're not even going to think about kids until we're both really ready for them.''

''I don't know when you're going to be ready for them,'' she said. ''You're forty-three years old right now.''

He stared for a moment somberly into his beer glass.

''Look. I've tried to explain it to you,'' he said. ''We have cash flow problems. Now please, don't start in on me.''

''I'm not starting in on you,'' she said. ''I'm not starting in on anything.''

They ate in silence. He tried to break the oppressive mood just once with an almost apologetic comment on the excellence of her cooking, which she couldn't have cared less about at the time.

''There's a movie tonight,'' she said. ''Maybe we could go.''

He smiled. He took her hand. She knew what was coming next.

''I'm sorry,'' he said. ''I have an appointment with Will Hartley tonight. He has some pretty important doubts about the new contract Buster's offering this year. Will's organization has to prepare for any contingency, you know.''

She was sweating. The kitchen fan hummed ceaselessly in the background.

''Aw, I'm sorry, honey,'' he said. ''It's the only time we could meet.''

''It stars Dana Andrews,'' she said. ''I don't want to miss a movie with Dana Andrews.''

''Then why don't you go?'' he asked. ''For God's sake, just go. You can even take the convertible.''

''I don't want to go alone,'' she said.

''Then telephone one of your friends,'' he said. ''Everyone's in the same boat, you know. I don't think Larry Foos is up for a movie tonight. I saw him this afternoon and he's working double shifts. Why don't you phone his wife? She might want to go with you.''

''I don't want to go with just anyone,'' she said. ''I want us to go together. I want to spend a night with you.''

''You spent last night with me,'' he said, ''and the night before that. And last Sunday night. . . .''

''Make love to me then,'' she said. ''Break off that meeting and let's just go to bed. We'll throw open the windows and turn on all the fans." She stopped. She knew that wasn't working with him. "Please take me to the movies," she said. She kicked herself for her pleading tone of voice.

He drained the last of his beer and pushed his plate to one side. He considered her a moment, hardened, distant. "To hear you talk," he said, "you'd think I don't spend enough time with you."

"I'm sorry," she said. "It's not you. It's just tonight."

"I'll do the best I can," he said. "I'll come home early."

"Never mind," she said after a moment. She looked at her hands, surprised to find she was nervously tearing a matchbook to bits. "I guess I'll just go alone," she said.

He almost never came home early. He was the kind of man who settled deeply into conversation whether it concerned his business or just the tales and outright lies of farmers, ranchers, range boys at the bar. He seemed able to laugh easily in bars when he seldom laughed anywhere else. He generally stayed on in the saloon until closing time. She had learned that about him. She didn't expect him home early. She did the dishes and mopped the kitchen. She brushed her hair out quickly and took off alone for the Arcade Bingo & Theater, grateful he had left her the convertible.

The theater was filled with babies. Almost every woman she knew was sentenced for years to walk in short, childlike steps as she pulled one kid along by the hand and boosted another on her hip. As she looked around, it seemed to her the babies alone far outnumbered the adults. They crawled by the dozens over the seats. They toddled up and down the aisle, tripping over their little white shoes and bursting into screams. The soundproof, glassed-in baby booth at the back of the Arcade was filled to capacity before the lights had even dimmed. Bonna St. Louis and her brood nearly filled the booth all on their own. Bonna could barely raise a hand to wave at Marge as she paced back and forth with a baby on each arm, her two redheaded toddlers scribbling on the glass with candy bars.

When the lights suddenly dimmed, the place exploded with cries. A group of rowdy high schoolers began to boo, hiss and flip popcorn at the squalls as Dwayne Vandergrin, manager of the Arcade, tried to catch them at it, his glowing red flashlight stabbing around in the darkness. It was nearly impossible to hear the newsreel in what seemed to Marge a plague of babies, the tiny bald heads bristling everywhere in the projector's glow like the white fluffy seed heads of milkweed in a weedy pasture. She turned and looked at Bonna again. She thought she saw Bonna gesturing through the glass of the booth with one of her babies. She was asking Marge to help. Marge turned quickly away. Somebody had to watch the movie. Later, Bonna would be grateful enough that Marge could fill her in on the scenes she'd missed.

Marge came home in tears from the movie. She couldn't stop crying on the drive home. She thought it was silly to cry like that but she still changed into her nightgown, curled up on the bed and let loose. At first, she cried because of the movie, then she didn't know why she was crying, thinking she had no reason to as she did. She raised her head and saw the clock on the night table. She realized how long she had been lying there alone, and on sudden impulse she picked up a capsized shoe Jim had left on the floor and let it fly full force at the wall he'd covered with his photographs. One of the thin black frames slid down the wall and hit with a crash.

It was the picture of his mother. Marge saw it suddenly changed as she picked it up, as if some hateful word was about to burst out with a hiss through the woman's clenching teeth. Marge went to the kitchen for a broom, dustpan, dishrag. She swept up the glass and rehung the picture. Then she did the best she could to scrub the scuff mark off the wall. She straightened his photographs. The one that showed him as a curly-haired youth with his arms lovingly around a dog was the one she liked, a leg of his knickers torn and the dirt showing plainly on his shoes. Most of the others were portraits of himself in military uniforms. There was the one showing a young man in his first uniform, just out of law school when he had never seen a war, the only picture in which he was smiling. The next showed a young first lieutenant with creases in his forehead and a startled look, his eyes focused off to one side as if unsure of sudden attack from that direction. Then his hair was suddenly gray, all action shots taken in front of army trucks, numbered buildings, mountains of supplies, his dark eyes steadily receding into the shadows of his features, his cheeks hollow, a look of determination on his face. Marge started to cry again for him, for all he must have been through, for the sad lost look in the last photo as he stared out from the archway of a ruin with something missing, something taken away from him forever. The picture of their wedding hung beside it, a little removed from and twice as large as all the rest. She looked at the crowd in the photograph, watching the two of them walk back up the aisle as if they were strangers. Even her father had something cold, distant about him, uncertain of himself in front of so many people, his dark jacket too long in the arms, his hair pulled back with one quick sweep of her hairbrush at the last minute, a child himself who had just given his daughter away. But she had been happy. That much she could see, moved to tears then too, but in a dream, as if marriage alone was a kind of solution.

She remembered that night. Arriving in an icy rainstorm at the Johnson Hotel in a city that was awash, the gutters roaring, squalls of sleet blowing down from the hills. Cabs were lined up in the circular drive of the hotel, a building that stood ten stories high and looked like what it was, the redbrick extravagance of an English lord among the simple wood and brick homes that made up the hill and most of the city behind, or the squat wooden shop buildings with their square false fronts and tar roofs along the street below, and scarcely two blocks farther toward a rushing creek, the row of low rambling tin shacks of the pawnshops and Indian taverns. Men in windblown raincoats struggled with their suitcases through the revolving doors. Bellhops and parking boys were on the run. A doorman in a top hat and red huntsman's uniform blew his whistle into chaos, the rain pouring off his cloak in dark red stains down the legs of his pants.

She pushed through a revolving door, out of breath from a mad dash across the sidewalk. Then her feet, wet through her nylons and the open toes of her shoes, sank into a rich world, the warmth of the thick red carpet like a sheepskin under them. She caught her breath at the sight of the lobby paneled in dark carved wood, at the huge glowing oil paintings of hunting scenes, men in red coats blowing trumpets over their hounds, brass and gilt everywhere in heavy designs, glass chandeliers that glittered like a fairy tale over a crowd of hurrying men. The hotel was packed with conventioners. Men stood in lines three deep in front of the clerks' cages. Bells were ringing. Voices were raised. Trunks, bags, boxes attended by porters were wheeled, carried, dragged around the potted palms and across the vast red desert of the lobby like the burdens of Africa. But what struck her most was that she had never seen so many men, all of them in suits, not a one in a military uniform. She wondered how many yards of cloth it had taken to make all the new suits. And there was something else, a feeling around these men of a party about to begin, a victory party, a long and feverish celebration of prosperity. They were the lucky ones. She couldn't help but think of the men she knew who might have been with them but were not. Then again, as she learned in the next few days, she had never met men like these. The men she knew would be pulling hydraulic hoses and clevis pins, lifting their heavy implements on and off three-point hitches the same way these men slipped light folders of pages into their briefcases, snapping the buckles closed, or the same way they sat pleasantly over their drinks talking thousands of dollars in deals. There was something entirely new to her about them, her first introduction to a world Jim had roamed freely, a world of men meeting around long tables in banquet rooms, knowledge shared among them like loaves of bread baked out of the latest in tax reforms, partnerships, charts with broad curves indicating the growth of nations. No desperate faces, no young boys with peaked hats making their last phone calls before shipping out. As she stood there in the lobby viewing this world of the lucky and the rich, the truth sank in. The war was over. Nothing could ever bring the nightmare back again.

She waited as Jim pushed his way through the crowd to the desk. It was to be a working honeymoon for him. But he had been good about that, the trip really serving as a last-minute excuse to get married so quickly. He only planned to leave her for half a day of conferences. He had given her a book of checks all her own in the car and she looked forward to the chance to practice signing her new name, Mrs. James D. Vogel, over and over again as she went shopping while he worked, knowing somehow that he'd be good about that too, not saying a word about how much she had spent on them both until they were home.

She had bought a nightgown for that night. She and her mother had driven all the way to Sturgis for her simple wedding outfit and her hands had found the nightgown on a rack in the store, as if her hands were superstitious about such things. It was a petite size, but she took it anyway, knowing somehow it would fit. She was caught by its soft shimmering fabric and most of all by a pattern of embroidery along the breastline, gold, green and blue threads intricately sewn like the eye of a peacock feather. And when Jim returned with the key and the bellboy was finally pushing open the door to their top-floor room, she felt confirmed in an omen, rooted in a sense of her own premonition. "Peacocks," she said as he carried her through the door. "Look, honey. Look at them all. It's perfect," she said.

A hundred blue-green eyes stared up at her from the bedspread, a whirling storm of exotic feathers all over the room, in the print of the high drapes, in the wallpaper in the bathroom. Jim had ordered all the right things for the room and busied himself with them—champagne in a silver bucket, baskets of fruit and flowers, a cold-plate supper waiting on the table under covers. She was too excited for any of it. She threw her arms around his neck, hugging and kissing him giddily. She grabbed up her small suitcase and rushed into the bathroom. "Just wait till you see this," she said, and shut the door with a laugh.

She was careful. Everything had to be right. She put on her soft gown, the feeling in it full of a love as simple as her hand as it arranged and rearranged her hair into different styles. She finally held it back with a length of gold ribbon. She put on a little makeup, just a little touch. Then two or three droplets of perfume, watching the hand that looked transformed by its rings in the mirror, the small diamond reflecting a greenish color from her gown. She remembered the little cloth purse in her suitcase. She unzipped it and pulled out a diaphragm, thinking it looked ugly,

116

out of place, like a corrupt brown bubble that rises to the surface of a pond. She had driven all the way to a doctor in Deadwood to get it, too shy to talk about such things with Doc Monahan. She carefully raised the hem of her gown, holding it in place with her chin. She squatted a little, feeling ridiculous in this position, a tube of jelly in one hand and the device in the other, the whole process reminding her of greasing down a tractor bearing and shoving it home with two fingers. She straightened her nightgown, checking and rechecking herself in the mirror. She felt her heart beating. She reached a hand out for the doorknob, hesitant, scared. Slowly, she pushed the door open and walked into the room.

"My God," he said, and the tone of his voice made her feel it with him. "Just look at you."

They made love with the lights on, quick and excited love. He was tired from the day, the long drive, the wine, and soon fell asleep. She lay awake listening to him breathe, still aroused. She would never have thought of herself as unsatisfied, she simply didn't think that way, the meaning of desire itself still an unspoken mystery. And she was satisfied. She already had what she had wanted most, to be pretty for him.

She got out of bed quietly so as not to wake him. She lit a cigarette, walked over to the window and looked out. A hard rain was falling, gusts of rain drumming against the windows. They were high up, as high as a mountaintop, and the lights of the city at night were like a handful of colorful Indian beads scattered out over dark wood. Somewhere in the streets the red lights of a police car sped through the rain, flashing, flashing, buildings lit for an instant as it passed, then vanishing in the darkness. She turned away from the window. She wanted nothing to do with the world below, with the thought that somewhere out there there was trouble in the streets. She flipped off the lightswitch in the room and climbed back into bed, straightening the covers, pulling the hundred peacock eyes of the bedspread up over her own. It was a moment of fulfillment as she turned and pressed herself against him, holding him warmly in his sleep, a satisfaction in the way the curves of their bodies fit tightly together like a matching pair of spoons.

Marge looked around their small, orderly bedroom on Yampa Street. She saw the clock on the night table and realized how long she'd been standing there alone, waiting for him. She checked the photos in their thin black frames, two short ranks of them on the wall, thinking she'd tell him one of them fell to the floor when she was cleaning. She got ready for bed, washing, putting up her hair. She hiked up her nightgown, squatted down on the toilet and reached in with two fingers to take out her diaphragm, still in from last night and left there all day according to the directions. She washed it off and put it back in its little purse. Anyway, she figured Jim would be too far gone when he came in that night. No need tonight to save millions of potential sinners from their mistakes, as he had put it once.

She went to bed and tried to sleep. But she couldn't sleep. Every few minutes, she heard something that made her think he was coming in, the breeze working at a loose rain gutter, a similar old car engine passing in the street. She got out of bed and went to the kitchen for his bottle of Scotch though she knew that two or three drinks usually kept her awake all the more. She drank quickly, wrinkling her nose and making a face with each sip, the taste reminding her of medicine. She fought back a sudden urge to put on her clothes and go get him. She dropped another icecube into her glass and went into the living room. She sat down on the couch and started to put her feet up on the coffee table, moving aside the Ward's catalogue she had left lying open that afternoon.

On impulse, she picked up the catalogue, a kind of itch in her fingers as she flipped through the tissuey pages, feeling a heat at the back of her neck as she did, knowing what she was going to do. She went to the kitchen for a pen and filled her glass. She smiled, sauntering down the narrow hallway, passing a mirror on the closet door and stopping a moment to look at herself. She was astonished at herself, astonished at how pretty she was, at the light smooth tan of her skin, at the way her mouth looked as it smiled, aloof yet confident, relaxed—that was it, relaxed, as she felt the whole world outside could relax now in such changed conditions. She was aroused at herself, not in any sensual way but in the way the world itself seemed aroused, in a headlong and productive rush of factories working overtime, in the sound of machinery digging all day in the streets, the *clapa clapa clapa* of hammers echoing in the distance—all caution thrown aside in a sudden conviction of security, in a newfound sense of her own powers. She wished she had a window in her belly, that's what she wanted, so she might see the future there. She smiled at herself in the mirror. She tipped her drink in a kind of salute.

In the living room, she tore out the yellow forms in the middle of the big catalogue. With a kind of fever, she flipped back and forth in its pages, filling in the numbers on the form for a new chest of drawers, a set of the most expensive dishes on the page, a wringer washing machine, a new set of fancy printed sheets, a bedspread with a feathery pattern, two pairs of short-heeled pumps just then the rage, bathrobes and slippers for the both of them, a box of pale blue stationery bordered with columbines, a new set of tires for her car, a new rake, hoe and other things for the garden, then, finally, a crib and a playpen, both including a whirling mobile of little plastic birds. She moved the pen to the bottom of the page. Working slowly, she signed his name there, copying his signature perfectly, the way the letters of his last name flattened out in a kind of bumpy line. She folded the page and sealed it in its postage-free envelope. Then she used a clothes-pin and clipped it to the mailbox for the postman.

She stood in the doorway, feeling the new breeze from the east, usually a sign of rainstorms, grateful that it might be cooler in the morning. She realized all the windows were still closed from the afternoon and she left the door standing partway open, going through the house, sliding all the windows up. She climbed back into bed and soon fell asleep.

Jim woke her, trying to be quiet. There was nothing that could wake her faster than when he tried to be quiet. His heavy breathing in the room. His knocking into things in the darkness. He struck a match sometimes, still not sure where the lightswitch was in their new house. She woke up to the sight of him in the weak yellow glow of his matchlight, overlooking a collection of tiny bottles he had knocked over on the dresser top while feeling around.

"Is that you?" she said, jolted awake by the noise.

"It's just me," he answered, blowing out his match. "Go back to sleep."

"What are you doing?" she asked.

"I didn't want to wake you by turning on the lights," he said. He struck another match and found the lightswitch this time. "I've been out with Will Hartley. Really had a great talk, hon. Good ol' Hartley. He was in fine form tonight. He was out with a new man in town, name's Joe Petrini. Says he plans to build a combination bowling alley and dance hall. I told him that's just what we need here, a good dance hall. He might even hire me to help with the financing agreements. Just think, honey, dancing every night of the week," he said. She made room for him. He took his usual sudden turn, flopping straight backward onto the bed. "Joe Petrini," he mumbled. "Wonderful guy. Really first-rate. We got to talking. He just finished serving in the air corps, and as it turns out, he might have been the poor bastard who accidentally ground-strafed us at Anzio."

"Maybe I'll get to meet him someday," she said. "Someday when you have the courtesy to invite me along."

"Aw, honey, you know I would," he said. "But they just don't bring their wives."

"You know, Jim, I wasn't lonely tonight. I don't think I missed you for a minute," she said. "I saw a beautiful movie. *The Best Years of Our Lives*. It was a beautiful movie. . . . Jim?"

"Hmmmm . . ."

"You'll fall asleep in your clothes again," she said.

"Naw, just resting," he said. "Just a minute."

"My dad used to fall asleep in his clothes," she said. "Sometimes, he'd be telling us kids a story. Around the beginning of the story, he'd be sitting on the parlor carpet, us kids all over him. Pretty soon, he'd make us sit back and he'd lie down on the carpet, and his voice would get slower and slower. Then he'd be asleep, right in the middle of the story."

"Uh huh," he groaned as if he was listening.

"None of us kids ever woke him," she said.

His eyes were closed, his breathing soft and steady, a line of spittle forming on his lips. She leaned over and started to unbutton his shirt.

"Oh, gee," he said suddenly, sitting upright with a jerk. He tried to help her with the buttons. "Need . . . glass of water, hon. O.K., O.K., I got it," he said, tearing his shirt off and tossing it on the floor. "Please, hon," he said. "Just a glass of water and couple of aspirins."

He fell back sprawling on the bed. She went into the bathroom for a glass of water and shook out two aspirins from around the cotton in the bottle. He had rolled to his stomach and was sound asleep by the time she stood over him. She took the aspirins and drank the water herself.

She thought of the day she had told her father she was going to marry Jim, walking out across the smooth and freshly planted autumn field to tell him. He reacted without surprise. He nodded just once to let her know he understood, checking the grains of winter wheat in the last bin of his drill, long on experience with forces out of his control.

The pounding of the diesel tractor almost drowned out his voice.

"Petie, I just don't think he's the one for you," he said.

He reached a hand down and pulled her up on the tractor after him. He scooted over on the seat. He put his hard wiry arms around her and held her there as he let her take the wheel, easing the tractor into gear, dust rising like smoke behind them, letting her spell him a few turns around his field.

She stood over the bed looking at her husband, at the shock of gray hair spread like fringe over his high forehead, at the way his lips hung open loosely as he snored, at the way the lines of his body sloped gradually back to the twin mounds of his behind, raised a little, straining the seams of his pants. She picked up his dangling, sleeping hand and squeezed it once as if to reassure him. Then she gently rolled him to his back, hardly breaking the rhythm of his breathing. She unbuckled his pants.

"What in hell am I going to do with you?" she said out loud.

But she knew what she was going to do. She leaned over and quietly pulled off his boots.

part
two

1

The sound of the western coyote is a high-pitched yapping doglike bark. I've never heard the legendary lone mournful howl from them. I'd probably go for my rifle if I did. As it is, I fire off five or six shots before bed to quiet them down long enough to fall asleep. When the pack gathers over a carcass of deer or antelope, over a lamb or a stray dog, the noise builds in pitch to a bickering song. They feed. Then the sound changes, unmistakably. Somehow, coyotes have learned to laugh. And they're doing it now. They're laughing out there.

Nights, coyotes range through the streets of this town. They've been so bold about it so long even the dogs hardly notice. It's still tough to see them—gaunt gray shapes that scatter across the untended yards, through the shells of houses, in the distance down the street. Nobody does anything about them. Scraps of paper, cardboard, old backyard trash swirl through this town like tumbleweeds. There are only old people left here now.

When I first came back to this town, I walked four miles from the freeway junction. I had a hard time getting the bus driver to let me off out there near an old peeling billboard in the alkali flats. There wasn't much to see on the flats but there was plenty of room to see it in—sparse brush under a lightly falling snow.

"The Jack Rabbit line takes no responsibility," the driver said. He pulled my suitcase out of the bus's belly. "You're crazy."

The Nowell junction was colder than I expected. The wind picked up and blew the snow like dust devils. I had to stop and change hands on the suitcase whenever I felt one had frozen to it. I searched for stars but they were hidden. The moon shone through the clouds with just enough light to see. The road was badly potholed. The ditches on either side were overgrown with grass bent and twisted under the weight of ice, reflecting in the eerie half moonlight like two long lines of crystalline flames. As I walked, I began to feel a strange sense of clarity, as if the mind was on the verge of some deeply and personally revealing thought. Then I realized what that feeling was—a heady, throbbing sensation brought on by overexposure to subzero cold.

My ears were ringing with cold. I cursed myself for wearing a cowboy hat and tried to pull it down over my ears. By the time I reached this town, marked on its outskirts by the sagging chain-link fences of the old Preston-Hill tractor sales yard, I was too cold to feel the impact of the moment, the way the litter mixed with the snow in windblown swirls, the way each bare tree lining the streets seemed ingrown haphazardly, dark branches in arthritic knots. This town was a shambles. I'd expected about as much. But not so far gone as it was.

I passed Beatrice Ott's house. A light burned in the downstairs hallway. I stopped, amazed. I remembered her hundredth birthday, years ago. A television crew drove all the way from Rapid City to cover the party. Everyone wore a tinfoil hat. Everyone yelled and blew a paper horn. Beatrice licked her lips. She looked overwhelmed at the hundred lighted candles on her cake. The camera hummed. She raised an arm to shield her eyes from the lights. She puckered her lips. Everyone leaned in with her and helped blow out the candles.

The TV announcer pushed his microphone close in over the cake. He leaned over and kissed Beatrice on the cheek. He smiled at the camera. "Well, Mrs. Ott," he asked, "how does it feel on this special occasion?"

"Terrible," she said. "How'd you feel if you was a hundred years old?"

On Main Street, the office of Doc Monahan didn't have a front wall. It looked as if something powerful had knocked it out. There was nothing left but a huge jagged hole with snow dusting in over the fallen beams, the hanging fixtures. Next door, I cupped my hands to my eyes and looked into the window of The Cove Café. A forest of chairs sat upside down on the tables. The floor looked clean. There were some new rodeo posters on the fly-specked walls along with the old ones, a good supply of gum, candy and ammunition in the glass case under the cash register. I was about to start for my mother's house again when I noticed way in back. The jukebox was gone. The wall looked newly painted where it had been.

I walked past the municipal bar. The pool game was frozen just after the break. Two half-empty bottles and a line of used glasses shone in the dull finish of the bar mirrors. The old boys must be drinking less, I thought. Or there were fewer of them left. The bar had a woman's torso carved into one end, sweeping up and out like the figurehead of an old wooden ship. By the glow of a beer sign I could see the paint was still on it, the large red lips still clearly raving an aria at the street. Beside her, so that at least one player could lean back and drape his arm over her shoulders, the poker table sat with cards spread out as if the boys had left in the middle of a hand. That was just exactly as it should be. I checked the time. It was late, almost midnight. The bus schedule home had never been predictable.

I saw the dark movement of a dog or a coyote at the end of the street. It scooted quickly into the shadows of the abandoned plant building. The Nowell-Safebuy turkey plant, once this town's major industry, stood at the end of Main along its only broad curve toward the highway. The building stood gutted and empty, the high arched windows out, the tall brick smokestack broken off at its top by the prairie winds. The yard was heaped with scrap metal, tangled wire, rotted posts, turned-over troughs long since peppered with bullet holes. On the side toward town, the fence between it and the yards no longer standing, there was a small house overgrown with brambles. A stovepipe ticked loosely back and forth in the wind. For an instant, I thought I saw smoke coming out of its china hat. Then nothing. But I half expected the patched-up door on that shack to fly open and an old man in longjohns to jump out barefoot in the cold. I remembered once stopping by that house to urinate into a pile of weeds. Mose Johnson had suddenly stepped up behind me. I couldn't stop. There was nothing I could do.

"Sword fight," he said. He was drunk. A loud and powerful flood crossed my thin stream like a pair of swords. He laughed. Mine didn't stand a chance. "At your age, you think your pecker's just for pissing," said Mose. "Ain't that right?"

I couldn't look at him. I watched the brown weeds curling in the steam.

"Boy, when you're as old as I am, you'll know damn well that it's the truth."

I sidestepped. I finished and backed away.

"You ain't old," I said. "You just look old."

He turned on me. He chased me off with a yellow splattering rain at my boots. It was the last time I ever saw him. My mother didn't think I was old enough to witness his funeral. And I guess the family didn't know him well enough.

I took a shortcut through the backyard of Anita Foos's house. The lights were on all over the house. Anita was probably still awake upstairs. I was quiet so I wouldn't scare her. She sat up at her husband's desk. Month by month, she went through all his old receipts the way she used to for him. Larry Foos had been the best mechanic this town had ever seen. But he had never run his business right. Anita always found bills he hadn't collected, sheafs of accounts he had forgotten to pay, disordered papers stuffed haphazardly into a crudely numbered system of old parts boxes. Anita did her best to make sense of them. She rubbed the strain from her eyes. She bent back over her ledger books and filled them with neat lines of figures, stopping to punch the buttons of an antique adding machine to calculate exactly Larry's bills and taxes.

Anita lived as if it was still twenty years ago, the best year Larry's business had ever had, also the year she had finally made Larry agree to take a long vacation. Though they didn't have any kids, Larry unable to have them as a result of high and prolonged fevers, they had never been known to take a vacation except for a day or two hunting and fishing in the hills. But that year, their small new house built just around the corner from ours, Larry's business secure and with five employees already, Anita made reservations for Hawaii. Larry was having a difficult spring, more tractors to diagnose and repair than he had ever done, so many that they soon no longer fit in his shop and parking lot. A line of broken-down tractors began to grow up the street from his garage, Sheriff Meeker threatening to have them all towed if they weren't moved soon. Larry worked day and night under pressure. Everyone needed a crop in. Everyone depended on him. His health began to fail. The recurring malaria that had bothered him ever since his service in the marines during the war gripped him with its sweats and exhaustion. Doctors at the VA hospital in Sturgis prescribed every drug in the book. They advised Larry to take a few months off from his job. But he couldn't do that yet. He single-handedly overhauled forty-two tractors that season, not counting the work he oversaw for his crew. By June, his skin looked waxen, polished. His veins stood out like taut wires on a rack of bones. The week before he was due to leave on vacation, while helping his crew hoist a tractor engine as big as a car, he was stricken. He died of a heart attack on the floor of his shop.

Anita suffered a psychotic break soon afterward. She was hospitalized at the Sturgis VA, but there was only one psychiatrist there and the ward was badly overcrowded. She didn't have children, had no one to be responsible for but herself, and she was let out after a few weeks. She came home. It was really better that way. People here had long considered mental illness a kind of eccentricity not too far removed from everyday life. They called Anita "touched." Or they simply said she was grieving.

Anita began to generalize everything in her past. It was as if to her all the events of her life from childhood to her husband's death were happening simultaneously. It was a characteristic of her manic-depressive illness that her personal history was all immediate, removed from notions of time. She came into The Cove Café some days frantic with energy. Her hair was braided the way she used to do it as a girl. She chewed gum and chattered nonstop for hours. She put on garish makeup. She plugged dime after dime into the jukebox when it would only run on quarters. She danced on the tabletops. Then suddenly, she started to cry, bitterly, over the smallest things, over something as small as the verse of a jukebox song or as small as the flight of a barn swallow across the street.

Even years later, Anita came into The Cove early each morning with her husband's ledgers. My mother served Anita's coffee. Anita opened her books and showed them off. "Marge, look how good Larry's been doing! He's got so much work now he's just had to go out and hire two new men. One of 'em's a convict just let loose from State. They say he's already been at it with Ruth Collins. Imagine. Only two weeks out of the pen and he's in that kind of trouble. But we'll make it. Nothing can stop us now. I just gotta figure out where to go. Now where would you go, Marge? I've never seen so many places to go!"

Anita brought out all her brochures on California, Hawaii, Florida—sunshine resorts—her pictures of palm trees on gleaming scimitars of beach, the pamphlets tattered at the edges, the colors faded. My mother played along. She conspired with Anita on where to go, told her how much fun it would be to see the ocean. When they settled on Hawaii, Anita clapped her hands together. Everyone who came into the café that morning would be shown the same ragged picture of a catamaran riding the waves, the fat brown paddlers grinning at the camera through an ocean spray.

Everyone knew. But it was still strange to me and Anita was frightening. I remembered the last time I had visited. My mother sent me over with a sack of day-old bread. Anita invited me in but she seemed suddenly frantic that I was there. The living room was strewn with clothing, Larry's socks to match up, his shirts and coveralls to iron. "Oh, damn!" Anita said. "I wish your mom could pick a better day!"

I stood in the hallway with the sack of bread. Anita rushed around her house putting up all bottles, ashtrays, knickknacks, anything breakable, on her shelves. She saw me as a toddler and she was babysitting. I was seventeen at the time. I set the bread down in the hall and went out. Anita chased me into the street. She took me by the hand and yanked me up the steps, scolding. I didn't know what to do. When I tried to leave again, Anita took off her belt as if she was going to strap me. I finally telephoned my mother. After Anita spoke to her, it was as if I weren't there at all.

The snow stopped falling. I turned the corner at the end of the block. All the houses were empty now but ours. I tried not to think of the other houses. At the time, I wasn't a man who gave in easily to sentiments. I had that harsh conviction of youth that the only worthwhile struggle was my own. A big part of that struggle was to control my strongest feelings, as if a man had to harden himself in order to succeed. Besides, I'd never wanted to come home again.

My mother's house loomed in front of me, set back from the street on a gentle rise. It was a large house, twelve rooms, just the number of empty seats to fill in a jury, as my father had described it once, this house that was a testimony to what he had once achieved in this town. I stood for a minute on the walk by the mailbox, a miniature Swiss chalet on a post with a bright red flag, a tiny rooster weathervane on the roof, which listed a little in the sudden calm. The front windows of the house were partly over-grown by the shrubs. The paint was peeling. A rain gutter was down. Nobody had shoveled the walks. As I went up the steps, the black metal railing was loose and rattled against the concrete like a short quick peal of bells.

I saw her through the front windows. She was asleep in her housecoat. The housecoat was sheer and hung on her like a thin veil of Irish lace. A bottle of gin sat on the table next to her, almost empty. She didn't look as old as I expected. Her hair was up in pins under a ruffled cap. Even from the porch, I could tell she had dyed the gray out. But she was thinner than I remembered. And there was something about her face, I couldn't tell what. I stood awhile, watching her sleep. Suddenly, I wanted to turn around and leave. If it hadn't been so cold I might have left. I thought a moment whether I should let myself in or knock. I knocked softly. I knocked again.

"Is that you? Is that you?" she called out. The door flew open and she was there throwing her arms around my neck and crying out, "Kurt! Kurt!" Her voice was high and there was a thickness to it. "Kurt!" she said, and hugged me for a long time. I held her back but awkwardly, with one arm, the other not wanting to let go of the suitcase.

She pulled away and kissed me. I set the suitcase down.

"Damnit, Kurt," she said. "You should have phoned! I could've got Dan Gooch out there with a four-wheel drive!"

I followed her into the house.

"I thought you'd surely be here by supper. I got supper on for you now. Get your things off there, you're all wet. I waited up. You see how I waited up." She laughed. "Damn! You should've phoned!"

This house pressed in. The walnut moldings looked darker than I remembered and there were cobwebs in the high corners. There was a stale smell of dust, perfumes, and of the coal heat. Newspapers and magazines lay scattered in the front room. The TV glowed with a pale blue snow, the picture rolling.

"You must be hungry. And cold. Come on!" She was almost singing. "Now why did you go and take the bus? We could've picked you up in Rapid! Come on here now. Before your supper dries out anymore."

I followed her slowly down the hall. I watched her feet. They limped a little as she walked. I thought of the hours she must have spent on her feet that day, how she had sometimes complained of tired feet. I remembered taking her feet in my lap as we watched TV, massaging them, gently cracking the bones. Her thin yellow housecoat billowed as she moved. She wore nothing underneath. Her skin shone through the robe. I'd never thought it so strongly before—how beautiful she was. Or must have been. I wondered if she had dressed this way for me. But then she had always dressed scantily at night.

"Just leave your things there in the hall," she said. She disappeared into the kitchen. "Come on now!"

Setting the suitcase by the closet, I started after her down the hall again. I stopped, a moment, in front of the door to my father's study. As a child, I used to wait long hours in front of that door for my father to come out. I pretended not to. I would never have thought of myself as waiting. I beat my fist into a baseball glove. I pitched a tennis ball at the door. She used to punish me for it when she saw the marks. I caught. I pitched. I caught. I used to imagine I heard a voice, the way a strong wind can make the grass sound as if it talks. There was no one inside. I pitched. I knew my father used to go in there to be alone, to do his work. I was almost never allowed. She used to go in sometimes. Then I was sent in to fetch him things—his cigarettes, his beer, his mail—or to be told to quiet down. I remembered a white telescope in a wooden case. I threw the ball hard. I remembered the day I helped him pack his books, his papers, his pipes, his army ribbons, his Civil War swords, in grocery boxes. I helped him carry them out to his station wagon. Then he drove away.

In the kitchen, she brought out my supper. She pulled a sheet of foil off the plate and folded it into a square so she could save it. She kept scolding herself because the porkchops had dried too long in the oven. She pulled them, half-eaten, off the plate to fry them again. Then she hovered over me with hands that couldn't keep from adjusting her cap or smoothing imagined creases in her housecoat. She waved cigarettes that switched hands in a kind of nervous juggling as she talked. She talked on.

"It's fine luck you coming home with Christmas just around the corner. It's been so long since we had a Christmas! You'll see how fine it'll be. We'll go up in the hills just like we used to and cut a tree. This'll be the year for a fiiine Christmas, you bet it will! You're going to stay here for it. You're going to be here for Christmas, aren't you?"

"Of course I'll be here," I said. "You think I'd miss it?"

"Do you have any money with you? You can't have Christmas without some kind of money. Not much. But some. You did bring some money, didn't you?"

"Oh, a few hundred," I said.

"A few hundred? Really? Well. I've got a couple of hundred saved myself. But there's a lot to do with it, too. Got to make it stretch for everyone. So now I won't worry. It's gonna be some fine Christmas!"

I ate, hungrily. She tried to sit in the chair across the table but couldn't keep still. She whirled around the kitchen, filling my glass before I'd emptied it. It had been a long time since I'd had three glasses of milk with a meal.

"You look so fine now," she said. "You're really handsome now. You're getting more handsome as you get older. I'll bet you got more women than you can count. Sure you do! Don't tell me any different because I won't believe you. I'll bet they're handsome women, too. Tall. I'll bet you like 'em tall and kind of smart. Even smarter than you. I'll bet you like 'em tall and smart, so you can let them do all the talking.''

I didn't say anything. She asked questions about women as if she had forgotten the difference between sons and friends and there are a lot of questions sons just won't answer.

"You never brought one home," she said. "It always hurts when I think you never brought one home."

She started to cry. I didn't know what to do. I reached out and put a hand firmly on the small of her back. That seemed to help. "Oh, God," she said, crying. "Just look at me. I really don't do this. It's just so good to have you home!"

I thought how little she knew me. In the years since I'd gone, I'd telephoned on holidays or once a month. I'd wired her money twice. In return, she wrote weekly letters as thick as a book, "big fats" as she called them. Whenever I read them, I felt helpless. I didn't want to know what happened here. Sometimes, I left her letters for days without reading them. But in recent letters, something was wrong. Something unstated. In the last one she had said it more directly: *A man came to see me about Grandpa's estate. No reason to get our hopes up but something just might come of it. He was out in the gumbo talking to Dan Gooch today and offered him two hundred thousand for his place. Two hundred thousand! Can you believe it? Of course old Dan wouldn't sell if he was down to a pea. Which he isn't. But I don't know. I ought to do something but pay the taxes. But then it's not mine or won't be soon. I don't want to make a move without you. That's what I told the man. I said I've got a son that takes care of business. I'll give him a call as soon as you get here. . . .*

She went down the hall to freshen up and blow her nose. She came back with her bottle of gin. She poured some in a glass and dropped in a couple of olives and some ice.

"How about one for me," I said. She looked at me strangely.

"I'm sorry," she said. "I should have offered one before. Jesus, I'm sorry! I guess you weren't quite drinking last time I saw you."

She fixed me a drink. She carried it over to the table.

"That man who came," I said. "How much did he offer for the farm?"

She froze in her tracks. She stared at me soberly a moment. She lit another cigarette and took a turn to the sink and back, dropping another icecube in my glass.

"I never said he made an offer," she said.

"Aw, come on," I said. "How much?"

"He didn't really offer," she said.

"Damnit, you can tell me," I said. "How much?"

"Forty thousand," she said. "We're not selling it for that."

I nodded. I finished my drink. But I knew the price she quoted wasn't enough. Something else was going on. She turned to the subject of Christmas again. Before I went to bed in the room I'd left eight years before, I had to agree with her several times what luck it was to be home with Christmas just around the corner. When I asked, she said she hadn't told anyone in town I was coming home. I let it go at that. We hugged and kissed goodnight.

In my bedroom, I was struck by the familiarity with which I moved. I caught myself unpacking my few clothes into what seemed their customary bureau drawers without a thought. I knew comfortable pathways through memorabilia—how not to bump into any of the hanging models of warplanes I sat with in front of the TV, painting detail after detail as a boy, or what game boxes would slide off the top shelf of the closet when I opened the door. The bed was turned down and waiting. Though it was cold, I opened the window at the foot of the bed. Photographs of school athletic teams still tacked to the small bulletin board all these years, curled at the edges like gray scrolls, scraped against each other in the breeze. Model airplanes came alive at the end of their threads. I wondered when it was war had become such an interest to me. I looked around the room and wondered how children had ever been raised this way, in a room that had everything—a set of drums, a trumpet, books, medals, trophies, two rifles, desk, chair, comic books, posters tacked up over every available inch, empty jars, tanks and cages for pets in the closet, three different styles of dress cowboy hats stuffed carelessly on the shelf just under the war games, a tiny Japanese TV on the bureau directly facing the bed. I wished with the intensity of prayer that I was long past this room. It was like praying for a world in which history is no longer needed.

I turned out the lights and climbed into bed. I closed my eyes and heard for a while the humming bus engine I had slept to the night before. I was almost asleep when the coyotes started. It was a lone, high-pitched *yip yip* and then *yip yip yip yip* in the distance. There was a silence. Then a chorus of them joined in from somewhere close, singing, barking, yipping and yowling as if they had a megaphone, and then I realized they must all be gathered together like a pack of ghosts in an abandoned house. They probably hunted mice in the old houses. But the sound they made was like laughter, that was it—a happy noise. I got up and closed the window. I went back to bed and tried to sleep. I couldn't sleep.

I wondered again why my mother had ever stayed on here. But I knew why. Her divorce had left her with a small monthly check for me. It had also left her with the house. But by the time the papers cleared, it was too late to sell the house—there was nobody left in this town to buy houses. And there was more than that. There was a yellowed document she kept in a metal box, stating that an act of Congress granted her father and his "heirs in perpetuity" deed to a farm. We might have left this house and moved out to the homestead, but the old farmhouse there had stood abandoned after my grandmother died and the weather soon made it not fit to live in. She didn't have the income or credit to get a loan to develop the land and even if she could have found a willing banker, she would have lived in fear of not making the payments and losing everything. So we lived on in this house even though she believed her life had gone wrong from the moment she set foot inside, as if the walls themselves could influence events. "This is the house where I woke up one morning spiritually dead," she once told me. "Now your father, he never did have any spirituality. Forgive me for saying it, but all he ever thought about was money."

She was up to something, of that much I was sure. But I didn't have the foresight to know just what.

Coyotes sang out, barking, laughing, having themselves a party. There wasn't a chance of sleep. Anyway, I was so tired I was awake. I turned on the lamp. I looked around the room and didn't like what I saw, what it made me think, what had happened here. I sat up in bed a long time, smoking. I stared into space. The coyotes finally settled down.

Through the window, an egg-shaped moon lay on its side in the branches of a cottonwood. A cloud moved in and left the room in darkness. I thought of the day ahead, of seeing her people again. I hoped it would be good to see them. I thought of how she hadn't told anyone in town I was coming home. And how I should have expected she wouldn't tell anyone. It was like sometimes a man waiting for rain won't mention the clouds.

2

This house is one of the finest houses in town, on the same low rise as the Whitcomb house, across the street from the Carlson house, which once took up almost a full half acre in rambling brick but was eventually torn down for salvage.

At the housewarming, the day this house was finished, my mother wore a low-cut dress she knew was a little too exotic for a Sunday, wearing it for coolness as she worked with Grandma Vera to check on the pies in her new electric oven, as she slaved over her beans, her dips, her salads, and as she scolded us kids for playing rodeo with my father's pet Belgian hares.

She organized the ladies on a grand tour of the new house. She showed off her colorful tile kitchen floor, her refrigerator complete with tiny ice machine that spilled the cubes down a sparkling glass chute. The kitchen wallpaper was a blue rooster pattern ordered all the way from England. A simply finished round plank table stood in one corner by the window, a single yellow blossom in a clear glass vase making the corner look like the background of an austere painting.

Nobody said anything. Through the window over the sink, she saw Jim on his way with a pan of hot drippings from the barbecue. "There we go," he said, holding the pan up, weaving in and around the crowd of ladies toward Grandma Vera waiting at the stove. Grandma reached out her mittened hands to take the pan from him. "Wait! Not yet!" he said, leaving the pan with her and taking a quick turn to the refrigerator for a jug of white wine.

"I made gravy when you were in knee pants!" Grandma Vera said. The women laughed a little and watched as Jim splashed wine into the pan, curling two fingers and kissing them like a master chef.

"Jim's just showing off his *sav-wor fare*," my mother said.

"That's *savoir faire*," he corrected her. Then he gave her a quick kiss on the cheek, nodded once to the group of ladies, and was out the door on his way back to the smoky cloud around the barbecue.

Women stood quietly in the thick heat of the kitchen. Marge led on into the living room. It must have struck them more like a small version of a great hall as much as a living room. The parquet floor spread out like a vast chessboard of alternating light and dark wood squares. The furniture was modern, curving chrome armrests on the couch and some of the chairs, an eclectic piece or two mixed in, left over from the little house on Yampa Street along with the braided rugs that seemed to her suddenly too dark brown for the room. And there were two things that didn't fit at all—a rocking chair that was an heirloom of Jim's family, with the howling face of an old man winter sculpted into its back, and near the fireplace, a small green marble statue of a boy and his dog in the worst of German sentimental style, the boy holding up a gilded clock that hadn't told time for half a century.

Women moved slowly across the living room, in parsimonious couples or in groups of three. They gathered near the fireplace. The fireplace rose massively off the floor like a fieldstone monument in modern design, all right angles, a rectangular slab of red sandstone raised off the floor for a hearth, a pattern of fossilized snails and a prehistoric leaf captured in its face. It took up nearly one whole end of the room.

Andrea Scott poked her head deep into the fireplace. She jiggled the damper lever. She drew back the glittering firescreens like the curtain on a mountainous stage. She licked a fingertip and reached it up into the flue. It came out clean. Others grouped closely around Andrea, running their hands over the hoary texture of the rust-colored stones.

"What do you plan on burning in there?" asked Andrea Scott. "Firelogs? You plan on burning plain old firelogs?"

"Why, this is lovely, dear," said Josie Carlson. "But it's so huge! Didn't you consider the size might be impractical?"

"She hasn't burned anything in it yet," said Andrea. "She'll have to burn whole trees in there."

"It doesn't have a mantelpiece," said Bonna St. Louis. "You should have Jim build in a mantelpiece."

"She'll have to set a bonfire in there."

"Well, this room is sure large enough it can use the heat," said Josie Carlson. "I've never seen such a room. And all these windows! Did you consider problems with the heat?"

"You'll have to ask Jim," my mother answered, sensing discomfort rising in them. Hands clutched tighter at purse straps. Faces turned away, staring through the windows. "But I don't believe I'd stand for any bonfires," she said. "You know who'd get stuck cleaning up the mess!"

A round of nervous laughter jittered through the room.

"Well, maybe you ought to put in some of them gas jets," said Andrea. "Jim just might save himself a piece of change on coal and wood. Ain't that right, Josie? Dan and me have gas jets and we're completely satisfied."

My mother looked to Anita Foos for consolation. Anita was her best friend, had just finished her own new house, and had stood with her in the fresh smell of sawdust under the skeletal frame, had helped her decide on which grain of spackling to use on the walls. She found Anita at the edge of the group, standing under the simple black iron chandelier that hung down near the stairs. Anita reached up slowly and touched it. There was a deep ringing sound as the chandelier began to sway, iron ornaments colliding. Anita had something terrible in her eyes. Her face was gray. She smiled tautly across the room. The tones of the chandelier faded into a hollow resonance like the last beating of an immense wrought-iron heart.

There were weekends spent on that fireplace, years of them it seemed. All of us—she, her son and her husband—dressed in old weekend clothes. We packed picnic lunches into the hills on hunts for just the right fieldstones. Each stone had to be a certain size, about the size of a gallon jug, and it had to have broad streaks of rust-colored lichens. How many hundreds of them had we knelt beside, considering, labored at turning up, only to find they were somehow the wrong stones, misshapen or discolored. We left God knew how many stones turned over along the creekbanks, or their boy made them tumble down the hills.

We all heaved and pulled at wheelbarrows loaded with special stones, bucking them up over fallen pine boughs, over runs and gullies, finally collapsing in exhaustion. They let the boy run off so they could lie back holding hands, resting in the comfort of the pines. At times like these, my father leaned over and romantically kissed her in his rare flush moments of total joy in gathering stones. They rested, breathing in the fullness of the afternoon as if this was the way people everywhere should be living.

Then something happened. Maybe it was their boy caught playing in bear droppings again. I was always getting into something. They had to chase after me for discipline, put up with my caterwauling. Or if it wasn't their boy, it was something else. The wheelbarrow lost one of its nuts or bolts. Clouds gathered for a drenching rain. Or my father complained there was too much cholesterol in his lunch, using a stick to draw diagrams of blocked-up arteries in the dust. No matter what happened, my father was on his feet, suddenly tense. "Let's get off our butts and get back to work now," he said, too seriously. "Come on! The sun'll be gone soon."

He attacked the wheelbarrow. It was as if he had to unload his fieldstones in the next instant or the results might prove disastrous. She was angry at him. His moods were so changeable. He couldn't just sit back and enjoy the simple pleasures of an afternoon. She left him straining alone at his wheelbarrow. She watched it get away from him. The stones spilled with a crushing sound. He cursed each stone bitterly. I tried to help, but he generally pushed me out of the way. He hefted each stone in again. Then he started off once more with the wheelbarrow, the tire jumping and rollicking down the hills. The expression on his face made her hurry after him, shouting, "Jim! Jim! What's the matter now!"

She caught up with him. He stopped, breathless, sweating. He sneaked his fingers over to feel his pulse. He came from a family in which the men had traditionally died young from heart attacks. But the fact was that almost every doctor clear to Denver had told him his heart was sound. She knew he feared for his health when there was something else that troubled him. He never acted the invalid. If she so much as pointed out the fact that he was feeling his pulse, they would soon be shouting.

She helped him with his wheelbarrow the rest of the way to the station wagon. By the time they finished loading, he seemed recovered. But we endured the long drive home in his silence. He acted as if we had all just shared an experience that should be mulled now, considered to its deepest implications. Once or twice, he apologized. He went to bed tired and depressed. Over fieldstones. Then later in the week, he left work early to hunt for them alone. We could always tell he had one by the sound of the station wagon's back door opening farther up the drive, almost to the kitchen window. He carried his new stone to the back of the old house, to a pile of them waiting for the new house to be finished enough. As he passed the kitchen, he showed his find to her through the window as she was fixing supper, posing there with his stone as if it was a kind of championship game trophy.

"It's going to be a new life," he said cheerily, his voice clipped and with an accent almost foreign. "You'll see," he said. He cleared the kitchen table. I helped him unroll the blueprints he spread out after dinner, over coffee and dessert. He marked changes on them long into the nights with a set of chrome-plated instruments, sometimes letting me poke the sharp point of the compass into the center of the rooms or hold the ruler as he drew lines. "You'll see how different it's going to be," he said. "We won't feel like the same people anymore."

At the housewarming, doors opened one after the other from room to room of my father's design. She no longer tried to show anything off. She just opened the doors and waited in the hallway, letting the others say what they would. She opened the door to the boy's room and saw immediately that it was a shambles. She had cleaned it that morning but the boy had found time enough. His model airplanes that should have been neatly hanging by their threads were scattered over the floor in bits and pieces. There were black marks on the wall over his bed. Target practice. How could he have done that? She watched a chameleon in its green phase— the one I called Frog because it almost never changed from green—scrambling hysterically in a mason jar. The mason jar had no top to it. There should have been four more chameleons. She reeled back, horrified. She made out the chocolate shape of the one called Stubtail lethargically sunning itself on the bedspread. Beatrice Ott tottered in and let out a wheezy shriek, grabbing at her throat. Marge gripped her by the wrists. Beatrice immediately calmed down. She helped Marge usher the others back into the hall and shut the door behind her.

God knows when the all-tile bathroom became a fixture in society. Most people in town wanted one. They were going in everywhere, in all the new houses, a characteristic of the decade, matching pastel fixtures springing up like a fervent tropical forest on tracts of dry brush country surrounding town, country parceled out in strings for foundations, sticks with little red flags fluttering at the boundaries of streets, water mains, sewers, sidewalks, driveways. The one in this house was large, as big as most regular bedrooms. There was a flaw in one corner, an extra set of copper pipes sticking up through the floor with surrounding globs of dried white caulking she had already worked at with a kitchen knife, a mistake she had caught at the last minute. The boy was underfoot, on his hands and knees pounding nails flat in the sawdust. Jim unrolled his blueprints. He measured with a tape. He checked the blueprints and measured again. "Our idiot contractor again," he said, looking at us both. "He must think people can dump and take a bath at the same time. If he weren't a friend of your dad's, I'd go ahead and sue. Just look at that cheap sheeting he used on the roof...."

The complaints, the changes, the revisions went on for years. They hired and fired three different contractors before they were done. And still there were mistakes. It seemed she couldn't go anywhere in the new house without bumping her shins into them.

Women followed her into the bathroom. She slid back the frosted-glass doors to the green, cavernous bath. "Come on," she said, trying to sound bright, trying to show off. "You should see this!"

Nobody responded. Marge picked at bits of packing tape on the new glass.

"Jim's mounted his shaving mirror in here," she said. "I think it's kind of fun. He doesn't like shaving anywhere but in the shower."

Andrea Scott and Bonna St. Louis slowly followed her over and looked in. Beatrice Ott and Constance Gamble looked in, faces moving in the concave shaving mirror with eerie expressions.

"I think it's kind of unusual," she said. Water drained across the room. "A man who shaves in there," she said.

"My Charles used to be just that same way," said Beatrice Ott. "Loved shaving in his shower. That is until he slipped once with a straight razor and I swear, he nearly gave me grounds for a divorce!"

Laughter had her thinking she was finally breaking the ice. She showed them my father's sandalwood soaps and oils. She gave a bar to Beatrice to take home for Charles. She was saved from what remained of her tour by my father's shout from downstairs that the barbecue was done. Her house was deserted in minutes. She made an excuse to Beatrice and sent her downstairs. She stood alone in the upstairs hallway.

She knew her own way outside. Down the stairs and out through the sliding glass doors of my father's study. She found herself nervously looking around corners, peering through the shadows of the stairway to make sure she was alone. She pushed the study door open cautiously and found the room was empty, warm-looking. Inside, she kicked off her shoes. She sat down in Jim's red leather reading chair and lit a cigarette. Festive cries sounded from the backyard. She watched columns of smoke drawn up through the lampshade until she caught herself staring. She lifted her gaze to his wall, covered floor to ceiling with hard-bound books. She remembered arguing with him about all the books, thinking they should keep them in common, as they had taken up three walls of the living room in the old house, her books and his, somehow feeling the best of them in his study now a kind of enforced separation of minds. Her racks of magazines and two small shelves of books in the front room with the TV looked like next to nothing compared to his. She wondered how long it would take her to get through all his books, mouthing the words, having to look up so many meanings, wanting to read them all. Then again, she saw how the dust of the move had settled on them. She would have to get to them first thing in the morning.

She stood up thinking she'd see what needed doing in the backyard. Then on impulse, she took a walk around his room with ashtray in hand, seeing his study complete really for the first time and feeling unmoored in it, drifting past the primitive features of a carved wood crucifix he kept not for religion but as a relic of his service in Europe during the war. She moved slowly past his other war memorabilia, his colored service ribbons, his Purple Heart in a wooden case, his officer's bars, three small chips of shrapnel removed from his arm in 1944, the gray battalion photographs once in their bedroom, now arranged neatly on his shelves. Across the room, there was a cabinet full of antique swords and rifles that he cleaned and polished on quiet evenings. She wondered just when it was war had become a kind of hobby to him.

Loud music, laughter, shouting from the backyard came to her with the same persistent deadening effect of a hard rain beating the windows. She turned and faced the windows. She saw Bonna St. Louis out there. Bonna had a fine china plate in hand. People crowded in the food line behind her. Wind billowed the sleeves of her husband's red nylon bowling jacket she was wearing, the jacket ballooning over her body. Bonna danced against the wind, looking around with a severe, impatient expression, searching through the crowd. Bonna found her husband, Erwin, and waved to him, then cupped her hand to her mouth and called out. Erwin St. Louis frowned into his beer mug. He waited just a moment too long before he pushed his way through the crowd and put his arm around his wife. Bonna took that arm, took that thick hand in hers, that workman's hand with one finger missing. Marge wondered what it was like for Bonna and Erwin, what they talked of at night, if it was somehow the same for them, if they lay awake with their plans. She thought of how they lived in a trailer house on five acres, kids, dogs, goats, a calf or two running wild. She thought of Erwin home from working turkeys, resting his arms in a ripped-up chair in front of the TV, most nights too tired to do anything but wait for supper on a table where the plates didn't even match.

Shouts went up around Jim. She watched him. She thought he looked foolish in the cowboy hat he wore on special occasions. Men whose names she didn't know were helping him carry the roasted pig to one of the picnic tables. They set it out in front of Jim. Jim poked a knifeblade through the crust, leaning his face in close and breathing in the steam. He grinned. He raised his knife and lopped off a quarter-moon-shaped slice. He stuffed the meat whole between his teeth, chewing it slowly and with a seriously discerning expression until he nodded his head once and swallowed.

Candidate for mayor Buster Hill moved in to help with the carving, white shirtsleeves rolled, his panama hat with the bright red *Three Cheers for Buster!* campaign button in the sweatband tilted back over his pale white forehead. "Who wants the part that went through the fence last!" Buster shouted, slicing it off. Then he ate most of it himself. Everyone laughed. A hundred men pulled at their beers. Buster handed a piece of meat to Jim. Jim stuffed the piece whole into his mouth. This was his afternoon. He felt proud this afternoon.

Kurt was suddenly there and Jim stopped his carving. He lifted the boy up on the table beside him. He waved an arm expansively to the men around him, showing off his boy, squeezing the boy around his small square shoulders, ruffling the hair on the boy's square head that looked somehow too large for the thin bones of his neck. The boy had features just like his father's. She had never noticed them so pronounced before. The boy sat gripping the edge of the table and swinging his legs. Jim raised his knife high. The knife came flashing down with quick execution. His father handed the boy a dripping piece by the bone. Kurt chewed it, looking mischievously happy he was at the center of a crowd, men lifting other women's sons to their shoulders, the dark shadows of cowboy hats moving over the ground before him like a flock of crows as everyone watched, waiting in front of him with plates in hand. Kurt suddenly reached out for his father's beer mug and hid his face in it. His father shouted. His father reached across the table for him. The boy ducked out from under his father's reach and laughter pelted the windows of the study. Kurt wiped his mouth with his sleeve. He set the mug back up on the table with both hands and ran hellbent across the lawn.

Jim draped one of his long arms over Buster Hill. Jim laughed, called out something, moved fraternally across the grass with Buster toward the beer. The barbecue was on. Grandma Vera and her friends had served up everything, the party moving on its own now like a programmed machine, everyone stepping in and dipping up the food. She saw Andrea Scott scrutinizing dish after dish on down the tables as if there were rattlesnakes in them.

Marge turned away from the windows. She knelt and pulled on her shoes. She emptied the ashtray onto a blank piece of notepaper and crumpled it, meaning to take it with her from the room. As she set the ashtray back on his reading table she stopped a moment, looking into it somehow unsatisfied, for one small moment wishing she, too, were made of glass.

She picked the ashtray up again. She moved over to the gun

cabinet and wiped the ashtray clean with one of his gun cloths, thinking he could never tell the difference. She set the ashtray carefully back on the reading table. Then she started to adjust his chairback into its exact position, brushing off the arms. There was a smudge that wouldn't come off. She took his gun cloth again and used one corner of it to scrub at the spot. She looked around. Suddenly, she shoved the reading chair against the tall bookcase. She climbed up on the arms and began to snap the cloth at his ranks of books.

Two hours later, my father found her in her new bedroom. The door was locked. It was Grandma Vera who had first noticed she had been gone from the party. My father had a key.

"Leave me alone!" she shouted in a high voice. A silence fell over the yard. People looked up at the drawn curtains of her bedroom. "Leave me alone!" she screamed.

There was a loud explosion of shattering glass. Nobody made a move, waiting, listening. My father had trouble shutting the bedroom door with pieces of broken ashtray in his hands.

Grandma Vera and Beatrice Ott tried to get my mother to come out. They knocked and called to her, gently, inside.

"I'm all right," she said. "Go away now. I'm just resting."

"She's wore out," was Grandma Vera's story, back in the yard. "She's worked so hard to make this move and get a party on!"

The party was breaking up, the sun on its way down over distant buttes. Crumpled napkins, cups, plates, bits of food were scattered over the backyard like a carnival grounds. Jackets and hats, wives and kids were gathered up. Cars pulled out of the driveway. Friends gave my father looks of commiseration as he stood in the front yard shaking hands, thanking each of them for coming.

Later, he gave me a spanking for letting his hares out of their cages. I ran around in the near darkness, herding them back into their new raised hutches painted the same shade of gray as this house. He sent me up to bed. I knocked on my mother's door to say goodnight but she must have fallen asleep. My father put records on his stereo in the living room, turning the volume up until the speakers were pounding, one of the records the *William Tell*

Overture—I knew that one because in the old house he put it on sometimes and laughed like hell when I came running in thinking *The Lone Ranger* was on TV. He built a fire in his new fireplace, really piling on the wood. Nothing was going to spoil the day for him. He mixed a drink and stared into his fire, his music rattling the windows, the huge flames taking off up the dark flue, flying up off the logs like brilliant orange birds. Finally, the house was quiet. He fell asleep on the couch in the living room.

In my new room, I crawled around on the floor in search of my pets, finding them where they liked to hide—in the cracks of the windowsills, clinging to the rough backing of my little chest of drawers, one of them hidden in the fold made by the bedspread tucked under the pillow. I still missed one, Stubtail, a funny-looking thing, the first one I had ever bought from the vendor at the Cheyenne stock show, who sold them chained to little cards, part of its tail missing and never grown back. Stubtail was usually chocolate brown and I hunted for him in the darker grain of the wood floor, under my chair, everywhere I could think of. I searched for him for days. At night, I left a small dish of meal-worms out for him. But I woke up each morning and found them untouched.

It was only months later that I finally discovered him, a transparent brown skeleton in one corner of the closet. I remember holding him up to the light and looking through him, looking through into his deepest parts, into his tiny fishlike bones, into the dark craters of his eyes, his skeleton crackly, delicate, like a thin dried leaf. I tasted it, just a little flake, a salty taste. I tried to get that skeleton over to my shoebox so I could save it, gently hoisting it in my palm. But it fell to pieces before I could get there. It crumbled to dust in the palm of my hand.

3

One afternoon, Buster Hill reached a hand out of his front porch hammock and discovered the bulldog pup he had named Buster, after himself, was no longer there. He awoke with a start and found the dog was running across the front lawn. It stopped by the paved road in front of the house and stood on its hind legs.

"Goddamnit, Buster!" Buster Hill shouted. The dog was dancing around eagerly, looking south down the street. Buster Hill looked after him through the unmoving shadows of the cottonwoods toward the hot dust of Main. A long blue Pontiac sedan with California license plates and a woman at the wheel slowed in front of Buster's curb. The door swung open a crack and, as the story goes, that bulldog jumped right in.

The blue car sped off down the street. Across the street, Josie Carlson said it wasn't so much the dog barking that made her look up from her iced tea as the sound of Buster Hill lumbering past, grunting like a wounded razorback. The blue car signaled for a left turn into the Baseline Road. It turned again like it would double back along Grove toward Main. Buster Hill broke through Josie Carlson's white picket gate, goring himself as he leaped over the backyard fence. He ran limping through a parking lot behind the house. The car made a right turn onto Main Street toward the highway.

Buster Hill caught up to the car at the intersection. He bounced along beside the fender. He was shouting loudly enough that Deputy Ben Perez and a few old boys scooted off their stools at The Cove Café. They watched through the new picture window of The

Cove as Buster Hill was leaping sideways down the street, bouncing high alongside that car like a man on a springboard. He shouted at an unknown, dark-haired woman, *"That's my dog! My goddamned dog! My damned dog!"*

He was stricken. He spun around like a quick whirlwind had seized him in midair and then released him. His huge bulk heaved face first dead in the middle of the street.

Deputy Ben Perez hustled out of The Cove and made sure Buster Hill was dead. The blue car turned north onto the highway. Deputy Perez ran off to wake Sheriff Meeker out of his afternoon doze at the municipal saloon. Sheriff Meeker stood for a long time over Buster Hill's immense carcass, still red-faced and sweating. Sheriff Meeker looked unsteadily toward the highway, muttering under his breath. He spat, turned, straightened up reasonably. He walked back across the street for the gun he had left on the hatrack at the saloon. He was still strapping the gun on, standing in the double doors of the saloon, when he stopped a minute, belted down a shot and tossed the glass back in to Dolores Moss. When he reached the middle of the street, he stopped again. "Dolores!" he shouted. "Dolores! Fetch me them keys!"

Dolores Moss threw his car keys out to him. The sheriff managed the rest of the distance to his brand-new black-and-tan Nowell sheriff's car, the one that had just been delivered the week before. He climbed in, steadied himself, talked on the radio. He had trouble getting the new car in reverse. A small crowd scattered when the car backed nearly full circle into the street, tires smoking. Sheriff Meeker went wailing off in the wrong direction out of town.

Doc Monahan flat refused to pronounce Buster Hill legally dead. He didn't want any part of what was sure to follow. Sam Carlson would have him wasting his time with autopsy papers, official hearings and testimony. Deputy Perez found the Doc in his office and told him the news. The Doc peered out his venetian blinds at the crowd gathering near the corpse. He asked Deputy Perez if he was sure Buster Hill was dead. "Then you go on out there and don't let anybody touch a thing," he said. He ushered

Deputy Perez out of his office. At his desk, he stuffed a pair of socks and a shaving kit into his black bag. Doc Monahan disappeared out the back way, leaving town by the back streets to avoid Sam Carlson.

It didn't take long for the news to spread. A crowd gathered in the street, standing back a good ten feet from the corpse. No one had even so much as turned Buster Hill to a more respectable posture, not even Sam Carlson, the new general manager of the Nowell-Safebuy turkey plant, Buster's second in command, his tie askew, sweat streaking his horn-rims, his bald head bobbing in that sea of onlookers who heard his shrill, woman's voice raised at them: *"Has anyone please seen what's happened, please? Is anyone here please willing to make a statement?"*

When he found Doc Monahan was no longer in, Sam Carlson sent people running off for the volunteer fire department ambulance. The ambulance was gone after a case of snakebite on the alkali flats. At the fire department, no one could get Sheriff Meeker on the police radio. Sam Carlson ranged through the crowd even more desperately: *"Did anyone see what happened here? Could someone please make a statement?"*

Dolores Moss finally thought to phone the Millis Mortuary, the newest member of the Chamber of Commerce since this town had grown sizable enough to attract a second mortuary. Darwin Millis and his son, Andrew, took their own sweet time putting on their best black suits, polishing up their wing-tipped cowboy boots and new maroon Cadillac hearse. It would be the family's first real public appearance, and Darwin hoped Willa Mason from the *Enterprise* would be out there with her Polaroid taking newsphotos of the scene.

Willa Mason was too stunned for photographs. Buster Hill, that man who had first brought the turkey-slaughtering industry to this town, that man who had built and organized Nowell-Safebuy turkeys into the huge vertical farm it threatened to be, who had put this town on the map within the national system of Safebuy supermarts, raising a million Safebuy turkeys per year, writing out the paychecks for a thousand farmers and workers who took care of them, that man who had fought her consistently for ten years about paving the streets with the cheapest possible materials in favor of low taxes and had finally lost—that man who had been her main source of front-page news had become an obituary. Willa Mason's hands held tightly to her camera as if it was a kind of amulet.

The crowd was growing. A kind of spontaneous generation had seized this town, borne from the shores of a shimmering white gravel sea where Buster Hill's body lay waiting to be moved. It was a hot summer's day. Several people felt faint under the sun. No one seemed to know what to do but Dolores Moss, who was already passing out free cold beers in front of the municipal saloon. The rest of the crowd was milling aimlessly, waiting for something to happen, a constant muttering rising off them like a steam.

The slaughtering line at the Nowell-Safebuy stopped at four thousand birds. Men in bloody green aprons poured into the streets. At the Tamblin-Hill grain elevator, the booming wind of the grain loaders suddenly died, leaving the same haunted atmosphere as the silence in a twister's wake. The First Bank of Belle Fourche pulled its shades. The Pacific & Western Railroad blasted its noon whistle intermittently, calling its workers in from the loading docks. A gleaming maroon hearse lumbered down Main Street, that dusty white gravel street laid out with strings and red flags, waiting for the paving crews.

This town pressed in. It took the strength of both Millis men and three plant workers straining to heave Buster's stiffened body into the hearse. Andrew Millis thought to cover it with a sheet. Men climbed in, cowboy hats huddling around that white tent as the door slammed. The hearse drove off and turned a corner, out of sight.

People stood then, not knowing whether to feel mournful or terrified, as if ready for either emotion suddenly to take hold of them. The crowd mixed solemnly in the heat, a small empty space at their center that no one crossed, like a hearthstone around which they still gathered, looking shocked, uprooted, as if expecting some final revelation that never came. Dolores Moss began calling drinks on the house at the municipal saloon, but it was the heat that finally moved them. The town slowly began dispersing, one by one or in small groups, toward the bar, The Cove Café, their homes, in out of the blast furnace of the afternoon. They left Sam Carlson still calling to them from the street. For eleven years, he had been next in line for promotion. He needed a statement of just what exactly had happened for his superiors.

4

The following season was the worst in history for raising turkeys. Sam Carlson pressed on with an industry-wide program of vertical integration. He continued Buster Hill's practice of contracting with farmers to buy turkeys a full season ahead of time at a fixed price on the day of delivery. That way, a turkey farmer could take his contract to the bank and borrow money enough to raise his crop. Those with a good history of delivery to the Nowell-Safebuy could even get payment at fixed prices in the form of company loans at a slightly lower interest than the bank charged. But a problem developed. For one thing, there was a growing turkey surplus in this country. Then the price of grain suddenly jumped by more than a third upward due to a huge international grain trade agreement overseas. By midsummer, calculating the Nowell-Safebuy's lower fixed price per pound against the higher cost of feed grains, every day a farmer kept his crop alive he was losing money.

The Nowell Farmer's Organization held meetings at the Rock Creek Church to discuss their problems. Those meetings became a theater of violent infighting, strong remarks thrown back and forth over just what to do, a pernicious wrangling over details. Most of the members of that group lived on such marginal credit that a single failure meant ruin to them. One splinter group, led by Will Hartley, tried to find new ways to market turkeys at a fair price—arranging transportation to distant cities and cooperatives of small grocery stores. Will Hartley received a phone call in the middle of the night, a hoarse voice saying, "Remember Will Green," and then hanging up. He assigned two drivers for each truck, both of them carrying shotguns, and a few truckloads were delivered to Omaha at a profit. Then even Omaha prices dropped straight into the basement.

Farmers grew desperate. Some even tried to sell turkeys door to door, plucked and slaughtered, in violation of health codes, in downtown Cheyenne, Rapid City, Belle Fourche, Deadwood, wherever they could get a price. But for farmers who had agreements with the Nowell-Safebuy, selling turkeys to anyone else in any form was in violation of their contracts. Sam Carlson threatened to sue. Against that threat and with a further rise in the price of grain due to drought conditions over much of the Midwest, a good number of the Nowell Farmers' Organization members decided on a radical course. They sent out press releases complaining of their problems, demanding legislative intervention to stop the vertical integration of farms, to pass a law against companies like the Nowell-Safebuy to keep them from buying up family farms in trouble. They invited television crews all the way from Omaha, Rapid City and Cheyenne to film the mass destruction of their crops. Most of the turkeys were piled in a trench and burned after slaughtering, then buried with a bulldozer. The prairie filled with black smoke whirling up day after day, rolling, tumbling, dark scarves of smoke blown for an instant to the shapes of godheads, vague monuments, black smoke tornadoes that scarred the summer skies with waste and violence. Even some farmers who had more favorable loans with the Nowell-Safebuy defaulted on their commitments.

My father paced around the kitchen, hands sunk deeply in his pockets. "It was really horrible to watch," he said. "I never thought I'd see such anger in Will Hartley and his friends. They dug a trench out near Rasmussen's, along the road. They must have dumped ten thousand turkeys in it. So they're all in trouble now. They'll be lucky if Sam Carlson doesn't sue."

"Who all was out there?" my mother asked. She painted a spicy red sauce over a pan of turkey. She had had to rent freeze locker space to fit all the turkeys she had bought from farmers passing door to door. She supported their movement. Her most evident support was that her family ate nothing but turkey for what seemed an eternity.

"Oh, about a third of Will's group," he said. "More than I thought would turn out. Don Hinkle backed out at the last minute. And Jim Claypool decided to butcher his turkeys, grind them up and ship them to a farmer in Iowa as hog feed. Can you imagine? I never knew hogs could eat meat. Anyway, it makes sense to get something out of them. Even company farmers were out there, like Jim Fuller and his family. And your father's friend Pete Bosserd would have been there but he broke his leg loading his crop. Will offered to go out and truck his birds in for him, but Pete said broken leg or not, he's going to drive them in himself in the morning. Please remind me tomorrow, your father wants to give Pete a bottle of my Scotch."

He was tired. His shoesoles dragged and scuffed across the tile floor, leaving fine trails of soot. He had ruined his pants. He had been close enough to the fires to have intricate patterns of small cinder burns on his white shirtsleeves. His face was streaked with black like a coal miner's face. His back and shoulders looked as if they might collapse under the weight of his fatigue and his difficult thoughts. She had seen this mood in him countless times—a depressed mood that no amount of talk ever seemed to penetrate, or at least no talk from her. The most she knew to do was turn his mind to something else.

"Honey . . ." she started. He looked at her gloomily.

"I'll go take a shower," he said. But he just stood there, watching her slide his supper into the oven.

"It really was terrible," he said.

"I can imagine," she said.

"No. You can't imagine it," he said. "It wasn't something

anyone who hasn't seen it could ever imagine."

"Well, it's done now. Isn't it?"

"No. It's not," he said. "It's just beginning."

"Honey, don't think about it now," she said. She slipped an arm under his. She reached up to push a few gray strings of hair from his eyes.

"It's all right," he said. "Just let me relax a little first."

"Then get out of here so I can get supper on," she said. "I'll come in later and rub your back."

"Don't bother," he said.

"Then get out of here right now," she snapped. "You're messing up my kitchen."

"I guess I'll take care of the hares," he said. Raising Belgian hares had become a kind of hobby for him. Part of the plans for the new house had included a line of neat hutches against the backyard fence to shelter the extended family of three hares he had bought a year or so before on impulse at a stock show. "Come on, Kurt," he said.

I followed my father outside. From the garage, I helped him carry the bags of wood shavings and green feed pellets, and a jug of vitamins.

"You know . . ." he said. He opened a cage door and pulled out a little tray. I filled it with rabbit food. "These hares really give me pleasure." He stuck a finger through the wire mesh of the cage and watched a hare nuzzling it before it tried a tiny bite. "What little time I have to spend with them. I guess I've never been much good at raising things. These guys probably wouldn't have survived this long if it weren't for what you and your mom do for them."

He pulled out a cage bottom like a drawer. I scraped it with a putty knife into a garbage bag. "I used to raise them when I was a boy," he said. "Hundreds of them. I had this dream of selling them to butcher shops. I wanted to help my mother with money after my father died. That was the Great Depression. Things were really tough then. Some people didn't have enough to eat. But it was all a big failure. The rabbits came down with a viral disease because I hadn't built the hutches right. They were too close to the ground. Not like these. We don't have to worry about these guys."

"What happened to them?" I asked.

"What do you mean?"

"To all the rabbits," I said.

"They all died," my father said. "In about three days. Now go turn on the hose. These guys look thirsty."

I ran to turn on the faucet. I waited by the house to turn the water off again, watching my father filling the little glass bottles and talking to his pets.

At supper, he didn't eat much. He twirled white bits of turkey on the end of his fork, daubed it through the sauce, sniffed at it once or twice, daubed it through the sauce again. He washed each little bit down with a glass of white wine. He looked at my mother strangely, without saying anything. She returned his silence. He crumpled his napkin and dropped it on his plate.

"I'm going to have to handle the lawsuits for Sam," he said.

My mother stopped eating. She looked as if she'd had the wind kicked out.

"Oh, Jim, no," she said. "Can't they find anyone else?"

"I wrote those contracts," he said. "I'll have to defend them point by point."

"Jim, no! It's not right!"

"Right?" he said, "Right? What the hell do you mean?"

"I mean . . . they're going under. They're liable to do anything."

"Don't you see that losing this case would be the best thing that could happen to them? What happens if they win? What?"

"Jesus, Jim, no. . . ."

"Oh, shut up. They made a business deal and came out on the short end. It has nothing to do with right or wrong."

"There are *families* out there! What are they going to do?"

"What everyone else does," he said. "They'll move."

"Jesus, honey. Please. There's got to be some other way."

"Can't you see the position I'm in!" he shouted. "Who built this house? Who?" My mother looked away from him, out the large dark wall of picture window. "Come on, Marge, half my work is for the company. What else can I do?"

"Quit," she said. "We'll make it somehow."

"There's not enough private practice here to make it," he said. "I'd end up suing my own clients to collect my fees. Don't be ridiculous, honey. What they're doing is wrong."

"Oh, we'll all be *proud* of you in court! Standing there in your suit and tie yanking the farms right out from under them!"

"Oh, bullshit," he said.

"Don't talk like that in front of your son," she said. She shook a cigarette out of her pack. Her hands were trembling. She crumpled three matches trying to get it lit.

"Sam'll buy time for any farmer who delivers," he said.

She didn't answer him. She looked over at me. I started to finish my food. There was no sound at all for a moment but the music of my silverware on the plate.

"They tried to asphyxiate them," my father said. "They drove a large, square-backed truck up to the trench. The truck had a hole drilled in the box and a hose that connected to the exhaust. But it wasn't big enough. It only fit two, three hundred at a time. They made a terrible noise. We had to walk down the road a ways to hear ourselves. Every few minutes, somebody checked to see if they were dead. It took a long time to kill them. When they opened the truck, there were dozens of turkeys still alive in there, flopping around, crawling over themselves. . . ."

"Honey, please," she said.

"Then Will Hartley called the others over to start shoveling the dead ones into the trench. They found some of them had managed to survive by crawling to the bottom of the heap. They started wringing necks. . . ."

"Jim! Please!"

"What in hell do you think I've been doing all day!" he shouted. "What in hell do you want from me!"

"God*damnit!*" She started to cry.

"What do you want from me!" he shouted. She pushed back from the table and ran from the room. "They didn't even shoot

158

them!'' he shouted down the hallway. "Will sent for barrels of diesel fuel. He burned most of them alive.''

She slammed the door of their bedroom. She threw herself on their bed and cried. She tucked her limbs up tightly on the bed, pulling the rough cover back enough to cry into the softer pillowcase. She could lie there alone for hours. Or he would come in and apologize. They might make it up and be kind to each other for several days. She waited. The front door slammed. The station wagon started up in the driveway. She ran out of the bedroom and down the stairs. She threw open the front door just as tires screeched into the street, a cloud of blue smoke rising into the summer evening.

"You sonofabitch!'' she shouted.

His car must have been doing sixty by the time it reached the corner. There was a loud crumpling fender sound as it hurtled over the curb making a high-speed turn a little too tightly. Then his car was gone.

My mother turned and leaned against the door. She saw me standing behind her, watching. Her face changed. "Come here,'' she said. She held out her arms. She hugged me, crying into my hair. "I'm sorry we fight,'' she said. "But sometimes we have to fight.''

I waited for my father to come home. Every time a car engine sounded distantly in the street I woke up in bed and crawled to the window at its foot. I looked out to see if it was him. But he didn't come home that night. He came in late the next morning. He said he had driven all the way to Cheyenne, then checked into a motel. They hardly spoke to each other for days.

5

A few nights later, as she told it, she awoke in the darkness. She was startled awake by something. She shivered. She thought it was the cold that had awakened her, as she gathered the sheets and blankets. Then she heard it again. She sat up and listened closely. Wind sound echoed through the screens. There was a light drumming of the rain on the windows, a loud clapping sound as the drainspout poured its flood of rain. In the background, there was a high shrieking—that was it, a sound like the yowling of cats but higher in pitch and weaker somehow, not like cats. She leaned over and shook my father. He rolled. He opened his eyes halfway and groaned. She listened. The sound had gone. She started to settle under the covers again when she heard it as loud as a scream.

She jumped out of bed. She ran over to the window and pushed it open. Nothing moved. Rain blew in a mist through the screen. The backyard was a patchwork of ominous, contrasting grays in fog and rain. Rain glittered like tinsel in the yard lights of the neighboring house. Across the street and behind the house, a sudden storming wind swayed the cottonwoods like dark grasping hands. A gale of rain stung her face through the screen. In the calm that followed, the steam of her breath floated back around her in a dispersing cloud. Nothing moved. Nothing moved out there but rain.

The next morning, my father rose early, as he usually did. A dawn mist glittered on the windows. She awoke to the sight of him pacing around their chilly bedroom thoughtfully a minute before he sent his body through brief calisthenics that served him more psychologically than for purposes of his health. He did pushups, situps, deep knee bends and toe touches, his joints crackling like autumn cornstalks. Arrowlike shadows moved violently on the walls. He finished. The window squealed as he pushed it further open. He stood in front of it a few minutes deep breathing before he lit up the first cigarette of his three packs a day. Then he put on his soft red robe and strolled casually downstairs to the kitchen to drink the first cup of his two quarts or more per day of watery coffee.

He sat down with the telephone. He checked in with the secretary at his law office at seven every morning, dedicated as she was to be at work at that hour, to remind himself of his schedule for the day. My mother rose to the sound of his voice on the phone. She drew on her robe. She joined him in the kitchen, poured a cup of coffee and began to fix his eggs. Out the kitchen window, she saw the backyard glimmering with rain pools and was taken by its beauty. Mist rolled in off the wild fields, an immense cloud rising with the sun. She hummed softly as she cooked. A mourning dove trilled, then called its three sad notes. Her eyes sought it out instinctively and found it sitting on the garden fence. It was close enough for her to see one eye the color of grenadine looking back at her. She stirred bacon curling in the pan. Around the back stoop, she watched dried rhododendron leaves rustle in the fresh wind as if something was alive in them. My father hung up the phone.

"I'll be out with the hares," he said. It was often his habit before he dressed and ate breakfast to step into the backyard to inspect his hares. He clucked at them. He poked his fingers through the cage wires like a curious child. He overwatered, spilled too much food in their cans, showered them with gallons of wood shavings as he worried over their cages.

"Whenever the rain comes from the south, it blows into their cages," he said. "We should really find a better way to shelter them. Maybe build little awnings or something."

"They don't mind the rain," she said. "Besides, you can't go pampering them. You'll wind up with weakened stock. . . ."

The outer door slammed by its spring. She cracked his eggs into the poacher. She saw him standing on the back stoop a moment, savoring the fresh wet morning. His face looked suddenly stricken. She froze. She remembered the sound made by a wounded jackrabbit kicking dead in the snow. That high squealing sound returned to her in the sound of my father's voice.

She ran into the backyard. She stopped. She sucked in her breath. The black-and-white hares were hung head downward all in a line. Wide blood trails splashed over the gray wooden cage frames into the mud and rain beneath. The hares hung stiffly, hind legs wired to the cages, their fur wet and drowned-looking. Each one had been butchered that way by experienced hands.

"Last night . . ." she started.

"Get back in the house," he said.

"I heard them," she said.

He reached out and touched one. He lifted it in his hand, something blue starting to spill out the neck. He let it fall back against the cage, the head swaying in the soft breeze as did all their heads, bare red cords left of their throats.

"Please," he said. "Please get back in the house."

I was at the screen door and by the look my mother gave me, I ran back upstairs to my room. The door slammed twice downstairs. In a moment, there was shouting. My mother was hysterical. She bounded upstairs with two small suitcases. She stormed into my bedroom and threw a suitcase up on the bed and opened it.

"We're going to Grandpa's farm," she said. "If he wants us there, then that's where we'll go." She tossed in some of my clothes, my gym suit, my school sneakers, working quickly, her face pale, her hands shaking. "As far as I'm concerned, we can stay there forever," she said. "Now get your notebook. Get your homework. Come on!"

My father was on the telephone as we passed the kitchen. He put the phone to his chest. "Call me at the office as soon as you get there," he said. She looked at him. "Honey, please," he said. "Come here."

She put her suitcase down and went over to him. He put his arms around her, one hand still clutching the phone. Her body sagged a little into his, her eyes closing, her cheek pressed hard against his shoulder. She didn't want to leave like this. "I'm sorry," he said. "I don't want you two involved."

"Then quit," she said. "Goddamnit, Jim, can't you see?"

"Look. If Buster Hill was still alive, none of this would have happened," he said.

"If you came to your senses once it wouldn't," she said.

"So you think it's my fault? Your mother thinks it's all my fault," he said.

"I feel like if we walk out that door, we might as well not come back," she said.

"You're upset," he said. "We're all upset. Now please. Just get to someplace safe, that's the important thing. This'll all blow over, I promise you. But we can't give in to these bastards. We simply can't," he said. "And I promise you something else. I'm going to make sure the bastards are caught. That much you can count on." He kissed her on the cheek. Then he held her firmly by the shoulders and looked directly into her eyes. "Just call me as soon as you get there," he said.

For the next several weeks, my mother and I lived at my grandfather's farm while my father stayed in town. I was driven in and picked up from school every day. For the first time, I didn't like it at the farm. Especially the way my Grandpa Ben talked. It was all a kind of vindication for him. "Even ol' Jake was out there today," he said at dinner. "Ol' steady Safebuy Jake," he said, "drove six thousand birds over to Rasmussen's. Shoulda had a hunk o' bacon with him so he could lick it once and be able to swallow again. Said this shoulda happened ten years ago, ten damn years ago for everybody, all of us in it together. And the beautiful thing is there ain't a thing the Safebuy can do about it. Not even with that sharpster you married," he said, looking quickly over at me. "Finish yer goddamn potatoes or you're a mollycoddle in my book," he said. "Hear me, boy? You ain't a mollycoddle, are ya?"

He reached his fork out across the table and stabbed a piece of meat off my plate. "That's too good for you," he said, chewing. He reached out again with his fork, helping me finish Grandma Vera's portions, which were just about killing me. "That's too good for you too," he said, helping me eat.

Grandma Vera cuddled me in bed next to her at night. Then Grandpa Ben woke me up early to carry two heavy slop buckets out to feed the two hogs he was raising for meat. Then I cut the twine on a bale of hay and kicked it out of the barn loft into the feedcrib. I dropped down into the crib. I jumped up and down in the hay, scattering it around so Grandpa Ben's two hard-mouthed geldings wouldn't bite at each other over a pile of hay. There was only one job I did that pleased him. After school, I went around the farm picking up bits of scrap metal, old pieces of frame from antique machinery, crumpled rusty squares of old roofing tin and old barbed wire, rolls and rolls of it pulled length by length up out of the earth along the old fencelines, finding pieces of metal wherever I could, even the heavy shell of an old gas engine strangely bolted to the ruins of what had once been a threshing machine. It was Grandpa Ben's beer money, the scrap of his generation that he sold for ten dollars a pickup load.

6

     That weekend marked the first of many shooting lessons. My father came early on Saturday to pick me up. My mother was sleeping in and he told Grandma Vera not to wake her. He gave a sack of frozen rabbits to Grandma Vera. She took them without thanks, her eyes narrowed, a hard look on her face like the looks I'd seen her give the occasional Indians who came to her door in summers on their long hot walks across the plains to the religious rites at Bear Butte. Grandma was polite, giving them food and drink on the porch, generous with them always, save for that look that said they could never be anything but strangers, they could never be trusted or invited in. My father didn't seem to notice. I was on the run with my jacket, slamming out past them and jumping into the car, glad to get to go with him. We drove back toward town in the direction of the smoking piles of the town dump, my father putting his arm over my shoulders and asking me about school and if I had missed him.

The town dump was a deep gash of ravine that stretched more than a mile like an enormous earthquake fissure in the prairie east of town. As we walked along the ravine, the wind mixed the acrid smoke and ash with the sharp sweet odors of the willows and sagebrush. My father's cowboy boots sank unsteadily in the sand. The wind ruffled his hair into disheveled peaks. He turned his coat collar to his ears.

I followed several paces behind him. He kept his eyes fixed ahead, between the high gray walls of sand through mounds of blackened tin and old rusted scrap metal, the white, rust-streaked shells of gutted appliances jutting up like careless grave markers in the smoking landscape. Crushed car bodies that looked as if they had been driven off the short cliffs were scattered in sun-baked pieces half buried in the sand. Magpies swarmed over the carcass of a dog dumped off by the ruts of a dirt road ahead. The birds craned greedily over the bones with their sharp blue beaks. It looked as if the wind should sweep them out of the ravine as it did small squares of cardboard, bits of paper, shreds of rags sucked up and whirling over our heads. The magpies spread their blue-and-white wings out to keep their balance. They called to each other—a loud cawing like the sound of crows but more like laughter than the sound of crows.

"Why don't we shoot at the magpies?" I asked.

"We can't shoot the magpies," he answered. "It's against the law. All birds of carrion are protected. Besides, they seem like decent birds, for scavengers. They look like they're dressed in tuxedos. You know why I like them? Don't you know why?"

"No," I said.

"Don't you know why?" he asked again.

"I don't know," I said.

"If we shoot the magpies, what happens to the dog?"

"What happens to the dog?" I asked. "He's dead."

"He stinks," my father said. "The dog stinks if the magpies don't clean him away."

I watched them. They tore bits from the carcass, then they spread their wings and danced up like goblins in the wind.

"I don't like the magpies," I said.

"That may be," he answered. "But they're necessary. A part of the natural order to things. During the war, I was once in a situation where it was impossible to carry off our dead. We were pinned down and couldn't get to them. We were all grateful for birds like the magpies and other birds, huge vultures as big as eagles."

He grunted as he leaned over for a tin can that still had its colorful label. I followed along behind him, collecting cans.

"Germs," he said. "Germs something like the germs that gave you the chicken pox make the dog smell."

"The dog has the chicken pox?" I asked.

"No," he said, and laughed. "Something like the chicken pox." He spilled an armful of tin cans at my feet. "Go ahead and set up these cans. And would you be so noble as to stack some of them on top of the others?"

I picked up all the cans. I carried them to one wall of the ravine and stacked them on a knoll of sand in neat lines like so many files of tin soldiers waiting to be shot. I made pyramids of cans behind the files. I finished. I scrubbed the soot off my hands onto my jeans. I trotted back to where my father stood watching me, my tennis shoes kicking up small clouds of ash.

"Now stay behind me," he said. "Always at least five or six feet. Stay to one side and don't move around."

He waved a hand at me like the conductor of the school chorus. I followed the hand's instructions, moving behind him and to the side just far enough that he could still see me in his periphery. He took a large black pistol out of his coat pocket and snapped the clip in.

"This is the forty-five," he said. "It's going to be very heavy for you to hold. I'm not sure your arm is strong enough to shoot it accurately."

"I can shoot it," I said.

"Good," he said. "Very good. But let me warn you, it has one hell of a kick to it. You have to fight to keep this gun in your hand. Hold it like this"—he held the gun three inches from his nose—"and it'll give you a black eye. The forty-five is one of the most powerful pistols ever made. Look at the size of the bullet. Look. Anywhere it hits a man, anywhere—on his thumbnail, for God's sake—it'll knock him over. . . . Are you listening? Kurt?"

"Yes," I said.

"Once you shoot a man with the forty-five, he shouldn't get up again," he said. "The first rule is never to point this gun at anyone, not at *anyone*, unless you intend to shoot him. The only reason to use the forty-five is to kill a man," he said. "Do you understand?"

"Yes," I said.

"Are you sure?" he asked. "If a man with a gun threatens you or your mom, you'll pick up the forty-five and shoot him?"

I nodded.

"Good. Now I want you to watch me very carefully. I want you to watch how I shoot and try to do exactly as I do. . . . Are you ready?"

I nodded again. I watched him reach his left hand across to free the safety catch. The large black pistol balanced naturally in his hand. He turned and squarely faced the targets. He planted his feet in a wide stance. He crouched, testing the spring in his knees, the pistol stabbing out about level with his chest and gripped firmly with both hands. "You should learn to shoot like this," he said. "To make your own body small like this, by crouching. You'll be a small target in case the man coming at you has a gun."

The pistol seemed to hang in midair an instant before his hand squeezed the grip. A shot rang out loudly and echoed along the walls of the ravine. Magpies flew up all at once and screamed. He fired again. The gun jumped in his hands but he turned the force back downward smoothly and fired again. A red can shattered. It flew up high against the ravine wall, then clattered end over end back into the sand. With each shot, my father anchored his feet more firmly in the earth. His back tensed. I heard the dead whining of a ricochet and a tin can exploded in front of me, the green paper label springing off in a crumpled star. His pistol kicked back and down, back and down in precise rhythmic arcs as he shot it again and again. Files of tin soldiers jumped up and kicked away. Pyramids fell into heaps. Then a startling silence overtook us. I felt a painful ringing in my ears. My father still stood there tensed in his crouch position and ready to shoot again.

"How many!" he shouted through the ringing in my ears.

I jumped back. I couldn't answer.

"Goddamnit!" he shouted. "How many!"

I looked at my feet. I tried to hear how many gunshots by remembering. I looked slowly toward the empty shells scattered like bright coins on the ground. I moved my eyes quickly and tried to count the targets.

"Seven," I said.

"That's good," he said, lowering the pistol. "That's very good. I didn't even tell you to count them. Now remember that. You have to reload after seven shots."

My father took a long stride back and held the gun out toward me by the barrel. I took it from him, surprised by the weight. He pulled out a clip and showed me how to dump the empty one and reload. He showed me how to push new bullets into the spring-loaded slot of the empty clip. He reached over and freed the safety catch on the pistol, then stepped around behind me. I raised the gun, crouching, extending my arms which shook with the heavy weight I could barely hold out. The front post of the sights jerked up and back, wavering unsteadily across a line of bright cans as I tried to aim.

"Raise it up now," he said. "Make the target sit on the post."

I held my breath. The big gun shook and trembled. The front post swayed around like a sapling in the wind. I pulled the trigger and his pistol jumped right out of my hands.

7

Nothing happened. Whoever murdered my father's hares was never caught. His other fears were unjustified—there was little reason to expect that the eighty or so farmers out burning their crops should resort to violence. There was also no reason to expect such an action could have changed anything.

Sam Carlson decided to make up for a drop in turkey prices by an increase in volume. The Nowell-Safebuy geared up for its most active harvest season ever—six thousand turkeys a day slaughtered, plucked, processed, packed a dozen different ways. Most farmers on contract delivered. Sam even bought up birds from a hundred miles away to make up the difference. The streets filled with a comic harvest parade of turkeys driven in trucks or simply herded in on foot—tens of thousands of snowy White Holland hybrids strutting in vaguely martial formations. They were followed by their generals, farmers in billed caps and faded bluejeans who pushed them along with stockpoles and electric prods until they were safely contained in the wire compound of the Nowell-Safebuy yards.

The Tamblin-Hill grain elevator towered like a huge tombstone at the head of this town. It was lit up and booming day and night with truckloads of grain from surrounding fields. But it rained hard in August, just when the seed heads were ripe, knocking the kernels loose. The wheat that was lost added to an unseasonably high cost of grain. Times were hard. But according to the small farmers, times had always been hard. Doc Monahan treated his usual quota of minor burns, deep cuts and multiple fractures due to carelessness in the fields. He treated his usual quota of lacerations from the Nowell-Safebuy. Larry Foos fought off his recurring malaria as usual and worked double shifts repairing harvest machinery in states of constant breakdown. The municipal bar had some of its windows busted, as happened every harvest in the brawls of tired men letting out their frustrations. Where Main curved into the Baseline Road, the odor of the turkey yards thickened and all but condensed into a steam that wafted through town on sluggish summer winds. The harvest ended with the usual wild and drunken week-long party. A carnival came through and set up rides in a nearby field. Bright banners went up along Main and the permanent billboard with *Nowell Roundup Rodeo* by the highway was repainted and bordered with flags. The only exception that year was at the rodeo, where a range boy three-quarters Sioux named Dan Gooch took all the prizes. People looked forward to the next white man who could beat him.

We moved back into this house. Though a loaded forty-five was kept in a kitchen drawer, my father was no longer afraid of violence. More real fears began to have their effect on him. Because he was known to represent the Nowell-Safebuy in their case against Will Hartley and the others, he lost more than half his caseload. No farmer in this county would come to him. Even company workers who heard about his suits for vast damages from men around tavern tables, men who shared the union spirit of the Amalgamated Brotherhood of Butchers and Meat Workers, fulfilled their need for lawyers in Belle Fourche. My father's morning phone calls to his secretary left him depressed. He complained to Sam Carlson and raised his fees. The Nowell-Safebuy was willing to pay almost anything to win its case.

There was trouble in this house. They argued about money. My father slammed downstairs and locked himself in his study to work on the case. I was sometimes called in to fetch him things—a fresh pack of cigarettes, a beer, cups of coffee. He looked up from his books and squeezed me around the waist. "You can be anything you want to be," he said. "But God save you, don't be a lawyer. You'll have to look thieves, liars and petty cheats directly in the eye and come up with excuses for them. And other kinds of law require an inborn ability to turn a courtroom argument in on itself—like turning a shirt inside out—and make another lawyer sound like a fool." He stared ahead for a moment, thinking. "This case is a little different," he said. "This one's a question of willful intent. *Capisce?*" he asked, using a word he had picked up in the service during the war. I was eight years old. He must have known I didn't understand. I nodded to him that I did. "Will the court decide it's the company's intention to force unfair prices on its farmers? And is the destruction of crops without even pretending to pay back the company a fair remedy for farmers in trouble? Of course, none of these questions has any meaning if the contract is full of holes in the first place. That's where I come in. I'm going over every point. And in the end, the answer becomes who the judge turns out to be. That's something I refuse to worry about, since it's totally out of my hands," he said. He sucked deeply on his cigarette and let the smoke come out in a kind of sigh. He was worried again who the judge would be. "You go to bed now," he said. We hugged and kissed goodnight. "I'll see you in the morning."

I left him alone in his study, smoking. I don't know when it was he started sleeping in there. First one night, then another, then it was every night he slept on the couch. My mother used the Sears credit card and bought herself a portable TV for her bedroom. They argued about money. "What else do you want me to do!" she shouted. "You're down there all night hunched up like a monkey on a grindstone!"

Each night, she closed the door to their room and turned on her TV. She lay in bed and watched, drinking. Through the plaster walls of my bedroom, I heard the sound of her TV like a far-off beating of drums. She lay awake long after her programs had turned to snow.

My father argued his case before Judge William "Link" Smith at the district court in Belle Fourche. Counterargument was presented the following morning, in front of Will Hartley and the others named in the suit. It was the end of October. The long wait began. It would take weeks before Judge Smith could write his decision. With nothing to work on and very few private cases, the Nowell-Safebuy fee wasn't enough even during the weeks of waiting and my father's mood grew desperate. He cut his secretary to one day a week. He made it clear he was running the family savings into the ground just paying for this house, the two cars, his office, all the food, the charge accounts, my mother's TV, everything. It seems most families have the same argument and exist at times as terrified hostages of their incomes. Even happy families are broken. Christmas was just around the corner. They grew near to hysteria over money and I remember my mother shouting at him over a bicycle I had picked out in the Sears Christmas catalogue. He had told her no, it was too expensive. But it wasn't the bicycle between them.

"You can ruin his life!" she screamed. "But I'm not going to let you ruin his Christmas!"

"I have needs too!" he shouted.

"Shut up!" she screamed. "He'll hear us!"

"Then I'll get out," he said. "I'll take care of my needs elsewhere."

"I don't want you out, I want a divorce!" she shouted. "A divorce!"

Glass shattered. I ran to the head of the stairs, my heart pounding. He was on his way to the front door. She caught up with him and grabbed his arm, pulling him around.

"Where are you going?" she said in a changed voice. He shoved her aside. She balled up a fist and hit him in the face.

"Goddamnit!" he shouted. As she was coming at him again, he pushed out the heel of his hand and bloodied her nose. She fell to the floor in the hallway. My father slammed out the door and to his station wagon. He drove off in the middle of the night.

After he had gone, I watched her stand slowly up with her head back, using the bunched-up hem of her nightgown to stop the bleeding. I started down the stairs to help. "Don't you ever get to bed?" she screamed.

I stopped in my tracks. I watched her go into the living room to the liquor cabinet. The bottles were gone or all empty there but a tall green bottle of white vermouth. She took the bottle of vermouth into the kitchen. I heard her dialing the telephone. She dialed the municipal saloon and talked to Dolores Moss, asking if my father was there. Then she dialed the Park Motel on the highway to Belle Fourche. She kept dialing the phone, leaving messages for my father to call her at every bar and motel in Belle Fourche, then on the road from Belle Fourche to Sturgis, to Rapid City, to Hot Springs, clear across the state line on into Cheyenne. Then she started to cry. She sat down on the kitchen floor with her bottle of vermouth, just under the phone, and cried until dawn.

Christmas was just around the corner. My father came home late the next day, hung over and with a bouquet of flowers. They didn't fight much for several weeks. One or two nights, he even slept with her upstairs. But my father's mood grew darker, gloomier. We all managed to ride up into the hills and cut a Christmas tree. We decorated the tree, my father stringing the lights and my mother and I doing the rest as he stared out the front window at a falling snow. "Saint Nick'll be here before morning!" she said, happily. She and my father exchanged looks. She frowned at him. She pushed me upstairs to bed and kissed me goodnight, lying in bed holding me a long time before I pretended to fall asleep.

She rose quietly and went downstairs. I listened to the sharp crackle of wrapping paper as packages were brought out of closets. I heard the clicking of an English bicycle as it rolled across the living room. I closed my eyes. Something happened: a harsh word from downstairs—I don't know. Then I heard my mother's TV drumming on the walls. I got up and sneaked into the upstairs hall. The lights were on in the living room, and by the cigarette smoke drifting through the wide arch to the foot of the stairs, I knew my father was still sitting there. At the foot of the stairs, I looked into the living room. He was sitting on the couch holding his forty-five with both hands. He pushed the barrel into his mouth. He saw me and quickly hid the gun in a space between the couch cushions.

"Ho, ho, ho," he said, drunkenly. "S'a nice bike, huh?"

I was crying. He knew why. My mother's bedroom was just over the living room, just over his head. Boards creaked as she crossed her room. The sound of her TV came through the ceiling. Suddenly, my father pulled the gun out from under the couch cushions and pointed it at the ceiling, at her noise. He pulled the trigger. He fired once more, twice, then again and again and again and again as I rushed upstairs screaming, *"No no no no no!"* I threw open my mother's door. She was on the phone in her bedroom, shouting into the receiver: "He's trying to kill us! Help! Please help me!"

I saw the sharp splinters of a pattern of holes through the shiny wood floor. I looked up. Dust was still in the air. There were holes in the ceiling, clear through the roof for all I knew.

"Ho, ho, ho," I heard my father downstairs. He laughed.

"No! Don't go down there!" she screamed. "Kurt! Kurt!"

At the foot of the stairs, I looked into the living room. My father was sitting on the couch, the pistol aimed at his temple. He looked at me, looked me directly in the eye. He pulled the trigger. The empty chamber clicked.

"Merry Christmas," he said.

He grabbed up a jacket and was out the front door before Deputy Perez arrived in the patrol car, the siren wailing down the street. The deputy rushed in and calmed my mother. He looked at the holes in the living room ceiling and in the floor and ceiling of her room. He wrote out a report. He spent the rest of the night sitting in the patrol car in front of our house in case my father came home.

But he didn't come home. In the morning, my mother gathered all my gifts but the bicycle and took them to the old second car. We left my father's few simple gifts sitting alone under the tree. We spent Christmas at my grandfather's farm. We opened gifts. I helped him with chores in a cold wet snow. Over dinner, my mother told her parents her decision. "We're getting a divorce," she said. She looked across the table at me with a firmness in her expression. "A divorce," she said directly to me.

"Well, I hate to say it," said Grandpa Ben. "But, Petie, I never did think he was the right one for you."

I looked at Grandpa Ben through the partly dissected carcass of Christmas turkey. I started to cry.

"You hush up now," he said. "I'm going to make a farmer out of you."

"Just leave that boy alone!" snapped Grandma Vera.

"We're not staying here," my mother said just loud enough to silence them. "We'll stay at the house until everything's settled."

We returned home three days later. My father's gifts were gone from under the tree. I wheeled the bicycle into the garage, telling my mother there was too much snow on the ground to ride it. And I never did ride it, not even once. I had the ability to forget it was ever there, leaving it stand in a corner of the garage and serve as a rusting framework for cobwebs the rest of its life.

I didn't see my father for weeks. Then one afternoon in January, he phoned. He told my mother to get out of the house for a few hours. I stayed behind. He arrived with a station wagon full of grocery boxes. I helped him go through his study, packing up his books, his antique rifles, his Civil War swords, his plaques, his war medals, his photographs in uniform. He left the photo of his wedding stand alone on a tall empty shelf. I followed him upstairs to the guest room, where my mother had moved his clothes. He packed several suits, shirts, ties, socks, his shaving kit and other items into a large suitcase. It was heavy. He let me help him carry it down the stairs. Then I helped him carry the grocery boxes of books out to his station wagon, packing everything in until it was jammed so full we had to tie several boxes to a rack on the roof under a tarp that was too small to keep them dry. The time came for him to leave. He hugged me, crushing me against him. There were tears in his eyes. "I'm sorry," he said. "We just never got along. It has nothing to do with you," he said. "I just pray God we'll both stop hurting you now."

He climbed into the driver's seat and started the engine. He rolled down the window. He made a gesture that I should lean my head in and he grabbed me strongly behind the neck and kissed me again. "You'll stay with me summers," he said. "I'll phone every Sunday. Don't you worry, you hear? Someday, you'll even come live with me."

He let me go. I watched him back down the driveway and turn off down the street, thinking I would never see him again.

A few days ago, I found a metal box in the closet of his study. She must have shoved it into a corner of the top shelf after he left it behind. The box was locked, but the catch sprang easily with a screwdriver. Inside were mainly documents, papers once important but lost in time: his marriage license, his certificate to practice law in this state, the titles to cars I couldn't remember he owned, an expired passport and savings book, and along with them, in a legal-sized plain brown envelope, was the written decision of a judge. The decision was dated December 17 of that year, before that Christmas. I knew a long time ago my father had lost his case and his job. But I never knew exactly when. All that mattered was that he was relocated in Colorado, I could visit him summers, and he sounded happy enough on the phone. Neither of my parents spoke much about what had happened.

Maybe some of the sense to these events can be found in the pages of the court decision. After agreeing with my father's arguments for a few paragraphs, Judge Smith wrote: *The reason I shall decide instead for the defendants is found in the contract itself. I think it is too hard a bargain and too one-sided an agreement to entitle the plaintiff to relief in a court of conscience. For each individual grower, the agreement is made by filling in names, quantity and price on a printed form furnished by the buyer. This form has obviously been drawn up by skillful draftsmen solely with the buyer's interest in mind.*

The judge goes on to state that it was unfair for the Nowell-Safebuy to reserve the right to refuse any turkeys it wished without remedy for the grower. It also cites a paragraph in the turkey contracts that provides liquidated damages for Nowell-Safebuy in case of breach of contract without granting similar rights to the growers. The judge wrote of paragraph nine of the contract: *It will be noted that Nowell-Safebuy is excused from accepting turkeys under certain circumstances. But even under such circumstances the grower, while he cannot say Nowell-Safebuy is liable for failure to accept his turkeys at time of delivery, is not permitted to sell them elsewhere until Nowell-Safebuy agrees. This is the kind of provision I think akin to the idiom "carrying a good joke too far." What the grower may do with his product under the circumstances set out is not clear. He has covenanted not to store his crop anywhere except on his own farm and not to sell to anyone else. This provision establishes the defendants' claim that Nowell-Safebuy has undue bargaining power to set prices on the products it buys and undue power to depress prices in a regional market it virtually controls.*

I am not suggesting any excuse for the growers in this case, who have deliberately broken an agreement entered into with Nowell-Safebuy. I do think, however, that a party who has offered and succeeded in getting an agreement as tough as this one is should not come to a chancellor and ask court help in the enforcement of its terms. That equity does not enforce unconscionable bargains is too well established a legal principle to require elaborate citation.

This disposition of the problem makes unnecessary any further discussion of the separate liability of the defendants.

The Nowell-Safebuy suit for specific performance is herewith denied.

I don't believe a child can fairly judge his parents. There are so many truths to their stories that we will never know. Conscience comes down naturally from them. At the very least we carry them with us in our genes. They make laws for us, not us for them. And we follow those laws like a duty, despite ourselves, with little choice but to honor them or let them fall.

8

The turkey plant shut down. It didn't happen in a single day or month but over a period of two years, with steadily increasing expenses combined with low prices and declining volumes. The Nowell-Safebuy completely restructured its system of farms. The logical extreme of vertical integration was direct ownership of the land. When the smoke finally cleared from the

N.F.O. protests and the violent upheavals in local farm credit during hard times for farmers, the Nowell-Safebuy began to buy land. It was a slow process. For example, the Reary farm was overextended. Ben Reary couldn't get the First Bank of Belle Fourche to extend his loans or to refinance, couldn't get president David Whitcomb to give him what farmers called the guts and hide loan, "the loan it takes the banker a barrowload of guts to give and everyone involved stands to lose his hide."

Sam Carlson made a personal visit to Ben Reary's farm. He inspected the long steel outbuildings in which Ben housed ten thousand White Holland hybrid turkeys in tier upon tier of wire cages. He watched Ben push the buttons on his new Harvestore silo, like a huge thermos bottle standing between his turkey barns, which let loose its measured doses of dry, vacuum-packed feed with a powerful inrush of air. The feed moved out along mechanical troughs, corn spilling like yellow rain down long gutterways. At the first loud *whoosh* of the silo and the humming of the electric augers that moved their feed, ten thousand turkeys stood up in their cages. They pranced a little, shook out their wings. A call rose among them, a single gobbling cry quickly joined by another and another until as if by that one lone command, the entire flock joined in with a deafening shriek. Turkeys rushed forward in their tiny cells, some in excitement slamming hard against the wire. Clouds of white feathers drifted across the barn like an exotic snow. Beaks clattering in the metal troughs, ten thousand bald red heads reached out and stuffed themselves.

Ben Reary showed off his cornfields—four hundred acres of level gumbo that produced more than enough to pack his silo, more than enough even to sell locally to smaller growers. He showed off his tractor, as big as a small house, his discs and harrows and seeders as wide as a two-lane highway, which were costing him thousands of dollars per quarter just in interest. Sam Carlson produced a sheaf of papers, dozens of forms, prospectuses, statistical graphs, even a health insurance plan. He made an offer to Ben Reary to pay off all his loans, buy his turkeys and his barns, his silo, his tractor, everything. Ben would get several thousand for himself to count as equity for the work of two generations. And he could still live on in his new house, could still work the land, still wake up every morning to punch the buttons on his Harvestore silo controls and feed his birds. Sam would hire him as "unit farm manager" to work turkeys for the Nowell-Safebuy on a steady salary, just like the plant workers in town. The Nowell-Safebuy would take over all obligations. It would also assume direct ownership of the land.

The Reary family didn't know what to do. Ben Reary placed frantic ads in newspapers clear to Cheyenne and listed his place for sale with a half dozen realtors. But in such hard times, no one wanted to invest in raising turkeys. He finally had to accept Sam Carlson's offer. He sold his farm. So did Jake Ballock, the Bosserds, the Hinkles too, eventually. Even Pearly Green and his kids finally sold out to the Nowell-Safebuy, though they didn't agree to work for them.

That next harvest, Ben Reary and many other small farmers raised turkeys for wages. It was one of the smallest harvests many could remember; slightly less than eight hundred thousand turkeys were hatched, stuffed with grain, trucked to town, butchered, packed, frozen, shipped out of town again. Ben Reary climbed back into his empty Nowell-Safebuy stock truck, which still echoed with the sound of turkeys. He leaned forward over the wheel, sweating, silent. His wife, Connie, sat next to him. He reached into his shirt pocket and handed her the check. She slowly unfolded that check with a tired glance. She pressed her lips with the same determination she had always had, would have as long as she lived—the same ability to forget her dreams for now and make her man as proud as she could of what little was there. In prior hard years, they did their best to hang on to the land; that was most important. They paid what bills they could and made plans for the coming year, that better year they all expected, had to expect in order to raise spirit enough to keep working through snowbound winter months overhauling in preparation for spring. But Sam Carlson's program was working. They didn't own the land anymore.

Sam Carlson should have known. He should have been aware of the Bates Rubber Company's fiasco in northwest Colorado. Bates bought up hundreds of thousands of acres of wheat and grazing land, pumping millions of investment dollars into the most modern cattle feeders, into a fleet of tractors powerful enough to level mountains and into a new crossbreed of cattle that could grow to weights of up to two thousand pounds in eighteen months with the aid of growth hormones. Everything was beautifully described in color brochures printed by the thousands for stockbrokerage firms in the East, including graphed projections of vast profits symbolically represented to the potential investor by line drawings of a series of ever fatter steers growing across the page.

But Bates couldn't find enough workers willing to sacrifice for the land. It had to hire one and a half times as many unit farm managers as there had once been family farmers, with production remaining just about the same. Bates discovered after intensive sociological research that family farmers are willing to work eighteen hours a day if need be and not just for money, but to hold on to the land. There is an immortality given to the earth, a sense of expansive dream passed from immigrant homesteader through generation after generation of his children in a self-perpetuating vision of the meaning of freedom and wealth. Unit farm managers punched their time clocks after eight hours and drove home. Production dropped. It wasn't long before the Bates Land & Cattle Company began losing millions.

Leading agrieconomists in the East, most of them men who had never so much as once experienced the realities of scraping barnyard manure off their boots, suddenly stopped talking about the benefits of vertical integration. They sat discoursing around a brand-new topic called ''farm unit management problems.'' And the same thing happened here. Or almost the same. It wasn't long before even the Nowell-Safebuy began losing money.

The turkey plant slowed down, laying off two hundred workers. People hung on through the winter, optimistically talking of future recovery. Times grew harder. It was the year my mother's divorce papers finally came, her settlement being the house and everything in it, the second car, and a small monthly check for my support. She made plans to sell the house. A half dozen real estate agents poked at the rafters with screwdrivers, clucked their tongues at the patchwork and spackling on the floor and ceiling of my mother's bedroom. She had plans to sell the house and move us both to California where her childhood friend Rae Ott lived, granddaughter to the Reverend and Beatrice Ott. It was a place near the ocean. My mother had never seen an ocean. But times were hard and the offers that came in for the house weren't half of what she expected. She decided to hold out for better times. And as a year passed, she might have grown wise enough to sell the house for any offer she could get before the turkey plant completely shut down. We might have lived in California. But then my grandfather died.

Grandpa Ben died suddenly one night. He simply fell back gasping. He called for his wife, his voice slurred, his tongue thick. They had just come home from an annual celebration—that one night each year when they unfailingly left whatever kids and problems behind for a dinner out to commemorate the first time Ben had carried a lariat rope ten miles across the snow-covered plains from his homestead to the Norman place. As the story goes, the Norman family house was small, constructed so that if the five Norman girls had in mind to do some proper courting, they had to lower themselves through a trapdoor, climb down a rickety ladder into the living room, then sneak out past their parents sleeping there. Old man Norman sometimes scattered crumpled newspapers on the floor to make sure there would be enough noise to wake him.

Grandpa Ben used a soft lariat rope to get his Vera down out of her high window, sometime after the moon had paled. He crept around out there a long time in the fierce winter winds. He carried lumps of meat to bait the dogs. It wasn't long before Ben and Vera had a small fire going in the Norman harness shop, way off behind the barn. This went on night after night for several weeks before they were married. They had a proper wedding in a church. But they always celebrated their anniversary according to the date of that first cold winter night when Ben had stood in the backyard, the dogs whining and simpering as he jumped around half frozen, lariat rope in hand. On that anniversary, Ben and Vera left the farm, drove to Cheyenne, had a dinner out and spent the night at a motel. The afternoon after their last anniversary, Ben and Vera pulled in at home with Ben grumbling for some unknown petty reason or, as Vera thought, because he had such a hangover from the night before. Ben went on about his chores, taking care of a few chickens, his two horses, the few beef cattle he kept for family use, mending a stretch of fence between the house and old hayfield that was now being rented out for pasture. At supper, Vera noticed Ben had a fierce headache and that he was so thick-tongued it was hard for him to eat or speak. But she thought he must have been drinking a little to chase his hangover away. Later that evening, he fell back dead of stroke in the living room.

"Don't tell me nothing," my grandmother said after we arrived late that evening. There were no tears, no evident signs of grief. Only the harshness in her voice let on how pierced she was by death. "No. Don't tell me nothing," she said. "He did what he could. He worked like the hammers of hell. After we lost the boys, he just did what he could to get by. He left this place. That's what he left. And there won't be much left of that once the neighbors finish. That new pump in the barn'll likely be gone before morning. Somebody'll just drive on up in an hour or so and take it. Oh, they'll offer me something. A few dollars. But if we wasn't sitting in this house right now, you can bet they'd be going over the very chair I'm sitting on. . . ."

"Don't let 'em, Mama," my mother said. "You don't have to let them."

"You hush up now," said Grandma Vera. "You're the one who's going off to Florida."

"California," my mother said.

"One of them sunshine states," said Grandma Vera. "It don't matter much which one."

"But, Mama . . ."

"Don't you tell me nothing," Grandma said. "Ben and me used

to do it too. I remember when Simon Lisky died. Never knew the news of a death to move so fast. Almost everybody beat us to it. But Ben still picked himself up a rifle and some horse harness at the funeral. He paid the widow a couple of dollars. Then when it came to me going through that dead man's house, no matter what I knew about the pretty lamps Simon had, no matter how much Ben kept telling me to get in there and bring us out something, I just stood there and watched them other women. They jumped on widow Lisky's personal belongings like a flock of crows. I never seen nothing like it. That old woman just sitting there letting them do it because she knew the farm would be sold for a song and she was too feeble to go anywhere but a rest home. So she just gave her house away. There was a lot of things in there I could have had, too. But all I took was one of Simon's dogs. Simon always liked his dogs. So I fed that one better than the rest.''

My mother was sitting on the floor in front of Grandma Vera's chair. My mother leaned her head on Grandma's lap. Grandma stroked my mother's hair. After a few pets like that from Grandma's hand it was as if an inner strength my mother had kept balled up inside suddenly weakened. She broke down crying in Grandma's lap. ''Now I ain't saying I blame anybody,'' Grandma said. ''The men can come take anything they please, pay me anything they want. Just don't you let them touch this house. Just because your papa's gone, that don't mean they can have what belongs to me. I plan to stay on here. That's what I decided. Your papa would have liked me to turn the farm over to you right now. But, honey, I don't see why I should. You'd likely sell it out from under me or worse. Worse is you might want to move out here yourself. And I just don't want to see you with that kind of hard work and endless days. So I'm going to stay on here until the barn blows down. Nobody's going to farm this place. Nobody's going to put a hand to it until I'm gone. I'll put affairs in order, then just sit right here until I can watch out the window and see this place look just like it did when Ben first gave it to me. This place is mine until I'm gone. Then you'll get your chance,'' Grandma Vera said, still stroking my mother's hair, a gentle bitterness in her voice that made my mother raise her head and look. "You can come take anything you get a hold on," Grandma said, "when that happens."

My mother looked at me as if I could help somehow. I didn't know what to say. The expression on my mother's face suddenly changed. She returned Grandma Vera's bitter tone of voice. "Just don't you dare let the neighbors see him," she said. "I don't care what your side's tradition is. You know he didn't want a viewing. He told me once that if you tried to give him a viewing, he'd sit up howling drunk in his coffin."

"He's my husband," Grandma Vera said. "I can do whatever I want with him."

"We'll see about that," my mother said.

"It's already been seen to," Grandma answered. "It's done by now."

We buried my grandfather two days later, embalmed and in a fancy blue metal casket that cost every dime in Grandma's savings account. "He never would have stood for this," my mother said even as she helped Grandma clean Grandpa's brown wool suit. My contribution was to polish Grandpa's good black stovepipe boots with embroidery from Mexico. Then I waited in the car parked in front of the Millis mortuary as the two of them went into what Darwin Millis called his "slumber room" to dress Grandpa for his funeral. There was a last-minute argument with Darwin about whether he was legally allowed to bury Grandpa in the old-fashioned way—on his own land instead of in a licensed cemetery. My mother spent the next day driving back and forth from one county office to another to get all the new paperwork done, mountains of forms to sign indicating exactly where the private plot would be in relation to future county development plans, hundreds of dollars in fees required even then. With the exception of a few others, including my Grandma Vera's, it was one of the last such burials ever permitted in this state. The upshot was that even if a man owned ten thousand acres of the remotest wilderness, he could do anything he wanted or could afford to do but have himself buried on it.

The funeral was on Grandpa's farm. There was some last-minute tension about whether all the necessary forms were done in time, but finally the maroon hearse from the Millis mortuary in town drove Grandpa back home in his coffin. Pearly Cyrus Green, Will Hartley, Jim Fuller, Charlie Gooch and his son Dan, friends of my Grandpa's even though they were both mostly Indian, and Jim Claypool served as pallbearers. They carried Grandpa's coffin into the living room and set it up on painted sawhorses. Then they opened the lid.

Grandpa Ben looked dipped in wax. Someone had drawn dark lines around his eyes. His cheeks and lips were red. His hands were twisted around a cluster of red and white carnations, with one finger rudely projecting out of control, pointing toward his viewers. The expression on his face looked angry. He looked to me like he wanted to sit up and cuss out everyone in the room. A crowd gathered in front of him, dark suits and white shirts making them look like magpies among the colorful funeral wreaths, hands still compulsively brushing snow off clothes and hats as if to be neat and dry was a form of security against death. My mother stood on with a fragile sense of time and place, looking shocked, uprooted but for the support she gave her mother, who leaned against her arm. There came a moment when Reverend Ott in his white robes stood in front of us. He spread his arms like wings. Even the sound of weeping fell back across the room like a soft diminishing wind until it became a sound so frail and piercing it was almost inhuman, a sound like foxes whistling in the distance. We knelt down on Reverend Ott's signal. He surveyed us with an evident sense of personal importance, as if he was pleased somehow despite this death by his stewardship of a tribe again confronted by the higher realities. He slowly found a passage in the notes for his service and began to read the words as if they were in the prayerbook: "Lord, we shall return to greet each other without our burdens. We shall greet each other without our problems, our cares, our sins. Even without the guiding hand of the church, there is a place for all good men in heaven. . . ."

The Reverend Ott looked out over us as he prayed. Almost

everyone prayed with him. And everyone knew what he was saying, knew that my Grandpa Ben hadn't set foot in a church since my mother's wedding.

Reverend Ott finished his prayer. Everyone stood. People began to file by Grandpa in his coffin. Grandma Vera reached out and touched two fingers to his lips. My mother was crying. I was crying too, and I didn't want to look at Grandpa again. I went into the bathroom and locked the door. I sat on the stool and cried for the times I wouldn't see him, for the times I had had the chance to please him and did not.

Will, Jim, Pearly, Charlie Gooch and the others picked up Grandpa's coffin. Pearly passed a pint bottle of something to keep them warm. Then they carried the coffin out and down the porch steps, straining under its weight nearly two hundred yards through a fresh dusting of snow to a lone cottonwood behind the barn. Reverend Ott walked close behind them, in front of my mother, my Grandma and me, the crowd following. The pallbearers set the coffin down beside a deep grave they had dug the day before by the cottonwood, using pickaxes to break through the first layer of frozen ground.

Reverend Ott read the funeral service from the Bible. Everyone rose. They watched Pearly and the others lower the coffin into the ground. And even as my Grandma Vera threw handfuls of earth over her husband, even as we waited there a minute in silence while she said goodbye, the looting had begun. The homeplace suddenly became the scene of a kind of joyous farm auction with very little money and Pearly acting as a kind of auctioneer, taking haphazard bids, not letting things go for nothing but not bidding them up too high, either, Eunice Fuller following along behind him writing prices down in a notebook. Men scrambled this way and that through the sheds and coops, pawing through the barn and shop to pick up whatever they could find—old harness, plowblades, mower and rake teeth, buckets, tools, car and tractor parts. An old man fell to the ground with two huge tires over his shoulders. Women and children chased after random chickens for a quarter apiece, stuffing them in old grain sacks and cardboard boxes. Jim Fuller, quickly away from the gravesite, was already trying to get Grandpa Ben's old stubborn goat around the neck with a rope. In the corral, a group of range boys was laughing and hooting, one of them beating on a pan with a spoon, taunting Grandpa Ben's two hard-mouthed geldings, which were smart enough to kick around devilishly to discourage any easy approach. After a while, whoever could stay on them would take them home for forty dollars a head. As I walked toward the house with my mother and Grandma Vera, everyone was busy around us, everyone with an armload of something: Ben Hogan's fishing poles, his milking stools, his shotgun, even the old, worn-out pad from his tractor seat. Bits and pieces of everything my grandfather had ever built or worked on in his life were soon piled in front of the cars and pickups parked haphazardly in front of the house.

My grandmother went into the house to join the women setting out a buffet. My mother and I stayed outside, watching.

"Why are they taking everything?" I asked.

"If your grandpa were here today, he'd probably join them," my mother said. "He was always one for looting funerals. He was the kind who made a party out of the occasion."

"But, Mom," I said. "Don't you want any of Grandpa's stuff?"

"It's not mine to take," my mother said. "It's Grandma's now."

"But why, Mom?"

"Look. When Grandma dies, God forbid, this farm will be ours. We'll probably sell it. That's what everyone else is doing. So when the neighbors see a place that's going to be sold after a funeral, or one that's bound to sit idle, they come for things. That's the way they do it. And it's better this way. It's better than letting all this stuff sit around and rot. It's better the neighbors, your Grandpa's friends, end up with something."

As my mother was walking, she was suddenly knocked into by a man with a heavy load. She lost her footing and fell in the snow.

"Hey!" I shouted after the man. I helped my mother to her feet. I watched the man struggling to get from the barn door to his pickup with a load of tack and harness. He carried so much of it over his arms, head and shoulders that he looked about two feet taller than he should, a kind of weird giant with a bale of tangled leather for his head. He must hardly have been able to see in front of him.

"Damn you, Don Hinkle!" my mother shouted. Don Hinkle didn't turn to look in our direction. He kept right on going, a tangle of old leather traces dragging through the snow behind him.

My mother might have left him go at that, left that old man alone with his treasures if she hadn't seen it: "My bridle," she said. She turned to me. "He has my bridle! Don!" she called out to him. Don Hinkle didn't even break his stride. "Just you wait here a minute," she said. "Don!" she shouted again, louder. She had to run to catch up with him.

"Don, you've got something of mine in there," she said.

Don Hinkle turned. He nearly dropped his load, buckling under the weight, his face sweating, steaming.

"Oh, what a terrible thing," he said, "a terrible, terrible thing." He made an effort to shake his head in condolence under a heavy horse collar. "It's just plain grieving to me," he said. "A terrible, terrible thing now, Marge. . . ."

"Don, you've got something that belongs to me in there."

The man appeared to understand well enough. He smiled, showing the few brown teeth left in his mouth.

"Well, I don't know as I do," he said. "Ben already give all this here to me. Why, just last week it was! We was sitting in his shop. Just last week he said Don, Don, he said, when I'm gone, you go on and take all that old harness in there. Give Vera twenty bucks."

"I don't care about the harness," she said. "You can have all the harness you want and you know it. But you can't go taking my bridle."

Don Hinkle looked nervously away, out across the frozen meadows. He was staggering, some determined force still drawing him a few steps closer to his pickup truck.

"Marge, just last week it was," he said. "He said Don, Don, when I'm gone, you go on and take all that old harness *and* that bridle in there. Ain't much good left to it anyhow."

"You're lying," my mother said. "You've got my bridle and you know it's mine. I didn't ride with it much. I was never much of one for horses. But as I recall, the times I did ride it was over to your place to visit Carol and you used to admire that bridle. Now, Don, no hard feelings. I'll be grateful you found it for me."

"Well, I did find it in there," said the man with finality. He looked as if he was going to make a fight of this at best. "Ben gave that bridle to me just last week!"

Don Hinkle nodded his head once as if that was the end of it for him. He turned and started back up the lane, walking faster now despite his burden. I looked around somewhat bewildered, as if there would be anyone disposed to help us. The looting was on. A whirlwind of scavengers was busy pulling my family's homeplace apart with amazing efficiency. Men tottered in and out of the ramshackle buildings as if they owned them, arms loaded, bags and pockets bulging. A group was teamed up and straining at an old orange tractor with starting problems. Another, larger group was perched like a covey of gnarled old doves on the corral fence. There was a kind of rodeo in the corral, each of those old boys taking his turn with one of Grandpa's cut-proud geldings out there, stamping, panicked, the white showing around his eyes at every approach. Pearly Green sat with the others up there and watched, passing a bottle.

Near the corral, I saw the rusted end of a piece of pipe sticking up out of the snow. I ran over to it. I wrenched it up, the snow crust breaking like white glass. I was out of my head. But the pipe was too long to swing when I pulled it up.

"Hey!" I shouted to the men on the corral fence. I waved a hand toward Don Hinkle. "Somebody help me stop him!"

No one knew what I meant. Pearly Green raised his pint bottle at me like he was offering a drink.

"Help me!" I shouted.

"It's all right, Kurt!" my mother called out. "It's all right now."

I looked at her. Her face was severe, something showing in it that I had never seen before—like the faces of old tintypes of my family where the inflexible cast to the mouth, the deep lines around harsh, distant eyes tell of hardship, scant food, the deaths of children.

Don Hinkle's boots scuffed through the snow. One of his large brown hands slowly began to work its way into the tangled heap of harness he carried, a good deal of it dragging behind him in the snow, horse bells and buckles jangling like a childhood promise of a sleighride. Strap by strap, rein by rein, I watched that hand shaking something free. A dark hash of bridle dropped off into the snow. He kept right on going, not looking back, not even once.

My mother picked up her bridle. She straightened it out in her hands, dried it tenderly on her coat. It was a work of remarkable beauty, brown and white horsehair braided into a diamond pattern, the reins at least six feet long, fluted Spanish silver bells woven into the cheek straps and two large, dark green onyx jewels set into silver dollars where the headband joined that part that fastened behind a horse's ears. Suddenly, my mother turned and hugged me, squeezing so tight I couldn't breathe. I held her back, held her up, helpless to her grief.

Don Hinkle unloaded the harness in his truck. When he was finished, he looked toward us quickly once, then quickly away. He climbed into his truck and started the engine. He backed around in a neat circle, truck chains whistling on the ice. He stopped in front of the house. He honked his horn several times. His wife soon came out and traded words with him. He said something to her with an ugly expression on his face. She nodded at him once. She hurried back into the house for her things. Then she climbed into the truck with him and they drove off up the lane.

I helped my mother through the yard gate, stepping carefully along the slick, icy path. Inside the house, the women had already laid out buffet dishes, candles glowing over the food, the windows filled with warm blue abstractions of steam.

"You all O.K. there?" Pearly Green called out behind us. I nodded in answer to him and he grinned, red-faced, filled with a kind of celebration I would never understand. We waited for him. We joined him up the steps and into the house.

All that afternoon, through the slow movement of a kind of

disordered wake, that gathering of cowboys, I couldn't keep from thinking of Don Hinkle. My mother wrapped up her bridle and tucked it neatly away in her suitcase. She held a kind of humble court in the living room, relaxed more now and greeting each guest, really visiting with many of them for the first time since she had married and moved to town. She did a lot of talking with Dan Gooch, a tall, young-looking Indian. I didn't like the way she was talking with him. I mixed through the crowd, a small stranger shaking hands and explaining who I was when asked. Most men stepped back from me a little when I told them my name, or at least the ones who didn't know the family history. There was something in the way they looked at me. They hadn't forgotten what my father had done or whom he had worked for. Then everyone began moving down the buffet line and dishing up a plate.

I wasn't hungry anyway. I went outside. The short winter day was almost gone, an aura of violet over the horizon. I walked out toward the barn, all the doors left open wide and creaking in the light breeze. In the barn, everything was overturned, everything was stripped from the rusty spikes driven into the beams as hangers. I looked out the half gate into the corral. There was a horse there, all alone. He pawed with one front hoof at the frozen ground. He sagged a little, hung his head low. No one had been able to stay on him. Or no one wanted to take him home.

I found the hay bales in the loft. I pushed a bale out the loft door and it fell to the earth in the corral, bounced once and broke open. My grandfather's gelding smelled it and nickered, breath steaming out his nostrils. He looked tired. His hooves lifted slowly in the muddy, frozen ground. He looked up at me, then looked at the hay. He didn't know what to make of me. He took a short step closer. Then he threw his head up suddenly, pawing at the ground. He lifted his head and snorted at me. I stepped back into the darkness. I crouched there quietly in the hay and listened to the dry rustle of his eating.

I wondered what Don Hinkle would do with all the harness he'd taken. He didn't have a team anymore. Then I imagined him hanging it around his farmhouse as decoration, bits and pieces of a full six-horse hitch in the living room, part of a sulky rig complete with scattered implements in one corner of the dining room as there were antique implements arranged around my grand-father's house, displayed like so many exhibits in a museum. I imagined a set of horse collars and hames hung over the heating stove. I thought of bell straps hung up so they would jangle in a summer breeze. In my mind, I heard an old man's voice spinning tales and outright lies about that harness, stories of just how it was when he was a young man out there horse farming, *gee hawing* and slogging through sod-covered earth sowing homestead wheat with that very same tack hanging right there on his walls. And sometime that evening, with the fatiguing release of consciousness brought on by the presence of death, I thought I found the sense. Ownership was not to be confused with heritage. That harness would hang for years as decoration, until Don Hinkle eventually sold his farm or died. Then it would all be stolen back again from him.

9

That spring, the turkey plant began the last phase of a complete shutdown. Our house wasn't selling. And my mother had something else troubling her aside from parceling out the few hundred dollars a month for us to live on. "I've got to get Grandma to sign a will," she said. "We can't go off to California until I've done that much. We just can't throw it all away."

She started to make appointment after appointment with a law-yer in Belle Fourche to go out and visit Grandma Vera with various drafts of a last will and testament that Grandma was hesitant to sign. They got as far as putting the pen in her hand. Then she said no, all the terms had to be changed, an anxiety starting to become clear in these sessions that to Grandma Vera it was as if signing the farm away in a will was signing away her own hold on life. It didn't make sense. She didn't want my mom and me to move out to the farm. Then again, she didn't want us moving thousands of miles to California, either. I was usually in school when my mother was out at the farm hashing things over, not even sure how she was going to pay the mounting lawyer's fees. Or I was over at crazy Anita's or at Beatrice Ott's house being babysat over my objections because Grandma Vera refused to discuss her business in front of a child. My mother came to pick me up late in the afternoon, frustrated.

"When are we moving?" I asked.

"When I'm damn good and ready," she said.

"I don't like it here anymore," I said. "All my friends are moving."

"Just what the hell do you think I'm doing out there!" she shouted. "I'm doing this for you! That's your future out there!"

"I want to go live with my dad," I said.

She reached across the carseat and slapped my face. Then she grabbed me by the hair and shook my head until my teeth chattered.

"Don't you ever say that again," she said. She let go of my hair. She turned away and looked out the windshield. Then she folded her arms over the steering wheel of the aging blue Ford and leaned her head forward, resting it on her arms. She closed her eyes. "Someday, you'll thank me for this," she said.

The town was coming apart around us. The N.F.O. tried to raise enough money through federal loan programs to form a turkey farming cooperative and purchase the Nowell-Safebuy processing plant and machinery. After a history-making court decision in the dairy industry set a legal precedent, the federal government decided its loans to farm cooperatives could not be used to purchase means of production such as processing plants. Such cooperative ownership of processing was called "socialist agricultural policy" by editorials in many newspapers. Besides, the Nowell-Safebuy had other plans for its processing machinery. It planned to move its machinery to a small town in Minnesota, much nearer main arteries of transportation. The area was already heavily signed into vertical contracts with corn farmers who wanted to start raising turkeys.

The Nowell-Safebuy also had other plans for this county. An act of Congress was passed designed to help control the production of grain. Congress decided to pay subsidies to farmers for not growing crops. One of Sam Carlson's last decisions as general manager of the Nowell-Safebuy was to put all land purchases here on long-term financing. Then he announced a plan for the conversion of all Nowell-Safebuy real estate in this county into wheat farms. Much of the land could sit idle that way, federal wheat allotment subsidies paying the interest on the bank loans the Nowell-Safebuy had used to buy farms. Many years later, with the new technologies of chisel-plowing, with aerial seeding, with new pesticides and herbicides slowly sifting earthward in pungent yellow clouds under the drone of airplanes, with tractors as big as houses, with discs and harrows wider than any farmer here would have imagined possible, nearly as wide as a four-lane highway, two hired men eventually farmed the same number of acres it had once taken twenty families to farm.

The turkey plant shut down. Huge, eighteen-wheeler trucks backed into the long brick plant building. In a few days, the miles of steel track for the slaughtering lines, the immense, three-ton power generators for the freezers, the modern canning and packaging equipment, the steam defeatherers—all those beautiful machines were gone. A storm of ancient factory dust and bits of white feathers swirled through the deserted turkey yards. Men were out nailing *For Sale* signs in front of houses. Then after a long time when there weren't any houses sold, first one family, then another, then a few more slowly packed their things, struggled out across their lawns with furniture and boxes. Old trucks were loaded ten feet high. It seemed every car was strapped down with boxes, clothing stuffed into the spaces between people in the seats. There was weeping, work-sharing, the most immovable and comic possessions left as gifts. Then the squeezes among neighbors, the hand-waving as solitary vehicles strained to get out of this town followed by the last calls of friendship, the final calls of grief among the women.

This town was abandoned overnight. Not really overnight if it means one specific passage of darkness to a dawn when there was nobody here. It took much longer than a single night. Town stores and shops began folding one by one. A lot of the stock left in them was finally given away. Then the bank and the government offices announced a move to Belle Fourche, the county seat. The schools closed. What few children were left here would have to take a bus forty miles in each direction.

Panic set in more deeply. Families were leaving every day, more and more with an air of emergency. There weren't enough available trucks to carry off all their things. Farewells began to happen in an instant or not at all. People even grew afraid of telling neighbors where they were moving because their creditors might track them down. Some families were simply gone without a trace. Their houses looked as if they might come back—old clothes, unwanted furnishings, other assorted and scattered belongings piled in living rooms, in driveways, in the streets. What wasn't finally scavenged over the years by people passing through doesn't look as if it ever belonged to anyone now. This town is like a sprawling, ragged, sagging heap, washed by fifteen seasons of winter to the same shade of gray as a pile of old barn boards.

The one small resource this town had left was in antiques. It used to be that every once in a while, a random car full of curiosity seekers passed through town. Some came thinking it might be a place to gas up and eat. Nobody ever took down the *Nowell Welcomes You* or *Nowell Roundup Rodeo* signs by the highway four miles south. The Cove Café was still in operation, and still is, along with the municipal saloon and a gas station on the way to Belle Fourche. But the café didn't have much of a sign and it was hard to tell it was even there. Most cars just drove through slowly, the people in them looking at the abandoned buildings and wondering what human folly had ever built then abandoned such a town, far off in the plains. But sometimes people sensed the treasures here. They stopped to explore in the old houses, to search through piles of belongings gradually washing into the earth. They looked as if they were out for a day's hiking in the woods, in nature. A chimney from a kerosene lamp was treated with similar awe and reverence as an arrowhead or a flint knifeblade of the Sioux. Sometimes, these people even had children with them, and a dog, sometimes they had a dog too. It was strange to see children running through the yards again, followed by a dog. Cars full of people picked up countless old bottles, tools, furniture, knick-knacks. They inspected them, exclaimed over their treasures, carried armloads of booty to their cars.

Pearly Green, new owner of The Cove, used to watch for cars like this. At just the right moment, he shuffled out into the streets. He stopped the people from driving off. He told them what they intended to carry away belonged to him. Then he haggled over a price. Sometimes in the course of bargaining he sensed he was talking to an antique dealer and he upped his price as far as he could. He figured he averaged about fifteen dollars a car this way. Fifteen dollars.

It seems like nothing here is worth much anymore. There hasn't been a car full of treasure hunters through in months. An antique John Deere Model D tractor that might have been worth some money once stands turning to rust in the Preston-Hill tractor sales yard. The antique popcorn machine at the Arcade Bingo & Theater fell over somehow this year and all the glass on it broke. The hand-carved, gilt-edged velvet theater seats are warped into uneven rows, stuffing pulled out of them by the mice, the bottoms rotted through. The gaspumps at Neil's Texaco are frozen with rust, barely standing, looking like men with glass heads and fingers plugging their ears. Only an empty parking lot is left of the Dairy Freeze, trucked off whole one summer by an enterprising soul. The shop signs and street signs are all missing a few letters. They will continue dropping off into the potholed streets or the weather will wash them away. There is still a public library, a one-room brick building just down the street next to the old Whitcomb house. Pearly Green keeps the key to it at The Cove, just a large room with books on three walls, most still in readable condition. No one keeps track of them. Every once in a while, my mother or Pearly or Andrea Scott will go in and dust off the shelves and do a little rearranging. The last time I was in there looking for a book, it struck me that a historian of the future might best describe this town by what books have never been read here.

We stayed on in this town. I remember the year everyone was moving away, I came home one afternoon to find my mother in a new dress. It was a light yellow gauzy material, a western style to the top and a skirt that showed off her legs. Her hair was different, too—a much lighter shade of blond than her natural color. And she wore makeup, her eyelashes curled, dark lines drawn around her eyes with sharp definition. She was smiling, happy.

"Your mom's done it," she said. "She's pulled a rabbit out of a hat."

"When did you do that?" I asked, thinking she was talking about her new hairstyle.

"Today," she said. "Grandma Vera signed the will."

We sat down to dinner. She poured my tumbler full of milk, then raised up her martini glass. We clinked glasses across the table. I didn't dare ask her when we were going to move.

"There's only one hitch," she said. "Grandma Vera wants us to take over paying the taxes, and some other expenses for the land. You and me. Twelve hundred dollars a year at least," she said. She looked at me. I didn't know what twelve hundred dollars meant. "We just don't have it on what your father sends. Sooooo . . ." She grinned. She leaned her chin into her palm, her green eyes half closed and looking seductive. "I've got a job," she said. "Can you believe it? Me! A job!"

She laughed. She leaned over and gave me a big wet kiss on the cheek. Then she got up and went to the counter to pour herself another martini. She took a tiny sip and held the glass out elegantly. "I start tomorrow. It's mainly at night, so you're going to have to help. You're going to be alone a lot more. And I'm going to pay you to give me a hand around the house," she said. She must have seen what I was thinking. We were never going to move now. She ruffled a hand through my hair and playfully swatted my behind. "Now don't you go and look so glum," she said. "We got to get working!"

10

The period in our lives began when she was living at night. She dressed each evening in black pumps and a sequined cocktail gown with glittering fringe along the line of her small but well-shaped breasts, her hair piled on her head, with curls held in place by rhinestone barrettes, garlands of tiny blue flowers, jeweled combs and pins, her beehive sparkling in the dim lounge light with such ornaments. I used to watch each day as she sat in front of her dressing mirror deep into the ritual of her makeup. Thinking back on it, I realize how much of a relationship she set up with herself in mirrors, transforming her face, somehow arriving at a separate character from among the many faces she held within. She glued false eyelashes on her eyelids, dark green with shadow. She let the liner brush sweep up at the corners of her eyes like tiny wings, giving them a kind of narrowed, Oriental look. She clipped on her nametag over her left breast, from a distance looking like a set of pilot's wings but close up a pair of elk antlers with the name "Margie" printed in white letters on the deep-purple plastic. I was just home from the school bus. She laid out her instructions for the evening as she dressed—to do the dishes after supper, to be sure and turn the TV off by seven and get to my homework, to put a basket of laundry through the washer so she could pop it into the dryer after she got home. She asked me to check the time for her by the clock on the nightstand. Then there was the rush downstairs to eat our simple quick supper together at the kitchen table, mostly frozen dinners and the like in those days, if there was time enough the two of us often eating quietly over our open books, she snatching another page or two of the three novels a month that came in the mail, me with my juvenile stories of sports and wars. Then she fixed her pink lipstick, kissed me carefully on the cheek and drove off, forty miles to Belle Fourche and the lodge run by the Benevolent and Protective Order of Elks.

She turned the "Big Six" wheel at the Elks' Club. She sat behind a curving green felt bar in one corner of the lounge, the "hospitality corner" as it was known, making rapid change on quarter to one-dollar bets placed on numbers from one to six. She reached up and spun the heavy wheel, its leather tongues snapping loudly over the metal pegs between numbers, and she learned to call the winning numbers even before the wheel had stopped spinning, claiming she could close her eyes and tell which numbers were up just by the sound. She earned dozens of dollars in tips on busy nights. But her main job wasn't spinning the wheel until the bar closed, it was a kind of gentle discretion, an ability she learned to fend off the nuzzlings of usually married Elks, laughing them off, turning even the most obtuse behavior into polite jokes, her wedding and engagement rings clearly visible, sometimes even pulling a photograph of me out of her purse and relying on respect for motherhood to get her out of the most forceful stampedes of the horned and benevolent brothers. One rule the management was inflexible on was that whoever ran the hospitality corner never be seen leaving the B.P.O.E. lodge with one of its members. She turned in her till, counted her tips, drank down her complimentary employee cocktail and drove home alone.

She started to do everything at night. She fixed another drink in the kitchen, changed out of her seductive work clothes, her "uniform" as she called it, into jeans and a sweater. She played music, dried laundry, mopped floors and vacuumed carpets at 3 A.M. People left in this town thought it was crazy the way she dug in her garden all night sometimes, the lone beacon of her flashlight dancing in the vast emptiness of the plains as she spread the horse manure she had picked up in fields at night, as she planted seeds mainly by feel, as she weeded, careful not to ruin her nails, and picked the worms off her tomatoes. She was up canning vegetables in her ticking pressure cooker as the sun was showing color in the east. Then she rousted me out of bed, laid out my school clothes and lunch money, fixed my breakfast and ushered me off to the bus. She showered, climbed into bed and slept until just before I got home from school.

I don't know whether it was because of more than two years of loneliness following her divorce or because she worked so many hours soberly among drinkers that she started to drink too much herself. I remember one night in particular. A Friday night. I had stayed on after school in Belle Fourche because of a scout troop meeting; our pattern was for my mother to pick me up at my friend Joe Benaro's house after she got off work the nights I had scouts. She was later than usual that night. I complained that she was so late, the Benaro family long since in bed and leaving me dozing on the couch, waiting. She bribed away my complaints with hamburgers and french fries to go at the all-night truck café and by letting me hold the wheel for most of the long straight highway to Nowell. At home, as we waited for our hamburgers to warm in the oven, she poured a tumbler full of gin and dropped in a couple of icecubes. She drank it down before the ice melted. Then she filled her glass again. I was talking to her all the while, turning the pages of the new boy scout catalogue and making lists of all the expensive, officially approved gear I thought I needed. She pulled her tips out of her purse and shoved them at me. "There," she said. "You can't say your mom doesn't bring home the bacon." She counted out the bills, forty-two dollars. "Take it," she said.

"But, Mom . . ." I started, pointing to pictures of camping gear that cost way more than that.

"Here then, damnit," she said. She dumped her purse over in my lap, coins scattering, rolling across the floor. "You can have tomorrow's too. Then that's it. That's all she wrote," she said. She slammed our burgers and fries on the kitchen table, still wrapped in their white paper. "They got a lot of damn nerve to sucker kids out of that kind of money," she said. "A lot of damned nerve."

"But, Mom, I gotta have the backpack and frame," I said. "Joe Benaro's got a backpack and frame."

"I think I'm gonna call the Benaros," she said, "right damn

now. Tell 'em what kind of nerve they got.'' She stood up out of her chair and started for the phone.

"No! Mom!"

She put the phone back on the hook.

"O.K., then," she said. "You'll just have to make do. Like I make do. Like I've made do all my life," she said, sitting back down again. She looked at her hamburger like some small dead animal on the table. She picked at her fries, one of them getting tangled in the fringe of her dress on the way up. "So you're going to make do," she said again.

"Yes, ma'am," I said.

"All right then," she said. "Eat your burger and get to bed."

"What about this other one then," I said after a minute, turning the pages of the catalogue in search of the picture. I looked up at her. A french fry dangled out the corner of her mouth like a rumpled cigarette. Her face went suddenly slack. Her eyes shut off, wide open. Her body tilted slowly forward and she went down that way, face first into a cardboard tray of fries.

I helped her up out of her chair, her arms groping around my neck, catching hold of my boy scout kerchief. She was still out but walking, or trying to walk, leaning into me, her legs buckling at the knees. We struggled this way up the stairs to her room. I didn't exactly put her to bed. I got her close enough somehow and just let go of her and she ended up there. She stirred, rolling to her stomach, her arms flailing at her back, fingers searching for the zipper of her dress. "Jus' a sec'," she mumbled. Then she passed out cold.

There's a moment in every boy's life when he reacts a certain way to his mother. For many it is triggered by a smell, a certain perfume he's suddenly aware of, for others a chance innocent intrusion into a bedroom or bathroom, or God knows how. For me it happened that night. I knew she wanted out of her dress and I tried to get her out of it, finding the hook, then unzipping the dress slowly, watching the taut sequined fabric parting like a glittering sea over the soft muscular curves of her back. I tried to get her arms out of the harness of her sleeves, hard to do as she lay flat on her stomach. Then I stopped. I just left her that way, asleep, half tangled in her dress. I shut the door to her bedroom, not even turning off the lights. I walked stiffly down the hall to my own room, overwhelmed and embarrassed by my own awakening.

I don't know when it was exactly that she started to date new men. There was one she met at the Elks' Club, a Yugoslav rancher by the name of Jake Yoblanock, much older than she was, and rich, owning ten thousand cows just across the border into Montana. "Jake's a kind of friend," she said when I asked her about him, one afternoon when he had taken us both up to the rodeo in Spearfish. Jake was off getting us both a popcorn. I didn't like him. And I couldn't understand some of what he said through his thick accent. "He's helped me out a lot," she said. "More than you know. He might even get us a loan someday for this idea he has of taking Grandma Vera's farm and turning it into a dude ranch for all these tourists," she said, pointing around to the rodeo grandstand full of parents and kids, kids mostly, tourists on their way back East from Yellowstone or on their way there via the national monument at Mount Rushmore. "And you know, Kurtie, I been thinking that's not half a bad idea, to make the place pay again."

But things didn't work out with Jake. He gradually became slightly less than a steady friend and more of a regular customer at the Big Six wheel. And she spun that wheel, night after night, her own fortune somehow tied to it now, snapping around the hundreds of little pegs, waiting to see what number might come up in that deep-purple carpeted hall with its generally bad country band twanging away steadily in the background. It was a club formed by a brotherhood of businessmen, of pillars of the community, and somehow, no matter whom she met there, the men were either married or none of them seemed right. She dated another man, a Bradley Parker, a soft-spoken clerk for the Great Westward sugar refinery, which was just on the point of being sold to the Mormon Church as part of its effort to corner the market in western sugar. But Brad was leaving the Elks and converting to Mormonism, partly for genuine religious reasons, partly because he had the idea that he might stand a better chance to keep his job at the refinery that way, and my mother's style of life just didn't fit in. She kept the wheel turning, that heavy antique implement of chance making the muscles of her left arm about a full inch thicker around than the muscles on her right arm, the way she sat on her high stool and had to reach up with that arm to turn it, the numbers ticking by, her other hand making quick change across the table for the winners and losers, the vast majority of them simply losers.

One night, Dan Gooch was an invited guest at the Elks' Club. Even though Dan was only three-quarters Indian, his presence at the Elks caused quite a flap, that brotherhood having strange restrictive rules about association with anyone but white men. Blacks and Indians weren't allowed to become members and technically weren't even allowed through the door. But Dan was well known to everyone in this part of the state, still walking on a pair of knees busted so many times from champion rodeo rides they were dark and bruised-looking, the joints like ground glass. He limped a little, just a shade, as he walked. He limped into the Elks behind Sam Preston, once part owner of a tractor sales yard in Nowell. Dan was used to the kind of treatment he received at the Elks' bar, and he was just about to turn and leave when he saw the "hospitality corner" and my mother. He went over and sat down. My mother took a chance at her job and made the cocktail waitress finally bring Dan a drink. Dan was the son of a good friend of her father's, had served as a pallbearer at his funeral when there had been nobody else at the last minute. They started to talk between spins of Big Six, Dan winning thirty or so dollars right away, which drew the attention of many benevolent Elks sitting in the bar. Dan was long on experience on how to avoid that kind of trouble. Folding his money into his pocket, he asked Marge to meet him later, for breakfast. She started to say no. But there was that certain link he had to her past, to her father, to a life of days.

The first I knew there was something serious between them was one winter night, a cold night following a blizzard. The snow was drifted as deep as the window ledges in the living room, the temperature twenty below, cold enough that the radio and TV stations were broadcasting regular stock warnings.

She had gone dancing with Dan at the Holiday Inn on the new highway to Rapid City. Most of their dating was a long drive away, at least as far away as Deadwood—almost a hundred miles from anyone they knew. Dan was still married, though he lived separately from his wife and kids, in a small house on the opposite side of his seven-thousand-acre drylands ranch from the house he had built for them. That night, as had happened before, Dan drank to keep up with his date and when Marge so much as looked across the room or danced a shade too close to another man, Dan sank into a quiet rage. Finally, he tossed a couple of bills on the table and stomped out into the parking lot. She had to gather up her things on the run and chase after him or he'd simply start his pickup and drive off with a screech of tires, leaving her stranded almost a hundred miles from home. She ran into the parking lot, her coat trailing her by the sleeve, things spilling out of her purse onto the ice. "You sonofabitch!" she shouted. She caught up to him at his pickup. "I'm not your goddamn property," she said.

Dan turned and let her have it. That was his problem. A few drinks, and thousands of years of a certain attitude of men in his tribe rose in him with violence. According to him, Sioux men had rarely held back with their women. If his squaw didn't please a man, he used to backhand her one and send her off to chew hides. This wasn't to say he didn't love her. Love had nothing to do with it. A woman needed discipline, needed to be told what to do. And if she kept displeasing a man, he used to trade her away for whatever he could get.

Dan let my mother have it, slapping her across the face so hard she fell back against a car. She lost control herself. She threw herself at him, using her nails and catching him at the neck. He made a fist and let it fly full force.

"Somebody call the sheriff!" she screamed. She sat doubled over on the pavement, one hand pressed against her face. "Help me!" she screamed.

Men came running out of the lobby to help. Dan tore off full speed out of the parking lot, his pickup fishtailing dangerously on the ice.

I was still awake, the colorful map of a war game spread out over the floor of my room, dice clicking in my fist when there was a knock on the door at the house. I ran downstairs and opened the door. It was Dan, a tall man all shadows against the snow, his cowboy hat in his hands, the hands working nervously at it, twisting the brim.

"So your mom ain't home yet," he said.

I shook my head no.

"I got to talk to her," he said after a minute. "I expect I'll wait."

There wasn't any reason why I shouldn't let him in. He wouldn't take off his coat or sit down. He circled around the living room like a caged prisoner. From time to time, he stopped at the windows. He parted the curtains and looked. It wasn't long before a car pulled up, tire chains ringing over the heavy layer of packed snow in the street.

"Look," I said. "She's in a sheriff's car."

Dan didn't say anything. He sat down on the couch, waiting to face whatever might happen.

The sheriff let her out of the car. The door slammed and the car made a wide slow U over the tire ruts in the snow, then picked up speed and drove off into the night. I noticed for the first time that Dan's pickup wasn't parked in front. No matter who had given her a ride home, she'd come in not knowing he was there. She moved slowly up the steps, her coat clutched together with one hand against the subzero cold, her other hand holding a bunched-up cloth over the left side of her face. I opened the door for her.

"Mom! What happened?"

"Damnit, Kurt, you should be in bed," she said. "It's two in the morning."

"But, Mom . . ." I started. She was moving down the hallway and looked into the living room. She let the cloth drop to her side, her eye purple and swollen. Dan Gooch stood up off the couch, slowly.

"You come home alone?" he asked, a strange tone in his voice.

"Get out of my house," she said quietly, almost a whisper. "And don't you ever try to see me again."

"Margie, I . . . I just came to say I'm sorry. That's all," Dan said. "I should have learned a long time ago that when a man hits a woman, he'll be paying for it the rest of his days."

"That's just like you," she said. "You're more sorry for yourself than what you did to me. Just look at it. I can't even go to work with an eye like this."

"Did he do that to you?" I asked, trying to put myself between them.

"You're not so old I can't give you a whipping!" she screamed. She slapped her wet cloth at my ears. I ran for the stairs. I stopped halfway up them.

"I never had a reason to say I'm sorry to a woman before," he said. "But I am. And it ain't ever going to happen again."

"You're damn right it won't," she said.

"I just kinda thought we might have a talk or something," he said. "Maybe work this thing out somehow. . . ."

"Get out!" she shouted. There was a long silence. Then I saw her struggling in the hallway, both hands pulling Dan toward the front door by the flaps of his sheepskin coat. Dan's body was limp, letting her have her way.

"Aw, please, Margie," he said. "We got to talk, honey. . . ."

"I ain't no goddamn honey," she said. She pushed him out the door and slammed it behind him, turning the lock home.

"Margie!" he called out. Both heavy fists landed on the door with a slam.

She went to the back door and locked it. Then she moved around the house checking the windows, the basement door, any way he could get in. On her way back through she caught sight of me on the stairs. I ran hellbent for my bedroom before it was too late.

"Margie, please!" Dan Gooch called in to her. "I ain't leaving till we have us a talk!" he shouted. "You hear me? I'm gonna stay right here! So you got two choices. You either let me in to talk or you find a frozen carcass on your steps. Margie! You hear me? A frozen beef!"

There was a long silence, long enough that I thought maybe Dan had second thoughts and had finally gone home.

"All right," he said. "If that's the way you want it, I'm taking off my coat. I said I'm taking off my coat!"

Not a word from her. I thought I heard her light footsteps going up the stairs. I was sure when I heard the sound of her bedroom door closing. I waited a long time. Then I snuck out of my room, just once, quickly, going to the window in the upstairs hallway that looked out over the front yard. I looked down, part of a gabled roof in the way, but just able to make out the dark shape of the man sitting cross-legged on the steps, his bare chest thrust out, his head held high, the cloud of his breath like smoke, his eyes fixed straight ahead in a kind of trance, a lone Sioux on a mountaintop waiting for the spirits to take him, his hat, shirt and coat tossed in a heap into the bushes.

"Wow," I said. I snuck back into my room. I tried to find something in the scoutbook to tell me how long it would take him to freeze to death at twenty below. As far as I was concerned, anybody who could black my mother's eye deserved nothing less.

She knew how long it would take. She waited just long enough for him to be in real danger, long enough to be sure. Then she let him in. She hadn't slept with any man but my father in this house. She had been raised to believe a woman simply didn't sleep with a strange man in the same house with her child. But she took Dan into her bed that night, half frozen, no apologies left in him. They were quiet about it, the floor creaking as they passed, her shushing him as they felt their way down the dark hall.

Later, I heard the happy noise of their talking in the kitchen. The smell of bacon frying was enough to get me up. It was an hour before dawn. She was in her housecoat and fuzzy slippers, wearing nothing underneath. She quickly pulled her housecoat closed as I walked in.

"It's an hour before you have to get up for school," she said.

"But, Mom, it's Saturday," I said. I looked at Dan. He was fully dressed, showered, his hair combed back, his brown fists busy with biscuits and butter. He smiled at me.

"The boy's likely hungry," Dan said. "You hungry, Kurt?"

"Well, go on upstairs then and get dressed," she said. I did what I was told. By the time I was back down in the kitchen, Dan was finishing his breakfast. She poured his cup full of coffee again, a cup from her best set of china.

"Damn good breakfast," he said. "Don't just stand there, boy. Pull up to the chuck, it's your turn now. I got to get going. Work starts out at the ranch at six. You look like you could learn a thing or two about working," he said. He stood up from the table. He put on his hat and coat and got ready to leave. She followed him down the hall, an arm around his waist. In the doorway, he kissed her, and she let him, in front of me, maybe a little extra in front of me, the both of them telling me something.

"So how do you want your eggs, Mister Mind-your-own-business?" she asked me back in the kitchen.

"You going to marry him?" I asked.

"Why shouldn't I marry somebody? How many times has your father been married?"

It was true. He had just gone through his third marriage and divorce.

"Don't worry," she said. "I'm not marrying anybody." She opened the refrigerator and took out a piece of meat. She held it over her eye, her fingers testing the puffiness.

"He sure got you a good one," I said.

"The man says he loves me," she said. "I know that's hard for you to understand. But it means a lot. If a man can say that much to you, you should give him a second chance." She cracked my eggs one-handed into the pan, doing them sunny-side up, the way she knew I liked them best. "Besides," she said, "maybe I'm just getting tired of living at night. And there's not a man in this world who'll put up with that forever."

11

We both got jobs at The Cove Café in Nowell. Each morning before school, my chore at The Cove was to set the tables. I pushed a little cart through the dining room. I folded green paper napkins into triangles and laid them out. I made the silverware jangle as I picked through it on a tray. Next, I set out cups turned over in their saucers.

Behind me, my mother moved along the counter checking the place settings. She poured coffee for Pearly Green and smoked her cigarette. The feeder bus for school in Belle Fourche pulled up in front of the big window and honked its horn. I abandoned my dishcart, gathered up my books, pulled on coat and boots and ran outside, the door slamming behind me.

"What did you forget?" asked Mrs. Tilson, a large, friendly woman who chewed gum with a cowlike stoicism as five kids already chattered away in the van. I turned and rushed back into The Cove for whatever I had forgotten—sack lunch, trumpet case, homework, gloves. My mother caught me on the second time out. She kissed me. I slammed through the door wiping lipstick off with my sleeve.

My mother served Pearly Green's coffee. It was part of the old man's metabolism that he had to drink twenty cups of coffee a day or die from lack of conversation. He was in a good position to talk as owner of The Cove. He was known to everyone. He had been a farmer thirty years, a turkey rancher most of that time. He had lost his youngest son, Will, who had run off after the truck hijacking, ashamed he was the driver, giving up on this county for good, though no one had ever proved who did it. To Pearly, it was as if

209

he had seen the words of the prophet written along the highway to Omaha. Before there was a calling in of loans and the turkey plant shut down completely, he sold his farm. He parceled out the pie from that to his four remaining kids to give them their start in life. Both his daughters had married and moved to Minnesota, only a two-day drive away. His eldest son had gone through troubles, a short prison term for assault, then he'd grown his hair long in middle age and become a beekeeper and tofu maker on a community-owned farm in Oregon. His other son, Terry, the kid he was by far the proudest of, was off somewhere in Saudi Arabia getting rich in concrete form construction. Pearly took the money he had left. He put a down payment on the coffee shop when the Nilsen family fled to the South.

The Cove had been close to failing ever since. Pearly, a widower, didn't seem to mind. He lived on his Social Security and the steady mortgage payments from his farm, the coffee shop barely scraping by, each year a small declared loss to offset Pearly's taxes. My mother did most of the work for him. She also took in the money. She paid herself first. Then she paid the bills. But mostly, she and Pearly gave the place away.

Each morning, Marge pushed the door open at seven in winter, at dawn the rest of the year. If Pearly wasn't already on his hands and knees tinkering with the antiquated café machinery, piecing it together with bits of wire, salvaged scrap metal, the splattered beads of his primitive soldering jobs making the pipes look like candles thick with silver drippings, she found him at the counter, mouthing the words of a book. The book would be any volume of the pre–World War I celebrated eleventh edition of the *Encyclopaedia Britannica*—remarkable for its scholarship of the day— that Pearly had resolved to get through ever since his youth. And it wasn't until age sixty-two that he had taught himself to read well enough.

Pearly would be hunched over his book, one hand holding down the pages and following the words, the other hand pulling at his earlobes, pinching at the end of his nose, tugging at the brim of his tattered brown cowboy hat or busy with smoking. He was a nervous man. He jiggled a foot or a knee as he read, his body always moving, responding to every word, his hands shifting the book back and forth on the counter like a steering wheel, his legs punching out suddenly at times as if at the clutch and brake pedals on a tractor.

Some days, Pearly left a small gift on the counter for her. He had a hobby of carving miniature wooden animals that he gave to everyone. He wrapped them in tissue paper and tied tiny labels around their necks that said *buffalo* or *condor* or *elephant* or *fox*, or any number of other animals he found pictures of in his encyclopedia. But when they were unwrapped, they always looked somehow like the same animal. The poses were a little different—a crouch or a run or a pawing at the air—but they all looked crudely the same. They all had peppercorns for eyes. Marge kept a complete menagerie of those wall-eyed wooden gargoyles arranged on shelves and windowsills, perched around the café kitchen where she worked.

When Pearly left her a gift, it was usually one of his animals. But sometimes, when the weather was right, he took down a soup bowl, filled it with water and left it on the counter for her with a single colorful blossom floating in it. Whatever the gift was, she was always surprised. She kissed Pearly on his leathery cheek. She sent her hands chasing along his ribs. She laughed as he pushed her grumpily away. "Go on and put a pot on," he said. He finally looked up from his book. "Or pull the shades and get ready to go all the way," he said, poking at her playfully.

She made the coffee and served it to him. She listened to the latest news from his encyclopedia, looked at the recent exotic snapshot from Arabia and shared whatever else was news with him. She cooked his breakfast. She poured a second cup of coffee and listened. Only rarely, when an event out of the past or simple loneliness had weighed too heavily on her the night before, would she tell him something of herself. He listened. He was an old family friend and had seen her the day she was born. Since her father's death, she had felt what it was to be an orphan, as everyone must be orphaned, and life was somehow easier for her as she

211

filled Pearly's cup, confiding in that one man who might have understood.

Marge kept much of what was left of this town alive. They passed through The Cove each morning. She cooked food for at least half of them. Mail was delivered every day and she sorted it, stuffed it in small wooden postboxes along one wall, selling stamps and taking in mail too, though Pearly did most of that. Once a week, she collected grocery lists for those who couldn't drive. Dan Gooch drove her forty miles in his four-wheel-drive pickup to the county seat to purchase food, drugs and other necessities. The town came to her for what they needed, to sit in her booths, eat the food she cooked for them, drink out of her cups. Everyone had good credit. Neither she nor Pearly had ever been known to go out collecting bills.

Will Hartley gimped in, fired up and still reciting the speeches inspired by the late J. G. Patton, onetime president of the Farmers' Union. Will recited speeches the same way he wore the same pair of boots for ten years. He patched them, tucked in the loose threads, sewed new patches over the old until it looked as if he walked in a pair of ragged boxing gloves. Will and Pearly got into terrible arguments about vertical integration in turkey farms. Vertical integration. There was a lot of talk about what had happened to this town.

"Vertical integration's no better'n a state of chattel slavery. That's a goddamn fact," said Will.

"You either do it that way or there ain't enough money in it for the company," said Pearly. "You seen what happens. The company shuts down. You raise five thousand pullets and have to sell or eat 'em all yourself. That's partly 'cause of all you suckers in the damned cooperatives. If that ain't communism, I don't know what is."

"Now hold on there," said Will. "I vote and pay taxes same as anybody else."

"Paid," said Pearly. *"Paid* taxes. A lot of good it did you."

"You're a born scab," said Will. "You'd of undersold any one of us. You'd of undersold your own sons."

"Damn right I would," said Pearly. "There's some things more

212

important than sons. But I was smart enough to sell the farm before that happened.''

They went on and on, haranguing without end. On the occasions when they grew close to violence, Marge told them she wouldn't serve them for a week. That usually quieted them. Or Will and Pearly took off for a pool game down the street.

Alice and Louis Kawczech walked in. They were one of the oldest married couples left in this town and they weren't doing well. Alice was first through the door. She had once been a husky woman. Now her big bones showed through her skin, her cheeks looked hollowed by a spoon and cast her face in a kind of permanent scowl. Louis followed her in, waddling, chewing on the stub of his cigar. He reached up about chest high and closed the door behind them.

Louis was short, at least a hand short of five feet. He was also fat, lately growing suicidal about his eating, even announcing in public that he'd resolved to eat himself to death. He hadn't always been that way. He had been a trim, small, soft-spoken man, a man who knew the stories, news and gossip of most of the people who had once lived in this town. He didn't tell stories now. He lived his life as if nobody had a past. If a person left the room, the town, or died, Louis didn't want to remember him. What mattered to him was what was around him at the time. It was as if he had come to the conclusion he knew nothing else for sure.

Louis had been happily married and barbering for thirty years. Then the turkey plant shut down. There wasn't enough hair left here to keep a barbershop open more than one day a week. Louis's sons left for distant cities where they both found jobs, married, telephoned on holidays. He kept the Nowell barbershop open as long as he could. Then he spent a year traveling all over the state looking for another job, trying to find another small town in need of barbers, but the jobs were all filled or no one would hire him. Or maybe he just missed this town too much. He came back to stay on, like everyone else who stayed on, scraping by on a few dollars, an insecure pension, the sound of a few good neighbors' voices.

Saturdays, Louis strolled from home to his shop. He chased the mice and insects out. He cleaned the rust spots off his razors, dusted off his towels, fired up his water heater. He dragged a small stool that made up for his height around for old familiar heads sitting in the barber's chair or on chairs pulled up around a magazine table where the subscriptions had all expired, ragged heads all bunched together there waiting for a good pruning like a cluster of gray rumpled shrubs.

Alice watched Louis eating at The Cove. She seldom ordered anything for herself. She drank coffee and blew cigarette smoke at his food. She watched each forkful of blueberry pancakes as if it was a poison. "You already had two porkchops at home," she said. "What are you trying to do, make *ten* pounds today?"

Louis bent to his food with genuine purpose. He pushed his mouth down just inches from his plate, seemingly afraid he might lose a forkful if he ate from a greater distance. He rested his forearms around his plate as if protecting his meal. He was going to eat. He started eating so much at The Cove, Alice growing more upset about it, that Marge had had thoughts of cutting him off. "If there's one thing on this earth nobody can take from Louis," said Pearly, "it's the right to eat himself to death. It ain't your place to stop him. It's almost a guaranteed American right, same for him as for anybody."

Marge prepared for her day, cooking and serving a dozen breakfasts, stirring up yesterday's chili, cutting leeks into a homemade potato soup. Though she couldn't see from the kitchen, she listened for the customers to come in and knew who it was by the sounds. After Pearly, Will, Anita Foos, the Kawczechs, Andrea Scott was usually in. Then Sam Preston some days if he was out driving, and Dryhole Davis, the retired oil drilling con man, might ride along with Dan Gooch if Dan drove in for lunch. And there were others: Keith Morgan, who used to sell insurance in this town, a few truckdrivers for the large grain hauling firms who took a short detour because they liked the food. In later years, there were sometimes a couple of enlisted men in blue uniforms, winged stripes and colorful kerchiefs making them stand out as air force boys, in for a hot meal on their way back from a twenty-four-hour shift deep underground in the missile silos that spread out across the prairie clear to Cheyenne. But mostly there were the

214

regulars, Pearly, Will, Keith and the others, men who hung around the coffeepot waiting for a game of cards or pool to start up down the street. She knew from the way most of them sounded just coming through the door whether she should drop what she was doing at the stove and run out to serve.

When Andrea Scott came in, Marge felt a cringing along her spine. She heard Andrea's battered, mufflerless pickup growling down the street. That pickup had white crosses painted on its doors and Andrea drove it fast, even in the worst blizzards. It *whumped* over the drifts, *whump whumping* through them in sprays of snow. It seemed miraculous the way that pickup could get through anything.

Andrea was a kind of self-appointed evangelist for the Church of Jesus Christ of Latter-Day Saints in Belle Fourche. She had made a conversion from Methodism about the year the economy collapsed in this town. She moved to Belle Fourche for a time with her husband. But her husband had eventually divorced her because she bought an old pickup, quit all drinking and smoking and began to spend her days out unofficially proselytizing for the Mormons. She invited herself into people's houses to quote the Bible and Joseph Smith and to hand out pamphlets. Her favorite pamphlet was an eighty-pager titled *Who Then Can Be Saved?* In order to achieve a little peace from Andrea's persistent sweet requests, Marge talked Pearly into letting Andrea stuff copies of her favorite pamphlet in the metal racks along with the menus. Then one day, Doc Monahan came in, shortly before he died of alcoholism. He sat at the counter down from Pearly, the thick pamphlets bristling in the menu racks. The Doc reached for a menu. In the process, he flipped one of the pamphlets aside in irritation, muttering. Marge served his coffee.

"What's that you said?" she asked.

"Aw, just this goddamn thing," the Doc said. He picked up *Who Then Can Be Saved?* "You ought to get rid of it. She says it's something for the soul. But what those people have done is discover a type of literary chloroform."

Pearly told Andrea to take her pamphlets back.

But Andrea's presence alone was a form of evangelism. She

215

roared down the icy street at thirty miles an hour, slammed on the brakes and slid in broadside in front of The Cove. She banged through the door with her yellow braids flying, calling out the Lord's good morning at the top of her lungs. She sat down and ordered breakfast. If the place was especially busy, when Marge took her order, Andrea leaned out over the counter beaming with sisterhood. She clamped Marge's wrist with a strong hand, blue eyes glittering with self-conscious holiness. "You look *so* tired," Andrea said. "You ought to fly on out of here. Go on and get yourself some rest! Go on now! If you need someone to take over, I'll look after things," she said. She reached a free hand up to straighten a lock of hair on Marge's sweating forehead. "You know there's nothing in the world worth you getting ill. I'll look after things!"

Marge stewed there a moment in silence. But anger or rejection was just what Andrea expected, after which she carried an air of dignified martyrdom. Marge thanked Andrea politely. She stood there waiting for the order as Andrea looked at her with pity. Andrea patted her wrist fondly and let it go. "You might add to your shopping list that Beatrice could use a hank of number five rainbow yarn," Andrea said. "You know how she'll get if she runs out!"

Marge could feel Andrea coming, a kind of premonition. The woman baited her. But she wasn't about to crack enough to tell Andrea off, to tell her that she had never seen such ignorance in pursuit of God.

She went about her day. Like any waitress, even here she had to put up with small humiliations, the strange truckdrivers who passed through and made rude leading remarks, the rush of the lunch hour when the six or eight tables filled with hungry souls, all demanding service at once. The place was busy enough that she worked hard well into afternoon. When the jukebox was still there, she plugged quarters painted with nailpolish into it, repayable at day's end, and turned the volume up so she could hear it in the kitchen. The Cove gradually emptied of customers. She ran the large sinks full and steaming. She faced her pots and pans, her tubs of dirty dishes, scraping them into Pearly's slop bucket, the ham rinds frozen in their grease, the cigarettes stubbed out in half-eaten bowls of chili, dipping each dish into the suds, then holding it slowly out under a scalding shaft of water and the winding motion of her sponge.

It was winter when she started at The Cove, a hard winter. The north wind that had gathered across a thousand miles of flat grasslands raked this town with a force that made the old buildings sing their age until they finally collapsed, one after the other over the years of winter. This town became a shifting landscape of scrap heaps and fallen trees. During storms, it filled with the sound of aching beams, the drumming of sleet and snow blown against the roofs, walls and windows. In the sudden, gusty winds, a man's spit could freeze before it hit the ground. There was so much snow that it could drift up to ten feet high across Main. Or snow it seemed from a hundred miles of surrounding bare land could invade town unexpectedly on the winds, an army of white moving drifts with tactics to barricade the streets for days. Then the wind would shift and the drifts might blow off into the prairie again in an hour's time.

The winds had always been unpredictable. There had been some winters when ropes were strung along the walks so people could pull their way up the street, hang on as they coasted down the street. December marked the beginning of a season that tested the strength of everything—on the range, whether a man's haystack was sheltered enough so it wouldn't drift in completely, whether his fences could stand the weight of snowdrifts, whether he had a barn strong and big enough to shelter his cows or sheep so the snow wouldn't form great walls around them in the fields, the drifts slowly closing in on them, isolating them out there without food or crowding them in until they trampled each other. It also tested whether a man's mind was sound enough to keep him from getting lost in ground blizzards, even in such a short distance as from house to barn, from street to home, and find himself wandering in confused circles until he froze.

Someone was always freezing in winter. It was a season of hardship and mourning. Yet if the wind was blowing at anything less than its peak strength, the old people who had stayed on here still left their houses. They made it through the weather as they could, wrapped up tightly in woolens, in sheepskin coats, in arctic parkas, maybe with a cane to test the ice. They felt their way blindly through the snow to The Cove Café, for coffee there before their cardgames, their pool, their jukebox, their television, their drinking, really not much more than that. Entertainment was hard to find. They gathered at The Cove because it was harder for them to wait out a storm alone.

Beatrice Ott was one of the few who considered herself too old to leave her house. Whenever a storm blew up, my mother kept her company on the telephone when the café wasn't busy. But Beatrice was getting feeble. She fell asleep sometimes just talking on the phone. It was all she could do to get into her backyard in spring and scratch out some kind of garden for herself. She used to tell people that the year she couldn't raise a single potato would be the year she died. Each spring, her garden shrank a little closer to her back stoop. She closed off the second floor of her house. She limited her movements to three rooms—from kitchen to bathroom to the parlor where Dan Gooch had set up her bed.

Beatrice still cooked for herself. She kept herself alive. Every Saturday, my mother and Dan Gooch brought coal for her stove, her mail, her feed grain and groceries, her hanks of yarn. Beatrice woke up early each morning to fix herself a breakfast of soaked and rolled unshelled barley, the same kind that's used to feed stockyard animals. She swore by it. It was cheap—about eight dollars a hundred pounds. And she managed to live on just about an exclusive diet of feed grain.

She also fed cereal to her birds. In spring and summer, she threw her kitchen windows wide. She scattered old bread and barley on the counters, the floor, her table. She clucked and coaxed out the window. First one, then another, then several more of the myriad swallows, sparrows, plain robins, obnoxious blackbirds hopped up onto the sill and flew in. Beatrice claimed to recognize certain visitors from years before. She had names for some of them, the ones tame enough to perch on her table. She ate her breakfast talking at a cloud of birds. Then she fixed herself up in one of her long, coarse gray dresses with a silver brooch and a collar that rose to her chin, her hair gathered in a neat bun in Victorian style.

Until the turkey plant shut down, Beatrice Ott had been a religious force in this town. She was the organizer of the Women for Christ Auxiliary, the Rock Creek Bible Day Camp, the Young Women's Christian Swimming League, countless church suppers and backyard sales. After the turkey plant shut down and she buried her husband, Beatrice gave up on her civic and church activities. She retired to a highbacked parlor chair to write letters to her daughter, her granddaughters, her great-granddaughters; that all her family were girls was a pleasing thought to her. She became a devoted viewer of daytime TV. But mostly she knitted, huge quantities of goods. She knitted wild-patterned sweaters with a dozen colors and tiny animals crocheted into them. She knitted enough mittens and socks to last this town a season. She knitted fancy ski masks with eye and mouth holes and twin pom-poms over the ears. She fashioned masterpieces—shawls with so many bells and beads strung into them they played a music wherever they moved, long flowing afghans fine enough to hang as tapestries. Each Christmas, she wrapped a box of her woolens as a gift for almost everyone in town.

People used to visit Beatrice just to see what fine patterned creation was spilling out of her lap, trying to get her to let on just who it was for. Once, word spread that Beatrice was knitting an entire dark brown jumpsuit complete with hood and drawstrings. A lot of the surprise in Christmas that year was watching Andrea Scott, the latter-day saint, open her box to find that jumpsuit and a note from Beatrice that said, "Merry Christmas, since you don't even have Brigham Young's good sense to come in out of the cold."

Andrea wore that suit several winters out in the cold, on her own personal missions through the blizzards. She pulled it on each morning the same way everyone else in this town had pulled on something made by Beatrice almost every winter morning for twenty years. Then there came a winter when it was different. When people opened their Christmas boxes, they told each other Beatrice wasn't long for this world. They pulled out sweaters with one sleeve a foot shorter than the other. Mittens drew all the way up the arms like evening gloves. Ski-mask hats sat on their heads like woolen teacups. It seemed as if Beatrice must have lost any ability at all to distinguish colors. And everything had so many missed stitches that it was a pile of unraveling strings in a matter of hours.

Something was happening to Beatrice. It was getting harder for her to see right and there was arthritis in her fingers. People began to visit more frequently, to sit talking to her mild gray figure, watching her fingers painfully stumbling through each stitch and some plain, shapeless piece of knitting already unraveling in her lap. Beatrice held up the piece and asked if it was passable. So many people told her how fine it was without knowing what it was that Beatrice came to the conclusion it might be best to give up knitting altogether. She closed up her box and started using it as a footstool. In spring, she planted a few potatoes near her back stoop. Then she sat not knowing what to do. Once a day, she hobbled out to hoe the potatoes. There was nothing else to do.

My mother spent at least an hour every Saturday with Beatrice, after the café had closed and she had finished her shopping in Belle Fourche. She sat in the sunlit parlor with her, watching the birds swooping in through the windows complaining for their feed. "I just pray it happens quick and painless," said Beatrice. "That's all I pray. And I ought to get rid of the birds, too. Tell them to go find someone else to freeload on."

Beatrice so convinced herself she was going to die that she quit feeding the birds.

"Oh, don't be foolish," said my mother. "You got a lot of good years left."

"You're not saving Louis Kawczech from the grave," Beatrice answered. "Why don't you go on and preach to him?"

But by the way Beatrice still cocked her head proudly against her chairback, her lips pursed in condescension, her chin held high, a sharp chin that looked like she kept a plum pit under her lower lip, and by the way she put on her flopping straw garden hat and still bent low enough to hoe potatoes, and especially by the way Beatrice kept calling out her husband's name in a kind of breathy desperation as if she were going to join Charles in the next instant, my mother knew Beatrice had too much energy left in her to die. She even brought a young doctor all the way from Belle Fourche to make sure Beatrice didn't have some physical ailment that was making her feel so morose. The doctor examined Beatrice and in the slow cheerful tones he reserved for children and the elderly, he exclaimed amazement at her good physical condition. Aside from cataracts that would soon grow operable and severe arthritis crippling her hands, he said there didn't seem to be anything wrong.

"I'm a hundred and two years old," said Beatrice. "Isn't that wrong enough for you?"

She sat through the remainder of that spring mostly alone, even the birds having left her now that she didn't feed them. My mother began to think there was nothing she could do. It looked as if Beatrice was right—if she tried hard enough, she just might will herself to death. Death was all she ever talked about. And like the birds, people in this town slowly quit visiting. Nobody wanted to hear her talk of death but Andrea Scott, who became a frequent, hardly tolerated visitor as she tried to convert Beatrice to her own personal visions of the latter-day saints.

My mother still visited on Saturdays, taking me along sometimes. We found the old woman slumping a bit more in her chair each time, her feet up on the knitting box, her eyes focused at the ceiling expectantly, as if her prayers that the roof would fall down on her head were about to be answered. At times, both cramped hands rose up from her lap. She closed her eyes. She sat that way a long time, her painful fingers pressed together in a ramshackle steeple, waiting, not speaking to her visitors. It seemed there *was* nothing anyone could do.

One autumn evening, I was lying in bed looking through the new Sears Christmas catalogue. A big part of Christmas was decided in October from its pages and I used to stare for hours into the full-color fold-outs of race cars that zoomed right off the page, at the pictures of kids grinning maniacally over their thousands of plastic army men waiting to be shot. I wanted everything. My mother used to lie in bed with me as I turned the pages and traded one fantasy for another. We were doing this when my mother suddenly took the catalogue out of my hands. She began looking at an ad for what seemed like an amazing machine, something called Knit Magician. It stood tall as a building in the foreground of a tinselly family scene—an elderly woman with her grandchildren, all of them smiling, all of them in pajamas, all pointing to a display of bright woolen articles the old woman was showing the kids how to make with the Knit Magician. My mother kissed me goodnight, letting me look one last time at a picture of whatever plastic junk it was I wanted. Then she took the catalogue downstairs and filled out an order form.

Four weeks later, she opened the box and was disappointed. The machine didn't look anything like the picture in the catalogue. It was just a small children's toy, a yellow plastic box with a contraption inside. There was a narrow slot at the base and a large hole on top. The box had a red plastic crank that made it look a little like a meat grinder. Yarn was fed in through the slot at the bottom, and when the crank was turned, thin tubes of wool grew snakelike out of the hole on top. The machine didn't do anything else but that—knit long and apparently useless wool snakes. My mother couldn't imagine what could be made out of them.

My mother put the machine in a paper bag along with some baked goods from The Cove. She sat down across from Beatrice in the parlor. They drank tea. I was allowed to watch the television if I kept the volume down.

"You know, I been thinking," said Beatrice. "Maybe Charles could have stopped you from marrying that man. He could've steered you back to the Cooney boy. He might've saved you the shame of divorce."

"The Cooney boy didn't know which end is north," my mother said. "And all I'd be doing is cooking for Cooney construction in Idaho. That's not much difference from what I'm doing now," she said.

"You could've met a different man," said Beatrice. "You

could've met a good man like my Rae did. I blame Charles for it. Not you. You were young and didn't know what you were getting into. Then again, you probably would've talked Charles into the idea. Charles was always running around saying, *You may be right, you may be right.* He lacked severity. He was never convinced himself without a good deal of reflection, either. And Charles was a mighty slow reflector. I used to tell him his thinking was like a false thaw. Everything got soft and muddy for a while and then it just froze right up again. I still think that about Charles. The way some men have minds like steel traps—like that SOB you married—Charles, he had a mind like a false thaw. . . .''

Beatrice had never forgiven her husband for a certain loss of faith, or ''spirituality'' as she called it, in the weeks before he died. Charles was bedridden with chest pains when this town was at its worst stage of panic. Almost everyone was out of a job. The bank closed its doors. Government offices moved to Belle Fourche. Entire families began to disappear without a trace to get out from under debts. And when the panic was at its worst, several hundred souls who hadn't moved on as yet flocked to the Reverend Ott for spiritual guidance. He knew they wanted fire-and-brimstone, an accusing fist battering down at them from the lectern until they repented for the Sodom they had built themselves. Severity was what they needed, what they had to have to leave this town with the only peace of mind they could have had—the peace of mind of simply having themselves to blame. Reverend Ott stood up out of his deathbed knowing his congregation would look to him for those final words in confirmation of what they already held to dearly as conviction, that somehow they had brought disaster upon themselves.

But he said nothing of the kind. His weak, ninety-year-old body crept feebly down the aisle. The pews were filled with the largest crowd gathered at his church since Buster Hill's memorial. As the reverend mounted his lectern, the only sound to be heard above Mrs. Carrie Anderson at the Hammond organ was the sound of weeping. He surveyed his flock several minutes as they wept, a congregation blooming with white rumpled Kleenex as women bowed trembling faces into their folded hands, weeping in grief at the last sermon they would ever receive in this town and for their neighbors gathered for the last time in that place of family worship. Beatrice sat in the front pew watching her husband, her demeanor an example of strength for everyone. Reverend Ott removed his spectacles and polished them on the black cloth of his ministry. Then he raised his hands. He strained to hold them up until there was silence.

He cleared his throat. He reached into his coat pocket and pulled out a small banner of newspaper. He leaned his head weakly toward the microphone, licking his lips. "I'm going to read to you from the only faith this country's got left," he said. He smoothed the news clipping out on his lectern and began to read from it in a parched, decrepit voice: "November hawgs . . . thirty-seven cents, up one half. Spring lamb . . . thirty-four cents, down two and one half. Prime steers . . . thirty-six cents, off one cent and one quarter. October turkeys . . . twenty-six, that's down two cents. Hard winter wheat . . . two dollars and seven cents this December. Corn . . . two dollars and sixty cents, that's down fifteen cents. . . ."

As he kept on, some in the congregation walked out of his church. Others sat disturbed but telling each other the reverend would soon get to the point. He finished reading from the newspaper. There was a long pause, the reverend looking out to see who was left, his eyes large, blue, grandfatherly behind the thick lenses of his spectacles. People coughed, whispered. Children's shoes clicked in the benchlike pews. "This is what the Lord says," he said. He turned to a passage in his Bible and began to read with his voice of prayer: *"Ho, every one that thirsteth, come ye to the waters, and he that hath no money, come ye, buy and eat; yea, come, buy wine and milk without money and without price."* His voice was gravelly, low, growing weaker as he read on to that conclusion based on faith alone: *"Instead of the thorn shall come up the fir tree, and instead of the brier shall come up the myrtle tree: and it shall be to the Lord for a name, for an everlasting sign that shall not be cut off."*

"Amen," he said, closing the Bible. People weren't sure all at once that the prayer was finished, and a staccato scattering of "Amens" answered his. "Thank you," he said. "May God bless you all."

That was as much as he was going to say. He motioned to Mrs. Anderson to strike up the recessional hymn. Reverend Ott didn't even attend the informal meeting and coffee hour in the parish hall after the sermon. He went home to his bed. Later that week, he died of old age, a man who no longer believed in miracles.

Beatrice spent a time trying to reorganize the Church of Christ Reformed. But its dwindling board of directors couldn't find a minister willing to settle here. Soon, there weren't enough people left here to make a congregation. The church was sold to Great Westward Sugar, Inc. Back bills were paid and what was left of the money was set aside to provide Beatrice with a small pension fund. The church building itself was converted into a seasonal warehouse for beets and potatoes.

That afternoon, years later, as my mother listened to Beatrice talk on about the past, she reached casually into her paper sack for the Knit Magician. She set it in her lap. She started to turn the crank like it was the most natural thing in the world she could be doing. There was a grating sound of plastic teeth, gears, spindles, bobs, grinding away. Beatrice looked closely in the direction of the sound. She tilted her head toward it as if any movement at all was tiring. Then she sat straight up, a little startled at what she saw.

"What is that, Marge?" she asked.

"It's a knitting machine," my mother said. "I was just thinking last week how much I could use a good pair of wool socks. I never learned how to knit. My mother was always good at sewing. But she never seemed to take to knitting, so I never learned. You know, when I was married, I never had to worry about things like that. Jim went out and bought whatever I asked him for. He was good for that much, anyway. It's sure not like that now."

"You going to knit with that thing?" asked Beatrice.

"I sure plan to," Marge said. "I don't know any other way to knit. This machine is for people like me who never learned how.

It's easy. All you got to do is turn the crank. See? Here goes. . . ."

"Let me see that a minute," said Beatrice.

My mother got up and showed her how to work the machine. Beatrice was fascinated. She reached out a hand like one big knucklebone in an old leather purse and found she could turn the crank easily. She peered down through the hole on top as if she couldn't quite see in well enough. She turned the crank once, twice, watching the circling rows of white plastic teeth grating out their stitch. "It knits a circle," she said with amazement in her voice. "It does a straight stitch. But it does a straight stitch around in a circle."

She scowled then and handed the Knit Magician back to my mother.

"Not much you can do with that, I expect," she said.

"There's not much I was ever able to do when it comes to knitting," my mother answered. She sat back down in her chair. She sat still a moment. Then she began to turn the crank on the Knit Magician furiously, pretending to be absorbed in the workings of the machine, peering downward into those polyethylene insides with their jumping strands of wool. A bright woolen bloom began to spill out the top.

"What's that you're knitting?" asked Beatrice after a while. She had to raise her voice over the sound of the machine.

"A pair of socks," my mother said. "Good wool socks. This first pair's for Kurt. Then maybe I'll knit up another pair for Will Hartley. You know how the weather always gets through his boots."

"Well, that's the wrong kind of yarn you got there," said Beatrice. "That yarn's too thin for good socks. The pair won't last a month. You need a thicker yarn than that for socks. That's good scarf or thin sweater wool. Anyway, it's not any good for socks."

"I can't figure out how to get the ends knitted over right, either," my mother said. "But I'll tackle that problem once I finish the knitting part of it."

Beatrice watched her every move. My mother increased the speed of her cranking. The ball of blue yarn was jumping around in her lap, it unraveled so fast. The end of a long blue woolen snake began to trail out over her knees.

"Give it here once," snapped Beatrice. "Hand that thing over here once now," she said. "You'll never figure it out."

It wasn't long before Beatrice had cranked out what looked to be two pairs of heelless socks or thumbless mittens. She was busy trying to figure out how she could get a heel into them or a thumb on when we left her sitting alone in her parlor. As I was going out the door, I turned. I looked at my mother standing over Beatrice, caring for her in a way her own mother wouldn't allow, for Beatrice and for all of them. All the rest of them.

I held the door open for my mother and as we left, Beatrice hardly seemed to notice that we'd gone. She waved a hand limply in our direction as if waving at smoke. She poked at the small machine in her lap. She held it up to her ear and shook it. She turned the crank, slowly. She pressed her face down close to it and looked through the top, squinting one eye, peering into it as intently as if she could see to the very center of the earth.

12

Dan Gooch moved in. I was away with my father on summer vacation and it was a celebration for two, Dan cowboy-rich from selling off part of his three thousand sheep in anticipation of a drop in prices. He had rolls of hundred-dollar bills in the pockets of his jeans. He threw out the old black-and-white box in our living room and replaced it with a color TV/stereo console in black walnut as big as the dining room table. He bought a new washer and dryer, wrapping his arms around them and carrying them in himself, hugged against his chest. He had the engine of my mother's blue Ford rebuilt by a friend on the reservation. And he bought her clothes—jeans and western shirts, a leather jacket with fringe, a different pair of boots to match each outfit, and a dozen flimsy, see-through chemises and things she wore at night. He took her out to dinners, to the dog races in Rapid City. On Saturdays, they rode to Belle Fourche to buy supplies for The Cove and some of the old people left in this town. They looked forward to a summer alone, without his kids or me, cowboy-rich and with a chance. But a few weeks after Dan moved in, Grandma Vera died.

I was off visiting my father. Each June, I took a trip to visit him, often in a different place. He had usually just bought a vacation home or was just selling one or, worse, had just lost one in a new divorce. I spent the month of June in the Colorado rockies, on a beach in Florida, in a small cabaña near Mazatlán, Mexico, in a large camper on the Alkan Highway to Dawson Creek. He moved from job to job doing corporate law, always highly paid but never satisfied. He spoke of each new vacation home and each new job as if it was something permanent, looking to the future as an extension of his present condition. But almost every time I saw him, he had changed jobs, homes, girlfriends or wives. He is presently living in his sixth vacation home on a cliff in Oregon overlooking the Pacific. He has just concluded his fourth divorce. And he's looking to get married again.

While I was away, my mother discovered one afternoon that Grandma Vera had moved into her car. The car didn't run anymore. It had been parked behind the house years ago and tall weeds grew up around it. Grandma Vera had packed all her canned foods outside and piled them in the back seat. She had brought her magazines and newspapers to the car too, and made a space for them on the floor in front. She stretched out on the front seat to sleep. She reached in back for a jar of fruit or vegetables, opened it, then ate her meal. She wore her pink bathrobe and an old housedress underneath. When my mother found her this way, it was clear she had been living in her car for days.

Grandma Vera had become incontinent. She didn't want to mess up her house and couldn't keep up with it, so she moved out to the car where all she had to do was throw the driver's-side door open and jump into the weeds. That was her reasoning. Everyone else said she had finally gone around the bend with senility.

My mother tried to get Grandma Vera out of the car. Grandma rolled up the windows and locked the doors. "You're all holed up in there like a bear!" my mother shouted. "You're living like a goddamned bear!"

"You just want to carry me out like the trash!" Grandma said.

"Come home with me then," my mother said. "I'll take care of you. You know I will."

"Oh, pshaw," Grandma said. "One mother can take care of three children, but three children can't take care of one mother. You'll find out."

"I *will* take care of you," my mother said.

"You just leave me alone now," said Grandma Vera. "You're getting my windows dirty."

"What's wrong with you? Mama! What!"

Grandma Vera fixed a stare through the windshield. That was all she was going to say. My mother found a bar and tried to pry the car door open, but it was an older car and the steel was too tough. She didn't want to break the windows. She finally went into the house and telephoned Dan Gooch. Dan came out with his cutting torch. He cut quickly through the lock, Grandma Vera coughing dramatically as her car filled with fumes. Dan reached in to pull Grandma Vera out of her car. She cracked a jar of peaches over his head. My mother and Dan fought her, Grandma hitting at them with her fists and shouting, "Let me go! Let me go! You're not my boss!"

They finally pulled her out. Dan held her in his arms as she kicked, squirmed, hit him about the head.

"Now what do we do?" he asked.

My mother knew there must be something wrong. She decided to take Grandma Vera to the hospital in Sturgis. Grandma cried all the way there, afraid of the inevitable. She knew my mother had a job, a child, enough to do. Taking care of her now was almost a full-time task. When the doctor told my mother Grandma Vera's systems were failing, out of control, Grandma Vera looked at her and said, "No child of mine's going to take care of me. No, sir. That's the bottom line. All I want is for you to take me home. I'll manage. You'll see, Petie. I can manage."

It was the first time she could remember her mother calling her by the nickname her father and brothers had used.

"Come on home with me," my mother said. "Please."

"Nooooooo," Grandma Vera said. "Noooooooo. . . ."

Dan Gooch pulled my mother aside. "Marge, it ain't right if you let her go home," he said. "And it ain't right for her to live with you, either, not the way she is. When they lose control, it's all over," he said. "I know. The same thing happened to my dad."

"What else can I do?" she asked.

"The Pioneer Rest Home," said Dan Gooch.

The doctor agreed.

"No!" Grandma Vera said. She pounded her fist against the wall. "You can't force me!"

"Look, honey," Dan said. "It's only in Belle Fourche. You can visit when we go in for groceries."

My mother decided to take Grandma Vera to the Pioneer Rest Home in Belle Fourche. The rest home was a large house, really, overlooking the Belle Fourche River. The staff set Grandma up in her new room. They instructed her to lie down on the bed as they put in an IV because she seemed so weak. The nurses left the room.

"You're not my boss," Grandma Vera said to my mother. "None of you are." She pulled the IV out of a vein in her hand. "You're not tossing me out like the trash."

Grandma Vera fell into a deep depression. She hardly moved out of her room at the Pioneer Home. The staff set her up in a high-backed geriatric chair facing the windows that looked out over a neat lawn, a slow curve in the muddy green river, flowering dogwoods in which birds were singing. When my mother visited the next day, all Grandma said to her was, "Bring me a jar of well water from the farm. That's why so many die here. The water's poison."

My mother brought a jar of water from the farm. She also brought some of Grandma's jars of canned food from the back of the old car. Grandma took a sip from the jar of water. "It doesn't taste right,'' she said. My mother opened a jar of pickled beets. Grandma took one bite and wrinkled her nose. ''These don't taste right, either,'' she said. ''Makes me think you've been messing with my jars again.''

The director of the Pioneer Rest Home took my mother aside. He explained it was common for residents to be depressed the first few weeks. He advised her to wait a month. He promised Grandma's condition would improve.

She died in three weeks. The official cause of death was heart attack, but Grandma Vera's heart simply stopped beating. It happened early in the afternoon, as she sat in her geri-chair facing the windows. I was away on a fishing trip and couldn't be reached. By the time I checked in by phone, the funeral was over. Grandma was buried next to my Grandpa Ben, under a lone cottonwood behind the homestead barn.

''She just checked out,'' my mother said on the phone. ''She willed herself out.''

''But how?'' I asked. ''How did she die?''

''Look, Kurt, the quality of life was gone,'' she said. ''She went on to something better. That's the way we've got to think of it. She went on to something better.''

I didn't like the sound of her voice. There was a long silence.

''But, Mom,'' I said. ''What happened?''

''Let me talk to your father,'' she said.

I didn't know what to do. It would be the first time in seven years they had so much as spoken to one another. I was telephoning from a coin phone in the hallway of a large fishing lodge in northern Idaho, made out of cedar logs three feet through and built by the Harriman family for Teddy Roosevelt in the days of railroad ranching. There were deer heads, moose heads, antelope horns, the sad glass eyes of dead cougars and mountain goats looking down at me from the walls. Just around the corner, my father was sitting at the bar getting very drunk in that mausoleum of hunting trophies. We had had a miserable time. He had brought a new girlfriend along with us on the trip, a twenty-eight-year-old law student from Oregon he had met a few months before. They had argued most of the time. Nobody had caught any fish worth talking about. My father had a Band-Aid over his cheek where the girl had hooked him trying to learn how to cast a dry fly. She was now in the billiard room making time with the boat boy while my father was at the bar. I didn't care. I had already moved my sleeping bag out of our little cabin and down by the lake so they could have at it in peace.

"I don't know," I said. "I'll try. Hang on."

My father was talking politics with the bartender. As usual when he talked politics, he pointed his finger as he spoke. "Now the trouble with these liberal programs is they don't leave room for the wealthy. You think about it. What kind of a country would this be without the wealthy?"

"Dad . . ." I started.

"Don't interrupt," he said. "The wealthy built the West," he said. "Like this lodge. Like the Harrimans. And they're still going strong."

"Dad. Grandma died," I said. He looked at me, caught for a moment with his finger poised in midair. "Mom wants to talk to you."

He ordered another drink. He took it with him to the telephone. I waited, looking out across the deserted tables of the cocktail lounge to the pool table where the boat boy was reaching around Jean's tight T-shirt, encircling her with his arms as he racked up, moving the triangle fluidly, searching for the spot. A moosehead looked on with stoic expression. The bartender turned his back on everyone and counted his tips. My father walked slowly back into the room, hands sunk deeply in his pockets, a sad look on his face. He sat down on the stool next to where I waited. He put an arm around my shoulders. It felt good, his arm around me. "I'm sorry about your grandma," he said. "Really I am."

He looked at me. Then he looked past me to Jean and the boat boy in the other room.

"It's O.K.," he said. "Everything's O.K."

"What did she say?" I asked. "What did she say about Grandma?"

"Aw, nothing much. She was pretty upset," he said. "Look. I

hate to cut the trip short this time. But maybe it'd be better if you went home early."

"Sure," I said. "I want to go home."

"You're a good man, Kurt," he said. "You got a tough row to hoe. I'll drive you down to Idaho Falls and send you back in the morning. O.K.?"

"O.K.," I said. He reached into the back pocket of his fishing pants for his checkbook. This was a ritual when I was sent home. He always wrote out my mother's monthly check for me to take back to her. It was usually a small check, the amount of my support. This time, he wrote one out for two thousand dollars.

"Don't you lose this now," he said. He folded the check and tucked it into the snap pocket of my western shirt. "That should help with the arrangements," he said. He put his arm over my shoulders again. "And tell your mom . . ." he started. He looked at me, unsure. Then he looked at Jill and the boat boy, at the bartender counting out his till, through the dark window behind the bar at lines of small white waves on the moonlit lake. "Aw, shit," he said. "Just give her my love."

My mother and Dan Gooch picked me up at the airport in Rapid City the next afternoon. She sat close to him on the front seat, Dan putting an arm around her waist as he drove, fast, with one hand. My mother didn't mention Grandma Vera. She was full of talk about the farm. "The farm's ours now," she said. "We've got our work cut out for us." She looked at Dan. "All of us. Dan here's got some ideas. He's had his hired men out repairing the fences. That's a start anyway. It'll take a while, but we're going to turn that farm into a showplace. Isn't that right, Dan? Into a showplace."

Dan Gooch was a sheep rancher, and a successful one, as his family had been ever since they had moved off the Rosebud reservation to seven thousand acres of the driest, most desolate prairie fifty miles east of Nowell. He was three-quarters Sioux and one-quarter white man, on the part of his father, with greenish-brown eyes and the aristocratic Roman nose of the Sioux. But he was all rancher, as his father had been before him, a man who loved horses, antelope hunting, high-heeled cowboy boots, wide-brimmed, high-crowned hats, silver belt buckles studded with turquoise. His idea of a good time was a six-pack of beer, a lariat rope and a mean horse. He roped the horse in a corral, snapped the rope at it, yanking its head one way and another, shouting at it, spooking it. Then he wrapped a loop around the horse's nose in a kind of halter and climbed on its back without saddle or bridle and rode it out until it stood shivering, legs spread, sweat coming off its hide in a foam. His idea of fireworks on the Fourth of July was a case of miner's dynamite. He stood on the riverbank, pulled out a dynamite stick, lit the fuse, then tossed it to the very center of the slow, snaking, muddy green river. He laughed like hell when everyone standing near him was soaked with spray or even knocked over by the shock of the explosion. He had been married once, to a Cheyenne girl, and he had at least six children that he spoke about. His kids were never allowed over to our house, not even once. Dan's ex-wife thought it would be harmful to them to see Dan living with a white woman. It was a strange relationship. Even after their divorce was final, if Dan's ex-wife wanted to date another man, she had to phone Dan up first, tell him who her date was and ask permission. Dan generally agreed, unless the man was one of his own hired hands, usually some distant cousin, nephew or uncle up from the poverty-stricken Rosebud reservation to earn a little extra money. Dan spoke ill of reservation Indians. It bothered my mother how Dan sometimes spoke of his less fortunate brothers.

"There's very few of them worth anything," said Dan. "They get a trailerhouse out in the Badlands, then throw their garbage out the back door. When the pile gets too big, they just move the trailerhouse. And you can't count on most of 'em to work, either. That's why I don't pay till the end of the month. When I paid at the end of the week, half my hands went on a drunk till the money was gone. Then they came back begging for their jobs. Hell. Don't seem like there's a one of 'em worth the name anymore."

"You shouldn't talk about your people that way," she said.

"Hell. My people are different. My people got off the dole and went out and built themselves something. Like your people. My people are a hell of a lot more like your people than some of those reservation bums. And my people haven't forgotten their religion, either," he said.

We were all in Dan's pickup, early one morning. Dan was going to drop us both off at The Cove Café on his way out to his ranch. My mother looked out the window at some of the abandoned buildings of this town, buildings with windows boarded over, making them look somehow like lines of blindfolded soldiers waiting to be shot. The sidewalks were fissured and out of kilter, like after an earthquake.

"Just go on and take a look at what my people built," she said.

"You know that ain't what I mean," he said. "A man in this world's got to go out and get some. That's all. He's got to go hunting as many times as it takes until his belly's full."

"I suppose you think the same way about me," she said. "Or don't you?"

Dan laughed. "Well, with you and me, Margie, it's different. No more hunting required," he said. "We both got the inborn ability to cut our losses into jokes and have a good time. Ain't that right? Ain't we having a good time?"

"We're having a fine time," she said. Dan pulled the pickup up to the curb in front of The Cove. "I just don't like to hear you talk that way. I get too much of that kind of talk."

"I ain't talking about the ones who still got their religion," he said. "I'm talking about the ones who don't know and don't care who they are anymore."

She scooted over on the seat so he could throw an arm around her neck and kiss her, his fingers, thick with silver rings, running through her hair.

"See you tonight, honey," he said. "We got hay out there, so expect me late."

Dan was religious. When he, the color TV, the washer, the dryer and everything else moved in with him, he also brought his medicine stick—that's what my mother and I called it. Dan just called it his "medicine," his *wopiye* in Sioux, though I never heard him use that word for it; I don't think he knew more than a couple of hundred words in his own language, just enough words to practice his religion. It was a grimy-looking leather pouch hanging by a thong at the end of a long stick carved into a snake's body with a crow's head, the wood dark orangish-brown like it had been hung in smoke, a single yellowed eagle feather hanging from a loop halfway down the snake's body.

Dan kept his medicine in the closet of her bedroom, back in a corner near where he hung his best clothes. About two days a month, he took the medicine stick with him and disappeared, not coming home at night, out practicing his tribal religion, for which he served as a kind of helper, a kind of deacon if Christian comparison makes any sense. Dan was also a Christian, not the kind who went to church every Sunday, but baptized and confirmed, and he went sometimes, once or twice even going with us in Belle Fourche. He didn't find the two religions in any way exclusive of each other, the one being a family practice, something for the wife and kids, the other being a kind of secret society he joined in with the men of his tribe. They painted themselves, sat in sweat lodges, smoked herbs, sang songs and danced, different rituals for every season and every moon of the season, a world of animal spirits called down into the bodies of men who danced out their stories and saw visions born of exertion and fasting. Dan didn't say much about his religion when I asked. It wasn't something he was supposed to talk about. I asked him how to join.

"Nobody joins," he said. "You let it be known that you're willing, and then they take you. In the middle of the night sometimes, five or six helpers just walk into your house and take you with them. It's an honor when they come. They help you get reborn, sort of. Mostly young men, boys about your age, but age doesn't make any difference. You don't eat or drink anything for as many as five days and nights, and sometimes you don't sleep, either. A medicine man feeds you spirit food, like feeding a baby, and he teaches you how to talk. Then you go off alone and get a new name, and an animal, like a hawk or a fox, and you learn to dance the animal. And you can never tell anybody. If your enemies ever find out your name, or even your animal, they can get the better of you."

"So they never take white men," I said, disappointed.

"Oh sure, they took plenty of white men once. And still do take some," he said. "There's some that say that's the only way to save us, to take white men in. But white men don't make good dancers," he said. "They generally spoil the dance."

"What else do they do?" I asked.

"I've already said too much," he said. He threw an arm around my shoulders and gave me a friendly squeeze goodnight. I lay awake thinking there was something in what he'd told me, a hint or something, and I'd let him know I was willing to join, or be taken. Nights when Dan took his medicine stick and went out, nights generally but not always of a moon just starting to wane, an egg-shaped moon that seemed to rest in the high-crowned branches of the cottonwood in the yard, I left my T-shirt, my jeans and boots on a chair by the bed so I'd be ready. I waited in bed in the darkness, listening, hoping to be taken. Then, after a while, I knew nobody was coming for me.

Their relationship didn't last long. But my mother gave it a try. Before I came home early from vacation when Grandma Vera died, she had let Dan and his medicine move in. They had already figured out what to do with me.

"Your dad's been married three times already," she said. "I deserve a chance too. It's been a long time," she said. "And I think it's better if we started out alone. Just us. It has to be that way to see if it'll work out. Dan's going to move some sheep out to the farm. He's going to hire you to stay out there and look after them. He'll pay you the same as he pays any hired man."

"You mean any hired Indian," I said.

"It'll be good for you," she said. "It'll be good for you to get out and do some real work for a change."

"But, Mom," I said. "I work!"

"It looks silly. A boy your age working like a waitress."

"I don't want to be out there all alone," I said.

"I don't give a damn what you want," she said. "I deserve a chance. You hear me? A chance!"

There wasn't much I could say. Dan had leased the farm from her and had it planned for me to tend four hundred ewes with lambs. The day came when I packed a knapsack full of old clothes, a larger knapsack full of books from the library in Belle Fourche. I also moved out several jars of fruit flies left over from a school biology experiment, larvae left to hatch out while I was away. I didn't want to asphyxiate them, kill the little white eggs at the end of the term. They had gone wild in their jars. I planned to let them loose on the farm—my own little crop. The next morning, I helped Dan move three truckloads of sheep from his dry ranch. On his ranch, it took four full acres to raise enough grass to feed a ewe and a lamb. On Grandpa Ben's farm, it was one acre, even though it had been fifteen years since it was last seeded to grass.

Dan loaned me a sheep dog by the name of Boots. He showed me my job, how to get Boots to herd the flock into the old corral each day, then how to worm them, doctor soremouth with iodine, how to paint brand, dock tails, make young rams into wethers. Dan also left me with a .30/30 Winchester, five boxes of shells and a 30,000 candlepower, hand-held spotlight on a long cord plugged into a car battery rigged up with a wire handle. It wasn't easy to drag it and the rifle around.

"You got to watch out for the coyotes at night," he said. "You hear 'em out there close, you get up," he said. "You make sure them sheep are down by the house at night and when Boots starts barking, you get out there with the spotlight. I lost ten percent of my flock last year to coyotes. I can't take that kind of loss this year. Can you shoot?"

"Sure I can shoot," I said.

"Let's see you once," he said. He worked the lever action of the rifle and handed it to me. I looked around for something to shoot. I saw a sparrow sitting on a piece of fence, not too far off across the pasture. I'd never actually shot an animal before. But it was there, a tough shot. I aimed. I pulled the trigger and the sparrow was gone. I wasn't sure I'd hit it, couldn't tell if it had just burst into nothing or jumped away. I handed the rifle to Dan and ran, tall grass whipping at my pants. I looked along the fence. Then I saw it, a lone, severed sparrow foot still gripping the top wire. I brought it back to him. I put it in his hand.

"Nice shot," he said.

"My dad taught me how," I said.

"Well, we'll see," he said. "I'll give you a five-dollar bonus for every dead coyote you can show me."

He was paying me a hundred fifty dollars a month, including groceries.

"You'd best be careful or I'll break your bank," I said.

Dan Gooch laughed. He turned and headed for the house. The house had fallen on hard times. In the years since Grandpa Ben had died, Grandma Vera had found it hard to keep up. Even the electricity was gone. The insulation on the wires had recently been chewed through by the mice and my mother didn't have enough money to rewire. So the power had been turned off to the house in fear it would burn to the ground. Some of the windows were broken out and covered with boards. The roof leaked in a hundred places, large brown stains spreading over the ceilings. The place was filled with mice. They nested in the old cupboards. They pulled stuffing out of the old furniture and scattered it around. Dan helped me clean out one room, the living room, where it would be easier to jump out onto the porch at night with the rifle in case the coyotes bothered his sheep. We moved one of the old, mouse-eaten beds to the center of the room. We set up a few kerosene lamps around the room and on the kitchen table. We finished about an hour after sundown. The lamps were lit, cheerily glowing around me.

"I'll check on you about every other day," said Dan. Then I watched out the window as he climbed into his pickup and drove off up the overgrown lane.

I didn't sleep much that night. The mice were having a party in the kitchen. I could smell them too, a strong rodent odor all over the house. Every time I closed my eyes and started to fall asleep, I woke up thinking I could feel their little sharp claws running over my skin. I tossed, turned, itched all over. And there were noises, the old house groaning in a light breeze, other more distant creaks and shudderings that left my heart pounding in the weird yellow glow of kerosene in which I was sure I could see the dim outlines of ghosts.

The next day, I hardly worked. I made sure the sheep were grazing close to the house. Then I wandered around the homeplace, thinking just what could be done out there. I almost had myself convinced that was my future—the homeplace. I'd never have to worry about a job. There was enough work out there for generations.

I headed for the barn, exploring, beating back the weeds. I formed a rough, L-shaped map of the homeplace in my mind, three hundred and twenty acres, all of it fenced. There had once been a hundred and sixty more, but my grandfather had had to sell that during hard times. The pastures needed reseeding, or planting into a crop. And what I might get started on right away was the barn, tightening it up. It might even be the right size for a small feedlot, if there would ever be enough money for grain, or if it didn't cost too much to get the old well in the barn working again. I looked at the barn close up, seeing the faded outlines of what had once been the family brand, ᴐ℞. *Lazy you are,* I thought. I wondered what was in my grandfather's mind when he had chosen such a brand.

The first really hot wind of summer raised the dust around me, flapped the rough tin patches on the barnsides, spun the listing barn-roof weathervane rooster like an insane propeller. The old boards creaked and groaned. Up close, that barn looked as if it could fall whenever it chose. It looked even older than I thought it was, made of rough, hand-cut beams and planks, most of them cracked, bowed now, the old square-cut nails pulling out of them on their own. The roofing shingles were warped into mad tangles that snapped in the wind. The doors were off their hinges. Inside, there was a steeply rolling landscape of rotted hay and manure and a deafening buzzing of a million flies. The old troughs were strewn around, in pieces. The stanchions were frozen somehow, unmovable, covered with the droppings of birds as if someone had splashed white paint over them. The barn beams leaned every which way. I found the remains of two old rubber boots and what must have been my Grandpa Ben's coveralls, hanging empty on a nail. When I tried the wood ladder up to the hayloft, it broke under my weight. I tried to correct a warp above me, in the loft floor, by pushing against it with an old pitchfork handle. When I did, a shower of rotted wood rained down. I caught the strong, rancid odor of a skunk somewhere around the feedcrib. I opened the door to the feedcrib. I moved a pile of old burlap sacks and found a deep, swirling layer of mice that scrambled up the walls at me. I walked back out to the center of the barn, into a broad shaft of sunlight pouring through a missing section of the roof. I stood, rooted there, opening and closing my hands as if I wanted to grab onto something, but there was nothing within reach. My stomach turned. I felt a sudden weakness from the hot stench inside the barn and the hopeless, slow crying sound of its beams. The best thing to do would be to plant a truckload of Dan Gooch's dynamite right where I was standing.

I searched for the well. I thought, *If only there's a working well.* I tried to remember if it was somewhere in the barn, near the troughs. I dug for a while through that compost and couldn't find it. While digging, I did find an odd, pincerlike tool the function of which I couldn't imagine. I also uncovered the bones of some small animal, the skull easily pinced by the tool, through the eye sockets. I played with that creation for a moment. I put it around my neck and wore it like a pendant. Then a horde of tiny biting insects poured out of the skull down the front of my open shirt.

I dug around the barn for about an hour without finding the well. Then I moved out of the barn, poking through the weeds, stumbling over the odd fallen boards and tangled wire. I tried to remember if my grandfather had had to carry his water in buckets from the corral. Or if he had hand-pumped it in through a pipe from the well. I searched for a pipe, kept searching for the well. I knew it would have a cement collar. It would be a slightly raised plateau of cement around a simple hole in the ground, hand dug by my Grandpa Ben, probably covered over now by a piece of planking like the hundreds strewn around. I started lifting up planks. I found nests of white worms under them. Then I lifted a board and jumped back ten feet. A black-and-yellow cornsnake raised up and hissed. It was as thick as my arm, longer than I was tall. I gingerly stepped forward and pinned it under my boot. Then I caught it behind the head, its tail whipping at my pantlegs. I toyed with it a few minutes, letting its toothless jaws strike viciously at my fingers. I carried the snake into the barn. I opened the door to the feedcrib. I tossed it into the crib. The mice scrambled away, hundreds of them diving under cover from the snake. I thought it would be a kind of paradise for a snake. But it just coiled there, black tongue marking time, its head raised up and watching me.

I was ready to give up my search when I found the well, under a pair of boards in the feedcrib corner of the barn, the rusted skeleton of an old hand pump beside it. I turned the boards over and sniffed down into the hole. I didn't think it had the right smell. I found a large stone. The well collar was just big enough to poke my head in after I dropped the stone. I waited. Seconds passed, long as arteries. I found another stone and dropped it in. Somewhere, deep, deep into the earth, I thought I heard the sound of it hitting dry bottom.

I couldn't sleep again that night. The mice were doing ballroom dances in the living room, some right under my bed. Then an owl started hooting so loudly it must have been on the roof, or in one of the upstairs rooms. I was scared. I didn't know why. I reached out and touched the cold steel comfort of the rifle. I rolled to my side and tried to sleep again. I listened to the owl. Its hooting cut through the sound of the prairie wind that set the house to creaking, the old screens to fluttering, and that raised a cloud of ash in the coal-burning stove. As the last hoots were lost in the wind, Boots raised his nose, his chain collar jangling loudly on the porch. He sniffed a long time, snuffled, sneezed. His claws clicked nervously on the porch as he circled around for a time. Then he lay down, lowering his nose across his paws again. I sat up in bed. "Goddamn you, Boots!" I said. "Shut up!"

I struck a match to light a lantern. Mice scampered into the corners, one of them diving into an overturned boot.

The dog growled. Then he suddenly whined loudly and jumped off the porch. Outside, spread out across the lower meadow, all the sheep started bleating at once. I jumped up out of bed. Naked but for a pair of socks, I grabbed up the lamp and rifle and danced to the front door, fumbling at the rifle's safety catch. I jumped out onto the porch. I stopped, shivering, shining the powerful beam of the lamp across the meadow. I watched to see how the flock was moving. When they scattered, there was a coyote or a wild dog dragging one of them down. When they bunched together, there might be something circling them, a coyote or a wild dog, maybe a fox, or there might be nothing. They were bunched together now, some of them trying to climb each other's backs, a moving white mass of sheep. I waited. I shined the light around, watching the dog travel back and forth around the flock with his nose to the ground. From time to time he stopped and looked in my direction, pricking up his ears.

I was too late. The lantern beam rested on the abandoned carcass of a lamb that had been dragged almost to the edge of the meadow, onto the lane. I wondered what I should do. I knew Dan would likely want me to pull on pants, boots, jacket, and hike down along the edge of the meadow to take a position downwind of the carcass. If I was lucky, in an hour or two I'd see the shadows of coyotes slip out to drag their kill across the lane into the brush. But the chances were the coyotes would sense I was there. I'd watch until morning without seeing them. I doubted I could stay awake long enough, not out there. I thought of how I'd feel waking up from a sleep I didn't notice to find the carcass was gone. I decided it was pointless to spend the night out there. I pointed the rifle high into the air. I fired off six shots, one after the other until the chamber was empty. The rifle shots all but scattered four hundred sheep to the four winds.

I damned the coyotes. I damned whoever it was who had the bright idea of me living out there in the first place. I shivered on the porch, the night breezes cold as a desert wind at night. I closed my eyes, wishing for a moment I was sitting with a girl named Lola Mae from biology class, thinking of her rich profile, smelling her light perfume in memory. I counted the days until summer ended.

I stood on the porch, the beam of the lantern fixed on the dead lamb, a streak of red across its heels, until I was sure the stars were fading. The cold finally drove me back inside. "Boots!" I called. "Come here, Boots!"

Boots dutifully took up position again on the porch, wagging his tail at me.

In bed, I found I still couldn't sleep. I lit the lantern again, and with the rifle across my knees, I sat up reading one of my books, one of a series about a young British naval lieutenant who swashbuckled his way across adventurous faraway seas. That's where I wanted to be—firing cannon into the French, capturing sailing ships and bringing them home for a prize. I read until I heard the first birds of dawn.

"I ought to fire your ass!" Dan Gooch shouted, yanking the sheet off my body. It was ten o'clock in the morning. "You got work to do, goddamnit! You ain't here for no vacation! Just look out there! Go on! Look!"

He pointed outside. The coyotes hadn't even bothered to drag the carcass of the lamb into the brush. They'd just eaten most of it where it lay, leaving the rest.

"What's the *matter* with you, boy?" asked Dan. "You're lookin' weak! Positively puny! What'd you do all day, just lie around pulling your pecker off?"

"I did what you said!" I shouted. "I was up all last night! All night! And if it's not the coyotes, the mice keep me awake!"

"Shit." Dan Gooch spit snoose out onto my floor. "Mice never hurt nobody."

"Well, I need a cat up here. One that'll stay around."

"Hell. The damn dog'll chew it to pieces," said Dan.

"I need some poison then. Bring me up some mouse poison."

"Aw, the dog'll eat it. The sonofabitch'll eat anything," said Dan. "And just what the hell is all this about mice? I ain't talking to you about no goddamned *mice!*"

"I can't sleep!" I said. "They're running all over me!"

"One day," he said, "one day on the job and you're sleeping in."

"What the hell's it to you," I said. "You got what you want."

"Boy, I ought to kick your ass until your nose bleeds!"

"You go on and try," I said. "Right now! Come on!"

Dan Gooch laughed. I was jumping around, the bed between us, getting ready to run out the back way if he took me up.

"Boy, don't you ever offer to fight a man unless you got your pants on," he said. "Come on, now. Get 'em on."

He went out and stood on the porch. I put on my clothes and followed him out, not sure what he was going to do. He pointed to what was left of the lamb. "You go on and drag that across the meadow so it don't stink up the place," he said. I grabbed the carcass by the heels. It fell apart in my hands. I had to kind of bundle it up, hide and bones, and carry it that way. Dan followed me. "Now you can't just wait for 'em to show themselves," he said. "You got to work at it! You go on and spend the night in that ditch over there, or over here, depending on which way the wind blows. You don't want 'em to catch your scent. Here," he said. He reached into his hip pocket for a pint bottle of whiskey. "I'll leave you this for the cold."

I dumped the carcass out of my arms, watching it tumble down a small hillock into the brush. I turned. "No, thanks," I said. "I'll get paid a lot more than a hundred fifty a month to spend the night in a ditch."

Dan kicked angrily at clumps of brush. Sheep scattered around us.

"Shit fire but I should have expected as much," he said. He started back to his pickup. I don't know why, but I followed him. "What the hell's the matter with you? Your dad teach you everybody can make a living sitting on his ass?" He climbed into his pickup, slamming the door. He reached a hand, his right hand, for the ignition. I leaned in through the window and grabbed his wrist. I squeezed it, hard. My other hand was ready to knock his chin off if he so much as moved. He froze there, looking at my hand on his wrist, keeping him from turning the key. I squeezed it as hard as I could, gritting my teeth, hoping to crush the bones. He looked at my hand on his wrist a long time, the knuckles turning white. Then he looked me directly in the eyes and grinned. I let go.

"You just go on and get to work," he said softly. "Hear me? Just do your job." He started the engine and shifted gears. "Here," he said. He tossed me out the small bottle of whiskey.

"Don't drink it all in the same night."

I watched him drive off up the homeplace lane, a column of dust rising after him.

I went back into the house thinking of breakfast, then decided I didn't want to eat. It was almost noon. The sheep would be taking to the shade soon and it would be harder to herd them. I drank a cup of coffee, splashed water over my face. I set out from the house determined to work. I'd work until the light was gone. "Come on, Boots!" I called. "Sic 'em, Boots!"

I waved a hand toward the corral, making a circling gesture. Boots saw what I wanted. He bunched the flock together, running hellbent after the strays, barking at their heels until they were so close they could hardly move. I opened the gate to the corral. Boots and I herded the flock inside. That dog even knew how to take the end of the gate in his mouth and close it. That was the end of the job for him. He lay in the shade of the loading chute and watched.

I carried a leather bag, like a saddlebag, over my neck and shoulders, a knife and a canteen on my belt. I started through the flock, almost all of them yet unpainted and needing their summer care. I found an old ewe and straddled her. I reached under her jaws, pulling her head up with one hand while the other squeezed her jaw muscles until her mouth opened wide. She kicked, hard, once or twice. Then she went completely limp, sinking to her knees in dumb submission.

I reached into the bag and pulled out a short plastic tube. I poked the tube down her throat, the way Dan had shown me. Then I clapped a hand over her mouth to keep it closed. I felt in the bag for a large white pellet and dropped it down the tube. I covered her nostrils with my palm until she swallowed. That way, she wouldn't lose weight, grow weak or even die from worms.

I pulled the tube out and her mouth hung open, tongue lolling like a dog's in mid-July. She let out a loud, forlorn bellowing. It was as if she didn't know enough to be properly scared until it was too late. I wondered just what this lambing machine was worth now, how many lambs were left in her. I looked at her teeth, almost worn to the gums. I felt her bag, large with milk, the teats distended and chewed-looking. I guessed she had one more year at the most. I reached into the bag for the paint marker. I painted a rough green *G,* the Gooch family brand, on her wool and turned her loose.

Her lamb nuzzled at my pantleg. It butted me once. It suckled at the crease in the seat of my jeans. I grabbed it up and straddled it. I looked at its mouth. There was a crust of scabs on its lips and gums from the soremouth disease. After giving the lamb a worming pellet, I pulled my knife out of its scabbard. I lifted its head and spent a while scraping the scabs on its lips and gums open with the knifeblade, slitting the gums a little with the sharp point, blood trickling from its mouth. I pulled out a squeeze bottle of iodine and covered the open wounds. That way, the lamb's mouth wouldn't close up with soremouth and it would grow. I squeezed alcohol over the knifeblade and wiped it off on my jeans. Then I squeezed more alcohol onto the knife.

I restraddled the lamb, facing its long tail. I grabbed the end of its tail and in one quick movement, I pulled it tight and cut upward with the knife. I threw the tail over my shoulder. I sprinkled blood stopper and anti-infection powder onto the wound. That way, in three weeks' time, it would heal into the bobtail characteristic of sheep, which made them worth four more cents a pound for simple reasons of configuration, a kind of symbol they had been cared for. Also, that long tail wouldn't catch burrs in the brush or get hung up on barbed wire. I pulled out the paint marker and painted Dan's brand on its new white wool.

I threw the lamb on its back, holding it down by pressing my boot against it. It kicked at me and cried out once, a small helpless sound. The entire flock seemed to answer it at once in a concert of bellowing. Then the lamb gave in completely, relaxing. Its orange eyes rolled in its skull as if it would die in this position if it could.

I wiped the sweat off my forehead with my shirtsleeve, looking around. I drank a swallow of water from the canteen. On the horizon, I watched a tractor as big as a house moving steadily, a bright red mechanical insect creeping along in the distance, dust trailing it like smoke. It was part of the Nowell-Safebuy's new wheat-farming operation on land that had once belonged to Jim

Fuller. Now it was part of forty thousand acres of wheatland the Nowell-Safebuy farmed with maybe a half dozen employees. They seeded it in the fall. Let the airplanes spray it once in the spring. Maybe sent a tractor out like that one, once in a summer, to sweep the weeds off fallow land. Then just waited. That was all. Waited for the combine crews to harvest all the grain, working their way up north all the way from Texas. Doing it that way, it was possible to take this one state and raise enough grain to feed the entire Indian subcontinent with a bare minimum of human toil. And, like my father, I believed it was right that way. Nowell-Safebuy wheat farms were so much more efficient than what I was doing. The point was food, quantities of food. It all looked so easy, that tractor driver in his air-conditioned cab, that wonderful machine crawling across the face of the same earth it would have taken my ancestors forty years to plow. What matter if a whole style of life was gone? What matter if the earth no longer served a single family, a small parcel of immortality for the common man? All that was lost to me, as lost as a cherry orchard in which people no longer knew the meaning of cherries, as lost as the unwritten language of a long-expired race of men. All that mattered was food, the wheat on the hill, the hay in the meadow, the mutton under my boot. Whatever method could raise them best and most efficiently would win the prizes of the earth. There was little beauty to it, in my mind. There was only sweat, and maybe a certain sense of unspeakable smallness in my soul in that of all the generations behind me, of all the lost tribes of my forefathers who had dug potatoes, milked cows, sown grain, picked fruit from primeval gardens, it had all come down to me in a knowledge I only wished to lose.

I leaned back over the lamb. I ran my fingers through its wool, picking here and there at burrs until my fingers were slick with lanolin. I thought of what Dan Gooch had said his own father used to say: "They say Jesus Christ raised sheep, but he weren't fool enough to stay in the business as long as I have." At that moment, I knew what he must have meant. I leaned over the hind end of the lamb, feeling for the wool pouch of its scrotum. I squeezed the little white sac, probing at its roots until it filled. With the knife, I

248

cut the tip off the pouch. I squeezed out a tiny blue testicle like a robin's egg. Then I leaned my face down close to it, breathing in the dust of this ritual surely as old as the domestication of mankind itself, feeling for it with my lips. I took it between my teeth and bit down gently. That was the ancient way, the Indian way, the Greek way, the best way because there was less bleeding than using a knife. I pulled my head back slowly until the coiling vessels snapped free. I spat it all out over my shoulder. I leaned down and removed the other one that same way. I poured blood stopper and anti-infection powder into the wound, knowing that way this lamb would gain more weight in the months before market and the breeding of the flock could be controlled.

I let the lamb go. It just lay there awhile. I had to kick it gently a couple of times before it stood up on its own. It cried to its mother. The old ewe came running, letting it hide under her body. I tipped my hatbrim up and let the wind cool my forehead. I tasted blood on my lips, spitting, already feeling tired. I looked around. There were a lot more undoctored sheep than it seemed. My face and eyes burned from the Sioux's holy sun. I knew at that moment this was not my future—not this farm, this labor, not this whole sphere of human toil. I would do anything I had to do to get away.

I took another drink from the canteen. I looked at the sun, high, far too high. Then I caught another ewe, straddled her, and set to work again.

13

They had had a fight. I knew they had because a strange man drove my mother home long before the bars had closed. I looked out the window and saw him help her up the walk, though she looked O.K., steady on her feet, talking pleasantly with the man. But then I saw one side of her piled hair was fallen in a mess. The man was Joe Petrini. Since he'd gone broke in Nowell, Joe had opened a successful dance club and cocktail lounge on the highway to Deadwood.

She thanked Joe at the door, kissed him on the cheek, and let herself in. She went into the front room and I heard the stereo/TV console go on with her "alone records," as she called them— Frank Sinatra and Tony Bennett and the like—letting the full-throated orchestras, the oceans of violins, wash over her mood. She went upstairs and changed for bed. Then she came back downstairs in her robe and slippers to sit on the couch in front of the stereo. I found her filing and painting her nails when I walked in.

"Where's Dan?" I asked. It was the wrong thing to ask.

"If he's got any sense at all he's out soaking his head," she said.

"I don't know, Mom," I said. Her arm had dark bruises above the elbow like blue-black stripes where Dan had grabbed her, squeezing for all he was worth. "He do that to your arm?"

"What's the difference?" she said. "I can wear the blue uniform. The sleeve on that ought to cover it."

"Jesus, Mom," I said.

"Don't you ever do that, Kurt," she said. "Don't you ever manhandle a woman."

"No, ma'am," I said.

"Break windows, break dishes, smash everything in the house and go out and shoot the dog if you have to, but don't you ever raise a hand to a woman," she said. I shook my head no. Tony Bennett was piping up full force, the violins rushing headlong to a crescendo of sympathetic chords. "That sonofabitch," she said. "He's probably off with his ex-wife right now."

"I'm sorry, Mom," I said.

"That's no grief of yours," she said. "That's sure no grief of yours."

"Can I rub your feet?" I asked. That did it. She smiled. We didn't need him. The night was only half gone and we were O.K., just the two of us, getting along no matter what happened. It seemed our whole life was like that. We were just sitting there on the couch, watching TV, me rubbing her feet, gently cracking the bones. Something bad happened. Or something good happened. And we just kept on like that, the two of us, the TV glowing like a colorful hearth, her feet in my lap and my hands, warmly, fluidly, squeezing them.

"Sure you can," she said. "You go put some popcorn on and I'll see what's on TV."

I ran off down the hallway to the kitchen.

"Put your slippers on!" she called after me. "The floors are cold!"

I was just shaking the popcorn out of its bag, a tiny cascade of yellow kernels dropping into the hot oil, when I heard Dan's pickup out front. I slapped the lid on the popper and started back through the long hallway. I was stopped by a loud smash, a heavy blow, to the front door as Dan kicked it open, the little brass and rubber stopper wrenched out of the wall, jingling across the floor like a coin, the doorknob sinking into the wallboard, tearing through it like paper, white dust raining down. Dan reeled through the doorway, knocking into the wall coming in. He looked me directly in the eyes.

"Where's that white whore hiding?" he said. "You hear me!" he shouted, leaning into the wall, his fists clenched, his head raised a little and looking upward toward the ceiling, thinking she was upstairs. "You goddamn whore!" he shouted at the ceiling. He was crying. Tears rolled down his cheeks. He straightened up a little. "Where is she?" he asked me, a small whining in his voice.

"I'm in here, Dan!" she called out, cheerily, a mocking cheerfulness. "Kurt's just making popcorn and we're watching TV," she said as if reminding him of basic facts, of some reality to his gone world. He looked off toward the front room, something missing in his eyes, an animal spirit replacing it, baring his teeth. He staggered in.

"Please, Dan," she said. "I can't take much more of this."

He was on the warpath. With a violent sweep of his arm, he knocked open bottles of nail polish and remover off the table, pitched against the wall like splattered abstractions of frost-pink blood. Then he grabbed her by the wrists and yanked her off the couch like a rag doll, the coffee table going over. "What was you doing with Joe Petrini in that car?" he said, his teeth clenched.

"Have you gone crazy!" she shouted. "You left me in the parking lot!"

"Let her go!" I shouted. She was struggling to get her wrists free, kicking at him, pulling back. He let go suddenly and she fell off balance, her knees buckling under her, her body going limp and slamming into the couch.

"Please, Dan," she said, starting to cry. "Please, please, please . . ."

"You want this white whore, boy, you can have her," Dan said. "I'm getting out of this whorehouse right now."

"Get out then!" she screamed. "Get out! Get out!"

"Damn right I will," he said, a tight mean smile crossing his face. He looked at the TV, the blue picture rolling. He leaned over the cabinet, hugging his arms around it, and with a loud crash he pulled it away from the wall, dropping one end, the picture going black. "You ain't gonna have Dan Gooch to go chippy around on anymore," he said, dragging the long console through the door.

"You just hold on there!" she shouted, following him into the hall. "You bring that back!"

"When I go, what's mine goes with," he said. He dragged the console through the front door, still standing open, bouncing the

TV down the concrete steps, glass shattering inside.

"I'll call the sheriff on you!" she shouted. He didn't even drop the tailgate on his pickup. He just threw that heavy piece of furniture in, letting it go over and land on its back. She tried to slam the door on him and lock it, but the door wouldn't close. "Dan, please," she said. "You don't know what you're doing!"

He pushed past her in the hall. I stood back out of the way as he shoved the French track doors of the utility nook open. He muscled up against the washer. He tore it off its fixtures with a groan, black hoses snapping free with an onrushing flood.

"Goddamn you, Dan!" she shouted. She tried to leap onto his back, beating at his neck and back with her fists. He just kept dragging the washer like she was no more than a mosquito, one steel leg of the machine digging a long shallow trench in the hardwood floor. I turned off the faucets in the utility nook and stopped the flood.

"That's mine!" she shouted. "You traded the old ones in on it!"

He kicked the washer out the door. It tumbled end over end down the concrete steps. Metal screeched against the pavement as he dragged it on the walk. My mother turned in the hall and ran for the stairs.

"Mom!" I shouted.

She was back down the stairs in an instant. She had something in her hands, a long, dark wood snake, the feather half crumpled at its middle, the leather pouch of Dan's medicine swinging at one end like a hobo's provisions. She made a dash for me back near the kitchen. She pushed Dan's medicine into my arms just as he was on his way back through the front door, ready to have a go at the dryer. "Hide this!" she whispered. "In back! Quick!"

"But, Mom, he'll kill you," I said.

"Go on!" she hissed, pushing me into the kitchen.

I ran out the back way. I thought of the garage, a heap of old potato sacks in the corner near the bicycle. I stumbled around in the darkness, knocking into things. I heard the dryer going down the front steps. Then silence. An odd, prolonged silence. I searched around, feeling in the garage for something, anything. I found a short shovel, the blade heavy, sharp. I whipped it through the air, testing its weight. I stood at the back door gripping the shovel, waiting for her to scream.

"Go ahead," she said inside, her voice low, sounding even calm. "Hit me. Just once and I'll leave it buried out there. I'll leave it out there until it rots."

On his way out, Dan tore the front door the rest of the way off its hinges. His pickup started up and he drove off. I watched the red eyes of the taillights round the corner out of sight. I dropped the shovel, smoke suddenly billowing out the back door from the kitchen. I rushed in, coughing. I burned my hands getting the flaming popcorn popper under the faucet.

"He'll be back," she said later, at work in the rubble of the front room, setting the coffee table upright, sweeping broken glass into a dustpan. "Tomorrow. He'll be sorry as hell and bring everything back," she said, me watching her with my hands held out in front of me, buttered and wrapped in gauze. "But this is it for him," she said. "This is the last time."

She was right about him bringing everything back. He turned up late the next afternoon, after her shift. He had the TV, washer and dryer with him. But he didn't say he was sorry, didn't ask her to take him back. He didn't say a word. Silently, his mouth firm, his greenish eyes as dead as glass, he positioned the TV back where it belonged and hooked up the white cubic machines. He even brought new hinges for the front door and tinkered with it, quietly, not quite able to get it to hang straight again or to close all the way. The TV/stereo console sat lifeless with a shredded cord until she could pay to get it fixed. The stereo never worked again. And the washing machine broke down from time to time after that; for seemingly no reason at all it stopped in midload with a loud buzzing alarm.

I fetched Dan's medicine for him, carrying it awkwardly in my gauze mittens. It felt heavy, painful to hold, the crow's head watching me as I carried it, held before me like an offering. Dan was sitting in his pickup in front of the house, waiting. She stood by the open window, her blue uniform not covering the bruises.

She was talking to him. She didn't want it to end like this. They fell silent as I approached.

My hands outstretched, I raised the medicine up to him. He took it from me, nodding at me just once, not looking me in the eyes. He dropped the medicine casually on the seat beside him, his head held high, his eyes fixed straight ahead, staring off through the windshield. He started his empty pickup and drove off, just like that. And no other man ever lived in her house again.

Later, only weeks later, she and Dan Gooch became friends, a coming together on different terms. He had gone back to his wife and kids by then, eventually remarrying and even giving up drinking. But he still drove the long miles from his ranch to The Cove sometimes for lunch, or he stopped off there on his way to Belle Fourche or Sturgis for parts. And he helped out at times, with Beatrice, Pearly, Louis, everyone, still riding with her on Saturdays for groceries. Our lives went back to normal, she working at The Cove with me helping in the mornings. We went on in this house, this town, most of my own activities through school in Belle Fourche, the only real difference being that I bought an old car with my summer earnings and no longer rode the bus to school.

Two winters later, two more summers herding sheep for Dan, who still kept his lease arrangement for the farm, I was admitted to an expensive college in the East on a program called Grass Roots Talent Search—a way to put rural kids into a different category of admission than city kids to make up for their generally inferior educations. I took a quick and practically meaningless degree as far as making a living is concerned, as many students did in those days. I grew my hair long and hitchhiked around for a year. Vietnam was a full-fledged war by then. I was due to be drafted and I knew it, my number coming up in the first call, so I joined the navy in hopes of staying clear of the action. And once I'd gone, I didn't come home for years. Hitchhiking across the country, I took northerly or southerly routes so I wouldn't pass anywhere near this town. I wrote letters or telephoned. She had had the chance to visit me for my college graduation; I'd invited her and even chipped in for plane fare. But she found out my father was also attending and she canceled out, not wanting or able to see him, not even there. I recall the night of my graduation, my father took a group of us students out on the town and ended up in bed with a pretty blond girl who lived in the room directly over mine and I was grateful my mother had stayed home.

I remember waiting in Rapid City for the bus to take me to college. It was an early admission—before I'd even begun my senior year in high school—and though I had the letter of acceptance since May, it was late July before I finally told her about it. She had thought she had me with her for one more year, then only had a few weeks to get used to the idea of my leaving. We sat in the shabby coffee shop at the bus depot, hardly speaking. She didn't want me to leave that soon.

"It seems like all your life, you wait for your child to grow up," she said. "Then when he does, you know it's all happened too soon. It's like my roses. I found a whole thicket of them along the creek when I was a girl. Little yellow roses. I cut one off and brought it to Grandma Vera . . . a fine, big one, as big as my fist, with dark green leaves. Grandma said she'd save it forever. She'd press it in her Bible. I remember that just like it's today. Then the other day, it just fell out of the Bible at me, straight out of Leviticus after all those years. It had turned brown and grown thin as paper, so thin I could see right through the petals, so thin I could make out print through it. But I still saw it just the way it was that day too, big and full, in the hand that was giving it to her. The same way I can look at you and still see the day you were born. And look at you now knowing you won't come back, not ever really. And it seems like everything's like that," she said. "It all just happens too soon."

14

Christmas was just around the corner. She woke me up early the morning after I first came back to this town. The dawn's orange scarves billowed over the horizon.

"Come on!" she called. "I got the day off! We're going shopping!"

She set a steaming cup of coffee in my hand. I spilled a little, propping myself up in bed.

"I feel sorry for 'em. Pearly Green's the only man I know who dumps pickle relish into chili," she said. "I got breakfast on downstairs. Hustle up now! There's ice on the roads!"

By the time I pulled on my clothes and was down the stairs, she was on the telephone to Dan Gooch. I sat down over a hot plate. I didn't have much of an appetite.

"Dan's going to let us use his pickup," she said. She sat down. "We've got a lot of shopping to do. Eat up now! Let's see. . . . We'll have to make a list. Now Pearly," she said, "I got a surprise for. Chris Vandergrin down at Rapid Amusements repossessed the jukebox. Pearly was only two payments behind on the new one, 'cause the old one just flat quit, and by God, they took it out. Well, I figure it's a gift for me, too. I wasn't sure I could swing it until you got here. I got that cheap Dutchman to give it back here for the payments." She laughed. "Dan I don't know about. Got any ideas?"

"Oh, we'll just wander around Randall's store and find something," I said.

"You can pick that out. O.K. . . . Anita I'm getting a collected Elvis album. I don't know why, but she threw all her records out. Just tossed them in the trash barrel and burned them. She misses them now. And Louis I'm baking rum cakes for. . . . Alice? What do you think?"

"Alice Kawczech?" I asked. "Is she still alive?"

"Nothing for Alice," she said. "Just for spite."

"Something to wear," I said. "She must be needing something to wear."

"Slippers," she said. "Not too expensive. Christmasy slippers. . . . All right. Beatrice? Now I don't want to get her handicrafts. Seems like she's busy enough with what she's got. That one's got me stuck. . . ."

"A pet," I said. "A parakeet."

"Out of the question," she said. "Her house is damn near a nature park."

"Then I don't know," I said. "Perfume. Or something for her bath."

"Maybe," she said. "But Beatrice is acting frail about baths. Andrea or I have to be there to watch. You know I don't mind doing it, but I really don't want to encourage her too much. If you know what I mean."

We were still stuck on what to get Beatrice when Dan Gooch pulled up and honked his horn. My mother and I bundled up. I made sure to get my money out of a small secret pocket in my suitcase. On second thought, I took my checkbook too. I was surprised that an old pair of rubber farm boots in the closet still fit. I went down the stairs and outside ahead of her. Dan was standing impatiently in the driveway, by his truck. It was a pretty day, the light wind just a hair above freezing, a strong morning sun making the snow-covered streets as bright as an ocean beach.

"How's it going?" I asked Dan cheerfully. I didn't like the way he looked at me, as if weighing something. We shook hands.

"Looks like the navy's lettin' you get out of shape," he said. My mother shut the door to the house and started down the steps. "Marge, didn't you show the boy my news clipping?" he asked.

"Oh, I forgot!" she said. She opened the house door again and rushed inside. I saw her figure through the living room window, going through a pile of scattered papers.

"So how is she really?" I asked.

"Ain't my place to say," Dan said. He looked through the open window of his pickup at the dashboard clock. "I got to make an auction in Sturgis in forty minutes," he said. "In your Mom's old car, that's a gamble."

"You're not going with us?" I asked. Dan didn't answer. "I see. She's just trading vehicles with you. Thanks, Dan. Thanks for doing that."

"There's one thing nobody's ever been able to say to your mom and that's no," he said. Dan reached into the pickup cab and honked the horn again.

"Hey, Dan," I said. "Doesn't Chris Vandergrin still have a delivery truck?"

"Now don't you go and spoil things," said Dan. "Your mom's waited a long time for this."

"Here it is!" she called. She waved a rolled-up news clipping and hurried down the icy walk. The clipping was from the Sunday magazine supplement of the Rapid City paper. The cover photo showed Dan grinning, cowboy hat tipped back over the dark mess of his hair. He grinned, long brown arms cradling five tiny lambs.

"That's the first set of quintuplets successfully raised west of the Missouri," he said. "It's part of a program I'm on with American Breeders. We're giving hormone treatments so every ewe on the ranch has twins or triplets. Then there was this one," he said. "Quintuplets. Had to feed 'em with toy bottles from my daughter's doll. See there? Aw, well, you can't see it very good in the picture. Anyway, I'm keeping ahead. A fellah's got to keep ahead these days just to stay even."

My mother gave Dan the keys to her old car. Then she kissed him quickly on the mouth. He backed away a little, keeping his eyes on me the whole time. "Thanks, Dan," she said. We watched Dan drive off in her old blue Ford.

She handed his keys to me. I opened the door for her.

"It's nice to see a gentleman back in town," she said. "Seems like there's been a shortage."

There were few surprises on the ride to Belle Fourche. The studs on Dan's tires whistled past the open fields as we drove. Those vast wheatfields looked desolate in winter, the snow blowing up off them in steamy blasts revealing patches of brown fallow earth. No houses stood in those fields. We must have passed a dozen high steel buildings marked with the yin-yang-like logo of the Safebuy. There were a few other emblems on buildings nearer Belle Fourche—of companies like Bates, Cargill, Cooke Industries, and the Great Westward sugar company. The fields themselves stood abandoned in winter. Maybe a caretaker at most drove the long miles from Belle Fourche once a day to check on things; or on farms nearer the town, maybe there was a night watchman. As we neared Belle Fourche, we passed junctions that had once marked highways leading to other towns—towns like Wall, Cedar Tie Crossing, Bear Creek—towns, like Nowell, that had been steadily fading over the years, the square false fronts of the buildings falling in, the boarded-over windows on the main streets giving those towns the same desolate appearance as towns laid waste by war.

I disliked those towns. I had long ago come to prefer the towns that lived, like Belle Fourche, where I had gone to school. It is possible to stand on a mesa overlooking Belle Fourche at night and see the town glittering like a rhinestone buckle set into the plains. I knew the neat, damask layout with its rows of new houses for the farm managers, the ag engineers, the heavy-machinery operators, the Great Westward refinery workers, the shopkeepers who took care of their needs, their families, their lawns. There were shopping centers, movie houses, bowling alleys, bars, ways to live in comfort. From the main street of Belle Fourche it was possible to hear the deep grumbling of diesel engines at the railheads, the Burlington Northern gondolas being loaded with grain and beet pulp. A skyscraper grain elevator worked day and night, huge tandem trucks with company brands humming quietly in line, waiting to pass through and take on their loads. It was always a relief to come off the prairie into Belle Fourche, a gateway town into the Black Hills. Life seemed prosperous there. It even felt tens of degrees warmer in winter than on the plains, as if the cold had granted a longstanding truce to that one small hollow in the earth.

We went shopping. We wandered around Randall's Department Store in the Belle Fourche Mall, buying simple gifts—a bright printed silk scarf for Andrea, a record for Anita, a book on the birds of the West for Beatrice Ott that was mostly colored photos with large print she could read with her lighted magnifier, a box of golf balls for Keith Morgan, who had lately taken to using his putter as a cane, a pair of pink fuzzy slippers for Alice Kawczech, a straw fishing creel for Dan Gooch. There was a crowd out, no one I recognized. There were a lot of new people in Belle Fourche, enough of them ranging up and down the aisles like finicky cattle on rich grass that it was a small triumph to get in ahead of them at the checkout stand. I reached for the wad of bills in my jeans. "I'll toss this into the hat," I said. "And you can pick up the slack later."

"Nothing doing," she said. She pulled out her wallet and made two neat stacks of bills and change for the exact amount.

"Aw, come on," I said. "You get the next one."

I picked her money off the counter and pressed it into her hand. Change dropped to the floor, quarters rolling.

"I won't have this now," she said. She waved her money at the salesgirl. The salesgirl reached out to take it, looking after us at the line gathering. "Hold on a second," I said. "This is on me."

The salesgirl looked at our few small items. She started to pack them all in one bag, laying the slippers in Dan's creel like two pink fish. She was patient. My mother and I picked up each other's money several more times. Then I took a five-dollar bill and leaned over the counter. "This is in it for you," I said.

Others in line were watching.

"Sorry. I'm not allowed," the salesgirl said.

But she took my money. As she was counting out the change from my hundred, she looked me directly in the eye, slipping a five-dollar bill into her apron. In the old days, my mother never would have let me get away with that. She would have stepped in with a ten-dollar bill and kept on fighting.

On our way through the mall, she stopped in front of the window of a small boutique. It was a curious place for Belle Fourche, put together with some sense of design, a new store, faceless mod manikins draped with vogue colors, black-and-white art photographs placed discreetly around to give the racks of clothing a gallery atmosphere. She was looking through the window past the manikins to something on a rack.

"Let's go in," I said. "Come on."

"Naw. We better not," she said.

"Aw, hell. We got the time. Try something on."

"No. I couldn't," she said. "I just couldn't."

"Come on. It's Christmas," I said. "Don't ruin the party."

I went in. She stood in front of the window a moment looking in at me, frustrated, then she followed me in. I was standing by the rack with a yellow bloomers outfit on it, kind of gay-looking.

"That's not right anyway," she said.

"Go on. Try it on," I said.

"I told you it's not right," she said. She picked it off the rack and held it up to her body. I agreed. She could swim in it. "Anything you can find at this place you can get at Sears a lot cheaper," she said.

"Doesn't look like Sears to me," I said.

"Come on now. We got shopping to do."

"Just try something on and we'll go," I said. The salesgirl was on us in an instant, a tall and darkly pretty girl with a city accent. My mother had just started quickly going through a rack of sale items. I motioned to the girl I'd tell her when I needed her. My mother stopped on a plain red dress, pulling it out with a swoosh of the skirt and holding it up.

"This one's reduced," she said.

"Naw, I don't think so," I said.

"I don't know," she said. "It's simple. I like a simple dress."

"Well, let's see," I said. "Don't stop now."

I watched her begin to pick gingerly, more slowly through the racks of dresses. It was like watching a rusty piano player getting into a tune. She felt along the seams of a dress, looked at the tags, started to pull it out, stopped, then went on to the next one. One or two she pulled out and held up to her in the mirror, letting the fabric swish around her ankles a moment before she decided no, that wasn't it. Then she stopped. She pushed an arm in and spread a line of dresses back. A black dress was misplaced on the rack, actually off to one side and hanging a little off kilter. It looked as if it had hung that way since about 1957, maybe before. It had a low neckline, the suggestion of a slit up the side of a sheathlike skirt, a kind of cocktail dress I think they called it, the neckline, sleeves and hem bordered with a blue-gray fur. She stood in front of it a moment, unsure. Then she looked at the tag. She turned to the next dress on the rack and quickly pulled it out.

"Try that last one," I said.

"Oh, no, Kurt, I couldn't," she said. *"That* one?"

"It'd look great on you," I said.

"Who'd wear something like that in Nowell?"

The salesgirl was right there before I could motion for her. "The lady would like to try this one and the simple red dress over there," I said.

"But, Kurt," she said.

"You don't have to buy everything you try on," I said.

The salesgirl brought both dresses to a changing room, my mother following. Then the salesgirl reappeared with a cup of coffee in a dainty china cup. She led me to a large armchair in front of mirrors. I sat down, the salesgirl placing the cup on the small smoking table beside me. It was good coffee. I liked the idea of being served. "You just set up here?" I asked.

"We've been here six years," she said, looking at me strangely.

"I've been away," I said. "Town's changed a lot."

"Thank God for that," she said. The bell at her counter rang and she strode off down the carpeted aisle between her colorful if a bit sparse racks and tables, rock steady in her high heels. There was something too put together about her, too austere about the entire boutique, like a minimalist painting whose aim is to keep out any imperfection.

My mother pushed open the door to the changing room. She put an arm on her waist and kind of swiveled her hips a little, then she leaned against the doorjamb and looked at me a little perversely. "Hey you," she said. "Over here."

"Ma, that's beautiful," I said. "Come look at yourself."

She walked slowly, waist held in like a model's, chin held high. Gray feathery fur wisped around her neck, at her sleeves, at the backs of her legs. She stood in front of the mirror and looked. She took in her breath with a little gasp.

"I was only joking," she said.

"Turn around," I said. She did, trying to turn her head to look. There was something about that dress, a style that still recognized her youth.

"We'll take that one," I said.

"Kurt, no!" she said. "We haven't even tried the other one!"

"We'll need shoes for it," I said. "Not just any shoes are right."

"I've got the *perfect* shoes," she said. She was suddenly caught, imagining how her shoes would look. "At home. Italian shoes. But I haven't worn them in years! Oh, Kurt, really, where would I ever wear it?"

"Wear it Christmas," I said. "I've never bought you anything nice."

"That's not true! You always gave me such nice things."

"Not anything as nice as this," I said.

She turned and faced the mirrors again, a private moment when she absorbed her own image with a critical eye. "All right," she said. "Even if I only wear it once."

At the counter, the salesgirl was friendly at first. My mother had gone on ahead a little, by the door, as if she didn't want to witness the sale, as if pretending it could still be a surprise. The salesgirl wrote up her ticket, making pleasant small talk about where I was coming back from and how long I planned to stay. I started to take the cash out of my jeans, when I looked at the amount on the bottom line. I couldn't believe the figure. It was about three times the money I had with me. I wanted to say something. Then I looked at my mother, arms hugging our bag of gifts, a distant expression on her face, a worried look. I pulled my checkbook out of the pocket of my pea coat and the salesgirl grew suddenly cold.

"We don't take out-of-state checks," she said.

"Aw, c'mon," I said. "Here's every ID in the book. You know what they do to sailors who bounce checks?"

"Cute," she said, giving me back my green military card.

"Listen," I said. "How long has this dress been in the store? Come on."

"It's my job," she said. "I'm sorry."

I was already writing out the check, making sure to keep my thumb over the balance forward column on the stub. I tore it off and put it in her hand, even pressing her fingers around it. "You can count on the navy," I said. I picked the dress up off the counter, half spilling out of its box. She started to reach out for the box to take it back but the check was in that hand. "I mean this is my first Christmas home in eight years," I said, backing further away. "Now we've both done something nice."

I made it to the door a little too quickly. She started to call out to me but my mother took my arm and pulled me all the way out of the store. When we were just past the windows of the boutique, she poked me in the ribs, hard.

"I told you so," she said. "Now don't you feel like the biggest damn fool?"

She looked at my face. It must have been pale, sweating. She laughed.

"Your Grandpa Ben used to say, 'Watch out when you come lookin' for your inheritance. You just might end up paying for the funeral.'"

She laughed again. I laughed with her, relieved. We ducked into the mall Woolworth's for Cokes. But she was in a hurry. "It's eleven o'clock already," she said. "We got a jukebox to load!"

She changed her mind and told me to pull into a Safebuy as long as we were passing one. It was a new building, the bright red-and-white logo on a huge revolving sign over neat rows of houses on the flat by the river, the picture coming over the hill like a white printed circuitboard with each building a kind of component plugged into it in soberly logical array, that towering emblem standing over it all in perpetual motion.

Inside, there was everything. My mother had me take a second cart and trail along behind her. "I don't usually shop here," she said. "I go to Mark and Buy, where it's cheaper. But there's so much here you can't get anyplace else."

There were cranberries from Washington, rice from Louisiana, fresh vegetables from Mexico, fruits from every corner of the earth. The abundance was breathtaking. Pyramids of dates and walnuts from California, heaps of oranges, bananas, pears, boxes of miniature tangerines from Japan, candies from China, cakes, cookies and mince from England, wines from every country in Western Europe, and it was all packed, distributed, labeled with that same red-and-white brand. We shopped, my mother happily cruising along with her cart to the slow cheerful music from the speakers overhead, tapes of sound electronically manipulated to be slower than the actual Christmas carols, smoother than any music of reality, developed after years of patient psychological research in order to help create an atmosphere of receptive buying for Safebuy's holiday shoppers.

She tossed everything in sight into our carts. Six different kinds of cheeses, olives from Spain, pickles, cocktail crackers, pie fillings, bread crumbs, armloads of fresh vegetables, carrots from New Mexico, coconuts from Hawaii, boxes and bags and cans of items, a hundred different foods. She only balked once at a price. It was at a tiny box of Safebuy-brand figs from Algeria, several dollars. But it was just a moment, then she tossed it in the cart. "If the poor can't eat a fig on Christmas, then what's the point," she said.

We turned the corner at the end of the aisle. Stretching along one whole back wall of the meat department were lines of turkeys, wrapped in bright plastic string bags, a film of white frost glistening on their fat breasts lined up five deep and one after the other down the long row of freezer. I looked at them, inspecting their labels, most of them Safebuy brand from Minnesota, most of them injected with oils and marked "self-basting," most of them with a bright red plastic button that popped up erectly out of the breast when the bird was roasted. There were hundreds of them, all different sizes and kinds, but a lot of them were large—huge, in fact. Pasted to the yellow block wall above the freezer were cheery signs in red cursive with a stylized wreath drawing around the edges, stating simply "Merry Christmas from Safebuy," alternating on down the wall with "All America Loves Safebuy Turkeys."

I watched my mother pick out a huge hen, twenty-four pounds, the largest hen turkey I'd ever seen, then set it on the bottom rack of her cart. The price was a full seven times per pound what any farmer in Nowell had ever been paid for a bird. Down at the end of the freezer, past the boned turkey rolls, the packages of turkey salamis, hot dogs, hams, sausage patties, I found a few forlorn-looking frozen geese from Oregon. I picked the two biggest ones out and dropped them in my basket. "Tell you what," I said. "I'll offer to cook these and we'll skip the turkey this year. It's been a long time since I've had goose."

"We've got a lot of guests coming," she said. "We'll need those too. And for a lot of folks it just isn't Christmas without a turkey."

It lay at her feet, steaming, fat breast almost reaching her knees. She turned the cart and wheeled the turkey away on its little bier, the roof overhead a heaping pyramid of worldly bounty she still added to as she might add the final flowers to a long procession. I followed, solemnly, my cart piled high.

There were near to intolerable lines at the checkout counter. I was suddenly in a bad mood. I knew what was coming next. I pulled the bills out of my jeans and handed them to her before the clerk began to pull each item across a computerized electric eye, prices flashing in digital readouts almost too fast to read and reminding me of the quick red firing codes on the missile control boards of my ship.

I went to the foot of the counter, taking sacks from the bag boy and loading the carts. As my mother finished paying, she gave me a look. I knew that look: after shopping four hours, we were both flat out broke. Being broke is a double-edged feeling—depression at the same time as a sense of malevolent freedom, as if nobody could possibly get us now, as if there was nothing left to buy. It was like being wiped out early at the racetrack, then settling down for the first time to watch the horses actually run.

"Don't you worry about nothing," she said on our way to the truck. "I still got a week's pay and tips coming. We're gonna have a fine Christmas," she said. "With you here it's already the best I can remember."

As we got out of the truck at Rapid City Amusements, still in the same tin warehouse in back of the railroad depot, I could see a storm blowing in. Banks of clouds were spilling over the hills and quickly covered Belle Fourche like the lid on a kettle. Chris Vandergrin, broker of pinball machines, video games, jukeboxes, coin-op contraptions of every size and shape, had expanded his business. A large delivery truck sat parked behind the warehouse.

My mother went into the office, where I could see Chris through the window, gone bald since I had been a high school kid asking him to change the tunes on his jukeboxes. She came out of the office with a pink slip. A guy I didn't know drove The Cove's new jukebox out with a forklift and I helped him position it in Dan's pickup bed before he let it go. It must have weighed five hundred pounds, a handsome jukebox with push-button controls and whirling pinwheel lights, hundreds of different tunes, most of them country and western records by bands and singers I no longer knew. Light flakes of snow began to fall. "Hey," I said. "How about something to cover it? Or does it play better if it gets wet?"

The guy brought a piece of plastic a shade too small to cover the jukebox completely. I tied it on with packing string. My mother watched. "How are we ever going to unload it?" I asked.

"You and Dan can't unload it?"

"Me, Dan and a horse might be able to," I said. "Why didn't you just have it delivered? They got a truck here."

"We'll manage," she said. A gust of wind billowed the tarp up around me, the plastic crackling. "Come on. We've got another stop to make."

On our way out of town, she had me pull into a lot where they sold Christmas trees and simple wreaths of boughs decorated with red ribbon. "Just a sec," she said. I watched her jump out of the truck, all childish spirit of the occasion, running nimbly as an elf to a display of wreaths. She picked out two, put her arms through them and turned, flapping her arms at me like wings and laughing. She wrote a check for the attendant. Then she carried the wreaths back to the truck and tucked them forward in the bed, well braced by heavy sacks of groceries already soggy from the first flakes of melting snow.

"In for a penny, in for a pound," she said, tucking her checkbook back into her purse. "It's gonna be a fine Christmas."

I drove as fast as I could, thinking of the jukebox getting wet. But we seemed to be outrunning the snow as we drove toward Nowell. The landscape was gray, wet. I wondered how short the light would be that day. We said very little as we drove. Every once in a while, she chattered something about how pleased she was with our shop, how we had taken care of everyone.

"Now don't go giving everything away before Christmas like you always do," I said.

"It's a season," she said. "Twelve days. Any one of them's good enough."

I teased her about not letting her see her dress again until Christmas Day. She was happy about the dress. For a moment, it was a perfect feeling, seeing her happy. Then her mood changed. We were approaching the junction of highway 79 into Nowell. "Turn right at the junction," she said. "I want to put the wreaths under their tree."

"Hey, there's a storm coming," I said.

"I know," she said. "We got to do it before we're snowed in."

"But the lane's covered with ice."

"This pickup'll get through anything," she said. "You don't want to drive the lane, then I will. Now turn! Damnit, Kurt!"

"O.K.," I said. I had already turned in the wrong direction. I backed the pickup around and drove in the direction of the homeplace. "Has anyone plowed the lane this year?"

"Just keep driving," she said. She clutched her purse in her lap, her fingers working nervously at the clasp. I reached the homeplace lane and turned in, coming up against the barbed-wire gate. The lane didn't look as if it had been plowed. Waves of drifts moved in ripples across the muddy gravel. I got out of the truck and looked south. It wasn't snowing yet, but the snow was coming from the south, from the hills. The wind moved the old jagged posts of the gate, swinging them back and forth, complaining in their wire halters. I undid the gate. I climbed back into the truck. "Any stock still out here?" I asked.

She shook her head. I started down the lane a few feet and stopped. I'd forgotten to lock the hubs in for the four-wheel drive. I got out, shivering, kneeling down in the wet snow, turning the discs on the hubs. I looked down the lane again and at the deep ditches on either side, shaking my head. She didn't seem to notice. She looked out grimly at the fields, patches of overgrown grass holding up the snow like ragged, chaotic straw baskets. The fields had been neglected. Even more lost to the years than I remembered.

I drove the truck gingerly, sliding around like a pea on a plate. I held my breath. I got as close to the house as I dared, a hundred feet or so back, stopping up against a snowdrift as deep as the headlights.

"This is it," I said. "As far as we go."

She was already out of the truck. She uncovered her Christmas wreaths, shaking them, brushing snow off the ribbons. She held one out and I took it. She tucked her purse under her coat as if not wanting to let it get wet. Then she started off, the snow falling thickly and sticking to the ground. I followed. The barn was up ahead, half the old gray building down, much of it only skeleton, the roof bowing inward and frozen, a fixed moment of time, in a mid-sagging to the earth. I wondered how long it had been since the corral had been used. Rails were down. It didn't look as if it could hold stock anymore.

I moved ahead of her and pushed through a high drift on one side of the barn, packing down the snow and making a path. There were holes in my boots. My feet were already wet. She caught up with me and passed, bending her head into the stiff breeze. Ice crystals stung my face. A lone cottonwood stood on a small hillock behind the barn, as tall as an owl can fly, its branches sweeping upward, strong-looking. Its silvery-black figure stood out against a horizon as gray as a rubbing of pencil lead. But it was alive, moving in the wind.

There were three small broken branches on the trunk. My mother stood on her toes, looping her fresh green wreath over a peg of branch. I did the same, red ribbons fluttering out into the air. Then she knelt in the snow, taking off her gloves. She folded her hands and bowed her head. She was a woman who rarely went to church. But she believed in God and prayed. She closed her eyes as a child would and her lips moved.

"You know it wouldn't hurt you to pray a little," she said.

"Oh, I don't know," I said. "I wouldn't know what to pray to."

"Your grandpa never believed in God, either," she said. "But he still prayed."

"Maybe I just believe there's only one chance on earth. You get that one chance and that's it. The rest is bones in the ground."

"Don't you feel it?" She held her hands out like witching rods as if she could feel something, the way a well dowser can feel out water underground. "Right here? I think I always felt it here," she said.

"Right now I just feel kind of cold," I said. "These boots leak."

"What would you do with it, Kurt? What would you do with this tree? I mean if it was yours. Right now if you could do anything with it, what would you do?"

"What do you mean?"

"I mean if this whole place was yours. What would you do?"

I looked up at the tree. I guessed there wasn't one like it for miles, a cottonwood tall enough for an eagle to nest in, its shade in summer covering the whole distance to the barn. I looked at her, standing over the graves of her parents, my grandparents, marked only by that tree, waiting.

"I don't know," I said. "I wouldn't want to decide."

"I'm sorry," she said. She sat down in the lap of the tree roots. She unbuttoned her coat and pulled out her small saddlebag of a

271

purse. She blew on her fingers. She reached into the purse and brought out a stiff white envelope with a green bow in one corner.

"I wanted to do this here," she said. She held it out, watching me with a hardness in her eyes that made me feel something was wrong, wrong.

"Oh, Mom, please," I said. "I can't."

"Take it," she said.

"Look. I got to make Westpac in a couple of weeks."

"You don't have much longer to go," she said. "Only until spring."

"But it's yours," I said. "It's your chance."

"Take it!" She raised her voice. Then she tossed the envelope at my feet, into the snow. I leaned over and picked it up, brushing it off. I put it in my coat pocket.

"It's not Christmas yet," I said. "I don't have to open it now."

"Oh, damn you!" she shouted. She kicked snow at me. She stood up and ran past me, fists clenched, stuff spilling out of her purse. She kept on breaking a new trail through the snowdrifts in a straight line for the pickup.

"Mom!" I called. I followed, gathering her scarf, gloves, the stuff from her purse. By the time I got to the pickup she was sitting inside, seething, keeping her silence.

"Look, I'm sorry," I said. "What do you want me to do? Hey, listen. I've always thought you should sell it. Take the money and make a new life."

"Just don't you sell the family graves until I'm out there too," she said.

"Aw, no, Mom," I said. "Aw, please, no. . . ."

I was dazed, not thinking about the ice. The truck was in reverse, backing around like on its own. We slammed straight back into a snowdrift, so hard I bounced my head against the back window.

"I knew I should have driven," she said.

"We're not stuck," I said. "We can't be stuck."

Wheels spun hopelessly in the snow, front and back. I shoved the stick into forward, then reverse, then forward, the tires burn-

272

ing as the truck pitched a few inches farther out of the hole than
before. Then, suddenly, we jumped out too fast and were pitching
forward on the ice, straight for the ditch. I hit the brakes, the
truck skidding sideways, then sliding over into the ditch with a
crushing sound. The engine rattled, stalled.

We were as good as on our side. I had to use my foot to kick the
door open like an overhead hatch. I jumped to the ground. I
reached in and helped my mother crawl out, lifting her, as light as
her clothes, to the ground.

One small panel of glass on the jukebox was broken. Other than
that, it was over on its side in the truckbed, crushing bags of
groceries. I imagined the sound of two hundred records all
scratched at once at high volume. She stood on, saying nothing,
long on experience with trucks getting stuck, machinery breaking
down, the entire world coming apart when it is least expected. Her
lips were blue, trembling. She tucked her hands under her crossed
arms as if to warm them.

"Let's get you to the house," I said.

"The groceries," she said. "They'll freeze out here."

"I'll worry about them," I said.

I gathered up an armload of groceries, one of the sacks ripping.
I followed her to the old house. The front door couldn't be opened
without prying it off its hinges, so we went around back. As I was
climbing the short steps to the back porch, one of the boards broke
through. Groceries scattered into the backyard. I picked it all up
again and followed her inside.

Eight years had passed. Since I had last seen it, the house had
been looted several times. Someone taking shelter in it had even
burned a hole through the floor of my grandparents' bedroom. All
the plumbing fixtures had been ripped out and carried away. Even
much of the old impoverished furniture had been picked over by
scavengers. The rest was heaped around in masses of soggy stuffing, feathers, rags of fabric, old boots, papers, scattered jagged
glass from busted canning jars, old yellowed newspapers and magazines crumpled into piles, the ceiling in the living room warping
low over the desolation. All the windows were boarded over but

most of them had been smashed from the inside, the snow dusting in through the cracks in the boards. Little mud pots of swallows' nests were fixed in the corners, thousands of tiny gray feathers caught like moths in the billows of cobwebs.

It was a wonder the coal stove in the kitchen was still there. Maybe it was too heavy. It looked as if someone had tried to pull it from the wall. I put my shoulder to it and heaved several times to get the stovepipe to fit again. I tried to light a fire. I finally found a two-by-four and levered the stove back out from the wall so I could run a piece of ripped-out molding up the stovepipe. A rain of mud chunks, straw, feathers, the remains of swallows' nests spilled out onto the floor. I heaved the stove back in place. I started to go out for wood, but the snow was blowing so hard it was tough to see past the door. I used a pipe and pried some boards off the back porch, jumping on them to break them into little pieces.

She kept a steady run going from the truck to the house, carrying in everything that wasn't already frozen and stacking it in the middle of the old kitchen. It took a long time to get a hot fire going. The stovepipe was probably still plugged a little at its top. Most of the smoke went up the pipe but thin wands of smoke streamed out of the open oven door and upward, traveling across the ceiling to the wide-open drafts in the living room. The haze of smoke, the snow, the clouds made the day's light even shorter. I found an unbroken kerosene lantern on a shelf in the kitchen. It still had some fuel. I made a chimney out of the jagged shell of a canning jar to keep it lit. She finished carrying in the last load of groceries and went out to fill two dented pans with snow. She came back in and set them on the stove. Neither of us said a word for a long time.

"Is Dan expecting us back?" I asked.

"Oh, about six o'clock he'll start getting worried," she said. "But you know me. I'm never anywhere on time."

I nodded. I knew what to expect. Sooner or later, Dan would come looking for us and his truck. He'd commandeer a county snowplow if he had to and find us, searching along the roads first, then the farm.

She found three ragged cushions in the living room, digging them out from under the bare wire framework of what used to be the couch. I cleared the glass from against the wall with my boots. "Blizzard's coming in now," she said. She laid the cushions down, facing the stove. "It could be a long night."

"It's a shame what's happened to the place," I said.

"You got to live out here to watch it," she said. "Even then, every time you turn your back, you're picked clean. You're lucky there's any house here at all."

"I guess so," I said.

"I used to think about moving out here. Even after you left. Every spring I'd tell myself, This is the year. Just pack up the house, board it up and move out. But I never did it. I was just too tired all the time. Then the last couple of years it'd take too much to get the place livable."

"I'm glad you're not out here alone," I said.

"Don't you feel sorry for me because I'm alone," she said. "I've learned to like to be alone. And I could have done it out here alone, once. But I never would have thought of it then. I always thought I needed a man and just couldn't find the right one. And I had you to raise. . . . So I just paid the taxes. That's all. That's your mother's contribution. Fourteen years of taxes. They're yours now. Everything's yours."

She got up off the cushions and rustled in the grocery bags for a bottle of wine. She handed it to me. I dug the cork out with the blade of my pocket knife. Outside, the wind picked up, blasting snow and ice against the house, sounding like a hailstorm on the roof, then it died down again. I handed her the bottle. She got up and searched for a glass but couldn't find one.

"I want to know what's wrong," I said. "I mean, if you're sick or something, I want to know."

"My health is nothing you need to know about," she said.

"If it's something serious, I ought to be told," I said.

"What's serious is that I'm tired of it all," she said. "I'm tired of feeding my body. I'm tired of putting my body to bed, tired of getting my body up in the morning. And work . . . I'm so sick of work I don't know what to do. I'm tired of seeing, breathing, feeling, everything. I want something better."

"We'll find you someplace better," I said.

"I don't want to go anywhere," she said. "I'm too tired to go anywhere."

"That's it then," I said. "You just want to hang on here and die."

"Of course I don't want to die," she said. "I don't even believe in death. You may be right there's only one chance in this world, and thank God for that. Well, now I've done all I had to do with mine. I'm free of it. I've left you with an opportunity and you can do anything you want with it now. But for me there's something after. I know it. I know it and I can feel it," she said. We were quiet for a long time. Then she looked at me and said, "Human souls never die. They just trade places."

I went out on the porch for more wood. It was dark, hard to find the nails to pry against with my short pipe. But the wood was as dry as stale bread and crumbled to splinters under my boots. I came back in with an armload of little pieces. She had curled up on her cushions, staring off through the open door of the oven. I fed the stove, as much as it could hold. After a time, she fell asleep. She looked cold in her sleep. I took off my jacket and covered her with it, moving closer to the stove to keep warm. I sat up, smoking, waiting for Dan Gooch and the county patrol. I listened to her breathe. I had a sudden desire to roll her over a little and get the envelope out of my jacket pocket and open it. But I knew what it was. I remembered as a boy her showing me the deed she kept tucked away in a metal box. I didn't know what to do.

I remembered the way I had seen my grandfather dry his socks and I took off my boots, peeling off my wet socks and laying them out on the oven door like a pair of limp blue fruits hung up to dry. I thought of my grandfather out in the first spring sun *gee-hawing* to his team, pushing his horses to their limits to drag a single plowshare a half acre a day through thick clay sod. Then I thought of the others like him still alive—Pearly, Will, Dan and the rest, my mother with them too still waiting out there for something, still holding on, counting the years by illnesses and deaths.

But I knew what they were here for. It was like a secret now, an all-but-unobtainable secret once a wisdom strong enough to move whole tribes across mountains, whole nations across oceans, my own grandfather across half a continent in a Model T Ford that stuck in reverse gear on the journey so he had to back up the last two hundred miles. Then he found the house we were in, a seldom used line station for the railroad that he put on log rollers and hitched to his team, moving it inch by inch eighteen miles to this piece of dry prairie he could call his own. It was the knowledge of his generation that if at first you don't succeed at life, you can always learn to plow. I thought, *There must be other secrets now and I don't know them.*

A loose board upstairs was flapping in the wind. The house creaked, groaned, shuddered in the storm. I tried to make a space for myself and lie down next to her on the cushions, trying to squirrel my body in next to her under the coat. She stirred, rolling to her back. She mumbled something in her sleep. I got up again, not comfortable anyway. Then I don't know why—I wouldn't have done it if she was watching—I knelt down on the floor. It felt hard and cold under my knees. I pressed my palms and fingers together, shaping them into the little steeple she had taught me to make as a child. I closed my eyes.

"Dear God," I prayed. A moment passed. I opened my eyes again, sitting back on my heels. I listened to the stove. I didn't know what else I should say. I sat that way a long time, watching the fire through a crack in the iron until the glowing embers turned to ash.

CPSIA information can be obtained
at www.ICGtesting.com
Printed in the USA
LVOW12s2101120916
504272LV00001B/23/P